I0749319

BOOK FIFTEEN IN THE RAIDING FORCES SERIES

THE WAR THAT NEVER WAS

PHIL WARD

A RAIDING FORCES SERIES NOVEL

This book is a work of fiction. Names, characters, businesses, organizations, places, events and incidents are either a product of the author's imagination or are used fictitiously. Any resemblance to actual persons, living or dead, events or locales is entirely coincidental.

Published by Military Publishers, LLC
Distributed by Military Publishers, LLC
Austin, Texas

www.philwardauthor.com

ISBN 13-978-0989592239
ISBN 10-0989592235

Cover design by Stewart A. Williams
Map illustrations by Tom Houlihan

For ordering information or special discounts for bulk purchases, contact
Military Publishers LLC
3616 Far West Blvd., Suite 117, Box 215 Austin, TX 78731

DEDICATION

This book is dedicated to one of my most loyal readers, the late Camm Lary, Jr. His life was defined by his strength, not by the adversity he overcame. He always went the extra mile — as a young Cadet in physical training on the drill fields of Texas A&M University — and as an adult in physical therapy facing debilitating injury and disease. If you told him to give you ten reps, he gave you twenty. The student who carried a dictionary in his back pocket because he couldn't spell became a Delegate to the 1974 Texas Constitutional Convention, charged with rewriting the Texas Constitution. The child whom the teachers said would never learn to read became the school board leader demanding greater reading proficiency in elementary school. Stick to it. Never give up. Make it better for others. This was his nature; as a community leader, elected official, businessman, church elder, husband, father, grandfather, and as my cousin and lifelong friend. Gig 'Em.

Cover Color by Savannah

Randal's Rules for Raiding

Rule 1: The first rule is there ain't no rules.

Rule 2: Keep it short and simple.

Rule 3: It never hurts to cheat.

Rule 4: Right man, right job.

Rule 5: Plan missions backward (know how to get home).

Rule 6: It's good to have a Plan B.

Rule 7: Expect the unexpected

Ranks, Awards and Nicknames

Rank Protocol:

The first time a person is named in a chapter or after a chapter break their full rank and name is given. Addressing military personnel by their rank is a mark of respect. At all levels rank is earned and those who have it - from a corporal to a four-star general are proud of it.

Decorations:

In the British military officers are authorized to put the initials of their decorations after their name. In the Raiding Forces Series the protocol is the first time an officer is introduced in a book the initials of his decorations are listed following his name. After that for the rest of the book they are not.

In the U.S. military officers do not have the same privilege.

Nicknames:

In the British military nicknames are endemic. Radio operators are called Sparks, red heads are called Ginger, tall people are called Lofty but sometimes short people are called that too etc.

In the U.S. military there are a lot of nicknames but nothing like the British.

Raiding Forces
Ongoing Operations

OPERATION ACCOLADE
Pinning down the Germans in the eastern Aegean.

OPERATION ACHSE
Code name for the German operation to forcibly disarm the Italian armed forces after Italy's armistice with the Allies.

OPERATION FIRE EATER
The actual raiding of the islands in the eastern Aegean.

OPERATION JAIL BREAK
Evacuate ABCHQ building on Castelrozzo.

OPERATION LEAF EATER/
OPERATION LONG NECK
Diamond interdiction program / eliminate diamond smugglers. ***Command and Control team***—code name **CARD GAME**, consisting of Colonel John Randal, Major the Lady Jane Seaborn, Captain "Geronimo" Joe McKoy, Captain Billy Jack Jaxx, Master Sergeant Mack Beckwith, Waldo Treywick, Captain Pamala Plum-Martin, Mandy Paige, Beverly Blackwell and King.

OPERATION LEOPARD
Germany's invasion of Leros.

OPERATION POLAR BEAR
A three-pronged airborne and amphibious assault on Kos, launched by General Friedrich-Wilhelm Müller aka "The Butcher of Crete."

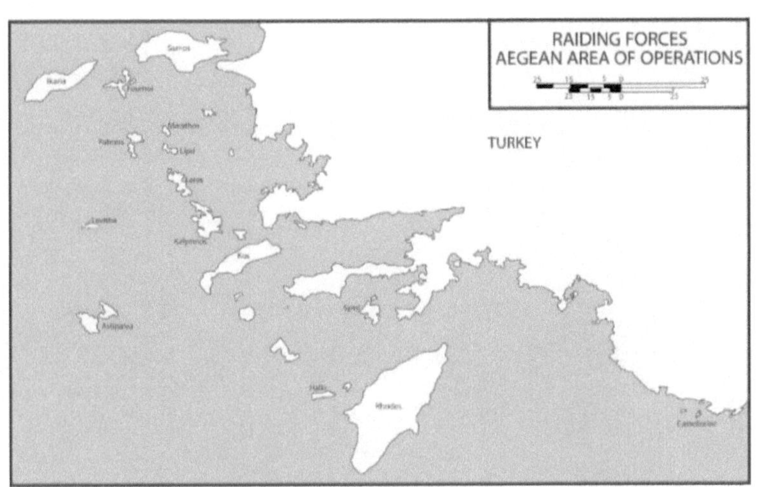
RAIDING FORCES
AEGEAN AREA OF OPERATIONS
TURKEY

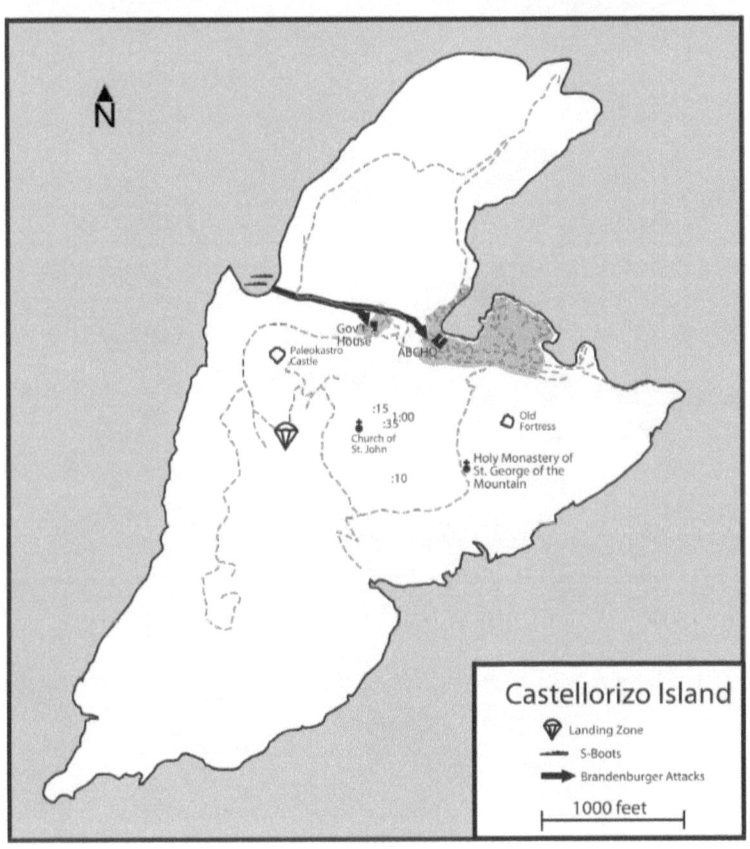
N
Gov't
House
ABCHQ
Paleokastro
Castle
:15
1:00
:35
Church of
St. John
:10
Old
Fortress
Holy Monastery of
St. George of the
Mountain
Castellorizo Island
Landing Zone
S-Boots
Brandenburger Attacks
1000 feet

1
"THAT'S ALL YOU'VE GOT?"

THREE C-47 DAKOTA AIRCRAFT THUNDERED across the turquoise Mediterranean in trail formation. Ten exhausted Rangers from the 575th Ranger Force were aboard each aircraft. The men were coming down from a week-long adrenaline high triggered by a night combat drop followed by six days of close-quarter combat in the vicinity of Benevento, Italy. They were the first Raiding Forces personnel to return to friendly lines following a high-intensity guerilla-style campaign conducted on a conventional battlefield far behind enemy lines.

The Rangers had been tasked with interdicting the 16th Panzer Division, which was making a road march to counterattack the U.S. Fifth Army beachhead at Salerno. Their efforts had temporarily stalled the road-bound Nazi armored division. They were leaving behind roads blocked by hundreds of felled trees, the rail line blown in places too numerous to count, and bridges so badly damaged they would need major structural repairs to support a tank, tank carrier, heavy artillery or even a fuel transport vehicle.

The reward for being the first to fight their way out from behind the lines was another mission laid on for later tonight 850 miles away.

Most of the troops were sound asleep bushed from the last week of constant hitting and running—as the Rangers liked to say, "Doing bad things to bad people". The planes' troop/cargo compartment offered plenty of room to stretch out. The C-47s were capable of carrying more passengers but tonight held just the optimum number for speed and fuel efficiency while transporting the minimum number required for the operation ahead.

Or maybe not.

No one had any idea what the Rangers would be going up against. Except the word was it would be top-tier Nazi fanatics belonging to the Brandenburger Küstenjäger (Coastal Raider) Battalion. The unit's identification might or might not prove to be true.

Colonel John Randal was mentally running through a checklist of what was ahead.

Situation: An element of the Küstenjäger Battalion of unknown strength had conducted a Commando raid on Advanced Base Castelrozzo (ABC). The attack came while the bulk of Raiding Forces personnel were away campaigning in support of the U.S. Fifth Army or stationed on Levant Schooner Flotilla vessels positioned along the Turkish coast to carry out pinprick raids on distant islands in the Aegean.

Mission: Drop on ABC.

Execution/Concept of the Operation: Conduct a night forced-entry airborne assault on Castelrozzo, retake the island, kill or capture the Nazi intruders, and rescue prisoners if any.

Operations Orders—or in this case a Frag Order (because it was a fragment of an order)—do not get much more bare-bones than that. This one was more like a fragment of a Frag Order.

There was zero actionable intel.

Col. Randal, Lieutenant Jake Novak aka "Jake-the-Snake," Master Sergeant Mack Beckwith, King, and the Lovat Scouts were aboard the lead aircraft piloted by Major General Sam Houston Blackwell—friends called him "Bronc," with Beverly, his University of Texas "Ten Most Beautiful" daughter, flying co-pilot. Major Jack Dance was the senior officer on the second plane, with Captain Billy Jack Jaxx in charge of the troops on the third.

They were the key players in the hurriedly assembled ad hoc Ranger Task Force.

The only information available at this point was a cryptic message from ABC Headquarters that German raiders had landed on Castelrozzo. Fighting had ensued resulting in a number of Raiding Forces personnel being KIA. Major the Lady Jane Seaborn, LG, OBE, RM, was unaccounted for.

At that point communications with Castelrozzo were lost and could not be reestablished.

Maj. Gen. Blackwell said, "What can you tell me about Brandenburger Commandos?"

Col. Randal said, "My information is they conduct national-level special operations for the Third Reich—specifically the Abwehr. The regiment contains a high percentage of foreigners or men with language skills. They have been known to operate in the other side's uniforms or civilian clothes. By all accounts it consists of highly motivated, extensively trained, picked men who do not adhere to the Geneva Convention."

Maj. Gen. Blackwell said, "Sound like bad actors to me."

Col. Randal said, "Reputation for war crimes, General—that's their MO."

Beverly said, "OK, for the last month in our spare time Mandy and I have been working up an enemy threat assessment for Sir Terry. Johnny's describing them exactly right, Daddy.

Brandenburgers are Germany's elite warrior spies. All we've been able to learn from MI-6 and SOE about the Brandenburger Regiment is it's a shadowy special operations unit directly controlled by Admiral Canaris, Chief of the Abwehr.

"Elements of the regiment have recently been reported in the Aegean AO."

At the time Lady Jane recruited the blond Tri-Delta Sorority girl to be her personal assistant she was an unpaid intern working at the Office of Strategic Services HQ (OSS) in Washington, D.C., on summer break from the University of Texas. Since joining Raiding Forces in addition to her other duties she was fast developing into a first-class intelligence officer.

Ordinarily, Beverly was laughing with a smile as big as Texas which made her fun to be around. But all signs of laughter had ceased the moment she heard that Lady Jane was MIA. The two were extremely close—almost like the sister neither one had.

Maj. Gen. Blackwell said, "The Brandenburger Regiment sounds a lot like the Nazi version of Raiding Forces."

Beverly said, "In an MI-6 intelligence report I read Canaris described them as 'brave ruthless men.' Doesn't take much imagination to understand what that means."

Col. Randal said, "At the start of the war when Hitler was gobbling up European countries, standard operating procedure was for Brandenburgers to precede Wehrmacht ground forces during the initial phase of an invasion. Their mission was to pave the way for the conventional assault units. They specialized in seizing strategic point-type targets on the line of attack by utilizing the art of deception.

"Then the conventional forces rolled through right behind them.

Beverly said, "The idea was to make it possible for German ground forces to storm in without being held up at the start line by a bunker complex, blocked railway tunnel or a blown bridge."

Maj. Gen. Blackwell said, "Pretty smart."

Col. Randal said, "Recent reports indicate out here they've been transitioning to small-scale Commando-type raids. Typically Brandenburger missions are characterized by surprise, speed, and violence of action. Most are raids of short duration—in and out fast, sir."

"So, what does that tell you, Colonel?"

"The Brandenburger Sea Raiders may be the advance element of a larger German reoccupation of Castelrozzo—which I doubt. The Nazis couldn't hold the island even if they did take it. My thought is the Abwehr specifically targeted someone."

Maj. Gen. Blackwell said, "And…?"

"If that's the case sir, the last two words in the definition of raid is *rapid withdrawal.*"

"Got it—what's the bottom line?"

Col. Randal said, "There's a chance the Brandenburgers exfiltrate before we can get there, sir."

"Not the assessment I wanted, Colonel."

Beverly said, "You suspect the Abwehr targeted Lady Jane?"

Col. Randal said, "It's possible."

Maj. Gen. Blackwell said, "I'm guessing those bad boys were coming for you Johnny, but you weren't home."

Beverly said, "Agreed."

Col. Randal said, "Wish I had been."

Beverly said, "Me too—seriously."

2035 HOURS.

THE THREE C-47S TOUCHED DOWN AT A ROYAL Air Force (RAF) base in Alexandria to refuel. Vice Admiral Sir Randolph "Razor" Ransom, VC, KCB, DSO, OBE, DSC, RN, was waiting when they arrived. As the Royal Navy's Director of Operations (Irregular) and the Chairman of Small Raids Inc., he was the commander of all small-scale naval operations in the Aegean.

The Admiral was Colonel John Randal's immediate superior.

Standing with VAdm. Ransom was Captain "Geronimo" Joe McKoy. He was back in Egypt after a whirlwind trip to the United States with Brigadier General William "Wild Bill" Donovan, Director of the OSS. They had needed to resolve his military status.

Both men were stone-faced.

Major the Lady Jane Seaborn was VAdm. Ransom's favorite niece.

Capt. McKoy and Lady Jane were longtime friends. She had introduced him to Raiding Forces back in the dark days in England when the Germans were expected to invade at any minute.

The troops deplaned and were trucked to barracks where they could take a shower, change into clean new U.S. Army-issue Paratroop M-42 jump suits, and chow down on a hot cooked meal. Everyone needed to draw ammunition, grenades, and demolitions. After the constant fighting of the last week most men had expended the triple basic load they were carrying when they jumped on Benevento.

The Rangers were wired tight exhibiting the kind of intensity that comes with having been constantly on the move in continuous action for days aware another mission was imminent—tonight.

The word was Lady Jane was MIA. To say the green-eyed brunette with the razor-sharp cheekbones and heart-attack smile was well-loved by the men and women of Raiding Forces would be a world-class understatement. She had adopted the unit shortly after it was formed—before it was Raiding Forces—and gave them their name.

Lady Jane took care of "her" troops, and they knew it.

Ranger Task Force wanted to hurt somebody—now.

Major General Sam Houston Blackwell, Col. Randal, Capt. McKoy, Major Jack Dance, Captain Billy Jack Jaxx, and Beverly were driven to the 10th Motor Gunboat Flotilla's Headquarters where VAdm. Ransom maintained a low-profile suite of offices. There was no sign outside. Those who had business with the Razor knew where his HQ was located.

Others had no Need to Know.

The group walked inside for an updated briefing. The atmosphere was tense. A Brandenburger raid on ABC was close to "worst-case scenario" for the island. Col. Randal had prepared a contingency plan called JAIL BREAK in the event of such an emergency—but it was not a good one.

VAdm. Ransom said, "At approximately 0200 hours night before last the Night Duty Officer in the Operation's Room at ABCHQ, Lieutenant St. Ledger, radioed RFHQ the island was under attack by German ground forces and Lady Jane was unaccounted for. Then the signal was lost. We have not been able to reestablish communications at this time.

"Jim Taylor has advised a German Forces Aegean radio intercept identified the attackers as a section of the 1st Sea Raider Battalion, Brandenburger Regiment. They inserted from a pair of E-boats.

“The majority of the people present on ABC at the time of the incursion consisted of small contingents of mostly female staff belonging to Raiding Forces, Small Raids Inc., MI-6 (Secret Intelligence), MI-9 (Escape), A-Force, Psy-Ops, and SOE. Castelrozzo was devoid of fighting troops except for the handful of Vulnerable Points Wing security personnel and the under-strength rifle company from the 2nd Battalion, Royal Essex Regiment recently rotated in to secure the perimeter of the island.”

VAdm. Ransom continued, “The bulk of Raiding Forces personnel remaining behind when the 575th Ranger Force deployed to Italy were away on operations or billeted aboard LFS schooners anchored in inlets along the Turkish coastline.

“The Brandenburgers landed on ABC away from the village. They marched overland avoiding detection by the 2nd Royal Essex coming in from the rear—land side. Then the Nazis attacked ABCHQ located in the palace complex constructed for Mussolini in better days.

“That is all the intelligence available to us at this time.”

The room was deadly still.

VAdm. Ransom said, “Colonel Stone and Captain Hoolihan press-ganged every mostly sober Royal Marine they could locate on shore leave in Alexandria—forty-nine Bootnecks. The Marines boarded four 10th Flotilla MGBs and set sail. Should be arriving off Castelrozzo in approximately two hours.

“Sir Terry is in command.

“Major Zargo is en route to ABC with a Greek Sacred Squadron detachment of approximately platoon strength but they shall take time to arrive having only LSF caiques for transportation.

“A wireless message went out from my headquarters to every Small Raids Inc. craft, primarily MGBs, PTs, and Levant Schooner Flotilla caiques, within one hundred miles of ABC.

The skippers were ordered to stand down from whatever mission they were on and make for Castelrozzo with all due speed. Upon arriving they shall land ashore any military passengers they happen to be transporting then standby off the island to establish a blockade to prevent the Brandenburgers from being reinforced or escaping by sea."

VAdm. Ransom said, "I intend to pin the intruders in place until the cavalry—meaning the Royal Marines, Rangers, and Greek Sacred Squadron—can arrive. While desperate times breed desperate measures, I cannot help but fear committing troops piecemeal to be a poor tactical solution. Nevertheless, it was the only option available.

"What say you, Colonel Randal?"

BRANDY SEABORN, THE MOST GLAMOROUS SKIPPER in the ragtag Small Raids Inc./ Raiding Forces navy, was at the helm of her sleek Italian MAS boat pounding hard for Castelrozzo. For once Captain Penelope "Legs" Honeycutt-Parker, OBE, GM, RM, was not onboard. When the Italians capitulated, the two women secured a boarding party of Royal Marines and raced to the nearest island known to be occupied by the Regia Marina. While the military situation was still fluid, they commandeered another MAS torpedo boat from the confused Italian sailors even though the terms of the agreement did not authorize them to do that.

The big-picture strategy was for the Italian Armed Forces to remain intact and fight on the Allied side. Brandy and Capt. Parker were not much impressed with the big picture. They were small-picture sailors who operated in the here and now.

"Legs" Parker had a command of her own but no fully trained crew which prevented her from being out tonight.

Brandy had been in the process of transporting a team of Veronica Paige's MI-9 (Escape) operatives on a clandestine mission for MI-6 (Secret Intelligence) about which she was not cleared to know the details. During transport she received a message from her father, Vice Admiral Sir Randolph "Razor" Ransom, stating Castelrozzo was being attacked by German amphibious troops. She immediately put about and raced toward the island at flank speed.

Her passengers, known in the intelligence trade as "Joes," were caught off guard by the turn of events, but they were all armed men. What four intelligence operatives could hope to accomplish against fanatical Brandenburger Commandos was questionable. Still, exigent circumstances demanded every man and woman do their duty.

All hands on deck.

Happening simultaneously, her father was briefing Colonel John Randal; her son, Lt. Randy Seaborn, was racing to the scene in his PT boat; and Brandy was arriving off the island away from the harbor where Raiding Forces Advanced Base Castelrozzo Headquarters was located. She decided to skirt the coastline to land the MI-9 team as close as possible to their objective—ABCHQ.

Sailing around a point hugging the jagged shore, Brandy spotted the silhouette of two German E-boats close in, sheltering against the wall of a sheer rock cliff. The pair of Schnellboots were potent fighting craft. More than a match for a single MAS boat.

Fortunately, she had Guns, the most decorated gunnery rating in the Royal Navy, manning her Thunderbolt mount. It consisted of four Oerlikon 20mm cannons augmented by six M2 Browning .50 caliber machine guns—this was an upgrade from the original pair of 20mm's on the gun mount. They could fire simultaneously at the touch of a trigger.

Brandy ordered, "Guns!"

Guns went on "G."

The Thunderbolt's 20mm Oerlikon cannon and the .50 M2 Browning heavy machine gun fire supported by the other three additional pairs of M2 Browning .50 caliber machine guns on the MAS boat roared to life. The massed fire vectored in on the target at virtual contact range for a sea engagement. There were so many tracers converging so fast that it looked as if a searchlight had been shined on the Nazi patrol torpedo boat.

It was hard to believe tracers were only loaded one every six rounds.

The sound and fury of the automatic weapons fire was deafening. It sucked the wind out of the air. The noise was not what one would have imagined. The effect of so much concentrated fire so fast was a yawning sound.

Low-pitched, like a heavy-duty chain saw being run in a cloak closet.

Guns was a true artist with the Thunderbolt and had done this before. He swept the port side E-boat stem to stern as if he were wielding a paintbrush. One moment the Schnellboot was a deadly Nazi fighting machine. The next it was a smoldering wreck floating dead in the water.

Shifting his fire, Guns transitioned to the second E-boat with the same result. The fight, if you could call it that, was over quick. Ten seconds, maybe less.

No one was counting.

Unlike in the movies, there were no big fireballs. Nothing blew up. Just two lifeless hulks bobbing listlessly in total silence shot to matchsticks in a matter of seconds. The mangled bodies of the Kriegsmarine crews littered the E-boat's decks.

Now the Brandenburger Sea Raiders had no way off the island.

COLONEL JOHN RANDAL WAS STANDING IN FRONT of a wall map depicting Castelrozzo Island in Vice Admiral Sir Randolph "Razor" Ransom's Operations Room at 10th Motor Gunboat Flotilla Headquarters. The Rangers who had flown in on the three C-47s were crowded around in a semi-circle, listening intently.

Because these were serious men and this was a serious briefing melodrama was kept to a minimum. Professionals only want to know who, what, when, where, and how many. The problem was there were no firm answers to most of those questions.

Col. Randal said, "All the intel we have at this time is that Castelrozzo has come under ground attack by what British Intelligence has reason to believe are Brandenburger Sea Raiders. We do not know in what strength. ABCHQ is thought to have been the primary objective of the raid.

"Admiral Ransom has signaled every MGB, PT boat, and LSF caique within a hundred miles of the island to sail for Castelrozzo. Their orders are to land any military parties they have onboard then stand offshore to establish a naval blockade. Colonel Stone and a contingent of Royal Marines in reinforced platoon strength are aboard four MGBs from the 10th Motor Gunboat Flotilla headed to ABC. Major Zargo is also en route aboard LSF caiques with an equal-sized detachment of his GSS Commandos.

"Immediately upon conclusion of this briefing we'll reboard our C-47s, fly to Castelrozzo, and conduct a night parachute drop. As you men know the island consists of rugged terrain but there's a plateau in the center large enough to construct a small airfield—the perfect DZ. We'll jump in and make an overland movement to our Objective Rally Point/Release Point which will be the castle on the escarpment above the village. From there we'll move to retake ABCHQ, Government Building, clear the harbor area, rescue any of our people being held, and then clear all other positions being occupied by the Germans.

"Once on the ground, you'll assemble in the same teams you've been operating for the last week. The teams will make up patrols which correspond to the chalk they flew in on."

This caused a stir. No one present had expected those teams to ever be utilized as operational units again. They were a random collection of paratroopers who had found themselves landing together or linking up by happenstance following the chaos of a 3,000-foot drop in high, mountainous terrain in the vicinity of Benevento, Italy, green-lighted by disoriented pilots who had no idea where the drop zone (DZ) was.

Per Col. Randal's orders jumpers had banded together upon landing in groups of no more than six Rangers. The teams had gone into business for themselves with the senior man present taking command. One team in the room had been led by a Private First Class—PFC Norvel "Horn Dog" Hansen.

While the ad hoc teams were less than optimal for unit cohesiveness on a mission of this type tonight a reorganization at this stage was not a tactically sound idea—at least not completely.

Col. Randal did plan to reshuffle the order of the officers and teams onboard the three C-47s for the Castelrozzo drop.

Col. Randal said, "I'll be in overall command. The senior officer onboard each aircraft will lead the Rangers on their chalks—organized into patrols of two teams each. The patrol leaders are:

"Lieutenant Novak, Chalk 1. He's been wandering around alone all by himself behind enemy lines for five of the last six days, so he'll probably enjoy the company."

The Rangers laughed.

"Major Dance, Chalk 2.

"Captain Jaxx, Chalk 3."

The men saw Col. Randal was in charge and on point in the delivery of his order seemingly unaffected by the news that Major the Lady Jane Seaborn was MIA. The Rangers noted he maintained his typical laid-back style while briefing possibly the most complex operation any military unit can be tasked to undertake—liberating prisoners.

Experienced special operations veterans pay close attention to details like that. A lot of things can go wrong on a mission like the one being briefed. Only one outcome is a success and they want the commander to bring his A-game to the fight.

Col. Randal's calm professional delivery as usual instilled confidence in men who had a long history of trusting him with their life.

The Rangers' estimate of the situation concerning their commanding officer's state of mind was way far off base. He was not feeling one bit calm or confident. Parachute onto ABC in the dark of night, kill or capture the Brandenburger Commandos known to be on the island, and liberate their prisoners—what could possibly go wrong?

To effect a rescue without loss of life to those being saved it is necessary to know *where* the person or persons to be liberated can be found at a certain *time* at a certain *place.* And Col. Randal had no idea as to the answer to any of those three things.

That was a problem.

Not making him feel any better was the list of female personnel known to be on Castelrozzo at the time of the Brandenburger raid: Lady Jane, Veronica Paige, Mandy Paige, Captain Stephanie Fawcett-Tatum, RM; Rikke Runborg; Lieutenant Bentley St. Ledger, RM; Alex "Cat" Gataki . . .

Col. Randal said, "The belief is the Germans will have taken some of our personnel prisoners—my guess is that's the case. Go in hard but keep in mind this is a rescue mission. We can't blow up everything. Team Leaders, keep your people under tight control.

"Once we're assembled on the DZ the order of march will be Lieutenant Novak, Captain Jaxx, followed by Major Dance. My command party will initially be traveling with Lieutenant Novak, then transition to Captain Jaxx's patrol when we reach our ORP.

"From there Lieutenant Novak's patrol will move down to sweep the built-up harbor area in the village. Major Dance's patrol will follow Lieutenant Novak out of the ORP. It will break off, proceed to Government House and clear it. Then stand by acting as Task Force reserve until we can develop the situation and get a better idea of what we're dealing with on the ground. Captain Jaxx's patrol, with my command party attached, will travel to and effect entry of ABCHQ to clear the complex.

"What are your questions?"

PFC Hansen's hand shot up. "Sir, you forgot weather. What's the forecast"?

A fair question since it is one of the items that should be included in a standard Operations Order, but one that had no business being asked—typical Horn Dog. They were going tonight no matter what the meteorological conditions.

Except for a few snickers a pin drop could have been heard in the room.

Col. Randal said, "Nasty."

Tension ratcheted down. Everyone laughed—a good leader can make that happen prior to a dangerous endeavor.

The instant Col. Randal gave the traditional, "This concludes my briefing," Master Sergeant Mack Beckwith pounced. He had PFC Hansen braced in a corner heels locked in a rigid position of attention. The young trooper found himself on the receiving end of a highly animated dose of old Army counseling, euphemistically described as "command guidance," delivered in a loud, verbose military manner.

The Sergeant Major was bringing smoke.

PFC Hansen would probably not be asking any more questions about the weather.

MAJOR GENERAL SAM HOUSTON BLACKWELL SAID, "That's it? That's all you've got?"

Colonel John Randal said, "Yes, sir."

Maj. Gen. Blackwell said, "You sure as little green apples adhered to rule No. 2: 'keep it short and simple'—yeah, I've memorized 'em.

"Heard better plans at a sandlot football game, Johnny."

They were riding in a khaki-colored Chevrolet staff car en route to the RAF airfield where the Rangers were to reboard the three freshly topped-off United States Army Air Force (USAAF) C-47 Dakota aircraft for the flight to Castelrozzo.

"Your married fiancée—whose sorry, no-good husband stiffed her on signing their divorce papers before shipping out to the China-Burma-India Theatre and who every single person I've ever talked to describes as big rich, drop-dead gorgeous with an even more beautiful heart—is MIA. Probably being held prisoner by the most diabolical Nazi thugs in the Third Reich.

"And your idea is to parachute onto Castelrozzo Island and '*develop the situation*'?

"That some kinda' Commando code for 'see what happens next'?"

Col. Randal said, "Pretty much, General."

Maj. Gen. Blackwell said, "If there's anything I can do to help stop this downward spiral in your life, son—you let me know."

Beverly said, "That's harsh, Daddy. Don't blame Johnny. It's not his fault there's . . ."

A horn started honking. Vice Admiral Sir Randolph "Razor" Ransom's command car was behind them. The lights flashed.

Maj. Gen. Blackwell ordered the driver, "Pull over."

He and Col. Randal exited and walked back to the other vehicle. VAdm. Ransom stepped out. They held a senior officers conference on the side of the dusty road as the trucks carrying the Rangers raced past.

VAdm. Ransom said, "My headquarters received a wireless message from Brandy moments after you departed. Upon arriving at Castelrozzo she fell in with the two E-boats believed to have delivered the Brandenburger Commandos to the island. Scratch a pair of Kriegsmarine motor torpedo boats.

"The Küstenjägers may not be aware of it at this point but they have no transportation home."

Col. Randal said, "What about the harbor, sir? There's always a caique or two tied up at the dock."

VAdm. Ransom said, "Randy is on station standing off shore aboard his PT boat at this time praying the Germans try to make a break for it. Brandy will be joining him shortly. The escape-by-sea option is off the table, gentlemen."

Maj. Gen. Blackwell said, "If the Brandenburgers are such masters of the art of lightning-fast raids why did they hang around ABC so long?"

Col. Randal said, "There's a chance they didn't find what they came for, sir."

Maj. Gen. Blackwell said, "That would be you then—they're making a major tactical mistake."

VAdm. Ransom said, "Affirmative. One they shall regret soon enough. Bring my niece home safe, Colonel."

The two officers locked eyes.

"Do my best, sir."

VAdm. Ransom said, "Before he sailed, Captain Hoolihan informed me he was issuing orders to his Royal Marines: Abyssinian Rules are in full force and effect."

Col. Randal said, "Good for Headhunter."

When they got back in the staff car, Maj. Gen. Blackwell said, "That Razor's one tough cookie. A man like him might not make such great father-in-law material. Still, I'm looking forward to meeting his daughter."

"For what it's worth, sir, the Admiral and Brandy welcomed me into the Seaborn family before Jane did."

Maj. Gen. Blackwell said, "Billy Jack told me she's so hot people rub her for luck."

Beverly looked at Col. Randal and rolled her eyes.

Col. Randal said, "He's not wrong, General."

Maj Gen. Blackwell said, "Yeah, I saw that picture of her Jack used to have in his plexiglass pistol grip. How did he ever get a woman like her to pose for a pin-up photo?"

Col. Randal said, "Brandy lives life to the max, sir."

Maj. Gen. Blackwell said, "So, how does sinking those two E-boats change the equation?"

Col. Randal said, "Good news and bad news. The Brandenburgers can't get off the island. Now prisoners are excess baggage, sir."

Maj. Gen. Blackwell said, "The hits just keep on coming."

At the departure airfield, the staff car pulled up to Chalk 1. The plane was easy enough to identify. A giant black silhouette of a bucking horse was painted on the left side of the nose under the pilot's window with "BRONC" emblazoned in script over smaller stenciled letters that read "Major General Sam H. Blackwell."

Next to the jump door at the tail, someone had scrawled in crude white chalk letters "KILROY WAS HERE."

It was not clear what that meant.

The Rangers were standing on the tarmac checking their equipment. Every paratrooper was responsible for sorting out his individual kit. In addition to their personal gear, each man had a British X-type parachute and a reserve lying at their feet. Tonight the reserve chute was for show. On this drop, the plan was to fly in low, get down on the ground fast, and hit the DZ in a tight formation because Col. Randal wanted to spend minimal time assembling.

Jump altitude was going to be too low to deploy a reserve—still everyone liked having one.

Maj. Gen. Blackwell and Beverly proceeded directly onboard to begin their preflight checks. Captain "Geronimo" Joe McKoy was talking to Lieutenant Jake Novak. He was fully armed to include his Winchester .30 M1 Carbine.

He liked it because it reminded him of a saddle gun.

Col. Randal said, "You're not . . ."

"Yeah, I am, John."

And that was that.

Lt. Novak was acting as Col. Randal's assistant jumpmaster on Chalk 1. "On board rigging an hour out, sound about right to you, sir?"

"Affirmative."

The former Pathfinder Platoon Leader from the 509th Parachute Infantry Battalion's Scout Company was a highly experienced paratrooper and a veteran of the North Afrika combat jump. He walked away to talk to the men in the stick. Lt. Novak intended to take advantage of every opportunity to spend time prior to green light with the Rangers in the patrol he would be leading. Even though he had been on the Benevento drop he was still the new player in a close-knit outfit.

Respect was earned not given in Raiding Forces. The Rangers were willing to cut Lt. Novak some slack up to a point.

Col. Randal had a record of selecting outstanding officers so he had that in his favor. Even so, "Jake the Snake" would have to demonstrate he had the right stuff—the men needed to see him do it.

Private First Class Norvel "Horn Dog" Hansen said, "How's the transfer to Raiding Forces working for you so far, El Tee?"

Lt. Novak said, "When we get on the ground assembled and prepared to move out you're on point, Norvel."

The men on PFC Hansen's team went, "Whoooa!"

People did not call Lt. Novak "Jake-the-Snake" because he reminded them of a warm cuddly pet.

Captain Karen Montgomery came around in a three-quarter-ton truck to drop off parachutes. Another truck came by to re-up ammunition and grenades for those who might have decided at the last minute they wanted extra. Nothing like an imminent operation to make a man rethink his ammo requirements.

There was none of the horseplay that typically took place at a departure airfield prior to a jump. Tonight the Rangers were conducting themselves as the professionals they were. No wasted time, no wasted movements, no wasted energy. Battle-hardened paratroopers going about the job of staging for their next combat jump.

Everyone was dialed in, tightly focused—impatient to get the mission under way.

The left engine of Chalk 1 backfired, wheezed, and slowly turned over.

The USAAF loadmaster came to the door of the aircraft.

Col. Randal made eye contact with Jake the Snake.

Lt. Novak ordered, "Saddle up, boys. Let's go! Next stop—Castelrozzo. Where Europe ends and Asia begins."

Col. Randal looked across the tarmac. Major Jack Dance was loading his men. Captain Billy Jack Jaxx was boarding his. When there were no Rangers left standing on the airfield he reached up, grabbed Capt. McKoy's outstretched hand and swung aboard.

The USAAF loadmaster slammed the door and spoke into his headset.

Almost immediately Maj. Gen. Blackwell began his take-off run.

Once airborne the three C-47s settled into a flying V. While the two follow-on pilots might not have been the world's best long-distance navigators they were skilled troop transport drivers and could fly a tight formation. Ahead was a two-hour flight to green light.

Destination—Drop Zone Castelrozzo.

LIEUTENANT JAKE NOVAK, aka JAKE THE SNAKE, was holding court in the back of the C-47 as it droned across the

Aegean. Colonel John Randal and Captain "Geronimo" Joe McKoy, sitting with Master Sergeant Mack Beckwith and Beverly Blackwell, who had come back from the cockpit to visit, were listening in. The former 509th Parachute Infantry Battalion Pathfinder Platoon Leader had the Rangers laughing.

"Join the army they said. It'll be fun they said. Volunteer for the paratroops they said…"

Col. Randal turned to Capt. McKoy. "Tell me about your trip to Washington."

Capt. McKoy said, "Donovan took me from the airport to the White House. We were ushered straight into the Oval Office. I've known the Roosevelt family ever since leadin' TR's mare Little Texas up San Juan Hill, which was actually Kettle Hill, over in Cuba—get a card from 'em at Christmas.

"So, we didn't waste much time dancin' around the how-dee-dos.

"First thing, the President's military aide reads out orders promotin' me to major general in the Reserve Army of the United States. Soon as that's done he broke out a second set of orders which he read, retirin' me on the spot—Boom!

"President Roosevelt said, 'Thank you for your service, General McKoy. Now get your ass on the next flight back to Egypt and stay on toppa' LEAF EATER—that's a presidential order.'"

Col. Randal said, "Roosevelt said that?"

"Word for word."

Beverly said, "Presidents use that kind of language?"

Capt. McKoy said, "Yeah, well, that's what the man said—direct quote. Then as we were headin' outta the Oval Office his military aide proceeds to hand over a telegram addressed to me care 'a the White House from my ol' quail huntin' buddy, the Governor 'a Arizona. He'd been informed I was bein' retired and wouldn't be available to command the state's National Guard Division when it mobilized for federal service like he intended me to."

Col. Randal said, "You were going to command a National Guard Division?"

"That was the Governor's idea, not mine. Never bein' a man big on rejection, even by a sittin' president of the United States—particularly one he didn't vote for—and bein' the hardcase he is, the Governor decided to rub FDR's nose in it some. His telegram was to officially inform me that due to the recent change in my military status, no longer bein' on the Army Reserve list and all, he was takin' the opportunity to advance me one grade in the Arizona State Guard."

MSgt. Beckwith said, "What rank does that make you now, Joe?"

"Lieutenant General."

Col. Randal said, "You're kidding."

"Well, it's only in the state 'a Arizona."

Beverly said, "Love it! There can't be more than thirty Lieutenant Generals in all branches of the military combined. And that's counting every theatre of operations worldwide. I know because when I was interning at OSS my job was to stick the pins in the wall maps."

Col. Randal said, "Congratulations, General."

Lieutenant General "Geronimo" Joe McKoy said, "Don't start that, John. I still want to be called 'Captain'—my stage name."

Col. Randal said, "I don't think that's going to happen."

COLONEL JOHN RANDAL HUDDLED WITH Lieutenant General "Geronimo" Joe McKoy and Lieutenant Jake Novak. King, Lovat Scouts Munro Ferguson and Lionel Fenwick, Beverly Blackwell and Master Sergeant Mack Beckwith were listening in. The senior Raiding Forces NCO insisted on being physically present any time his boss was involved in anything other than a closed-door session.

Sergeant Majors like to be accorded the privileges of their rank. They do not like to be left out of the command party. However tonight MSgt. Beckwith would be operating in a dual capacity: senior NCO for the ad hoc Ranger Task Force and one of the two team leaders in Lt. Novak's patrol—in charge of the men he had organized and fought with following the Benevento drop.

At this point in the operation Col. Randal was having second thoughts about the hurried Op Order he had issued earlier. It had not followed the traditional five-paragraph SITUATION, MISSION, EXECUTION, COMMAND & SIGNAL, and ADMINISTRATION & LOGISTICS format. In fact, it was not even a good frag order.

Had he been grading his performance, which is always pass/fail for tactics, he would have flunked himself.

It has long been known that the best way to get an idea across to the troops is by repetition. That concept had been hammered into him in all the military schools he had attended. Then reinforced by the two Master Sergeants, Hammerhead and Tiger Stripe, when he was detached from the U.S. 26th Cavalry Regiment to the Philippine Scouts Constabulary for anti-bandit duties. And finally at the British Commando Training Center in Achnacarry, Scotland.

Since Col. Randal had a few of his leaders on board Chalk 1 he decided to take advantage of the opportunity to go over the plan one more time with his key players. Without a doubt Major Jack Dance and Captain Billy Jack Jaxx would be doing the same thing on the other two aircraft.

Col. Randal said, “When we get on the ground Lieutenant Novak you take the lead. I’ll initially travel with your patrol. Private Hansen, I understand your team is to be the point element. You two Lovat Scouts link up with Horn Dog—lead Ranger Task Force to the ORP.

“When we arrive, General McKoy, King, the Scouts, and I will transition to Captain Jaxx’s patrol. Sergeant Major, I want you closed up tight with the lieutenant during his movement to contact. Jake’s never been to Castelrozzo help him get there.

“Major Dance’s patrol will follow Lieutenant Novak’s out of the ORP, then break off to secure Government House.

“Captain Jaxx’s patrol and the command party will depart last. Upon reaching ABCHQ his party will assault and secure the ground floor of the building. General McKoy, King, the Scouts, and I will pause to allow them time to make entry. Then we’ll pass through and proceed up the staircase to clear the second floor where Lady Jane has her suite.

“A follow-on team of Captain Jaxx’s men will then leapfrog us to clear the third floor.

“Questions?”

They all had questions but knew there were no answers, so none were asked.

Col. Randal said, “Everyone wants a chance to light up the Brandenburgers tonight but remember, we need prisoners. They can provide intel about where our people are being held—then you can smoke ’em.

“Exercise extreme caution you’ll be going up against the best Nazis in the business.”

Lt. Gen. McKoy said, “Dangerous as rattlesnakes. Treat ’em as such. But remember, boys, for our purposes a live prisoner is better than a dead bad guy.

“Can’t emphasize that enough.”

Col. Randal said, “Lieutenant Novak, when you arrive in the harbor area clear every building.”

“Yes, sir.”

Col. Randal said, “In the event you find yourself in a protracted firefight Major Dance will move to reinforce. Unless that is he’s tied down with problems of his own at Government House. In that case Captain Jaxx will come to your assistance, provided we’re not still engaged at ABCHQ.

“If that happens, you’re on your own—clear?”

Lt. Novak said, “Roger sir.”

“If the Brandenburgers are holding prisoners my guess is they’ll be concentrated somewhere near the dock. They’ll be wondering why the E-boats haven’t arrived. Expect them to be trigger happy.

“I say again—exercise extreme caution.”

Lt. Novak said, “Let me get this straight, sir. Kill all the bad guys, but we should try to capture ’em first. While we’re at it, try not to kill the good guys—who may turn out to be girls.

Col. Randal said, “You’re starting to show potential, Jake.”

THE USAAF LOADMASTER INFORMED COLONEL JOHN Randal, “Ten minutes out, sir.”

The jump light over the open door switched on red.

Col. Randal stood up and splaying his fingers on both hands arms outstretched, gave the command, “TEN MINUTES!”

There was the rustle of Rangers moving around on their bench seats checking their equipment for the thousandth time since the C-47 had taken off from the RAF airfield in Alexandria. Col. Randal moved up the aisle doing the airborne shuffle—never picking his boots off the deck to prevent any possibility of tripping. He made his way to the cockpit to effect last-minute coordination with the pilots.

Out the windscreen he could see a big full moon.

That may have been why the Brandenburgers had chosen this particular time to raid Castelrozzo—because of the increased visibility. It was fashionable for the Royal Navy to time their operations to the moon cycle. Possibly the Germans did the same. Col. Randal had long thought the practice originated as an excuse by the Royal Navy *not* to conduct a Commando raid which they saw as a misuse of their limited resources of ships.

Now, timing of airborne operations was being dictated by the phases of the moon as well. Theoretically, the idea was to give paratroopers better light to see by while assembling after they landed. Col. Randal believed the policy was a classic example of overthinking by rear echelon armchair-Commando staff officers possessed of strong opinions and little or no practical experience.

Raiding Forces went when ready—moon or no moon.

Major General Sam Houston Blackwell was sitting in the co-pilot's chair. Beverly Blackwell was in the command pilot's left seat, flying the plane. They had switched places for this last leg of the long flight from Italy because she flew the route often.

Besides, Maj. Gen. Blackwell thought it great fun to have his daughter be his airplane driver. He could sit back and watch the operation unfold. Bronc loved to drop paratroopers. A lot of moving parts were involved in the process of putting jumpers on the ground, on time, on target.

It was not easy.

Tonight the flight path required an off-island approach, then a hard dogleg to port in order to arrive over the drop zone without overflying Turkey or encroaching on its airspace. Beverly was banking the plane when Col. Randal shuffled into the cockpit. The hard turn was necessary because neutral Turkey was only a mile from Castelrozzo.

The exercise was a political fig leaf. The C-47 was *already* in Turkish airspace. Castelrozzo lay nearly two miles inside the three-mile territorial limit all nations claim.

Beverly glanced over her shoulder. "Confirm—where do you want me to green-light the drop, Johnny?"

"Dead center in the middle of the island."

"I can put you down closer to ABCHQ."

"Not necessary."

Beverly said, "OK, forget everything I said to you previously about heroics being overrated. Kick ass and take names, Johnny—rescue Lady Jane."

Maj. Gen. Blackwell looked over his shoulder and gave Col. Randal a wink.

That's when the thought occurred to Col. Randal that Bronc might have an ulterior motive for letting Beverly fly the final leg. The General may have been concerned that if Beverly were not flying the aircraft she might stand up, stroll back, and tailgate the stick out the door. No way to stop her—she was wearing a USAAF B-7 backpack-type parachute.

With Beverly it was a legitimate concern.

Maj. Gen. Blackwell said, "Good luck, Colonel. We'll talk about the 'Paratroop Advisor' deal under better circumstances. Have an idea I'm pretty sure will work for the both of us."

"Yes, sir."

"Get it done, son."

Beverly said, "Six in thirty."

Col. Randal shuffled back down the aisle, turned, and faced the Rangers arms outstretched holding up six fingers, "SIX MINUTES!"

Then he braced his canvas-topped raiding boots on either side of the door, reached up and gripped the rim that ran around the edge and arched himself out to make his initial jumpmaster inspection. This check was unnecessary. He had already had a look at the DZ out the windscreen from the cockpit. The other two C-47s were in trail, closed up tight. There was no Initial Point (IP), checkpoints, or ground signals to verify.

They were jumping on his command—not the light even though it would be on.

Col. Randal looked aft one more time to confirm the two trailing aircraft were where they were supposed to be then swung back inside.

"STAND UP AND HOOK UP!"

This was the command the Rangers had been waiting for. If anyone had been having butterflies about the jump they went away now. From this point forward it was strictly business.

The men were all switched on, dialed in, ready to go.

"CHECK STATIC LINE!"

There was the usual metal-on-metal grating as the troops rattled their snap links. This sound was always a rush. It meant they were doing it. No matter how many jumps a paratrooper had it was always a thrill to be standing up, hooked up, with the sound of the wind rushing in the open exit.

In some ways, the commencement of the jump commands was the best part of being a paratrooper.

"CHECK YOUR EQUIPMENT!"

Also, a needless command tonight. Unless someone's reserve had malfunctioned and the silk started to spill out onboard the aircraft creating a safety hazard all the Rangers were going to jump. In the event that particular failure happened, as it did on rare occasions, it was not unknown for a jumper to scoop up the reserve's canopy in his arms, hold it protectively against his chest and exit the aircraft with the rest of the stick.

No one wanted to be left behind on board—not tonight.

"SOUND OFF FOR EQUIPMENT CHECK!"

Starting from the back of the stick like a string of falling dominoes, "Okay, Okay, Okay . . ." rippled its way to Col. Randal.

"ONE MINUTE—CLOSE ON THE DOOR!"

King, jumping No.2, braced himself as the stick surged forward. The men shoved up tight against the parachute pack of the man in front until they reached him. For this drop it was important to land as closely compacted as possible—quick assembly being all important.

There was not going to be time to waste rounding up misdropped jumpers.

Col. Randal turned and arched himself back outside the aircraft. This final jumpmaster check was absolutely crucial. He was planning to go on green but not until he physically observed the C-47 fly over the shoreline—the exit was on his command and he had no intention of going until ready.

The wind tore at his new U.S. Paratrooper issue #3 olive drab M-42 jump jacket the Rangers had been issued to replace the jumpsuits they had been living in for the past week. The M-42 was a prototype. Office of Strategic Services (OSS) was field testing them prior to adoption by Airborne Forces.

Castelrozzo was dead ahead.

The beach flashed past below.

"LET'S GO!"

Then he was out of the plane head down on his chest, feet and knees together, hands clasped on the ends of the reserve parachute on his chest, elbows in tight and counting, "ONE THOUSAND, TWO THOUSAND, THREE . . ."

The British X-type parachute deployed. Known for its soft opening shock, it delivered tonight. He barely felt it. Col. Randal found himself floating free, drifting backward, at peace with the world. Then *WHAAAM*!

He was down hard.

That was quick. Beverly had dropped them lower than 400 feet, a lot lower. That was one of the benefits of having a qualified parachutist as a pilot. She knew it was critical for assembly on the ground to take place as fast as possible.

The tradeoff was risking jump injuries. With experienced jumpers it was worth taking the chance. Beverly made the right call.

Lieutenant General "Geronimo" Joe McKoy walked over. King was with him. Lovat Scouts Munro Ferguson and Lionel Fenwick appeared. Captain Billy Jack Jaxx, jumping the third plane in the formation, came down hot in a textbook, prepare-to-land position and did a parachute landing fall (PLF), about six feet away. The following two C-47s had put their jumpers out right over Chalk 1's position.

They might not be competent at pinpoint long-distance navigation but the Troop Carrier Command pilots were outstanding formation fliers. Col. Randal could not have hoped for tighter dispersion. Things were happening all around him. Men were coming down, doing PLFs, dropping their parachutes, shaking out their personal equipment, charging weapons, assembling.

Lieutenant Jake Novak had his people organized and ready to move out in record-breaking time. Major Jack Dance sent a runner to say his patrol was assembled. Capt. Jaxx jogged to the front of the column to report in person. "Good to go, sir."

Col. Randal said, “We’re traveling at this time.”

Lt. Novak ordered, “Move out, Horn Dog—Lovat Scouts to the front.”

The Rangers began their advance on Castelrozzo village a little over a mile away out of sight over the escarpment. The Task Force was in a column formation moving with a purpose. The men were loose weapons at the ready.

Out of nowhere Ensign Theodore Hamilton aka The Great Teddy, OBE, appeared, “Hey Presto” like one of his magic tricks.

He reported to Col. Randal.

“Where do you want me, sir? I brought your 45mm Brixia and forty rounds. Thought you might want it.”

“How did you manage to get here, Ensign?”

“Capt. Jaxx had space available on his plane.”

“He just let you strap hang a combat mission?”

“I may have slightly overstated my authorization sir. Had to be in on this one. Lady Jane…”

Col. Randal said, “Fall in on me then. Better hope those Nazis have spirited her away to Berlin by now, stud. Because if they haven’t Lady Jane’s surely going to murder you for tagging along this night.”

Ens. Hamilton said, “I shall take my chances as long as we bring her back, sir.”

Patrolling to the ORP did not take long. The Rangers were moving with authority. As they traveled Col. Randal ran through various tactical scenarios in his mind. He always thought better on the move in command going back to his days in the jungle hunting Huk bandits.

The problem tonight was not enough information for him to develop a cohesive scheme of maneuver. Raids are characterized by detailed planning, surprise, speed, and violence of action. Tonight there was virtually no planning because of an almost total lack of intelligence. And with Greek civilians on the island and the Nazis potentially having taken prisoners the violence of action would have to be toned down.

Rescuing people is a lot harder than it sounds.

Col. Randal dropped back in the column to march with Captain Billy Jack Jaxx. The two took the opportunity to go over the details of what was going to take place once they arrived at the ORP. Best guess was prisoners would be held at ABCHQ—provided the Brandenburgers had taken any. Clearing the complex with the handful of Rangers available was going to require split-second timing, crisp execution, and precision teamwork.

That was why Col. Randal was entrusting the HQ's capture to his young Small Operations Group (SOG) commander. In a fast-developing contact the two of them were almost able to read each other's minds. They could anticipate each other's actions. And there was one other reason—troops responded to Capt. Jaxx better than any officer he had ever served with.

Lieutenant Jake Novak halted the Task Force at the ORP which was also the Release Point. From here the three patrols would move out to their objectives. The position was located at the base of the wall around the castle built by the Knights of Saint John in 1306. The ruin was on a precipice overlooking Castelrozzo Village. When selecting a Rally Point it is desirable for the commander/patrol leader to choose an easily recognizable terrain feature.

In that one thing tonight Col. Randal had overachieved.

The castle was the most dominant terrain feature on the island.

The Rangers established a defensive perimeter. Col. Randal held a brief leader's conference in the center to conduct final coordination—repetition, repetition, repetition. In the military there is no such thing as overkill on repetition.

As Lieutenant General "Geronimo" Joe McKoy liked to say—"Too much ain't enough."

Col. Randal said, "At that point we'll evaluate the situation and adjust our tactics as dictated by developments—questions?

There were none.

Maj. Gen. Blackwell was right—the Concept of the Operation was pitifully short on detail and there was no Plan B.

But now at least the Ranger Task Force element leaders had their final marching orders.

Col. Randal said, "All right then, let's do this."

2
IMPROVISE, ADAPT, OVERCOME . . . MAYBE

LIEUTENANT JAKE NOVAK'S PATROL MOVED OUT OF the ORP first. Major Jack Dance followed with his people. The Rangers snaked their way down the steep switchback trail disappearing into the darkness.

No lights were showing in the village below. Castelrozzo was on 100% blackout during the hours of darkness. The Nazis had an airfield on Rhodes only a half hour away by air. While the Luftwaffe had more important targets to fly against there was always the threat of aerial attack.

Air raids had taken place in the past.

After the two patrols departed Captain Billy Jack Jaxx ordered his people to shrink the perimeter. The plan was to remain in the ORP long enough to allow Lt. Novak and Maj. Dance time to reach their objectives. Then he and Col. Randal would commence their advance on ABCHQ.

Since there were three entrances to the Headquarters complex Capt. Jaxx's patrol was broken down into three entry teams. The Rangers were going to hit all three doors simultaneously. The idea was to execute a dynamic entry with the intent to put force on force.

Colonel John Randal, Lieutenant General "Geronimo" Joe McKoy, King, Ensign Theodore Hamilton, and the Lovat Scouts would follow the team led by Capt. Jaxx through the main entrance. While the Captain cleared the Operations Room the command party would proceed up the oversized spiral staircase to the second floor.

Col. Randal, King, and Ens. Hamilton would proceed directly to Lady Jane's suite. Lt. Gen. McKoy and the Lovat Scouts would break off to begin sweeping the guest bedrooms down the hall where the Royal Marines, FANYs, WRENs, and other female personnel had their sleeping quarters. Once he secured the Operations Room, Capt. Jaxx's team would follow Col. Randal's party up the staircase and bypass it to clear the third floor.

Col. Randal did not have high hopes the operation would play out as planned. There were too many tasks, too much space in the palace and not enough Rangers and the mission had been hastily developed with much of it being coordinated on the move following the jump. There was no time to conduct a rehearsal which is essential when taking down a point-type target like ABCHQ. And the Brandenburger Sea Raiders, being hardcore experienced individuals, were not about to roll over simply because Raiding Forces showed up.

Capt. Jaxx had his two team leaders, Sergeant Fred Waltmier and Corporal Leslie Cooper pull in tight to huddle for last-minute coordination.

"Synchronize watches 0345 in thirty seconds—hack. We hit the doors at 0400 straight up. Any bad guys encountered prior to entry time need to be eliminated utilizing suppressed weapons. Keep it frosty boys."

Col. Randal adjusted his Rolex as he listened in. A present from Lady Jane. He always thought about her whenever he checked the time.

Right now he was trying hard not to.

In a low voice barely loud enough for the Rangers on the perimeter to hear, Capt. Jaxx ordered, "Move out—make it happen, boys."

Although none of the Rangers were members of Capt. Jaxx's SOG and the teams had never been in this three-element patrol configuration before tonight the men coalesced moving like a unit that had been working together for years. As the file started snaking its way down the narrow winding path, Col. Randal was running through the combination of possibilities of things that could go wrong—which is what combat commanders on an operation in progress do non-stop.

A highly experienced Special Forces officer specializing in long-range independent operations, Col. Randal was not happy.

No Plan B.

Barely a Plan A.

Chances of a friendly-fire incident—high.

No diversion, which can be invaluable when going against a point-type target. The purpose being to distract the opposition long enough for the assault team to get in fast—exactly what Raiding Forces needed to do. Unfortunately, a diversion was not an option. The Brandenburgers would likely respond by executing their prisoners.

For the same reason a feint was out.

Extraordinary care had to be taken in the execution of the Actions On the Objective because ABCHQ was where any prisoners would in all likelihood be located. The idea being to rescue them alive. The problem was Raiding Forces—and in particular U.S. Army Rangers—are trained to break things. They are good at kicking in doors and shooting everyone inside. Toss a grenade or two—even better.

Finesse was not their style.

By necessity the scheme of maneuver for Capt. Jaxx's attack on ABCHQ did not conform to the Raiding Forces rule to "Keep It Short & Simple."

While Ranger Task Force was thought to be fairly evenly matched to the Brandenburgers in terms of number of boots on the ground the Nazis were formidable opponents. They could not be expected to give up easily once the fight commenced. The Germans knew things would not end well for them if captured.

Finally, security troops from the 2nd Battalion Royal Essex Regiment were somewhere on the island. Lieutenant Colonel Sir Terry "Zorro" Stone, KBE, DSO, MC, and Captain Butch "Headhunter" Hoolihan, DSO, MC, MM, RM, were en route and would be arriving by sea any time now with a contingent of Royal Marines. Major Zargo was sailing for the island with a section of the Greek Sacred Squadron. Levant Schooner Flotilla caiques at sea on various clandestine missions had been diverted to land their armed parties ashore on Castelrozzo. These were good things except Ranger Task Force had no radio contact established with any of them which increased the chance of a blue-on-blue firefight in the dark.

A lot of things could go wrong.

As they traveled Col. Randal said to Capt. Jaxx, "You realize only one of our rules has been adhered to."

"That's a definite rodge. 'The first rule is there ain't no rules.' Got it working for us. We're good, sir."

Jack Cool.

Improvise, adapt, and overcome—maybe.

KING LED OUT ON POINT FOLLOWED BY THE LOVAT Scouts. They moved like big hunting cats. The Merc had his razor-sharp Fairbairn Fighting Knife at the ready. He was a specialist with a blade—his weapon of choice for close, silent work.

Colonel John Randal, Lieutenant General "Geronimo" Joe McKoy, and Ensign Theodore Hamilton fell in behind Captain Billy Jack Jaxx in the file. As the patrol moved, Col. Randal experienced the old familiar sensation he was looking down from above. This was something he experienced on operations from time to time—but never mentioned to anyone.

The feeling usually—but not always—evaporated as soon as the action commenced.

As they marched, Col. Randal said, "Ted, while I was away campaigning in Italy orders came through for your promotion."

"Sir?"

"You're probably not old enough to even be in the army much less be a commissioned officer—but there it is."

"Sir, are you having me on?"

"Negative, you can thank Admiral Ransom. He ordered me to put you in for it and the Duke confirmed the appointment. Congratulations, Lieutenant."

"Bloody fantastic, sir!"

Col. Randal handed him a pair of lieutenant's rank insignia, "These were mine when I was in the Ranger's Territorial Regiment before being moved to the King's Royal Rifle Corp. They're yours now, stud."

"I shall not let you, Admiral Ransom, or the Duke down . . . on my word, sir."

"See to it you don't."

Lt. Gen. McKoy was listening in on the whispered conversation. He handed The Great Teddy one of Waldo Treywick's custom-rolled cigars. The gift of a cigar upon promotion was a long-standing military tradition—at least in the U.S. Army.

Only it did not normally take place in the middle of a night movement to contact during a high-risk special operation.

Lieutenant Theodore Hamilton stuck the cheroot in his pocket. He was walking on air.

As the patrol traveled, Col. Randal continued working through the tactical problem. Lt. Gen. McKoy had a dictum he liked to quote from time to time which gave him something to think about, "When something starts goin' downhill, it picks up speed." With the corollary being, "Once a thing's snakebit, it stays snakebit."

Both were in full force and effect tonight.

The patrol came to a short halt. The Rangers knelt down on one knee, every other man facing out left or right. Weapons were at the ready. Most men were armed with the .30 M1 Garand rifles they had carried during the jump on Benevento a week ago.

Up ahead at the point King disappeared into the dark. After a short pause Capt. Jaxx had the Lovat Scouts move out. The rest of the patrol followed cautiously until the Scouts came to ABCHQ's main entrance.

A sentry wearing a standard-issue U.S. Army khaki summer uniform, clearly visible in the moonlight, challenged, "Halt! Who goes there?"

No one had any idea what the countersign might be. There was no way to know. Local passwords were established by the Vulnerable Points Wing commander and changed every twenty-four hours.

Besides, this was most likely *not* a VPW sentry.

King stepped out of the dark behind the guard and executed a vicious rear takedown and strangle hold his left arm locked around the German's throat. For added measure, the Merc rammed the 7-inch, double-edged blade of his Fairbairn Fighting Knife into the man's heart as the two fell to the ground.

Swift, silent, deadly—efficient.

As an added precaution, King snapped the Nazi's neck.

At least Col. Randal hoped the sentry was a Brandenburger. The challenge had been issued in flawless English. Now the Rangers were aware they could be engaging enemy personnel in American uniforms armed with U.S. Army weapons who looked like them and spoke their language—better than they did.

Capt. Jaxx signaled his two team leaders, Sergeant Fred Waltmier and Corporal Leslie Cooper, to move out to take up their positions at the entrances they were tasked to make entry. King and the Lovat Scouts fell back on Col. Randal. This put Capt. Jaxx's team in position to make entry through the front door first.

The lead Rangers in each of the three teams were armed with suppressed .22 High Standard Military Model D pistols to maintain the element of surprise for as long as possible. The idea was for Capt. Jaxx to lead the way inside to secure the Operations Room while Col. Randal's follow-on team raced up the stairs to Lady Jane's suite and effected her rescue—the happy-ending scenario.

Time seemed to stand still as the clock ticked down.

Everyone was wanting to go.

Finally Capt. Jaxx whispered, "Prepare to move out—move out!"

The entry team went through the front door at a rapid walk in a crouched position pistols at the ready. When making an entry slow is smooth and smooth is fast. Only amateurs rush in guns blazing.

The Rangers were stone-cold professionals. Hard men, tightly focused, ready to execute. It mattered not one bit to them they were going against the best special operations unit in the Third Reich.

King, followed by Col. Randal, Lt. Hamilton, Lt. Gen. McKoy, and the Lovat Scouts flowed in right behind them. Inside there were several lights on. Dim but enough to see by.

Possibly the Germans had been searching for something.

Capt. Jaxx's team broke left for the Tactical Operations Center (TOC). King, leading the command party, headed straight for the giant spiral staircase. They raced up the steps, abandoning "slow is smooth, smooth is fast" temporarily until reaching the landing at the second level. Then Col. Randal transitioned into the lead while Lt. Gen. McKoy and the Lovat Scouts peeled off starting down the hall to clear the bedrooms.

All twenty of them.

Inside the suite the door to Lady Jane's master bedroom was standing open. Col. Randal came upon a Brandenburger dead in the doorway face down. On the floor next to him was a .32 CZ Model 27 pistol with a silencer attached.

The suppressed CZ Model 27 was a sophisticated state-of-the-art weapon. It confirmed in Col. Randal's mind that these Nazis were in fact Brandenburgers. As he stepped over one of the bodies behind him King switched on the light inside the bedroom door. A second dead Nazi was on the floor also armed with a silenced CZ Model 27.

Both men were dressed in American uniforms.

On Lady Jane's rumpled king-sized bed a glassy-eyed Nazi was propped up holding a blood-soaked bath towel to his stomach. The man had lost a lot of blood. The bed was soaked and a large pool was on the floor where he had initially gone down after being shot.

There were morphine syrettes scattered around.

Someone had placed him on the bed—but who?

Gold oak leaves pinned to the Brandenburger's collar indicated he was a major in the U.S. Army which may or may not have been his actual rank. Was he the raid team commander? A silenced CZ Model 27 was next to him but the German was too weak to lift it.

Col. Randal reached out, picked up the weapon, and stuck it in his belt.

A fourth body was down by the open sliding glass door leading out to the suite's private pool. A mile in the distance sparkled the lights of neutral Anatolian Providence, Turkey, looking like something out of a fairy tale.

No blackout restrictions there.

Col. Randal said, "You the officer in charge?"

Speaking weakly but in impeccable English with no detectable accent, the Nazi said, "The infamous Colonel Randal, I presume—here to offer your surrender?"

Col. Randal said, "Tell me where Lady Seaborn is located. If we get her back unharmed I might let you live."

The Brandenburger appeared to be barely hanging on to consciousness. "Someone opened fire as we made entry and shot four of us. It happened so fast I thought it must have been you, Colonel. But perhaps Lady Seaborn was sleeping with some other highly skilled marksman in your absence."

Col. Randal said, "I'm not going to ask again."

The Nazi said, "Other than my statement of the obvious you can see for yourself I am not at liberty to discuss details of an ongoing operation. As you Yanks say—name, rank, and serial number."

Col. Randal said, "Is that what you're going with? I have a skilled interrogator standing by. She'll make you tell her the pet name your mother's first boyfriend gave her in kindergarten—last chance."

The Brandenburger glared at him.

Col. Randal ordered, “Lieutenant Hamilton, go downstairs, radio Brandy to land ashore and report to me immediately.”

“Sir!”

From the deck outside, King said, “This Nazi has not only been shot twice, his throat’s ripped out. Looks like Happy’s handiwork, Chief.”

“Good for him.”

Sgt. Waltmier’s follow-on team of Rangers, assigned to clear the third floor, thundered past, taking the stairs two at a time. Trailing behind them Capt. Jaxx broke off on the second landing and came into the suite. He wanted to check on the status of Lady Jane in person, and—he brought bad news.

For once there was no sign of his laid-back Jack Cool persona.

“Sir, you need to come down to the TOC; you’ll want to see this for yourself.”

As they were going down the spiral stairs, Col. Randal said, “Find any more Brandenburgers?”

“Three, sir—all dead.”

“I need a prisoner, Jack.”

“Understood, Colonel, you’ll see why we shot ’em. Brace yourself. It ain’t pretty, sir.”

They walked into the TOC. Lieutenant Bentley St. Ledger was dead in a pool of blood on the highly-polished marble floor. She had been shot in the face.

Point blank—execution style.

Col. Randal felt like an icicle had been jabbed through his heart. His usual reaction to people being killed or injured was an absence of feeling. Not something he would care to admit to or was proud of—it just was.

Lt. St. Ledger was different. She was special. All the girl wanted was to serve her country and be accepted as a member of

Raiding Forces which Bentley viewed as the family she never had due to her mother's six marriages.

Lady Jane loved her—everyone did.

There were three dead Brandenburgers sprawled on the floor. They looked like pin cushions from all of the small-caliber bullet holes. Col. Randal drew his suppressed .22 High Standard and shot each of them in the head one more time.

WHIIIIIICH. WHIIIIIICH. WHIIIIIICH.

The hard-eyed Rangers standing around did not say a word. Lt. St. Ledger had been a favorite of the troops. They would be wanting payback.

Lt. Hamilton said, "Mrs. Seaborn shall be ashore in zero five, sir."

Col. Randal said, "King, take an escort to meet her at the dock."

"On the way, Chief,"

Lt. Hamilton said, "Mind if I put a round in these Nazis as well sir? Bentley was my friend."

"Be my guest, Lieutenant."

WHIIIIIICH. WHIIIIIICH. WHIIIIIICH.

Col. Randal said, "Any sign of our people when you cleared the ground floor?"

Capt. Jaxx said, "Negative sir. Only Bentley. One of the Brandenburgers was down when we came through the door. She must have taken him out."

"Good."

"My boys shot the other two."

Col. Randal said, "Nice job men."

The Rangers began dragging the dead Nazis out of the TOC. Lt. St. Ledger was carried to another room and placed on a couch. Capt. Jaxx brought in an Oriental rug from the entry hall and covered up the bloodstain on the floor where she had fallen. He did not want people to see it. The two of them had been friends too.

She posed for a photo he carried in the plexiglass pistol grip of his Colt. 38 Super for a while.

King took two Rangers and started for the dock. Lt. Gen. McKoy arrived downstairs and trailed along with them. As they were departing a burst of firing broke out from the direction of the waterfront. To experienced ears the gunfire was clearly a brief two-way exchange of fire even though all the rounds were distinguishable as being from U.S. weapons—a .45 Thompson submachine gun and a combination of .30 M1 Garand Rifles and .30 M1 Carbines.

Lieutenant Jake Novak was in contact.

Col. Randal said, "Let's step out of the room for a minute, Lieutenant Hamilton."

When a senior officer says something like that to a junior officer it is generally, but not always, the precursor to an unpleasant experience for the subordinate. Lt. Hamilton wondered what he could have possibly done wrong.

He could not think of anything but that did not mean it had not happened; you never knew?

Col. Randal said, "Break out the cigar General McKoy gave you, Lieutenant. I'd like the privilege of lighting it."

He produced his hard-service Zippo with the gold crossed sabers of his old outfit the U.S. 26th Cavalry Regiment. The unit no longer existed having eaten their horses, surrendered to the Japanese Imperial Army and forced to go on the Bataan Death March.

"I have a change of mission for you, Ted. Effective immediately you're relieved from whatever secret stuff you've been doing for A-Force, SOE, or any other agency we've loaned you out to."

"Sir?"

"I'm assigning you to Beverly and Pam for the duration—meaning for as long as Raiding Forces operates in the Aegean. Any time either one flies a mission that calls for the plane to RON or land and remain on station for any protracted period of time you will be onboard to supervise camouflaging the aircraft.

"Is that clear?"

Lt. Hamilton said, "Affirmative, sir."

Col. Randal said, "That means you'll probably be involved in more missions than anyone in Raiding Forces—you up for that?"

"Absolutely one hundred percent, sir!"

Col. Randal said, "All right then, I don't want any more dead women on my watch. Make sure it doesn't happen on yours—that's an order."

Firing broke out from the direction of Government House. Major Jack Dance was in action. The situation was developing.

Now Col. Randal had to make sense out of it.

PRIVATE FIRST CLASS NORVEL "HORN DOG" HANSEN was pulling point as Lieutenant Jake Novak's patrol worked its way into the narrow strip of the built-up area along the waterfront. The moon was bright enough to reflect off the cobblestones. Waves lapped against the shore.

The beauty of the night was lost on PFC Hansen. At the moment, the Rangers were engaged in a deadly game of cat and mouse with an unknown number of highly trained Brandenburger Sea Raider Commandos. The problem was the bad guys were hiding somewhere inside one or more of the buildings with the advantage of cover and concealment while they were outside in the open attempting to wrinkle them out.

There had been a brief engagement when the Rangers first entered the village culminating in both sides going to ground. Now the patrol had tightened up edging its way carefully down the street moving by inches. Everyone had their backs against the walls of the storefronts lining it.

The Standard Operating Procedure (SOP) of ten-yard spacing for normal light infantry patrolling does not apply to clearing buildings.

Lt. Novak was directly behind PFC Hansen brushing against his back. In a situation like this it's a good idea for the patrol leader to be at the front of the column to make rapid decisions. It is also desirable to have the troops in position to be able to put instantaneous concentrated fire on a target if and when one should present itself.

The situation was tense.

Lt. Novak whispered, "What do you think, Horn Dog?"

"Army doesn't pay me to think, El Tee."

"Yeah, well give it a shot anyway."

"I'd say if we keep pushing up this street we'll flush 'em, or they'll try to ambush us, sir."

Lt. Novak said, "From inside they'll have a hard time bringing effective fire on us without showing themselves as long as we maintain tight position along this wall—don't move an inch out in the road."

"You got it, Lieutenant."

The tactics of taking down a fixed enemy position with some limitations on its fields of fire are not unlike a game of billiards. Everything is dependent on straight lines and angles. The defender does not have all the advantages as might be imagined.

For the Germans to engage effectively they needed to obtain a direct line of sight. Unless they opted for the almost-guaranteed-to-fail "spray and pray" technique of holding their weapon out a door or window and blazing away without looking or aiming.

Which would also have the undesirable result, for them, of giving away their position.

Lt. Novak knew these die-hard Brandenburgers were not about to commence fire until they had visually acquired a target. As long as the Rangers did not provide them one the Germans would have to expose themselves to engage. The purpose of the exercise was to force the Nazis to do exactly that.

Then kill them.

Small unit tactics are a high art form. Move and countermove. The slightest mistake can be deadly.

A block behind Lt. Novak's patrol Lieutenant General "Geronimo" Joe McKoy, King, and the two Rangers arrived from ABCHQ. They turned right and walked down to the dock to meet the MAS boat.

It was warbling up to the pier.

Clad in her standard uniform of rolled-up shorts, rubber-soled, canvas-topped raiding boots, and a leather bomber jacket to ward off the chill of the night at sea, Brandy Seaborn stepped off the boat carrying a .30 M1 Carbine.

"Any word on Jane?"

Lt. Gen. McKoy said, "Not at this time. We think we've got the Brandenburger CO. John needs you to interrogate him."

"With pleasure."

A short burst of firing came from Lt. Novak's patrol.

King said, "Time to go Mrs. Seaborn, stay close to me."

They moved along the pier back to shore. The Merc was careful to avoid exposing the group to any watching Brandenburgers. Occasional bouts of firing, no more than a few rounds at a time, came from Lt. Novak's patrol farther down the street.

As King turned off to lead the way to ABCHQ Lt. Gen. McKoy broke off to go to link up with Lt. Novak. When he closed on the patrol he worked his way past the rear security man up to where Sergeant Major Mack Beckwith was in the prone position immediately behind the tail end of Lt. Novak's lead team.

"What's the story, Mack?"

"Some Krauts holed up in that storefront straight ahead, General."

Staying well up against the wall, Lt. Gen. McKoy edged his way up the file carefully stepping around the Rangers some of whom were kneeling, others prone. He came to where Lt. Novak was having a whispered conversation with PFC Hansen.

They were trying to figure out their next move.

Lt. Gen. McKoy said, "You men come across any items of women's clothing laying on the ground when coming down from ABCHQ. . . . handbags, jewelry, anything like that?"

Col. Randal's JAIL BREAK plan in case of an emergency raid on ABCHQ called for those making their getaway or if captured to drop personal items to signal that they had passed by.

Lt. Novak said, "Negative, sir."

"All right then."

Lt. Gen. McKoy stepped out in the middle of the street and launched a 45mm round from Colonel John Randal's shoulder-fired Brixia mortar at the plate glass window of the building where the Brandenburgers were taking cover. The glass shattered. A bright flash came from inside the building followed by an almost instantaneous *BOOOOOM*!

"What you waitin' on Jake, an engraved invitation?"

So much for deliberate, methodical move versus countermove.

Lt. Novak ordered, "Move out, Hansen."

PFC Hansen shouted, "On me, boys!"

Horn Dog's team jumped up and disappeared into the cloud of smoke and dust billowing from the building. Two went through the destroyed window while the others knocked down the door. Shots rang out inside.

The Rangers were emptying the eight-round magazines on their semiautomatic .30 M1 Garands as fast as they could work their triggers—controlled fire which is superior to full automatic fire.

When Lt. Gen. McKoy and Lt. Novak walked in to inspect the results two Brandenburger Sea Raiders were down on the floor in the state of what Raiding Forces tended to describe as "seriously dead."

Lt. Novak said, "What the hell Horn Dog, do those look like prisoners to you?"

"Got outta hand, El Tee."

"Yeah, well, I'm going to let you explain that to the Colonel."

LIEUTENANT GENERAL "GERONIMO" JOE MCKOY moved up one of the cobblestone footpaths in the direction of the firing that had come from the vicinity of Government House. The island's administrative building was located above the village off to one side on the escarpment. The structure was large by Castelrozzo standards, but not anywhere near as big as the palace built for Mussolini—which the former Italian dictator had never stayed in.

Gunfire had been heard from Major Jack Dance's objective but it had died out.

Lt. Gen. McKoy had his 9mm Beretta MAB-38 submachine gun at the ready. The borrowed 45mm Brixia shoulder-fired mortar and its pack of shells was slung over his shoulder. He was comfortable working alone during hours of limited visibility. Not that it was as dark as it had been.

It would be sunrise soon.

He was doing the math—the sentry King had taken out, four dead Brandenburgers in Lady Jane's suite. Three in the TOC. And the two Jake the Snake's men had shot in the village. If the intelligence was accurate approximately thirty Nazis had landed on the island. At this point nearly a third of the raiding party were already out of action.

Numbers like that were a catastrophic casualty rate for the Brandenburgers. Any military unit that suffers 30% or higher casualties in a single engagement is considered combat ineffective. The term casualties include wounded—some of whom will be ambulatory, meaning they can still fight.

The German's losses were all KIA.

Lt. Gen. McKoy estimated that since Raiding Forces had seized the initiative the Nazis would scatter. In his experience the fact the Brandenburgers were not concentrated in a single location was telling. The Nazis had apparently been searching the island when Ranger Task Force jumped in. If that was the case he was beginning to have doubts the Germans would be holding prisoners—none had been captured or the Sea Raiders had already executed them.

They would be too much trouble to secure.

"Halt! Who goes . . . ?"

Lt. Gen. McKoy's 9mm Beretta M-38 submachine gun was at his shoulder and firing before the challenge was completed—an automatic reflex. The weapon was a gift from Major the Lady Jane Seaborn. She had arranged to have it modified to his personal specifications by Westley Richards & Company in Cairo. Lt. Gen. McKoy was an exhibition-class marksman who had his own ideas about what he wanted in a fighting weapon and his Beretta M-38 was almost perfect.

The Brandenburger was knocked over backward by a hail of 9mm rounds center of mass. The pattern could have been covered by the size of a coffee cup. It was extraordinary marksmanship under low light conditions against a target ready, willing and able to shoot back.

Anyone calling out challenges tonight had better have some kind of an accent. Precise pronunciation was not going to cut it. No one in Raiding Forces (with the exception of the women who had attended Swiss finishing schools) spoke precise English. For sure, none of the Rangers did.

And there was another thing.

In the U.S., Army recruits standing guard are taught to issue the challenge, "Halt who goes there—Friend or Foe?"

The person being challenged replies, "Friend." Only a complete idiot would ever respond "Foe."

The school solution response is, "Advance friend and be recognized."

At which point the sentry issuing the challenge additionally calls out the word identifier of the day. In response the countersign is offered. And they both live happily ever after.

Works great in training.

In an actual combat environment challenges never actually go like that. A soldier standing guard hears someone approaching and goes on red alert pucker factor kicking in full bore. Instead of the standard challenge taught in basic training he calls out "Halt" and the word identifier. If the correct authenticator is not instantly forthcoming, any right-thinking sentry opens fire.

It is not unknown for a guard walking his post in an active combat zone to fire off a few rounds and *then* give the order, "Halt…"

The Brandenburgers should have known that but did not. They were doing it by the book. The U.S. Army's book their intelligence contacts had provided them.

The results were proving fatal.

Lt. Gen. McKoy searched the Nazi and secured the man's M1928A1 .45 Thompson submachine gun and .32 CZ Model 27 with silencer. He added them to his own arsenal: A Colt Single Action Peacemaker with .45 ACP cylinder, a Colt 1911 Government Model .38 Super, a suppressed .22 Colt Woodsman, a Colt 1908 .380—he was a Colt man, and his bespoke 9mm Beretta MAB-38.

Finding nothing else of interest or intelligence value, Lt. Gen. McKoy moved on toward Government House. The sun was coming up now and it was getting light fast. When he arrived four Nazis clad in U.S. Army uniforms were lined up on the lawn—all dead.

The Rangers establishing the perimeter outside the complex started laughing when they saw him arrive.

Maj. Dance said, "General, are you sure you're packing enough firepower, sir?"

Lt. Gen. McKoy said, "Better to have and not need than to need and not have."

"What are we supposed to do now, sir?"

"Stand by here for new orders, Major. I'll go confer with John and then get back to you. He'll have a plan—always does.

"Don't reckon you got anythin' outta those bad boys before you shot 'em?"

"Negative, sir."

BRANDY SEABORN AND KING CAME DOWN THE spiral staircase into the TOC. Colonel John Randal was huddled with Lieutenant General "Geronimo" Joe McKoy, Lieutenant Colonel Sir Terry "Zorro" Stone, Captain Butch "Headhunter" Hoolihan, and Captain Billy Jack Jaxx.

Col. Randal said, "That was quick."

Brandy said, "Your Nazi is dead. I never even touched him, John. Too far gone."

"He tell you anything?"

"When I arrived, he said, 'Tell Gretchen . . . " and died without completing the sentence."

Col. Randal said, "Gretchen?"

"I found this in his paybook—mean anything to you?"

Col. Randal looked at the photograph. He recognized it immediately. SS-Hauptsturmführer Gretchen Von Coffenhauser. She was staring straight at the camera wearing her SS officer's billed hat, long black gloves, and thigh-high black boots. Clenched in one of her hands on her hips was a coiled whip.

She was naked.

"Liebe Gretchen" was scrawled on the back.

Capt. Jaxx checked out the picture. "I'm putting that one in my pistol grip, sir."

Brandy said, "I thought you shot her in Istanbul?"

Col. Randal said, "I did."

Lt. Gen. McKoy said, "I saw 'em wheel the gurney out of the hotel room. That Nazi woman was deader than world peace. At least that's what Pam and I thought."

Col. Randal said, "You're sure the Brandenburger said—'Tell Gretchen?'

"Positive?"

King said, "Affirmative Chief I heard him."

Mandy Paige and Alex "Cat" Gataki walked into the TOC. They were disheveled. Everyone started talking at once, excited to see them alive. The first JAIL BREAK participants to return.

Col. Randal said, "Give me a report."

Mandy said, "I was asleep in my room. Shots rang out down the hall from the direction of Lady Jane's suite. We had carried out practice drills for such an event. I leaped out of bed, shouted 'JAIL BREAK' as loud as I could—as per the plan—then ran to the back stairs.

"All the girls in residence were screaming 'JAIL BREAK' and evacuating the building as fast as they could. If the palace ever came under ground attack everyone was to run up the escarpment, scatter, and hide in abandoned houses. We had all picked out one to go to.

"I encountered Cat en route to mine. We hid out together the rest of the night, all the next day, and last night. When the sun came up this morning we heard firing, saw MGBs landing troops and decided to sneak down to investigate."

Col. Randal said, "Encounter any of our other people out there?"

"No, but a series of green flares is the All Clear everyone will come in once they see the signal."

Capt. Jaxx said, "I'm on it."

Col. Randal said, "After the initial gunfire here at ABCHQ did you hear any other shooting?"

Mandy said, "Negative, things remained quiet until we heard firing in the village this morning before daylight. Then more gunshots in the direction of Government House."

Col. Randal said, "All right. Go freshen up then get back down here on the double. I want you to help me develop a plan to locate the remaining Brandenburgers. We'll need the cooperation of the islanders.

"One other thing Mandy the Germans must have a collaborator on the island. The Brandenburgers wouldn't launch a raid without local intelligence. You're my Counterintelligence Officer.

"I need you to identify them for me."

Mandy said, "Really good to see you, John. I thought you were still away fighting in Italy."

"Some of us are back. Step over in the corner with me. I need a word."

Mandy said, "Something wrong?"

Col. Randal said, "Bentley's dead—Jane's MIA."

Mandy put her head on Col. Randal's shoulder and started sobbing. Everyone in the room tried to look somewhere else. Nothing to see here.

But there was.

Capt. Jaxx walked back into the TOC after firing off the green signal flares.

Col. Randal said, "Take Mandy and Cat up to their rooms. Fill them in on the details about Bentley. Lay it out the way it happened."

"Yes, sir."

Capt. Jaxx and Mandy were great friends. She liked to give him almost as hard a time as she did Col. Randal. Their relationship made him "Right Man Right Job" for the assignment—one Jack Cool would rather not have been assigned.

King came over. He had met Mandy at Habbaniya during the siege and the Merc had always been very protective of her. The four of them walked slowly up the stairs—Mandy was still sobbing.

There was no putting the genie back in this bottle.

After they were gone, Lt. Gen. McKoy said, "Rough day at the office, John?"

Col. Randal said, “I’d say so, yeah.”

Lt. Gen. McKoy said, “Don’t be too hard on yourself. Sounds like JAIL BREAK worked pretty good. Probably don’t feel like it right now, but that was some real prior plannin’ you did right there, John.

“No tellin’ how many people you saved.”

Col. Randal said, “Lady Jane put the final touches on the plan. I just came up with the idea. Never thought anyone would actually have to use it.”

Lt. Gen. McKoy said, “That’s why they call ’em contingency plans.”

Brandy said, “Jane had us conducting JAIL BREAK drills nearly every night while you were away. Veronica taught classes on Escape and Evasion covering MI-9 methods we could use if we were on the run. I was glad to have a mission come up so I could sail away and not have to participate in all the E&E training.”

Col. Randal said, “Do you have any idea which house Jane was planning to use as her hideout?”

Brandy said, “Veronica forbade us from ever revealing our secret place. In the event anyone was captured they would not be able to give away the whereabouts of the others even under torture.”

Lt. Col. Stone came over. “What is our next move, old stick?”

Col. Randal said, “Let’s see who comes in after the All Clear before we attempt anything else. Our evaders may have intel we can use. Get in touch with the commander of the security battalion. I want an explanation of what the Essex were doing when the Brandenburgers attacked.”

Lt. Col. Stone said, “Consider it done—he better have a satisfactory answer.”

Col. Randal said, “Be thinking about how we’re going to run the surviving Brandenburgers to ground.”

Lt. Col. Stone said, “Prior to the conflict there were over ten thousand people in residence on Castelrozzo. Once Italy and Greece declared war on each other the military-age men left to join the Greek Army. Once the Italians occupied the island everyone who could began emigrating to Egypt or Australia. The population dropped to slightly over a thousand, consisting mostly of single girls, married women waiting for their husbands to return home, and children.”

Capt. Jaxx said, “That’s why the troops like to stay here on stand-downs between missions instead of going to Cairo—lots of lonely girls.”

Lt. Col. Stone said, “What it means to us is that less than half of the twenty-five hundred houses on the island are being lived in. The rest are boarded up. Clearing all of the vacant houses will be a challenge.”

Capt. Jaxx said, “There’s no guarantee the Brandenburgers aren’t hiding in some of the occupied residences—holding the Greek homeowners hostage. We’ll have to physically check every house on the island.”

Lt. Gen. McKoy said, “Clearing built-up areas is hard, dangerous work. Our boys ain’t trained for it and we wouldn’t have enough men to do the job if we bring in everybody we got. Four square miles don’t sound like much—but it’s a lot.

“We’re gonna’ need some help.”

Captain Butch “Headhunter” Hoolihan came into the TOC. “Colonel, you need to step outside, sir. Come see what’s entering the harbor. You’re not going to believe what’s about to dock.”

Everyone walked out to get a clear view of the bay. The *King Duck* was steaming in. A raised deck had been fitted at the forward end of the Landing Craft Tank’s (LCT) tank deck. Sitting on the platform side-by-side were a pair of captured Tiger tanks with the barrels of their 88mm main guns sticking out over the bow ramp.

Acting Provisional Lieutenant Warthog Finley had arrived on scene to do battle.

Lt. Col. Stone said, "Looks like a prehistoric monster."

Capt. Hoolihan said, "Something out of a Jules Verne book."

Capt. Jaxx said, "That's a mean machine."

Lt. Gen. McKoy said, "If Warthog can hit what he's aimin' at with those German 88s it'll be mean all right—real mean."

Col. Randal said, "We need to find out."

LIEUTENANT GENERAL "GERONIMO" JOE MCKOY; Vice Admiral Sir Randolph "Razor" Ransom; Captain Cuthbert Bowlby aka "Curly," RN; Brigadier Dudley Clarke; Brigadier Raymond J. Maunsell—who like to be called "R.J."; James "Baldie" Taylor, Lieutenant Colonel Sir Terry "Zorro" Stone, Lieutenant Commander Adrian Seligman, Major Jack Dance; Captain Lionel Chatterhorn; Lieutenant Jake Novak aka "Jake the Snake"; Waldo Treywick; Captain Pamala-Plum Martin, DSO, OBE, DFC, RM, and Beverly Blackwell were gathered in the TOC for an officer's call.

Capt. Plum-Martin and Beverly had flown the newcomers to Castelrozzo aboard the Small Raids Inc. Catalina christened *Black Cat*.

The plane was painted black. The name was stenciled on the nose with a giant pair of slanted eyes that looked like they belonged to a Siamese cat. Only the eyes were visible—signifying the aircraft being, hopefully, invisible in the dark.

Colonel John Randal suffered through a repeat performance when he broke the news about Lieutenant Bentley St. Ledger to the two pilots in one of the side rooms. Capt. Plum-Martin had known Bentley long before the war. Beverly and Bentley were girlfriends.

Neither woman broke down but they were clearly devastated and working hard not to.

Col. Randal said, "I wanted you to hear it from me first."

Sounded pretty lame.

Everyone was standing by waiting for Col. Randal to begin his briefing. Most of the recent arrivals had rushed to the island because Castelrozzo was the springboard for launching intelligence missions out of Egypt into the Aegean and on to mainland Europe. All of them had detachments stationed there and none of their personnel were accounted for.

Capt. Chatterhorn had flown in because he commanded the Vulnerable Points Wing security personnel assigned to Raiding Forces. Keeping Castelrozzo safe was his responsibility. He was grim-faced, having just been informed that six of his men assigned to guard ABCHQ had been found dead in a building in the village.

Shot in the back of the head.

As Col. Randal was about to start, Major Zargo, the commander of the Greek Sacred Squadron, walked in.

Col. Randal said, "Here's what we know. A detachment of Brandenburger Sea Raiders landed on Castelrozzo night before last. Their primary target was ABCHQ. For reasons not known to us they chose to remain on the island the following day. Brandy arrived last night and sank their two E-boat transports stranding the Nazis on the island.

"A team of Raiding Forces personnel from the 575th Ranger Force under my command, styled Ranger Task Force, parachuted onto Castelrozzo before dawn this morning. We cleared

ABCHQ, Castelrozzo Village, and Government House. In total, fourteen Brandenburgers are KIA at this point in the operation. No Allied prisoners have been rescued. Known friendly losses are Lieutenant Bentley St. Ledger and six Venerable Points Wing security specialists—all murdered execution style by a single gunshot to the head—Bentley was shot in the face.

"Everything else about the current enemy situation is conjecture at this point.

"Between all of us we have over fifty people missing. An Escape and Evasion plan was in place in the event of a raid. Now that we've given the All Clear we're waiting to see how many of our unaccounted-for personnel come in.

"Ranger Task Force has been ordered to hold in place until we develop more intelligence from our returning evaders. There are still approximately twenty-plus heavily-armed Brandenburgers on the loose with over twenty-five hundred houses on the island to hide in.

"Raiding Forces is not capable of handling a clearing operation of this magnitude in any reasonable period of time. Half our troops are still behind enemy lines in Italy. Most of the rest are scattered all across the Aegean stationed aboard LSF schooners. So we're going to have to come up with a plan.

"This concludes my briefing."

Escapers and Evaders had started to trickle into ABCHQ by the time the session broke up. Captain Stephanie Fawcett-Tatum came in first, followed by a First Aid Nursing Yeomanry (FANY) who worked for SOE. Then more and more people began to arrive. Being a proponent of the 'P for Plenty' formula, Capt. Jaxx went out and put up additional green flares.

Capt. Plum-Martin, Mandy, and Brandy debriefed the first people to return. Almost all of them were female personnel. However there were a few male intelligence, communications, maintenance, and other specialists stationed on the island who had responded to JAIL BREAK.

The flood of people coming out of hiding required more help with the interviews. James "Baldie" Taylor and Cuthbert Bowlby pitched in. One thing became apparent. The Brandenburger raid had started to fall apart almost from the start.

From the moment the Germans attacked ABCHQ the operation had begun to lose momentum. Four of the team being killed was a serious setback and the loss of the mission commander likely proved critical. It seemed reasonable to believe the second in command made the decision to remain on the island to continue the search when the Sea Raiders did not immediately capture their intended target.

Part of the JAIL BREAK plan was for evaders to go to their preselected hideouts and then move to a position from which they could surreptitiously observe. Since virtually all of the houses on the island were built on the slope of the escarpment most included an upstairs room with an excellent view. The returning evaders reported seeing teams of Germans searching ABCHQ, Government House, and the village store-front buildings.

Veronica Paige's JAIL BREAK training had emphatically taught that hiding spots should never be in a location "the eye was drawn to," such as a large building or prominent terrain feature, so the Brandenburgers had never come close to any of the evaders during their searches.

Lt. Gen. McKoy, VAdm. Ransom, and Col. Randal were huddled in a corner of the TOC.

VAdm. Ransom said, "Based on what you have observed since you landed give me your assessment of what has transpired, Colonel."

Col. Randal said, "Commando raids depend on surprise, speed and violence. Limited time on target is of the essence—

less is better. In the initial stage if the assault does not go as planned raids can quickly lose their momentum.

"That's what happened here, sir."

VAdm. Ransom said, "Sometimes when things do not go your way it is better to back off, reevaluate, then return at a time more favorable for success. These Sea Raiders made a fatal error in judgment when they chose not to withdraw immediately.

"Now we have to make them pay for it."

Lt. Gen. McKoy said, "Never a bad idea to live to fight another day. These hardcases are learning the hard way you can be too tough for your own good. Maybe they believed their own press about being supermen.

"There's a lesson to be learned here."

CAPTAIN BILLY JACK JAXX SAID, "HAVE I EVER asked you for anything, Sir?"

Colonel John Randal said, "You've wanted me to introduce you to Rita and Lana, Mandy, Pam—punching up on that one, stud—a couple of the dancers at the Kit-Kat Club..."

"I'm serious, sir, have I ever requested an assignment as a favor?"

"No, you never have, Captain."

"I am now, sir."

"Let's hear it."

"Let me take down these Brandenburgers. I want the job, Colonel."

"Any idea how you intend to go about it?"

"You and me, sir, let's hunt 'em down. Kill every one of the murdering Nazi bastards."

Col. Randal said, "I can make that happen."

JAIL BREAK, THE ESCAPE & EVASION TRAINING, and the rehearsals worked as planned. Within the hour the evaders had reported back to ABCHQ. All accounted for.

Except for Lady Jane..

3
VISIONS OF A KNIGHT'S CROSS

IN THE TACTICAL OPERATIONS CENTER EVERYONE had a story to tell. The place was packed with people all talking at once. Many of them had thought the JAIL BREAK was simply another drill. When no recall was ever issued it had begun to dawn on people this was for real.

It took a while but eventually Colonel John Randal was able to develop a better picture of the raid.

Most of the JAIL BREAK evaders had not observed any enemy activity from their hide positions. Those who did saw men in khaki uniforms unlike the type worn by the former 575th Parachute Infantry Regiment or 10th Ranger Battalion personnel. The invaders primary weapons were U.S. Army issue.

No one reported hearing gunfire after the initial flurry of pistol shots from ABCHQ until this morning.

All the Brandenburgers killed so far had also been armed with .32 CZ Model 27 suppressed pistols. The handgun was an excellent choice for clandestine wet work. Based on the lack of shots heard Col. Randal came to the conclusion the Germans had relied entirely on their silenced handguns.

The prior planning, weapons, and tactics confirmed his opinion the Sea Raiders were professionals up to a point—

remaining on the island was a mistake. The E-boats had made a stealthy approach. Instead of landing on a beach which might have been guarded the Brandenburgers came ashore under a sheer cliff, scaled it, then made their way cross-country avoiding detection on their approach march.

Everything about the execution of the raid had been textbook perfect until the Germans reached their primary objective—ABCHQ. What went wrong? The unsilenced rounds fired by Lieutenant Bentley St. Ledger in the TOC and coming from Major the Lady Jane Seaborn's suite triggered JAIL BREAK.

The Brandenburgers never saw it coming.

The JAIL BREAK alert spread like wildfire to the offices and sleeping quarters of MI-6, SOE, A-Force, LSF, etc., located outside of ABCHQ. Within minutes of the assault on their primary objective the Germans' element of surprise had been compromised, the raid commander critically wounded, and five Brandenburgers killed. And all Allied personnel stationed on Castelrozzo Island were executing their E&E plan with alacrity.

The Brandenburgers momentum collapsed which is a hazard in the small-scale raiding business.

The Nazi's primary target—most likely Col. Randal—had not been located. The raid's second in command, on taking charge, had the option to call off the mission and withdraw or remain on the island to continue the mission.

Col. Randal believed the Brandenburgers were of the opinion there was time to continue their operation because they had met no organized resistance and did not believe Castelrozzo was likely to be reinforced anytime soon. The new raid commander may have had visions of a Knight's Cross dancing in his head.

The German's mistake was not expecting Raiding Forces to react so fast.

Col. Randal was quietly observing everything taking place in the TOC staying out of the way letting his people do their jobs. A lot could be learned by watching and listening. He had been carrying out small-scale operations for so long it was fairly easy for him to form an idea of the Brandenburgers' thought process based on the little bits and pieces of information coming in.

He was doing his best not to show concern about Lady Jane being MIA. He knew the importance of exhibiting "command presence" in the face of adversity. Nothing good would come from letting people know his true feelings no matter the situation.

But in his opinion it was bad.

Lady Jane Seaborn was missing. None of the returning evaders had seen any sign of her or Happy. There was no information forthcoming about what had happened after the flurry of shots came from her bedroom. The longer she remained unaccounted for the more likely Raiding Forces would not be able to rescue her.

Col. Randal knew that Lady Jane was likely dead.

The commotion in the TOC became more than he could take. There was a side room designated as "Col. Randal's office" that he had never used. He retreated there now to get away.

Captain Stephanie Fawcett-Tatum tapped on the door and stuck her head inside. "Lieutenant Finley to see you, John."

"Send him in."

Acting Provisional Lieutenant Warthog Finley, DSO, OBE DSC, RNPS, came bursting through the door like a runaway railroad train. The hard-drinking, two-fisted, former tugboat skipper was a take-no-prisoners sailorman, even when there were no prisoners to be taken.

If you were casting a part in a movie for a bull in a China shop—Warthog Finley.

Col. Randal said, "You've got a story for me, Skipper?"

No one ever called him Acting Provisional Lieutenant or even Lieutenant—it was always Skipper. Aboard his Landing Craft Tank he was the "Captain."

In a whiskey-ruined voice Skipper Finley rasped, "Me, Admiral Ransom, and Hank Rawlston was having a drink one day in Alexandria discussing how the conversion of those Australian Matilda tank engines to LSF caiques was progressing. Any time we have a chance the three of us get together to tip a few, tell sea stories…"

This was news to Col. Randal.

" . . . and the Razor mentions that the Royal Armored Corps was experimenting with mounting 17-pound guns on the chassis of U.S. Army Sherman tanks. I think he called 'em 'Fireflies.'

"The Royal Navy got wind of what the RAC was doing and decided it could be something that might work for them. The Admiralty had been looking for a shallow draft craft with some heavy firepower for close-in shore naval fire support. So they started running tests to see if it was possible to mount the Fireflies on a Landing Craft Tank to provide really close naval gunfire.

"The idea being a gunboat capable of going in right up to the beach and knocking out enemy gun positions at point-blank range. For troops making a contested amphibious landing, those 17-pounders could be a lifesaver.

"Then the Firefly tanks could land ashore and continue the fight. Royal Navy—smartest guys in the world."

Col. Randal said, "So, how did that work out?"

Skipper Finley said, "The navy found they could sit two Shermans side by side on the bow of an LCT, provided they added a reinforced support deck up top. Ain't much of a naval engineering problem so they tried it. Held the tanks easy enough only the RAC is still having problems making 17-pounders fit in the tank's gun turret.

"The Admiral, being a military genius in his own right when it comes to naval strategy and fighting ships, asks if I thought something like that might be useful for Small Raids Inc. Put a couple of tanks on the *King Duck*—support Raiding Forces.

"I said, bloody right. It would give us heavy firepower we can deliver up close and personal on distant islands to support our small-scale raids. It's pretty clear the Royal Navy ain't about to provide Raiding Forces any naval gun support in our slice of the war."

Col. Randal said, "I like it."

Skipper Finley said, "The only problem was two problems. We needed a pair of tanks. Nobody was about to give even one to Small Raids Inc."

Col. Randal said, "I can see how that would be."

"Hank says he knows where we can lay our hands on a couple of tanks nobody has any use for. There's this abandoned Desert Tank Battle School outside of Alexandria that was used to demonstrate Afrika Korp's tactics to new units arranging out here to show 'em what they might expect to encounter going up against Rommel.

"According to Hank, a couple of captured Tiger tanks was sitting at the entrance of the front gate to get the troops' attention when they showed up for class."

Col. Randal said, "I've seen those two Tigers."

Raiding Forces had recruited instructors from the school to serve in Desert Patrol when it had first moved to Oasis X.

Skipper Finley said, "So, Hank, he goes out one night with a tank retrieval vehicle and midnight requisitions the pair of 'em. The Razor orders the shipyard to start work on installing a top deck on the *Duck.* Then he goes out to recruit gunners."

Col. Randal said, "Tankers are hard to find now the war's moved on."

Skipper Finley said, "Turned out to be the easy part, Colonel. When GHQ broke up the Special Air Service after Stirling got captured, several new units were formed out of the unemployed troops. One was something called the Raiding Support Regiment.

"Some of those ex-SAS men transferred to it had been tankers before volunteering for the Special Air Service. They liked the sound of a seafaring life aboard an LST sailing the Aegean shooting tank guns at shore targets, eating good Royal Navy chow.

"Problem solved and about bloody time. I didn't give up getting rich being a tugboat skipper to haul freight to Castelrozzo ever since Raiding Forces quit landing gun jeeps behind enemy lines from the King Duck.

"I need a fighting ship, Colonel."

Col. Randal said, "Are those Tigers accurate from the deck of an LCT?"

"Negative, can't hit a bloody thing. We have to anchor first before a shoot so the Duck is stable. On the right kind of beach we can run the bow up on shore for a rock-solid gun platform. Only limitation is range—no long-distance stuff.

"All our ship-to-shore fire missions have to be line-of-sight."

Col. Randal said, "What about fire control?"

"We've organized radio teams to land in order to coordinate with the on-scene ground commander. They can use voice or wig-wag signal flags to talk to the Duck. Fire control is not much of a problem anyway.

"Once the target is marked my gunners can see where their rounds are impacting."

Capt. Fawcett-Tatum opened the door without knocking. "Phone call for you, John."

Col. Randal had never received a phone call in his office—he picked up the receiver.

Lady Jane said, "Meet me at the pier in fifteen minutes."

CAPTAIN PAMALA PLUM-MARTIN, MANDY PAIGE, and Beverly Blackwell had set up tables in the TOC and were interviewing everyone who had taken part in JAIL BREAK. While they waited their turn to be debriefed the returnees were sharing their experiences with each other. The evaders were eager to tell their stories now that they were safe.

The level of talent present in the TOC was arguably the finest group of intelligence and Special Forces professionals in any army in the world. However, everyone realized they did not have a clue what to do next. Other than to hunt down the Brandenburgers hiding on the island.

Only how?

Lieutenant General "Geronimo" Joe McKoy, Lieutenant Colonel Sir Terry "Zorro" Stone, Major Zargo, Captain Butch "Headhunter" Hoolihan, Captain Billy Jack Jaxx, and King were studying a large wall map of Castelrozzo. They were marking off sectors on the acetate cover to determine where the units coming ashore would set up prior to conducting a full-scale sweep of the island. Normally the location of friendly forces is marked in blue grease pencil and enemy locations in red. Since no one had any idea where the Brandenburgers might be there was no red on the map.

Vice Admiral Sir Randolph "Razor" Ransom, Lieutenant Commander Adrian Seligman, and Brandy Seaborn were discussing the blockade being established around the island.

Brigadier Dudley Clarke, Cuthbert "Curly" Bowlby, and James "Baldie" Taylor were interviewing the people who staffed their offices on ABC having been relieved from their duties of debriefing evaders.

Colonel John Randal made eye contact with Jim. He excused himself then walked over.

"I need Beverly and Mandy will you have someone sit in for them?"

"Everything all right, Colonel?"

"Jane's OK, but I don't have the full details."

"That is a relief—Cuthbert and I shall come back and sit in for them."

Col. Randal went to the debriefing tables.

"Mandy, you and Beverly on me."

As they were leaving the TOC Col. Randal made eye contact with King. The Merc followed. They walked down the cobblestone path to the village. Lieutenant Jake Novak's patrol of Rangers was taking a break in place.

Jake the Snake came over to report.

"We've cleared all the storefront buildings. No joy. Only the two Brandenburgers we killed when my patrol first arrived. General McKoy—he's hell on wheels, sir."

Col. Randal said, "Nice job, Lieutenant. Stand by here. Colonel Stone will have new orders for you shortly."

"Yes, sir."

Col. Randal and his party continued down to the dock. They proceeded along it to the end of the planking. In the distance a yacht flying the Turkish flag was approaching.

Signals were exchanged with the Patrol Torpedo (PT) boat standing offshore. The yacht came alongside. There appeared to be someone transferring from the Turkish craft to the motor torpedo boat but it was difficult to be sure exactly what was taking place from a half-mile away.

The PT boat powered toward the dock kicking up a rooster tail in its wake.

Major the Lady Jane Seaborn and Happy stepped off onto the pier. She was wearing traditional Turkish garb including a headpiece. When they recognized her Mandy and Beverly started screaming, laughing, and crying all at the same time.

The two girls had been convinced she was dead.

Col. Randal would not have wanted anyone to know how relieved he felt. As usual, he and Lady Jane acted like they hardly knew each other. Public displays of affection were frowned on in the military and not done by women of her class—except when they were.

There were big smiles and a lot of happy laughter all around from a group that had not been doing much smiling or laughing lately.

"I thought you were in Italy, John. Have you come to rescue me?"

"I did but it appears you were only vacationing in Turkey?"

"Happy and I were asleep when he alerted. My PPK was on the nightstand per your instructions. Men stormed into the room. I engaged as they came through the door—a double tap, center of mass as best I could see for each—exactly the way you taught me.

"Happy has been sleeping in a lightweight canvas harness in anticipation of a JAIL BREAK. We ran out on the deck, I snapped a rope on the D-ring, lowered him over the balcony, then I slid down. We had rehearsed the drill so it went fast.

"The two of us ran to the shore, dived in, and swam across to Antalya Province. The Turks took us in. However, the Province Chief would not allow my return to the island until he was convinced the fighting had ceased."

Col. Randal said, "You do know there are sharks in the Aegean?"

Lady Jane laughed, “A whole school of them were in my bedroom.”

Col. Randal said, “Happy can swim a mile?”

“Oh, yes he swims with us when we take our morning PT.”

“What’s with the costume?”

“I was sleeping in one of your khaki shirts. By the time we swam across most of the buttons popped off. I was practically naked. General Bakkal, the Province Chief, asked his mistress to loan me one of her outfits.”

Col. Randal said, “That’s some story.”

Mandy hugged Lady Jane, laughing and crying. “We have been terrified something dreadful happened to you.”

Beverly said, “When you didn’t come in after the JAIL BREAK all clear—it was awful.”

King said, “Impressive close quarters combat shooting, Lady Seaborn.”

Lady Jane laughed. “It was automatic—all the practice sessions with John and Beverly on the pistol range paid off.”

Col. Randal said, “You took out the German team leader and interrupted the raid’s operational tempo. The Nazis were never able to recover—nice job, babe.”

Lady Jane said, “I want your Browning P-35.”

“Why might that be?”

“Because it contains thirteen rounds. My Walther only holds eight.”

Col. Randal said, “Good reason.”

WHEN MAJOR THE LADY JANE SEABORN ARRIVED IN the Tactical Operations Center everyone in the room stopped what they were doing and stood up to clap. Her safe return took the primary stress factor out of planning the operation to secure

Castelrozzo. Now Raiding Forces could hunt down the Brandenburger Commandos still at large without having to worry about her being in the line of fire.

The gloves were off. There was no longer any pressing need for field intelligence about Lady Jane's whereabouts, so taking prisoners was not a priority. The mission was to find, fix, and finish the remaining Nazis.

And not take any unnecessary casualties in the process.

Lady Jane went upstairs to change and Colonel John Randal went with her.

When they were alone he broke the news about Lieutenant Bentley St. Ledger. Lady Jane went full-on poised. Her features looked like they were carved in stone which had the result of making her even more beautiful.

"I'm really sorry, Jane."

"Kill them all or better yet, let me."

Lady Jane sounded like she meant it.

Not knowing what else to do, Col. Randal went back downstairs.

Lieutenant Colonel Sir Terry "Zorro" Stone said, "Major Dance reports he has Germans trapped in an abandoned property not far from Government House."

Col. Randal ordered, "Lieutenant Finley, land your Fire Control Team ashore then have your LCT stand by for a fire mission."

"Wilco!"

Col. Randal said, "Colonel Stone, inform Major Dance to keep the Nazis contained. His team is not to attempt to assault the house. I say again, he is not to effect entry."

Captain Billy Jack Jaxx said, "Where do you want me, sir?"

"Escort the *King Duck's* Fire Control Team to Major Dance's location on the double. Take the Lovat Scouts. I'll meet you there."

"Moving now, sir!"

Vice Admiral Sir Randolph "Razor" Ransom said, "Mind if I accompany Captain Jaxx? I would like to observe Captain Finley's tanks in action."

Col. Randal said, "By all means, Admiral."

Beverly said, "Mandy and I want to watch."

"Negative, get back to your debriefing. I need to know everything that transpired on this island from the moment JAIL BREAK went into effect until right this minute. Something went wrong with our defense plan. We need to know what it was and fix it."

Mandy said, "As you pointed out John, someone on the island collaborated. Beverly and I have pledged to make it our life's work to identify them. I promise it shall not end well for whoever that person or persons turns out to be.

Col. Randal said, "Good."

Lieutenant General "Geronimo" Joe McKoy said, "King and I are on you, John."

"All right then, let's go."

Major Jack Dance had a guide waiting for Col. Randal in the village when his party arrived. They moved up the path to Government House. A short distance farther up the escarpment they came to where the Rangers had taken up a prone position forming a firing line in front of an abandoned house.

In better days the place had been a neoclassical mansion. Now it was boarded up. Probably looted by the locals like most of the other abandoned residences on the island.

Capt. Jaxx was already on scene with the two-man *King Duck* Fire Control Team. Down in the harbor the LCT was moving into position. Acting Provisional Lieutenant Warthog Finley was maneuvering to run the bow up on the shore.

Col. Randal asked the sailor with the radio, "What's the preferred method to mark the target?"

"Smoke grenade, sir."

Col. Randal said, "Tell Skipper Finley to stand by for a fire mission."

The three-level house was built into the side of the escarpment about fifty yards away. There was not a stick of cover. Any approach was going to be over open ground.

Col. Randal called a leader's conference.

"Major, I want your men to stage a demonstration—feint an assault. While you're creating a diversion we'll move up and put a smoke grenade on the target. When it's in place pull your Rangers back. I want them well out of the *King Duck's* gun-target-line.

"After Warthog shells the place to my satisfaction you make entry and clear the building."

"Yes, sir."

Capt. Jaxx, King, and Lt. Gen. McKoy were engaged in a heated debate.

Col. Randal said, "What is wrong with you people?"

Lt. Gen. McKoy said, "We all want be the one to place that smoke grenade, John—get us some big time payback."

Col. Randal said, "King, once Major Dance's diversion commences see if you can work in close enough to toss the smoke up on one of the balconies."

"Roger, Chief."

"Jack, you and the Scouts cover King then shift to a location behind the house and set up a blocking position—staying well back out of the line of fire from the *Duck.*"

"Yes, sir!"

A blocking position when employed by itself is called a roadblock or ambush. When a block is set up in conjunction with a maneuver element the combination is described as a "hammer and anvil." The maneuver element—or hammer—drives the enemy onto the block—or anvil.

Then both the hammer and anvil parties light the bad guys up.

Col. Randal was establishing a hasty hammer and anvil. When in the immediate proximity of a highly trained, well disciplined, armed, and hostile enemy, the series of movements to get into position can be complicated. The Rangers executed the maneuver effortlessly with parade-ground, drill team precision.

"General, you and Admiral Ransom stand by to advise me as the tactical situation develops."

Lt. Gen. McKoy said, "You can sure be a wet blanket sometimes, John."

VAdm. Ransom said, "I concur."

Lady Jane arrived with Happy and her two bodyguards, Rita and Lana. The two Kit-Kat dancers were armed with their favorite .30 M1 Carbines. Lieutenant Theodore Hamilton was with them. The Great Teddy was lugging Col. Randal's Brixia shoulder-fired mortar with the pack full of 45mm rounds.

Col. Randal said, "Not a chance, Jane, you're going back to the TOC."

Lady Jane said, "I am not!"

"That's an order."

"Happy hates Germans. He can track them."

"We've got them trapped. We don't need to do any tracking. Go home."

"No, John."

The signaler reported, "Captain Finley is good to go, sir."

Col. Randal said, "Happy stays. Rita, you and Lana escort Lady Seaborn back to ABCHQ. Make sure she remains in the building."

"John!"

"Fail to comply, *Lady Seaborn,* and I'll have King throw you over his shoulder and carry you down this hill."

Lady Jane stomped her boot in frustration, "You can be..."

Lt. Gen. McKoy said, "I already told him he was a wet blanket before you showed up."

Lady Jane said, "He is worse than that—these Nazis shot Bentley."

Col. Randal ordered, "Move out ladies."

"Do not let anything happen to my dog."

As the women started back down the path Lt. Hamilton said, "Sorry, sir . . ."

Col. Randal said, "I expect better judgment from my junior officers, Lieutenant."

"Lady Jane can be persuasive, sir."

Col. Randal said, "Raiding Forces officers are required to make difficult decisions under duress."

"Yes, sir."

Col. Randal said, "Let's see what you can do with my Brixia. On my command, take a crack at the double doors. Maybe go for one of the plate glass windows if you can hit it."

"Wilco, I can hit it sir."

"Major Dance, be prepared to execute your feint when Lieutenant Hamilton engages."

"Roger —standing by sir."

"Let's see what you've got, Lieutenant."

BLOOOOOP.

The round left the tube. It was visible in flight and arched like a BB fired out of a Daisy Red Ryder air rifle. The 45mm shell crashed through one of the two large plate glass windows on the front of the house and detonated inside.

Col. Randal said, "Nice shot."

The Rangers commenced laying down a base of fire as if preparing to assault. King sprinted the fifty yards to the side of the residence. Capt. Jaxx and the Lovat Scouts stood by providing over-watch protection ready to engage should any of the Nazis be foolish enough to attempt firing out a side window.

The Merc reached the wall of the house, slamming up flat against it. He pulled the pin on a violet smoke grenade—a color the Rangers called "goofy grape"—then tossed it up on the second-story balcony. As the smoke billowed out King retreated around back to link up with Capt. Jaxx and the Scouts who were in the process of shifting their position at a dead run.

The signaler spoke into his handset, "Smoke out—authenticate."

The radio broke squelch, "Goofy Grape."

Col. Randal said, "Execute, execute, execute."

The radio operator relayed, "Commence fire."

Maj. Dance ordered the Rangers to pull farther back off the gun target line. It was a good thing everyone moved fast because the two Tiger tanks, the mightiest armored fighting vehicles currently in the German Army inventory, opened as one.

BOOOOOM!

The first two ranging shots were marking rounds. Normally marking rounds are white phosphorous. Easy to see and to adjust from. Skipper Finley's Tigers did not have phosphorous rounds but that was not a problem.

The distance from the LST to the target was approximately four hundred yards. A chip shot for experienced tank gunners. The ex-SAS men had not had much gunnery practice lately but even rank amateurs could hit a three-story building at that range.

The pair of 88 marking rounds screamed in, smashed through the front wall, and blew up inside.

Col. Randal ordered, "Fire a battery of six."

The signaler relayed the command.

A battery of six fire command called for all six guns in a normal-sized artillery battery to fire one round. Since the *King*

Duck only had the two 88mm tank main guns each one would need to fire three rounds in rapid succession.

The two Tigers began to boom as fast as the loaders could slam in a fresh shell. The ship-to-shore fire support was impressive. The house was coming apart at the seams. Single family residences are not designed to withstand that kind of punishment

Tigers are typically equipped with two types of rounds, armor-piercing (AP), high-explosive (HE)—also described as high-explosive anti-tank (HEAT). Against another tank or a hardened bunker AP is the ammunition of choice.

For a civilian home HE will do the trick. The target was being blown apart. Pieces of the structure flew up in the air as every round impacted. The 88s continued to slam in rapid fire until the fire mission was complete.

Skipper Warthog Finley was back in the war in a big way.

Col. Randal commanded, "Maj. Dance—do it now!"

The Rangers re-formed on the move swinging into an online formation for a frontal final assault. As soon as the realignment was completed the troops went in—shooting, cheering, screaming Rebel yells. The attack would have been classified as a bayonet charge but Raiding Forces troops were not issued bayonets.

At that exact moment firing broke out to the rear of the building.

Capt. Jaxx, King, and the two Lovat Scouts opened on a Nazi who jumped out a ground-floor window trying to escape. Jack Cool was armed with his prized .30 "Baby" BAR modified to Colt R-80 Monitor specifications by the U.S. 27th Ordnance Battalion stationed outside Cairo. King carried his new Swiss 9mm Sig MKPS submachine gun—duty weapon of the Swiss Guard at the Vatican. The two Scouts had .30 M1 Garand rifles keeping their privately owned Westley Richards 7x57 red stag rifles slung over their shoulders for sniping work if needed.

The Brandenburger never had a chance.

Shot to pieces—hammered on the anvil.

The Rangers made it look easy.

Col. Randal, Lt. Gen. McKoy, VAdm. Ransom, and Lt. Hamilton followed Maj. Dance's assault into the house. They found Rangers downstairs in the living room standing around a dead Nazi who resembled a rag doll. He looked small and pitiful not like a ferocious Brandenburger Sea Raider Commando who shot women in the face.

Happy immediately attacked him.

The dog was ferocious. Absolutely wild. He must have been abused in the German military training system he had been schooled in.

Col. Randal had trouble pulling him off.

Lt. Gen. McKoy said, "Go ahead let the dog get some; ol' Happy's fired up."

Lady Jane was right the dog hated Germans.

Col. Randal said, "Guter Hund," which means "good dog" in German. One of a few simple commands he had been taught during the dog handler training Lady Jane had arranged for him. Whatever his reasons, Happy clearly despised his former masters, but he did respond better to some commands in the language he had learned as a puppy.

With the house secure, the Rangers reassembled in the front yard. Lt. Gen. McKoy held the bloody blouse ripped off one of the Nazis up to Happy's nose. The dog growled.

Col. Randal said, "Such" (pronounced "Zook"). Which meant "search." And it was on.

Happy liked this game.

MAJOR CLIVE ADAIR—THE FORMER "MAYOR OF Oasis X" and now the new "Mayor of Castelrozzo," Major Zargo, Captain Butch "Headhunter" Hoolihan, and Captain Lionel Chatterhorn joined the search for Nazi holdouts. Lieutenant Jake Novak brought his patrol up from the village to reinforce. Captain Billy Jack Jaxx was acting as the patrol leader, while Colonel John Randal served as dog handler.

Happy was working like he was possessed.

The problem was the majority of the villas on Castelrozzo were built into the side of the escarpment ringing the harbor. There were no streets, only cobblestone paths along a steep slope. Even with an aggressive dog the search was going to take forever.

Capt. Chatterhorn had a word with Vice Admiral Sir Randolph "Razor" Ransom. Then he walked up to the point element where Captain Billy Jack Jaxx, Colonel John Randal, and Happy were leading the way.

"Sir, the Admiral has agreed to arrange for a RAF Catalina to fly out the two dog teams I have at Raiding Forces Headquarters. They could be here in approximately two hours if I return to ABCHQ and place the call."

Col. Randal said, "Make it happen, Captain."

Capt. Chatterhorn said, "Be back shortly sir. I want to run these butchers down one by one and kill them with my bare hands."

Capt. Jaxx said, "Get in line, Lionel."

Three hours later the search was still on. Happy would pick up the scent and then lose it. Lieutenant General "Geronimo" Joe McKoy, who had a lot of experience working with bloodhounds in his U.S. Marshal Service days, was of the opinion that the Brandenburgers had scattered to go into hiding when they heard Lt. Novak's brief firefight in the village at sunrise. They could be shifting from location to location. The Nazis had to know at this point they were not getting off the island and they would be desperate.

Desperation makes dangerous men more dangerous.

There is a technical difference between tracking and trailing. Tracking is searching for a specific person. Trailing is following an unknown subject. Not that the book definition mattered. They were looking for Germans suspected of hiding in houses so they knew to look in houses.

Just not which one.

Happy was trained to lay down when he alerted. Nevertheless, Col. Randal kept him on a leash, bearing in mind Lady Jane's order to not let anything happen to her dog. Given the chance the Nazis would shoot the animal.

To protect against the possibility, the Lovat Scouts provided overwatch by moving by bounds with their 7x57 Westley Richards at the ready every time they approached a house. Covering movement can be done by "leaps" or "bounds." Leaps are like the children's game of hopscotch. Bounds means one person or vehicle advances while covered by another that remains stationary in place. The idea was to provide constant cover by fire.

Anyone peeking out a window of an abandoned house was going to be shot no questions asked.

Col. Randal called a halt to give Happy a break. Waldo Treywick, James "Baldie" Taylor, and Brigadier Dudley Clarke arrived to join the patrol. Everyone wanted to be in at the kill.

The operation was turning into a circus.

Col. Randal pulled Lt. Gen. McKoy aside. "Sir, I need you to exert some of your command authority."

Lt. Gen. McKoy said, "I liked it a whole lot better when…"

"It's not my fault the Governor of Arizona promoted you into the stratosphere, General."

"Yeah, but don't call me 'sir' again unless we're runnin' a game on some senior flag officer types."

"Yes, sir."

"I know you're joking, John, but I meant it about the sir business—cut it out. Enough's enough—you've always treated me with a great deal of respect no matter what my rank. Let's leave it at that.

"What's it you want from me?"

Col. Randal said, "Jack's about to let Lieutenant Novak take charge of the patrol in order to evaluate him for a slot in SOG. I want you to order all the strap hangers back to ABCHQ before we move out. The last thing we need is for one of 'em to get shot."

Lt. Gen. McKoy said, "I can do that. Say they're a hindrance to Jake's performance—all the gold braid lookin' over his shoulder. Not that he strikes me as the get-rattled type."

Col. Randal said, "I'd go back myself except Happy's only going to work for me or Jane."

Lt. Gen. McKoy said, "Yeah, unfortunately for you I'm guessin' there's gonna be some repercussions for that crack about havin' King sling Lady Jane over his shoulder. Sounded real macho, though, when you said it, though."

Col. Randal said, "I'm trying not to think about that."

LIEUTENANT JAKE NOVAK WAS ROTATING THE teams that worked directly behind Colonel John Randal and Happy. Master Sergeant Mack Beckwith's team would stay up front for half an hour and then Private First Class Norvel "Horn Dog" Hansen's men would relieve him and take the lead. The former 509th Parachute Infantry Battalion's Scout Company officer was handling the patrol with an ease that can only come from long experience commanding troops in the field.

He clearly knew his small-unit tactics.

On the next break, Col. Randal pulled PFC Hansen, a long-time SOG member and well-known critic of all things pertaining to officers, aside. "How did Lieutenant Novak do in your firefight in the Village?"

"The Snake acquitted himself well, sir."

Praise for an officer did not get much higher than that from Horn Dog Hansen.

Col. Randal quietly asking his NCOs how a new officer was performing was one of his standard practices. Horn Dog was not an NCO, having been busted more times than anyone could remember, but he was serving in the capacity of one and his opinion mattered. Col. Randal had no room in Raiding Forces for medium-level performers, fake toughs, or martinets.

What the troops thought about their leaders was important to him.

That said being an officer in Raiding Forces was not a popularity contest.

Col. Randal signaled to Lieutenant General "Geronimo" Joe McKoy, who had returned to the patrol after escorting all the "visiting firemen" back to ABCHQ. He moved up front with Waldo Treywick, who did not consider himself a visiting fireman, to where Col. Randal, King, and Happy were pulling point.

Down in the harbor a Catalina glided in, landed and taxied up to the dock.

Col. Randal said, "That should be Captain Chatterhorn's dog teams from RFHQ, General. Why don't you and Mr. Treywick go organize another patrol and take out one of the tracking dogs."

Lt. Gen. McKoy said, "Thanks John. Maybe you ain't such a party pooper after all."

Col. Randal said, "Take the Headhunter with you. I want Butch leading the other dog team patrol—make that happen."

Lt. Gen. McKoy said, "Can do."

Waldo said, "Get the old Abyssinian firm back in action. 'Right Men. Right Job.'"

Col. Randal said, "That's the plan."

After they left, King said, "You three hold Captain Hoolihan in high regard, Chief. He was your batman at one time?"

"My Number 2—like you. Baldie and I gave him a direct commission prior to the drop into Abyssinia. Butch thought we were joking . . . it wasn't a real promotion. He found out different."

As soon as the patrol moved out again Happy picked up a trail. It led straight to an abandoned villa. He went prone to indicate Germans.

The dog looked over his shoulder at Col. Randal.

He wanted to charge inside.

"Good boy!"

Capt. Jaxx said, "Showtime."

The signalman said, "Captain Finley needs to reposition the LCT. "

Lt. Novak said, "How long's that going to take?"

"Fifteen minutes, sir."

Lt. Novak ordered, "Sergeant Major move your team to cover the back of the house. Make sure to set up at an angle out of the gun target line. That way you won't have to pull back prior to the shoot."

MSgt. Beckwith said, "Yes, sir—moving at this time."

Lt. Novak said, "Do we need to mark the target?"

The signaler said, "Negative, sir. Captain Finley has been following our progress through his binoculars as we traversed across the slope. He has the target in sight."

"Horn Dog have your people stand by ready to go in on my signal."

"Yes, sir, El Tee."

"Lieutenant Hamilton, would you like another try with your Brixia mortar?"

"Affirmative, sir."

"On my command then."

Lt. Novak had all the parts of a classic small unit action—a miniature hammer and anvil—in place in a matter of minutes. There was no way the Brandenburgers would be able to escape. All they could do now was surrender. One highly popular dead girl and six executed Vulnerable Points Wing security men guaranteed no one was going to invite them to do so.

Lt. Novak studied the disposition of his troops.

The Fire Control Team signalman said, "Skipper Finley is in place standing by for a fire mission, sir."

"Light 'em up, Ted."

Blooooop—WHAAAAAM!

"Try a couple more."

Blooooop—WHAAAAAM! Blooooop—WHAAAAAM!

Lt. Novak ordered, "Inform Skipper Finley he is cleared to fire for effect."

From the harbor, firing in tandem, the Tigers roared, *BOOOOOM—BOOOOOM!* The pair of 88mm shells slammed into the building. Right on target. The villa shuddered as smoke and dust belched from inside.

The Tigers pounded away.

The command "fire for effect" ordered the guns to keep shooting until ordered to stop.

Waiting longer than absolutely necessary as the rounds pounded the house Lt. Novak finally ordered, "Cease fire!"

When the signaler announced, "End of Mission"—meaning the last round had left the tube, Lt. Novak shouted, "ON LINE. MOVE OUT. FOLLOW ME!"

Then he led PFC Hansen's team in the assault on the villa.

Col. Randal, Capt. Jaxx, King, and Happy traveled behind the screaming Rangers. Inside, the house was a shambles. Two dead Nazis were found on the second floor where they had initially retreated in an attempt to get away from Lt. Hamilton's .45mm mortar rounds.

Happy attacked immediately.

COLONEL JOHN RANDAL CALLED A HALT. THE patrol had been conducting search and clear operations for nearly eight hours now. No more Brandenburgers were located.

It was slow tedious work. Care had to be taken when approaching a building where someone inside might take a shot at you. The Rangers had only managed to check out fifty-one houses. There was no way to speed up the process. Hopefully, Lieutenant General "Geronimo" Joe McKoy and Captain Butch "Headhunter" Hoolihan had been able to clear another fifty between them, having gotten a later start. That would make approximately a hundred houses searched out of 2,500 or so that needed to be cleared.

There was a bright spot: no additional friendly casualties—Greek islander *or* Raiding Forces.

The Rangers were hungry, having not eaten breakfast or lunch, due to the urgency of running the Nazis to ground.

Happy would have kept working but he was tired. Col. Randal knew his men needed a break, a good meal, and a night's sleep in a real bunk. The patrol made its way down the escarpment to the village.

Col. Randal peeled off and took Happy to the shore. The dog deserved a swim. When the two finally reached ABCHQ the place was pulsing with activity.

Lady Jane was nowhere to be seen.

Col. Randal ordered, "Go find Jane."

The dog took off at a run.

Lieutenant Colonel Sir Terry "Zorro" Stone was standing in front of the wall map of Castelrozzo talking to Lt. Gen. McKoy, Capt. Hoolihan and Capt. Jaxx.

Vice Admiral Sir Randolph "Razor" Ransom was in conference with Cuthbert "Curly" Bowlby, James "Baldie" Taylor, and Brigadier Dudley Clarke. With them were two worried-looking senior staff officers Col. Randal recognized from Middle East Command's Plans Division. One glance told him they were not discussing a handful of Brandenburger Sea Raiders at large on Castelrozzo.

In another part of the TOC Captain Pamala Plum-Martin, Mandy Paige, Beverly Blackwell, Major Zargo, Major Clive Adair and Captain Lionel Chatterhorn were engaged in a discussion.

People were coming and going.

Normally the Tactical Operations Center was quiet, almost like a library, with only the occasional radio report breaking the silence. Messages would come in from time to time, scheduled commo checks or some inquiry or report. A FANY, WREN, or Royal Marine would log them. Occasionally a staffer would post a caique or LSF schooner's change of location on a map. But due to the time and distance constraints in the Aegean and the inability of Raiding Forces to respond to events from far-flung locations with anything resembling rapidity, the Operations Room usually ran at a tranquil pace.

Brandy Seaborn saw him.

"What did you do to Jane?"

"I . . ."

"She says you had turned into a bully and called her Lady Seaborn."

"That's true."

"Did Jane mention she was sleeping in *your* shirt when the Germans attacked?"

"She did—what's that about?"

"Women sleep in their lover's shirt when he is away if they really care for him because the scent of his body on the material is a connection when they are alone in bed at night."

"Really?"

"This is a difficult time for Jane. Her first Royal Marine killed. Be gentle, handsome—you hurt her feelings."

"Where is she?"

"In your suite composing a letter to Raquel—Bentley's mother."

"Thanks, Brandy."

Wishing he were anywhere else on Planet Earth, Col. Randal trudged upstairs to find Lady Jane reclining on her bed. She had a pen in hand and a blank sheet of her personal monogrammed stationary on her lap. Happy was beside her, being very still.

The dog was resting his head on his front paws watching with sad eyes.

Lady Jane was crying.

4
COCAINE, WHIPS AND CHAINS

CAPTAIN PAMALA PLUM-MARTIN SAID, "JOHN, WE need to talk."

Colonel John Randal was sitting alone in his office in the Tactical Operations Center at ABCHQ. He was rethinking everything. A lot had happened in a short amount of time. The German intentions for their raid on Castelrozzo and what he was going to do next were far from clear in his mind.

Col. Randal said, "OK."

Capt. Plum-Martin, the first handpicked member of Major the Lady Jane Seaborn's exclusive detachment of Royal Marines, an on-again-off-again MI-6 officer, CARD GAME member and one of Raiding Forces' pilots, came in and took a seat. She looked serious which was not typical of her but then today was not the normal day on Castelrozzo.

While it was true that a picture of Capt. Plum-Martin in a swimsuit deserved to be up on a billboard advertising suntan lotion—it would be a mistake to take her as nothing more than a pretty face.

Lieutenant General "Geronimo" Joe McKoy claimed a year of war was like a dog year. If so, that would mean they had worked together for the equivalent of nearly thirty years.

Not only did Col. Randal like her, he trusted her.

Capt. Plum-Martin said, "Istanbul—before you came out to Egypt. We need to go over the details. There may be loose ends."

"Like what?"

"Let's start with when Lawrence Grand of SOE's Section D sent you to the Middle East Command. What were his instructions?"

"I was to evaluate the opportunity for future Raiding Forces operations in Egypt. Jane's husband had turned up alive. She had disappeared. Larry said he thought it would be good to get me out of the country for a while."

Capt. Plum-Martin said, "Not the entire story."

Col. Randal said, "He asked me to do him a favor en route. Travel incognito, stop off in Istanbul, meet 'a person or persons known to me.' At first, I thought the contact was going to be General McKoy because his poster was in the lobby of the hotel when I checked in. However, when I met with the General he handed over the Browning P-35 he had been tuning for me, directed me to be in the casino at a certain time that evening wearing a tuxedo to be found in my room. Then he advised me not to go—said it was a bad idea.

"Sometime later you knocked on my door—you were the contact."

Capt. Plum-Martin said, "That was your complete briefing?"

Col. Randal said, "Well, you showed me a photo of a female SS officer, Hauptsturmführer Gretchen von Coffenhauser, who you said was working for the Abwehr in Istanbul. She was going to make an approach in the casino. The idea was for the Hauptsturmführer to pick me up and take me out on the town.

"Then kill me."

Capt. Plum-Martin said, "I gave you more information than that, John."

Col. Randal said, "You informed me you were running a sting operation. The plan was to use me as bait to lure a high-value target out into the open from an unknown location and then your team would kidnap that individual.

"Oh yeah, you also mentioned Miss von Coffenhauser was a bisexual S&M aficionado into cocaine, whips, and chains—a giver not a taker."

"I had no idea it was going to be you," Capt. Plum-Martin said. "Damn Larry Grand."

Col. Randal said, "That's what you said."

Capt. Plum-Martin said, "We went down to the casino together. Gretchen literally bumped into us when we walked in. I threw a glass of champagne in your face then stalked off as if we were having a lover's quarrel. What happened next was not part of the script.

"You two were all over each other."

Col. Randal said, "I was TDY on His Majesty's Secret Service following my . . . *your* orders."

Capt. Plum-Martin said, "Did Gretchen say anything to you or did she simply start ripping your shirt off? We found your tuxedo studs littering the stairwell."

"Not that I can recall," Col. Randal said.

"You managed to constrain yourself long enough to make your way up to her bedroom where you had sex and then she left you on the bed to run a shower?"

Col. Randal said, "I can neither confirm nor deny . . ."

Capt. Plum-Martin said, "Gretchen goes into the bathroom at which time her SS bodyguard appears armed with a syringe and a truncheon—you shot him?"

"Yes."

Capt. Plum-Martin said, "She hears the shot, runs out of the shower nude holding her Walther PPK—I have it here in my purse—and you shot her?

"That's what happened," Col. Randal said.

"I arrived seconds later to find you getting dressed," Capt. Plum-Martin said. "Gretchen and her bodyguard were dead on the floor. Almost immediately hotel security personnel entered the room. They covered both bodies with sheets and had them transported?"

Col. Randal said, "You were there."

Capt. Plum-Martin said, "As was Joe McKoy."

"Correct."

"No other conversation transpired between the two of you—absolutely certain?"

Col. Randal said, "Why the questions?"

Capt. Plum-Martin said, "Did anyone ever mention the possibility von Coffenhauser ran out with her pistol to *defend* you?"

Col. Randal said, "You're kidding."

"Negative, love, MI-6 floated the idea as a working hypothesis at the time," Capt. Plum-Martin said. "Everyone on my team saw the sparks fly in the casino. I attempted to abort the operation because the physical attraction between you two was so intense."

Col. Randal said, "That might be over . . ."

Capt. Plum-Martin said, "You should be aware of the possibility the Hauptsturmführer is alive."

"Really?"

"And she may be behind this raid on Castelrozzo."

VICE ADMIRAL SIR RANDOLPH "RAZOR" RANSOM came into Colonel John Randal's office after Captain Pamala Plum-Martin left. He shut the door. If this were a poker game that would have been a tell.

"We are not having this conversation."

Col. Randal clicked on.

VAdm. Ransom said, "In the last war, I was given a command consisting of a destroyer named *Yellow Jacket*, three trawlers, twelve drifters and a collier. My orders were to establish a naval base at Port Laki on Leros. My assignment was to patrol the Turkish coast between Samos to the north and Rhodes to the south—we were enemies last time around.

"At night landing parties of Royal Marines and sailors were sent in boats into the small coves to search for, seize or burn Turkish caiques. We would also go ashore, round up cattle and bring them back to the flotilla for victuals. Tactics were straight out of Blackbeard's playbook.

"The Aegean has historically been considered a strategic part of the world by the Admiralty. At the same time it has always been treated as a low-priority sideshow. In those days I was working off charts dated 1852.

"Essentially the same kind of support Small Raids Inc. has to contend with to this day. We are only provided outdated, obsolete equipment, boats and planes no one else has any use for . . . captured enemy gear and the like. Whatever we can scrounge or improvise.

"For FIRE EATER, conceived by higher headquarters as a wide-ranging raiding and intelligence undertaking across vast distances, the only troops I can provide Raiding Forces are the remnants of a handful of small special operations units whose glory days are behind them.

"As you are aware with the war having moved on the character of the conflict in our AO, which encompasses the entirety of the Aegean, has been altered. The Eighth Army is fighting in Italy. The mighty fleets have all departed for other seas. With the fast fleet of aircraft carriers, battleships and heavy cruisers gone, all that remains is what the Royal Navy condescendingly describes as the 'dust of the sea.'

"That is how the Admiralty thinks of Small Raids Inc.—the sweepings.

"On the other side the Balkans have always been of major strategic importance to Hitler. Oil, copper, bauxite and chrome come from the region. The equivalent of over twenty German Divisions are occupying Yugoslavia, Greece and certain strategic islands in the Aegean. Recent intelligence indicates the Führer is convinced the logical next step is for the Western Allies to move against the region in force, attacking through what Prime Minister Churchill calls the 'soft underbelly of Europe.'

"We, meaning the Allies, want Hitler to continue to believe that is exactly what the future holds. Dudley Clarke's A-Force is working round the clock to create misinformation designed to stoke the Nazis' fears to that end. What our side would like to see happen is for the Nazis to reinforce the region with additional divisions.

"However, beyond blocking the Aegean and holding a defensive line—called the 'Iron Ring'—Crete, Scarpanto, and Rhodes—German intentions in the region are unclear.

"While there are fundamental disagreements between London and Washington on strategic policy out here the one thing everyone on both sides of the pond agrees on is those twenty German divisions need to stay right where they are. Their entry into the Italian Theatre would complicate the situation. And when the Allies eventually do invade the Continent twenty extra divisions sitting on the beaches of France waiting for our troops to wade ashore would be disastrous.

"Pinning down the Germans in the eastern Aegean is called OPERATION ACCOLADE and consists of several different elements. Our part, the actual raiding of the islands, is as you are aware OPERATION FIRE EATER. For all practical purposes you will be the Officer in Charge Raiding Operations Aegean—though the infighting with Colonel Turnbull and GHQ Cairo over who is actually in command has yet to be entirely resolved.

"The reason I am going over all this with you again Colonel is because I never want there to come a day when you conclude small-scale raids against tiny islands in a remote backwater are not worth the sacrifice of blood and treasure."

Col. Randal said, "I hear you, sir."

He knew twenty additional German divisions in Italy would have crushed Lieutenant General Mark Clark's invasion at Salerno. Even one of them reaching the Allied beachhead in the first forty-eight to seventy-two hours would have thrown the invasion back into the sea.

VAdm. Ransom said, "One other point of note. This raid on Castelrozzo may be the precursor of larger German operations in the region. The Aegean has gone up in flames since you departed for Italy."

Col. Randal said, "I was only gone a week, sir."

"Quite a lot can occur in a week."

"That is a fact, Admiral."

"Immediately following dinner tonight I have scheduled an intelligence briefing to bring you up to speed on recent developments in the FIRE EATER Area of Operations."

"I'll look forward to it, sir."

VAdm. Ransom said, "Now on another subject, in the spirit of 'if anything can go wrong it will at a bad time,' I am the bearer of news that may prove disquieting for Jane."

Col. Randal said, "Lovely."

VAdm. Ransom said, "Her husband's troop ship was sunk en route to the CBI where he was to serve on Mountbatten's staff. Aerial reconnaissance reported Japanese surface craft near the scene, possibly rescuing survivors. Mallory may be dead or a POW, but he will most certainly not be signing their divorce decree any time soon.

"Poor Jane."

Col. Randal said, "I'm not sure how this news will play with Jane, sir."

VAdm. Ransom said, "The timing is not optimal."

"Yeah."

LIEUTENANT COLONEL SIR TERRY "ZORRO" STONE came in after Vice Admiral Sir Randolph "Razor" Ransom departed. The Errol Flynn look-alike playboy had been too busy sorting out a multitude of problems all coming at him at once to have a chance to speak at any length with Colonel John Randal.

The two officers had a lot of catching up to do.

Only now there was not time for more than a brief report.

Lt. Col. Stone said, "Finally located Captain Jones-Teasdale, the commander of the 2nd Essex Battalion detachment providing security on Castelrozzo."

Col. Randal said, "What's his story?"

Lt. Col. Stone said, "He only has eighty-six men under command. Not what one would describe as a full-strength line infantry rifle company. Certainly not the battalion I thought was to be stationed here."

"And why might that be, Sir Terry?"

"The 2nd Essex Battalion recently reflagged as the 11 Parachute Battalion—converting from infantry to airborne. Jones-Teasdale's command consists of the men in the battalion who chose not to become parachutists. As soon as they complete their three-month tour here on the island the troops will be transferred to a replacement depot on Sicily. From there they shall be shipped out to Italy as individual replacements where needed."

Col. Randal said, "So they're not happy campers."

"That would be in the way of a monumental understatement, old stick."

Col. Randal said, "What have Captain Jones-Teasdale's people been doing all this time with Brandenburgers running loose on the island?"

"Guarding potential landing sites around the perimeter," Lt. Col. Stone said. "In penny packets of troops who have never served together as a squad, platoon or company almost totally lacking in wireless communications scattered miles apart. They were supposed to put up signal flares in the event of an incursion."

Col. Randal said, "Not much of a plan."

Lt. Col. Stone said, "Captain Jones-Teasdale claims he never knew anything was amiss until receiving a report of firing coming from the direction of the village this morning."

"Have him report to Captain Chatterhorn. We need to tighten things up around here," Col. Randal said.

"Taking place as we speak. Chatterhorn was tearing a strip off the good captain as I departed to report to you. Not sure it is entirely Jones–Teasdale's fault. Securing the perimeter of a four-square-mile island is virtually impossible with the number of people he has."

Col. Randal said, "Why weren't there more security troops—a battalion was promised?"

Lt. Col. Stone said, "Safeguarding Castelrozzo Island has never been a priority for MEHQ or GHQ Cairo—as Jumbo Wilson's organization is now styled. Middle East Command Headquarters was downgraded while you were away—as befits the military backwater it has become.

"I repeatedly indented for additional manpower as did Captain Chatterhorn and Admiral Ransom. GHQ Cairo rejected our requests out of hand."

Col. Randal said, "What was their explanation?"

"We were being 'alarmists.' Heads shall roll on my word. Someone will pay."

The dashing Life Guard's family exercised enormous influence in the British military hierarchy. And while Lt. Col. Stone was the celebrated black sheep, which was not entirely a bad thing for a Stone, when he made a threat to seek redress for incompetence affecting the troops under his command it was a given the weight of the family would back it to the hilt.

His father, the Duke, was well-known for looking out for his family and his troops. The Stone family regiment, the Lancelot Lancers, was attached to Raiding Forces. His reaction to their being put at risk due to failure to act on the part of GHQ Cairo—even though there were no Lancers present when the Brandenburgers carried out their raid—was going to be outrage of epic proportions.

The Duke knew Raquel St. Ledger, Bentley's mother. Exactly how well had been a matter of speculation among the horsey set for years. She would be wanting answers about her daughter's death. In all likelihood he would be demanding an accounting from Lieutenant General Henry Maitland Wilson aka Jumbo, on her behalf.

There was no chance the Duke or Raquel would be satisfied with any response GHQ Cairo provided. Bentley was dead and members of the Duke's "family regiment," the Lancelot Lancers, serving with distinction in Raiding Forces, had not been properly supported by higher headquarters. There would be repercussions.

That was a given.

Col. Randal was outraged but trying not to show it. When the 575th Ranger Force flew out for Italy he had been assured adequate defense measures would be taken to secure Castelrozzo in his absence. Plans Division could have easily stationed a full battalion on the island or even two. There were infantry regiments garrisoned in Egypt not doing much other than standing by to be available in the event of an "internal" threat—meaning civil unrest.

Col. Randal was open to the possibility GHQ had failed to provide adequate security for ABC as payback for the Small Raids Inc./Raiding Forces rebellion against Colonel Douglas Turnbull's power play to take control of all Special Forces units in the theatre. He was also willing to accept that he had moved too fast in turning Castelrozzo into a forward operating base and had some responsibility for not consolidating the island's defenses prior to departing for Italy.

Nevertheless the lack of adequate troops allocated to defend Castelrozzo was inexcusable.

Sir Terry never made threats. He made promises. His word was his bond.

And he never quit coming.

Col. Randal said, "Don't lighten up on GHQ on my behalf."

Lt. Col. Stone said, “Not a chance there was no reason Bentley had to die the way she did. May take a while, but revenge is best served cold. General Wilson’s prospects for promotion to Field Marshal anytime soon have taken a hit—the Duke shall see to that.

“Actually, Jumbo has bigger immediate problems than my father or a stalled career. Following the briefing tonight you shall have a clearer understanding of all that has transpired while you were vacationing in sunny Italy. A sordid tale awaits.”

“Why not tell me now?”

“Why ruin the suspense?”

Col. Randal said, “Hasn’t been such a great day, Sir Terry. I was counting on you for the good news.”

Lt. Col. Stone said, “Dream on, old stick—military strategy concocted from afar in the wee hours over brandy and cigars rarely produces the results one hoped.

“There is no good news.”

Col. Randal said, “I was afraid you were going to say something like that.”

In the distance, the Tiger tanks began booming.

Strange how now German 88s were a comforting sound.

NOT LONG AFTER LIEUTENANT COLONEL SIR TERRY "Zorro” Stone left to resume his duties, Mandy Paige came to the office. The beautiful MI-5 counterintelligence officer did not have any pressing need to see Colonel John Randal. She simply wanted to.

“Is that mascara on your collar, John?”

"Could be . . . emotions have been running high around here."

"Stand by for another layer."

Mandy hugged him around the neck sobbing. Her second breakdown of the day. Like Major the Lady Jane Seaborn she had been brought up to never show any emotion in public except joy. But now her grief over Bentley's death boiled over again.

Mandy needed a safe place. They were in private. The two were friends. That was why she was here.

Col. Randal's day was not getting any better. He never knew how to respond to crying women. He and Mandy had been close since the siege at RAF Habbaniya during the rebellion of the Golden Square rebels. When all had seemed lost she earned his respect for her bravery and can-do attitude no matter how desperate things were.

Few people enjoyed Col. Randal's confidence to the degree she did.

If there was anything to say to make Mandy feel better he was unable to think of what it might be but he wanted to come up with something.

She kissed him on the cheek.

"I can always count on you to be there for me. You raise my spirits no matter how dreadful events are. Love you, John."

Since he had not actually said or done anything Col. Randal was not sure of his next move. "I love you too . . . just don't say I said that. Except it's OK to tell Jane. I'm pretty sure she knows."

Mandy laughed through her tears, "See, I am feeling better already."

Hoping to switch to a less emotional issue Col Randal said, "What's your takeaway from the interviews with the JAIL BREAK evaders?"

Mandy said, "Not one item of significant intelligence value, John. The Brandenburgers landed and advanced to ABCHQ unobserved. Their presence was only detected when gunshots rang out inside the building.

"Pam and I believe you to be the primary target but that is only speculation."

"Why me?"

"Beverly and I have been researching the Brandenburger Regiment for our Enemy Forces dossier. We have an idea of how it operates. If the Germans are in fact planning larger-scale operations in the Aegean in the immediate future the idea may have been to take out the Chief of Special Operations prior to commencing. Undoubtedly the Sea Raiders were not aware you were absent from the island.

"Taking you out would be classic Brandenburger MO—seize key pieces of terrain, defensive positions, and eliminate top enemy commanders in advance of an invasion by conventional forces."

Col. Randal said, "The Nazis couldn't be planning to seize ABC—there's no way to hold it if they did."

Mandy said, "There are a lot of other islands in the Aegean for the Germans to capture and you would be the top commander to react to any German occupation."

Col. Randal said, "That's why MI-5 only takes the smart ones."

Captain Billy Jack Jaxx knocked on the door and then stuck his head inside.

"Butch and I are heading out to the *King Duck.* We want to coordinate with the tank gunners. We'll be back in time for the Razor's briefing, sir."

Col. Randal said, "What're you coordinating?"

"We want to see if there's a more precise way to mark targets than smoke. Headhunter and I need to be able to direct the gunner's aim at a specific part of the building—like a certain window or maybe a door.

"Can't do that so well with smoke grenades, sir."

Col. Randal said, "Good idea. Take Mandy with you. You'd like to see the inside of a Tiger tank wouldn't you—for the intelligence value?"

"Absolutely."

Mandy had exactly zero interest in tanks, enemy or friendly, but she knew what Col. Randal was trying to do.

Capt. Jaxx said, "You've got eyeliner on your blouse, sir. Were you two making out in here?"

Col. Randal said, "Move out, Jack."

WALDO TREYWICK CAME IN NEXT. FIRST THING HE handed Colonel John Randal a handful of his custom-rolled cigars to replenish his supply. The two immediately fired up. Col. Randal did the honors with his hard-service Zippo lighter. Every time he broke it out nowadays he wondered how many of his old friends in the U.S. 26th Cavalry Regiment were still alive.

Col. Randal said, "How'd Rocky hold up during JAIL BREAK?"

"Fine. She'd picked herself out an abandoned mansion somewhere up on the hill to hide out in. Takes more than a handful 'a bloodthirsty Nazis to get that human heat wave's spirits down.

"She used to be one of 'em, you know."

"You don't suspect Rocky's the Brandenburger's contact on Castelrozzo?"

"Naw, the woman hates Germans. Only worked for the Abwehr because she had no other choice when the Wehrmacht invaded Norway. Them knowin' she'd already spied for the Russians and all—Nazis thought they'd turned her but they was wrong.

"Rocky's a world-class survivor."

Col. Randal said, "That's a good thing."

"Yeah well not bein' a spy now don't mean she wasn't real outstandin' at bein' one when she did work for the Hitlerites."

"So I've heard."

Waldo said, "Wanted to stop in and let you have a follow-up report on the diamond smugglin' interdiction program me and Captain Butterfield has been runnin' outta Cairo."

Col. Randal said, "Like to hear it."

He could use a change of pace.

Waldo said, "Our orders straight from OSS in Washington, D.C. is to disappear the smugglers. Not a hunnert percent sure on what that means entirely or why. The impression I got was we're supposed to kill 'em dead right there—DRT.

"But that ain't exactly how we been doin' it."

Col. Randal said, "Really?"

Waldo said, "Since nobody's fully explained to us *why* we was supposed to be makin' 'em vanish, other than it was a good idea to eradicate every diamond smuggler from the face 'a the earth like they was some kinda' germ, me and Captain Butterfield came up with another solution on our own. We got Mandy to cut a deal with Major Sansom. We catch the traffickers then he turns 'em over to the Egyptian police with a' ironclad guarantee they'll be held in prison until the war's over.

"They're as good as dead as far as being able to smuggle any more diamonds."

Col. Randal said, “What’s happened to you, Mr. Treywick? Back in Abyssinia you’d have slit a smuggler’s throat then eaten your lunch sitting on his corpse.”

Waldo said, “Could be I’m goin’ soft, Colonel. Hangin’ around the likes ’a Lady Seaborn and Rocky has had a civilizing effect on me. Women can do that to a man.

“In their own way they’re as dangerous as those man-eatin’ bad cats we used to fight.”

Col. Randal said, “That is a fact.”

“Besides, those Egyptian smugglers is just tryin’ to make a livin’. They ain’t real Nazis,” Waldo said. “Nothin’s gained by killin’ ’em.”

Col. Randal said, “Our orders were implied. You’re free to interpret ’em as long as you follow the spirit of the directive. OSS laid down the *what* but never explained the *why*. Lady Jane suggested the reason Donovan wants smugglers dead might be to prevent them from transporting some other strategic contraband.

“Some type of material that could end up in German hands we’re not cleared to know about.”

Waldo said, “I remember her sayin’ that.”

Col. Randal said, “Turning the traffickers over to the Egyptian prison authorities is a good plan Mr. Treywick. I like it. Should have thought of that myself.”

“Well, that’s what you got me for Colonel—ideas. You’ve had your hands full lately. Me and Captain Butterfield has been recoverin’ stones but the problem we got is not all them minor league criminals infestin’ Cairo’s underworld is cooperatin’ with The Three.”

Col. Randal said, “What does that mean?”

Waldo said, “They ain’t sellin’ to ’em ‘one hunnert percent exclusive’ like they’re supposed to. Our pet crime lords has got some competition. We're havin' to work round the clock at trackin' down all the diamond deals bein' dealt on the side."

"Donovan will be expecting a detailed report on that development," Col. Randal said. "He's not going to like the sound of it. Do you believe you're intercepting the majority of the stones?"

"Oh yeah, Major Sansom's intelligence outfit is the best there is. Ain't nothin' goes on in Cairo he don't know about . . . at least not much. The Major's got hisself an army of informants who'll drop a dime on anybody buyin' sparklers. And they'll tell who they're hirin' to run 'em to Turkey.

"Captain Butterfield keeps a spotter plane airborne pretty much all day, every day," Waldo said. "He tracks the caravans we got targeted from the minute they roll outta Cairo. When they get out in the middle of the desert he orders his Foreign Legion boys to swoop down on 'em in their gun jeeps.

"Sometimes the traffickers make a run for it."

Col. Randal said, "How's that work out?"

Waldo said, "Never ends well for the bad guys. Not with a spotter overhead and trigger-happy French Foreign Legion badasses in jeeps watchin' their money gettin' away.

"Once the drama's over the rocks is recovered and turned over to Mr. Big, meaning me. All the trade goods go to the Legionnaires to take back to Cairo to sell on the black market. Plus, they get to pocket any cash money that gets taken.

"The smugglers disappear into the Egyptian prison system. The camels get driven out to Oasis X to be sold to the Emir at a deep discount—Foreign Legion boys get that money too. Then that ol' crook brokers the animals to traders passing through the oasis headed for who knows where, parts unknown."

Col. Randal said, "A well-thought-out plan, Mr. Treywick—no fingerprints."

Waldo said, “Traffickers is gettin’ disappeared. CARD GAME gets the diamonds—which makes us all happy. Butterfield’s boys are makin’ money so troop morale’s sky high. And I’m gettin’ job satisfaction outta bein’ ’a anti-smuggler.

“Late-life change ’a occupation.”

Col. Randal said, “Good report.”

Waldo said, “Deal’s pretty slick if I do say so myself. All the evidence goes up in a puffa smoke—poof. Like The Great Teddy says, “Hey, Presto!”

Set a smuggler to catch a smuggler.

Right Man, Right Job.

AFTER WALDO LEFT COLONEL JOHN RANDAL WAS sitting alone again trying to develop some semblance of an idea what to do next. There was a scratching at the door. Happy pushed it open and slipped inside. The dog sat down and looked at him expectantly.

Either Happy wanted to go hunt more Nazis or Lady Jane had sent him.

Before he could figure it out Beverly Blackwell arrived.

“You’re not going to cry too?”

“No, Johnny, but I feel like it. Just wanted to see how you’re doing. I know Bentley and six of your men murdered has to be hard on your spirits.

“Thought maybe you could use a friend.”

Col. Randal said, “One of your University of Texas Ten Most Beautiful smiles would go a long way right about now.”

Beverly laughed, “Typical I came to cheer you up and you try to make me feel good.”

Col. Randal said, "It was a mistake to transfer Raiding Forces to ABC without proper security measures in place. I moved too fast. We've paid a price for it."

Beverly said, "Not your fault Johnny. I was in most of the same meetings you were. Everyone was in favor of the transfer of RFHQ staff to Castelrozzo.

"Besides, you thought we would be safer here after Lady Jane was shot in Cairo."

Col. Randal said, "Well I got that wrong."

Beverly said, "Don't second-guess yourself. That's one of your best traits. You make a decision, put it in action and take responsibility no matter the outcome.

"One of the reasons you're such a great leader."

Col. Randal said, "Is Jane in the TOC?"

"No, she's still in her room."

"Let's go see what she's up to."

When they reached the landing on the second floor music could be heard coming from the suite. Rita and Lana were playing one of Lady Jane's records on her turntable in the living room. The two ex-slaves were dancing with each other. The fact Nazi killers had been hunting for them for the last two days had not dampened the girls' spirits.

Beverly plopped down on a couch with Happy to watch while Col. Randal went into the master bedroom to check on Lady Jane.

She was sitting in front of her gigantic clamshell mirror putting the finishing touches on her lipstick—a color called Brandied Raisin. Having recovered her composure and redone her make-up it would not have been possible for anyone to know about the crying.

Lady Jane said, "I see Happy accomplished his mission."

Col. Randal said, "My first thought was the dog might be wanting to go on another patrol."

Lady Jane said, "I am sure he does. Happy thinks hunting Nazis is a great game. Right now, however, I would rather you to escort me to the TOC.

"Appearances have to be maintained."

Col. Randal noticed his 9mm Browning P-35 laying on the nightstand by the king-sized bed. Now it was sporting ivory grips with "Raiding Forces" carved on them. He had carried those grips on his pistols in Abyssinia to make him look like a *tillik sau*—big shot, to the natives.

After the campaign concluded the ivory was switched out for high-grade English black walnut. Lady Jane had installed one set of his ivory panels on her Colt 1911 .38 Super. She kept the grips belonging to his other pistols in her jewelry box.

Now she had the Browning's ivory stocks back on "her" pistol.

In the mirror she saw him checking out the handgun, "I shall be keeping it by my bedside from now on."

Col. Randal said, "Good plan."

"Thank you for coming to save me."

"Any time."

Lady Jane laughed trying to recover her spirits without much success. "In the future let's try to not make a habit of my needing rescue missions."

"Roger that."

They went back downstairs to the TOC where Lady Jane proceeded to work the room like a politician at a fundraising event.

Beverly said to Col. Randal, "She's a trooper."

Lady Jane was standing on the rug covering the bloodstain where Bentley had been executed.

Col. Randal said, "Yes she is."

VICE ADMIRAL SIR RANDOLPH "RAZOR" RANSOM was conducting a briefing on the situation in the Aegean Theatre of Operations in a room down the hall from the Tactical Operations Center. Attendance was restricted. Flannigan was stationed outside the door with a list. Lieutenant General "Geronimo" Joe McKoy was sitting one side of Colonel John Randal on the front row with Major the Lady Jane Seaborn and Beverly Blackwell on the other. Also present were Brigadier Raymond J. "R. J." Maunsell, Security Intelligence Middle East; Brigadier Dudley Clarke, A-Force; Cuthbert "Curly" Bowlby, MI-6; Captain M. H. S. McDonald, aka "Snow White," RN; Lieutenant Colonel Sir Terry "Zorro" Stone, Lieutenant Commander Adrian Seligman, Levant Schooner Flotilla; Major Zargo, Greek Sacred Squadron; Major Baltimore "Mongo" Farquhar, MC, Lancelot Lancers aka Lounge Lizards; Major Clive Adair, Phantom/Mayor of Castelrozzo; Veronica Paige, MI-9 Escape; and a surprise attendee, the professor, Doctor Layton Winthrop.

Notably absent were the two staff officers from Cairo GHQ.

At the last minute, Captain Billy Jack Jaxx, Captain Butch "Headhunter" Hoolihan, and Mandy Paige arrived back from their jaunt out to the *King Duck*. None of the three were on the list. They slipped into the back and took their seats.

No one objected.

VAdm. Ransom said, "This is a classified briefing. The purpose is to bring Colonel Randal up to speed on the evolving military environment in the Aegean. And to ensure that all of us in this room are on the same page as regards Allied—read British—intentions in the AO going forward.

"Conditions, as we understand them now, will likely change in the near future. In simple military parlance the situation is fluid. As it stands tonight: German forces have been driven from North Africa, the siege of Malta has been lifted, Sicily is under

Allied control, Italy has signed an armistice and our forces have invaded the Italian Peninsula.

"Mussolini was arrested by the Italian government. He was held incommunicado in a remote Alpine resort hotel awaiting trial for crimes against the people. A team of Waffen SS Commandos led by one Colonel Otto Skorzeny conducted an audacious glider assault on the hotel, effected a rescue, and spirited him to Berlin by air . . ."

This was news to Col. Randal. He made eye contact with Beverly. He wanted all available intelligence on the rescue in order to study in detail the means and methods the Germans used.

She nodded.

" . . . From Germany *il Duce* went on the radio to announce his escape and to give the order, 'All Italian Forces are to ignore any previous commands from the traitor Marshal Badoglio.' The burning question is are the Italians with us, against us or will they attempt to be neutral? The best answer is—only time will tell.

"My personal take is we should not expect much out of them other than lip service.

"Closer to home British operations were initially designed with the idea of bringing Turkey into the war on the Allied side. Prime Minister Churchill obsesses over the prospect. I tend to rate it a highly unlikely outcome as the Turks are not apt to take a gamble on the outcome of the war.

"That said, Turkey has quietly made concessions for Small Raids Inc. to station LSF schooners in remote coves along their coastline by turning a blind eye to our doing so.

"With the capitulation of Italy here in the Aegean OPERATION ACCOLADE was laid on in hopes of exploiting the Italian surrender. The purpose was to induce Turkey to enter the war on the Allied side, stimulate partisan movements in

Yugoslavia and Greece, weaken the Nazi hold over the Balkans, divert German forces away from the Allied invasion of Italy specifically at Salerno and to occupy Rhodes—the most strategic piece of real estate in the Aegean.

"The idea was to exploit the confusion created by Italy's sudden collapse by launching an immediate amphibious assault to capture Rhodes while simultaneously walking in and occupying some of the smaller Italian-held islands. We were presented a golden opportunity albeit with a 'time is of the essence' clause requiring immediate action.

"Rhodes is the key to the Aegean. The airfields located on the island give whoever holds it air superiority over the entire AO. In modern naval warfare, airpower is king. In the event control of the air is lost, surface ships can only operate under cover of darkness.

"At the time Colonel Randal and the 575th Ranger Task Force were departing for their jump on Benevento Rhodes was occupied by some thirty thousand Italians and sixty-five hundred Germans. The fantasy at GHQ Cairo was the numerically superior Italians could be persuaded to engage and tie down the Germans until such time as we were able to mount an invasion with 234th Brigade recently arrived from Malta specifically for the task.

"To that end, Major the Earl Lord George Jellicoe of the Special Boat Section and a party of two, Major Dalby—who overstated his parachuting qualifications, and Sergeant Kesterton, were dropped onto Rhodes with less than a day's advance notice to coordinate with the Italian commander, Admiral Campioni. The liaison mission, as envisioned by Colonel Turnbull and Plans Division, can only be described as suicidal lunacy in its inception.

"The word 'fantasy' comes to mind once again.

"Nothing went as hoped. Because he is not parachute qualified Turnbull planned to land by boat to chair the talks. He never arrived. Major Dalby was badly injured on the jump—turned out it was his first ever.

"However, Lord Jellicoe was able to meet with Admiral Campioni.

"The Admiral was a limp reed. He dithered—not able to make a decision. In Cairo, Jumbo never got around to assembling the troops for the invasion. Meanwhile, the Germans on Rhodes reacted with lightning speed. They occupied Admiral Campioni's HQ while the Admiral was considering his options.

"Lord Jellicoe was forced to hide in a closet.

"Despite outnumbering the Nazis nearly five to one, Admiral Campioni caved in. The bloody coward handed over the island without a fight. He did arrange for Jellicoe to escape.

"The failure of General Wilson to take advantage of the opportunity to walk in and occupy Rhodes is a military blunder which will likely affect operations in this part of the world for the remainder of the war.

"Prior to the Italian Armistice the Regia Marina's Aegean fleet consisted of six destroyers and thirty-odd MAS boats. Those vessels were seized by the Kriegsmarine during their OPERATION ACHSE. Added to the U-boats already operating from Salamis this makes for a formidable enemy naval presence Small Raids Inc. shall have to contend with going forward.

"In addition, several flotillas of Kriegsmarine UJ escorts and heavily armed F-lighters are en route from the Black Sea. German Naval Group Command South has other Nazi-flagged vessels sailing from as far away as France. This portends future Nazi military adventures in our AO as yet undetermined.

"For our part the Aegean Theatre is sandwiched between the Italian campaign and the Indian front in the CBI. Both enjoy higher priority. That did not stop the Prime Minister from sending out his 'play high and dare' missive to Jumbo Wilson. To date no less than seven ill-conceived plans have been put forward by GHQ Cairo to invade Crete, Rhodes, Leros, Kos and a number of other small islands.

"As pointed out the German airfields on Rhodes give the Germans air superiority—I shall return to that momentarily.

"President Roosevelt, General Eisenhower and the U.S. Joint Chiefs of Staff do not see eye to eye with Prime Minister Churchill in regards to the Aegean theatre. They do not believe ACCOLADE is a priority. In fact, they are convinced any involvement in the Aegean will result in a growing commitment of men and matériel

Which the Joint Chiefs believe will detract from the main effort against the Nazi power on the European mainland at a later date. It is abundantly clear the United States is not willing to provide aircraft, ships, men or matériel support for ACCOLADE/FIRE EATER.

"We have no choice but to go it alone in the Aegean with the lowest priority of any theatre in the war.

"General Wilson, wishing to reestablish his reputation with the Prime Minister after the Rhodes fiasco, acting against the advice of Admiral Cunningham and Air Marshal Tedder—who side with the Americans—ordered Colonel Turnbull to dispatch troops to Leros and Kos.

"The only units the Brigadier had to send were the Long Range Desert Group and the Special Boat Section. In addition Jumbo ordered the 234th Infantry Brigade, a garrison unit of questionable fighting ability, to speed up its plans to occupy Leros.

"The SBS parachuted onto Leros landing on a drop zone selected by Lord Jellicoe, who having recently escaped Admiral

Campioni's closet on Rhodes had traveled to the island by MAS boat. Shortly after arriving the LRDG, augmented by an additional fifty SBS operators, flew out to Kos thirty-one miles offshore.

"GHQ Cairo's plan called for Leros to be reinforced by 8 Indian Division. Another pipe dream. The division never sailed at least not for any place in our AO."

"The Prime Minister recognizing the loss of Rhodes changed the military equation in a bad way messaged General Wilson authorization to evacuate Leros if he so chose. For reasons of his own, most likely to make up for failing to take advantage of the opportunity on Rhodes, Jumbo decided to press on with defending the island despite having ceded control of the skies to the Germans.

"Which again is one click short of insanity.

"To conclude, one does not have to be a Napoleon to foretell what is about to happen next. Without air the battle is lost. As previously pointed out Wilson and Turnbull have built a house of cards on Leros.

Now it is starting to come tumbling down."

Walking down the hall following the briefing Col. Randal said to Lt. Col. Stone, "Why do I have the distinct impression things are worse than the Razor made 'em sound?"

"Because they are, old stick."

Lady Jane said, "Admiral Ransom painted a grim picture, Terry—the lowest priority of WWII."

Lt. Col. Stone said, "That he did."

Col. Randal said, "What's your takeaway, Terry?"

Lt. Col. Stone replied, "My best estimate of the situation is Raiding Forces and the GSS will be the only special operations units in the Aegean left reasonably intact after the Germans capture Leros—which they most certainly will."

Lt. Gen. McKoy said, “Yeah, I agree. Those boys on Leros are out on a limb. Waste ’a real good manpower.”

Lady Jane said, “We need to exercise care not to allow our people to be swept up in the absurdity.”

Lt. Gen. McKoy said, “You’re right on the money as usual, Lady Jane. When the smoke clears Raidin’ Forces is gonna need every trigger puller we got.”

Lady Jane said, “Who is at fault for this?”

Lt. Col. Stone said, “The blame starts in London then goes to the White House—with stops at Allied Forces HQ in Algiers and GHQ Cairo.”

Lt. Gen. McKoy said, “Sounds like there’s probably some payback in this deal for the Brits not agreein’ to let us invade across the Channel into France the way the U.S. Joint Chiefs of Staff and Eisenhower wanted to earlier this year.”

Col. Randal said, “It would have been a disaster. Our troops weren’t ready to take on the German Army. Besides the combined Allied navies didn’t have enough ships to support a cross Channel invasion and still don’t.”

Lt. Gen. McKoy said, “You ain’t wrong, guaranteed to fail.”

Lt. Col. Stone said, “Without doubt.”

Lt. Gen. McKoy said, “Say John did Pam happen to mention the possibility that the Nazi SS woman you shot in Istanbul is alive and well?”

Col. Randal said, “She did.”

“Karma comin’ back at you, huh?”

“Oh, that’s great.”

“I’ll tell you one thing you ain’t got to worry about . . . that giant bald-headed SS bodyguard ’a hers magically comin’ back to life. You dinged that bad boy with a 9mm round square between the eyes.’

“That was some fancy shootin’ right there.”

Col. Randal and Lady Jane peeled off and went upstairs to their suite. King was at the desk on the second-floor landing. Captain Pamala Plum-Martin had pulled up a chair and was sitting with him.

Col. Randal said, "Tell Stephanie to send someone to relieve you. We've got an early morning. Happy wants to hunt Nazis."

"Thanks, Chief."

Inside, Col. Randal and Lady Jane changed into swimsuits. They went out to the private pool on the deck. Happy was already there napping on one of the lounges.

The sun was sinking into the turquoise sea creating a kaleidoscope of spectacular colors. Col. Randal and Lady Jane sat on the steps in the pool unwinding. They were not saying much enjoying each other's company.

Rare fine moments like this had been few and far between for them lately.

Col. Randal looked forward to their time together. Being around Lady Jane made him relax and took his pain away. She never had an agenda.

He always knew where things stood with her—almost.

"There's no good way to tell you this Jane but you should know Mallory's ship was sunk en route to his new duty station. He's missing . . . possibly a POW. Jap boats were sighted in the area after the sinking."

Lady Jane said, "Mallory is nothing more to me other than a teenage mistake. I allowed my family to arrange my marriage to an adulterous narcissist because it was a 'good match.'"

"Pretty cold, babe."

"Yes, it is, babe—any chance he signed my divorce decree before sailing?"

"I don't think so."

As the light was beginning to fade a flight of six German Junkers-87 aka Stuka dive bombers arrived overhead looking like a flock of angry pterodactyls. They rolled in on their attack run coming straight down with dive sirens screaming. The ear-piercing, crazed banshee wail was intended to strike terror in the hearts of those below about to be bombed.

It worked every time.

The Ju-87 was an obsolete aircraft underpowered by modern standards. The Luftwaffe had been forced to pull them out of front-line service during the Battle of Britain because so many were being shot down. But because of the lack of RAF air in the Aegean the Stuka was virtually invulnerable. That was not the same thing as infallible. The German pilots got it wrong. They attacked a large building most likely mistaken for ABCHQ. It was the Long Range Desert Group (LRDG) barracks that were empty because all the troops had deployed to Leros and Kos.

With no advance warning and the air raid underway so quickly it was too late to move downstairs to the ABCHQ bomb shelter. Since there was nothing else they could do Col. Randal and Lady Jane stayed in the pool and watched the show unfold.

The Stukas blew the LRDG barracks to smithereens.

Happy was not so happy about the dive sirens or the explosions rocking the island. Neither was anyone else. Being on the receiving end of an airstrike is a life-altering experience.

Even if it hits the wrong target.

Lady Jane laughed, "You are always a fun date, Johnny."

A tall column of black smoke marked the impact of the bombs as the Ju-87's flew for home.

Col. Randal said, "That about caps it."

VICE ADMIRAL SIR RANDOLPH “RAZOR” RANSOM walked out by the pool as the Stukas were winging their way toward home. “A message arrived moments ago from GHQ Cairo over General Wilson’s signature ordering Raiding Forces to assume operational control of the Special Boat Section and the LRDG effective immediately.”

Colonel John Randal said, “Why would that be, sir?”

“Turnbull is transferring his flag back to the fleshpots of Cairo before the Germans invade the island. He and Jumbo need someone to blame. The destruction of the two irreplaceable Special Operations units on Leros will not play well when word reaches Whitehall they were mishandled by GHQ Cairo. Both organizations are great favorites of the Prime Minister’s—the LRDG’s exploits are legendary and Churchill was a close friend of Lord Jellicoe’s late father as was I.”

Col. Randal said, “We’ll have to make sure that loss doesn’t happen sir.”

VAdm. Ransom said, “There is no authorization to withdraw either unit from Leros.”

Col. Randal said, “I’m not going to stand by and allow my men to be captured, Admiral.”

VAdm. Ransom said, “I would be surprised if you did.”

5
NOT BY STRENGTH, BY GUILE

COLONEL JOHN RANDAL AND HAPPY WERE WITH Lieutenant Jake Novak's patrol. He felt he should be back in the Tactical Operations Center helping develop a plan of action for Raiding Forces in response to recent developments on Leros but Happy would only work for him or Major the Lady Jane Seaborn.

He was not about to let her hunt Brandenburgers.

One of the things most on his mind was that as of yesterday, the Special Boat Section and the Long Range Desert Group were under Raiding Forces operational control (OPCON). Both units were currently being misused as standard line infantry—a role they were not trained or equipped for. Exactly how he was going to rectify their situation was not clear.

Now that the two units were officially his responsibility he had to act—that was a given.

At breakfast, James "Baldie" Taylor briefed Col. Randal on both organizations' current status before he went on patrol. The SBS had already lost over a third of its troop strength executing missions the small-scale maritime raiding unit was not suited for.

The majority of the losses occurred on the island of Kos when the Germans invaded.

The story for the Long Range Desert Group was even worse. Their long-time commanding officer, Lieutenant Colonel Guy Prendergast, was being transferred to GHQ Cairo to be Colonel Douglas Turnbull's deputy in hopes of getting someone on his staff who actually knew something about Special Operations. He had turned over command to Lieutenant Colonel John "Jake" Easonsmith, DSO, MC, a highly respected officer in the LRDG. A new commander, no matter how long he has served in the unit or how respected he might be, always takes time for troops to adjust to.

Sent from Leros to Kos with a detachment of the SBS prior to the Germans assaulting the island, the LRDG was then ordered to carry out another hasty operation to seize and hold the nearby German-occupied 3.5-square mile island of Levitha. By any measure, the assignment was not the appropriate use of specialized reconnaissance troops whose motto was "Not by Strength, by Guile."

There was not much guile in what happened next. In compliance to orders the LRDG conducted a hotly contested, forced entry, amphibious assault on Levitha. It failed. As a result, the unit suffered more casualties in one day than it had in all the years spent behind enemy lines in the desert.

The New Zealand government was outraged by the mismanagement of its troops—Colonel Turnbull had inexplicably denied the LRDG's request to make a reconnaissance of the island prior to going in. Now, A Squadron (NZ) would no longer be allowed to serve under GHQ Cairo's control. It was being withdrawn and reassigned.

The Long Range Desert Group was shattered.

Currently the remnants of the SBS and LRDG were in defensive positions on Leros waiting for the Germans to invade. Evaders belonging to both units were still on the loose escaping and evading—E&Eing—on Kos. The hope was Veronica Paige's MI-9 Escape would be able bring some of them off.

Col. Randal was reasonably sure he had seen military incompetence the equal of Cairo GHQ's bungling of the LRDG and SBS, but he was not positive about that.

In the distance the Tiger tanks on the *King Duck* began booming. Acting Provisional Lieutenant Warthog Finley was engaging a target farther down the shoreline. The Vulnerable Points Wing dog team working with Captain Butch "Headhunter" Hoolihan's Royal Marines must have made enemy contact.

Col. Randal resisted the temptation to go to his assistance.

Happy alerted and indicated by lying down. The dog looked over his shoulder at Col. Randal. He gave the hand signal to "stay."

King moved up with his 9mm SIG MKPO submachine gun to provide additional firepower at the point of the patrol.

Lovat Scouts Lionel Fenwick and Munro Ferguson went to the prone to provide overwatch. Scout Ferguson was the spotter. Today he was utilizing a pair of captured German Swarovski 6x30 binoculars that were better at close-range observation than the Lovat's standard-issue Scout Regiment Mark II 20X spotting scope.

Before Lt. Novak's patrol could deploy a face appeared peeking out a second-story window.

Scout Ferguson said, "Send it."

BOOOOM!

The 7X57mm round from Scout Fenwick's Westley Richards red stag hunting rifle sounded unnaturally loud in the early morning air. Glass shattered. Nothing happened for a three count then a man fell forward crashing through the window down to the ground.

Caught off guard and now having to play catchup Lt. Novak dispatched Private First Class Norvel "Horn Dog" Hansen's team to establish a blocking position at the rear of the house on the run. He then ordered the remainder of the men, already moving into position under Master Sergeant Mack Beckwith, to launch their assault.

Lt. Novak's idea was to rush the house quickly. He wanted to take advantage of the surprise created by the gunshot. The Rangers went in hard and fast.

No one else was inside.

Col. Randal said, "Hope we didn't just shoot the homeowner."

King said, "Not unless he was in the 82nd Airborne, Chief."

Lt. Novak said, "Must be a uniform captured on Sicily. All-American unit patch, M-42 jump jacket, and brown Corcoran paratroop boots. Airborne all the way, sir.'"

Col. Randal said, "Nice work, Lovats."

As was typical the two Scouts did not respond—another day at the office.

As soon as he saw his chance Happy raced over and attacked the dead Nazi.

Col. Randal said, "Jake, we need a live prisoner."

"Gonna be tough, Colonel, with that hound around."

COLONEL JOHN RANDAL RETURNED TO ABCHQ. There were four patrols out with dog teams conducting grid searches now. They were going to have to take up the slack for the rest of the day. He needed to work on future plans with Lieutenant Colonel Sir Terry "Zorro" Stone.

Based on all available intelligence the military situation in the Dodecanese island chain was gearing up to become hotly contested. It was not entirely clear how Raiding Forces fit in moving forward. The state of events in what were called the "Italian islands"—even though they were primarily inhabited by Greeks—could best be described as fluid. Which is how the military likes to depict a confused situation without using the word "confused."

Col. Randal found Lt. Col. Stone in the mess hall sitting at a table with Beverly Blackwell, Mandy Paige, and Alex "Cat" Gataki. He pulled up a chair to join them. One of the orderlies, a local Greek boy hired by Major the Lady Jane Seaborn as a mess steward, brought a plate.

Lt. Col. Stone said, "How did your patrol go this morning?"

"Took out one more Brandenburger."

"At this rate it is going to take a long time to clear all the residences. We shall need to check out every one of them," Lt. Col. Stone said. "In the event we fail to locate all the Nazis when we are finished we have to start over again—some may circle back to their old haunts."

Col. Randal said, "We need to get the islanders involved."

Lt. Col. Stone said, "Acting on my instructions Major Adair placed Castelrozzo on round-the-clock curfew for the next seventy-two hours. Everyone is on lockdown. Not sure how much help the locals can be sheltering in place."

Mandy said, "The local phone company is working. We have a directory of every person currently living on the island. We can start calling to see if anyone has anything to report."

Lt. Col. Stone said, "Get with Stephanie—you two organize a phone bank. Use every Greek speaker you can lay hands on."

Cat said, "I speak Greek."

Her English was improving at a fast clip.

Lt. Col. Stone said, "Yes you do."

Mandy said, "Follow me, Cat, you can be my first phone operator."

Col. Randal said, "If you see your mother will you tell her I'd like a word?'

"I will."

Col. Randal said, "Beverly, are you up for flying tonight?"

"Always. Where to?"

"Leros."

"Johnny, our last trip to Leros didn't turn out so great."

Col. Randal said, "We'll fly in under cover of darkness. You drop me off. Then come back tomorrow night for a pickup."

Beverly said, "Anyone else going, or is it just us?"

"I'll get back to you on that."

Lt. Col. Stone said, "Are you quite sure about this?"

"I want to evaluate the island's defenses—check out the SBS and LRDG."

"We can send someone else."

"Negative."

Lt. Col. Stone said, "I am aware time spent on reconnaissance is rarely wasted, old stick. But we have issues that require your immediate attention. I have a long list of items put on hold due to your recent absence."

Col. Randal said, "Have to see it myself, Terry."

Lt. Col. Stone said, "In that case, I require your undivided attention for a full two hours this afternoon."

Col. Randal said, "I'll be in Lady Jane's suite at 1300 hours. We can meet in private. Take all the time you need, Sir Zorro."

As Col. Randal and Beverly were making their way out of the room they stopped by the table where Major Jack Dance and Captain Stephanie Fawcett-Tatum were having lunch.

Col. Randal said, "Things are stable here on ABC, Major. I'd like you to fly back to the Salerno beachhead. You need to be there to assemble your Rangers as they straggle back to friendly lines."

Maj. Dance said, "I was going to request permission to be allowed to do that, sir."

Col. Randal said, "Start shuffling people back to ABC as soon as possible. Keep Stephanie apprised of the numbers of people returning. We need to develop some idea of what our losses are going to look like at the end of the day."

Capt. Fawcett-Tatum said, "I shall have the duty pilot fly Jack out as soon as we finish our lunch, John."

Col. Randal said, "No rush."

He had fixed the two up on their first date. Then called Maj. Dance away in the middle of it to marshal with the 575th Ranger Task Force for immediate deployment to Salerno. A love life in Raiding Forces had to be . . . flexible.

Capt. Fawcett-Tatum said, "Thank you."

Before he and Beverly could make it out of the dining room Veronica Paige walked in.

"You were asking for me, Colonel?"

"I was—you have four MI-9 caiques. I'd like you to dispatch them to Kos. Ring the island to be on standby for evaders on the run. But be careful.

"The Germans own the place now."

Veronica said, "All Escape boats were signaled a change of mission to proceed to Kos the moment I heard word it was being invaded. Unfortunately one is so far away it will be days before it can arrive."

Col. Randal said, "Get with Commander Seligman. Commandeer every LSF caique as well. If he gives you any static, see Admiral Ransom. We may already be too late but we have to give it a try.

"Also, keep in mind MI-9 may have a change of mission of its own if Leros falls before you conclude operations on Kos."

Veronica said, "I am already planning for that eventuality, Colonel. As for Adrian, he has always been extremely supportive of my MI-9 work. I shall see him straight away. In addition I intend to speak to Baldie in hopes he may be able to provide SOE agents familiar with Kos to send ashore and search for evaders."

Col. Randal said, "That works—do it."

Veronica said, "Kos is a big island—over a hundred square miles. The Germans could not possibly have had enough time or the troops to secure the entire island. We shall do everything in our power to save everyone we possibly can."

Col. Randal said, "Talk to Major Zargo he might be able to supply some of his GSS men to help."

"I shall."

"Check in with Admiral Ransom he may have thoughts as well."

"Wilco."

Veronica refrained from mentioning she had already spoken to both VAdm. Ransom and Maj. Zargo. Even though MI-9 possessed the lowest priority of any M-letter agency in the British military intelligence system, it was a mission she was passionate about. She was tireless in her efforts to rescue escape and evaders on the run.

"Bring 'em back alive, Mrs. Paige."

Veronica said, "Our unofficial motto."

Happy, who had trotted up to Lady Jane's suite when they came in from patrol, was waiting for Col. Randal when he and

Beverly walked out in the main hall. He wanted to go Nazi hunting.

Col. Randal scratched him between the ears, "Maybe later, killer."

VICE ADMIRAL SIR RANDOLPH "RAZOR" RANSOM, Colonel John Randal, and Lieutenant Colonel Sir Terry "Zorro" Stone were sitting in the briefing area of Major the Lady Jane Seaborn's second-floor suite. It had originally been a private formal dining alcove. A small crystal chandelier provided the light for what was now a wall of maps depicting the FIRE EATER Area of Operations.

VAdm. Ransom said, "I shall not take up much of your time. You two men have much to discuss. What I would like is to provide you with a broad overview of how I see Small Raids Inc./Raiding Forces operations going forward.

"First, and I am sure this is foremost on your mind, Colonel Randal, is the question of the Long Range Desert Group and the Special Boat Section. They have been placed under your operational control and are at peril of being destroyed on Leros. The caveat is you do not have the authority to withdraw either unit until the emergency on the island has passed.

"Make your plans accordingly."

Col. Randal said, "Yes, sir."

VAdm. Ransom said, "Moving forward plan as if the Leros problem does not exist. Except bear it in mind at all times. We can do little that will have any effect on the outcome. But what happens to the island will impact how we conduct operations in the Aegean for the remainder of FIRE EATER.

"Do we understand each other, gentlemen?"

Col. Randal glanced at Lt. Col. Stone. They were being ordered not to notice the pink elephant in the room. The LRDG and the SBS were to be sacrificed. There was nothing Small Raids Inc. or Raiding Forces could do about it, so move on.

"I hear you loud and clear sir."

VAdm Ransom and Lt. Col. Stone both knew that response was not the same as a "Wilco."

Col. Randal had no intention of moving on.

Besides he and VAdm Ransom had already reached agreement on the subject.

VAdm. Ransom said, "Do what you do best Colonel—take charge. Develop an aggressive raiding program. Work up your small-scale raids until you achieve an operational tempo you can maintain for at least the next eighteen months.

"If you encounter interference by any outside agency bring the matter to my attention immediately or as I have heard you say—'if not sooner.' Your brief is to be entirely focused on taking the fight to the enemy. I shall deal with the military politics, departmental infighting and interservice intrigue.

"Questions? No?

"To wrap we three have a dream assignment. Licensed to raid targets of our own choosing in a theatre no one but the Prime Minister and the Germans care about. Churchill shall lose interest soon enough. Then we shall only have the Nazis to contend with.

"You develop tactics. Consult with me on strategy. I coordinate logistics, maintenance, transport, supply and bang heads as needed."

Col. Randal said, "We can do that, Admiral."

VAdm. Ransom said, "On your return from Leros, Colonel, you, Colonel Stone, Major Adair and I shall be flying to

Alexandria. Small Raids Inc. has a highly classified project we have been working on privately without your knowledge for some time now.

"It will change the game."

AS VICE ADMIRAL SIR RANDOLPH "RAZOR" RANSOM was preparing to leave Mandy Paige came rushing in. James "Baldie" Taylor, Cuthbert "Curly" Bowlby, and Beverly Blackwell were right behind. While Mandy was Raiding Forces' counterintelligence officer recently she had been doubling as the temporary S-2 until a decision could be made about who would take over the job full time. The unit was far too short on officers to pull one of the troop commanders in to become the intelligence officer (IO), which is typically how positions on battalion and regimental-sized staffs are filled. In past days Major the Lady Jane Seaborn and Captain Pamala Plum-Martin had both held the post on a short-term basis.

From inception Raiding Forces had never enjoyed the luxury of a permanent staff.

Mandy said, "Late breaking news from Kos."

Cuthbert said, "As you know the island is a strategic piece of terrain because of the airfield near Antimachia. Leros, with its ports and Kos with the airdrome, are mutually supporting—only thirty-one miles separates the islands. The terms of the recent armistice called for the four thousand-plus Italians stationed on Kos to support our troops in the event of an attack.

"The soldiers in the ranks did not see it that way. News of the ceasefire was greeted with wild enthusiasm by the Italians who hoped that for them the war was over. They wanted no farther part in it."

Jim said, "A company-sized element of our 11 Parachute Battalion was dropped in as reinforcements/stiffeners. Our paratroops were enthusiastically welcomed by the garrison. The Italians even spread straw on the DZ to make it softer for them.

"A contingent of fifteen hundred British troops, primarily 1st Battalion Durham Light Infantry, soon landed by sea.

"Life was good.

"Then a regiment of the German 22nd Air Landing Division with the 1 Sea Raiding Battalion, Brandenburg Regiment and the 5th Parachute Battalion, Brandenburg Regiment, personally led by the division commander General Friedrich-Wilhelm Müller aka 'the Butcher of Crete,' launched OPERATION POLAR BEAR—a three-pronged airborne and amphibious assault on Kos."

Cuthbert said, "Like on Rhodes, our side enjoyed a five-to-one advantage. However, once the attack began there was limited coordination between British and Italian units. No air cover was available because the German parachutists seized the airfield on their initial drop—the hay was most likely still out.

The Luftwaffe's troop transports encountered very little resistance because the island's antiaircraft artillery was rendered virtually useless due to the fact the ammunition intended for Leros had been delivered to Kos and it was the wrong caliber.

"The Luftwaffe's 10th Fliegerkorps was free to bomb and strafe at will."

Jim said, "1,388 British and 3,145 Italians surrendered and were marched off to Neratzia Castle to be imprisoned. That is a good count. We have an agent inside."

Cuthbert said, "Acting on direct orders from General Müller, 103 Italian officers of the 10th Regiment, 50th Division were given a sham trial the moment the fighting ceased. Then all of them were summarily executed by firing squad."

Jim said, "Even in Abyssinia we never saw a mass slaughter of Europeans on this scale. It is one thing to have rogue Nazi units like the 999th made up of criminals released from prison murdering civilians and committing the odd atrocity. It is quite another for German troops from one of their most elite divisions liquidate the entire officer corps of a division-sized unit on direct orders from their commanding general who was physically present to supervise."

Cuthbert said, "The Germans have no intention of observing the Geneva Convention in the Aegean."

VAdm. Ransom said, "I confess to being guilty of turning a blind eye to reports the Germans have not been adhering to the Geneva Accords in hopes they were not true. No more. Small Raids Inc. has been ordered by the Admiralty to conduct a 'piratical war against the enemy's lines-of-communication.' That is precisely the posture Raiding Forces shall take going forward.

"No quarter asked or given—prisoners can walk the plank for all I bloody care."

Beverly said, "We've had a lot of bad news to process in the last forty-eight hours."

Col. Randal said, "That's a fact."

Lt. Col. Stone said, "Now the Germans have an airstrip on Kos from which to fly ground attack missions only minutes away from their targets on Leros. And it is the perfect springboard for launching a parachute assault if the 22nd Air Landing Division so desires. Once the Germans make their move the situation is likely to deteriorate rapidly."

Leros was in the Nazi's crosshairs and the clock was ticking on when they would pull the trigger.

COLONEL JOHN RANDAL DID WHAT HE ALWAYS DID when given an assignment he thought could use the benefit of another perspective—meaning he was out of ideas. He met with Lieutenant General "Geronimo" Joe McKoy.

Waldo Treywick sat in.

Col. Randal laid out everything, the LRDG, SBS, Leros, Kos, the execution of 103 Italian officers. They studied the wall maps, measured distances and counted Raiding Forces troop strength present in the AO. While the Aegean Sea was not a major ocean like the Atlantic or the Pacific for one small raiding unit that had men scattered from Italy to the Congo it was a monster-sized body of water.

Col. Randal knew Raiding Forces was not likely to be assigned more troops. No new equipment was in the pipeline. The gear they were using, with a few notable exceptions, was obsolete, captured from the enemy or repurposed from some other use to fit their needs—like the Greek caiques powered by Australian tank engines.

In one fell swoop with the capture of Kos, the Germans had achieved virtual air superiority over the entire Aegean. They definitely enjoyed it over Leros. Now Small Raids Inc. boats would be limited to sailing at night and laying up under camouflage at some out-of-the-way place at dawn.

And that meant now a mission to a distant location might require days—or even weeks—at sea.

Col. Randal, Lt. Gen. McKoy and Waldo were highly experienced at operating behind enemy lines over vast distances while outnumbered with little in the way of support. They were skilled in the art of doing more with less, improvising and adapting. Even so, FIRE EATER was going to be a stretch.

A long range naval war is a logistical nightmare even under the best of conditions.

All three of them had Waldo's custom-rolled cigars clamped in their teeth. Unlit in deference to Major the Lady Jane Seaborn. Chewing on the cheroots was not much to help with the thought process but it was better than nothing.

Not that smoking would have done any better.

Lt. Gen. McKoy said, "Well, John, looks to me like you're just gonna have to figure some way to turn a lemon into lemonade."

Col. Randal said, "That's helpful, General."

Waldo said, "Remember that correspondence course you took while you was staking out the Mexican border back in the day bein' an Arizona Ranger, Joe? Business 101. 'The problem is the solution.'"

Lt. Gen. McKoy said, "Yeah, I do."

Waldo said, "I was discussin' how we use it in Raidin' Forces with Professor Winthrop the other day. He thought maybe we might get better results if we chucked in somethin' called 'Occam's Razor Blade.'"

Col. Randal wondered where this was going—their strategy sessions had a history of spiraling out of control as this one seemed to be doing.

Waldo said, "Mighta just been Occam's razor . . ."

Lt. Gen. McKoy said, "What's a razor *or* razor blade got to do with anything?"

Waldo said, "Well, Occam, he wrote hisself his own rule. I may not be quotin' the words exactly right but it's, 'the simplest solution is the best solution' or somethin' like that."

Lt. Gen. McKoy said, "That's pretty good, Waldo."

Col. Randal thought they seemed to be forgetting Raiding Forces Rule Number 2 "Keep It Short and Simple."

Maybe Occam's razor worked differently?

Waldo said, “We got us a lotta in’s and out’s to figure on before we can plug everythin’ into our formula. Raiding these little islands scattered all over the place . . . ain’t exactly sure I understand all the what’s and what nots.”

Col. Randal said, “Neither do I.”

Lt. Gen. McKoy said, “Nothin’ to it John just play the hand you’re dealt—think small.”

Waldo said, “Yeah, the problem is the solution married up with the simplest plan—that’s the way to go, Colonel.”

Col. Randal said, “I can always count on you two.”

He knew what Raiding Forces was going to do and even had a name for the strategy.

CAPTAIN BILLY JACK JAXX CAME THUNDERING UP the stairs. King sent him straight in with no announcement. Waldo handed him a cigar. He stuck it in his teeth.

“Got one, Colonel.”

Colonel John Randal said, “Say again?”

“A prisoner, sir. He’s slightly, well maybe more than a little slightly, concussed. But we have him and he’s alive.”

“Outstanding!”

“Headhunter and I worked out a targeting technique with Warthog Finley’s tank gunners. We load up magazines of M1 Carbine ammo all tracer. Two men armed with Carbines are designated to be our target indicators. When we identify a target, the two shooters split up to get as much separation as possible. On command both men open fire, sir. The tracers vectoring on a spot are easy to see from the *King Duck*.

"Then to make absolutely sure everyone is on the same page we fire a flare from a flare pistol at the exact same place. Even if it glances off the spotters can see where it struck the building—they get our intentions.

"Today was the first chance to try it. My point element spotted a Nazi observing our patrol from a second-story window. As rehearsed, my two shooters split up. Then on my command they began shooting tracers at the window.

"*Boom*! Just like that one of the Tigers fired. Dead on the money, sir.

"We rushed the house wanting to get in fast. The Brandenburger was upstairs unconscious on the floor. I think the gun loader screwed up, Colonel."

Col. Randal said, "What makes you say that?"

Capt. Jaxx said, "It was an AP round, sir. The shell whizzed through the walls out the back and ricocheted up the escarpment who knows where. There wasn't any detonation but the concussion from that 88 solid nearly zapping him put our Nazi down for the count.

"Worked like magic, sir. We've got a system now."

Col. Randal said, "Turn your prisoner over to Brandy. Then sit down with one of the Royal Marines and dictate your targeting instructions. Have Captain Fawcett-Tatum make copies for all the patrol leaders."

"Yes, sir."

"Good job, stud."

Waldo said, "Occam's Razor Blade."

As Capt. Jaxx was leaving, Col. Randal picked up the phone and rang the TOC. When one of the Royal Marines answered he asked for Captain Stephanie Fawcett-Tatum. When she came on the line he said, "Is Brandy still in the building?"

"Standing right here."

"Put her on."

"Hello, handsome."

"Brandy, I'm sending Billy Jack down. He's going to turn a prisoner over to you. Wring every bit of information you can out of him. There's no need to be gentle. The Razor has issued a 'no quarter asked, no quarter given' order for the duration of FIRE EATER."

"Why would Father do that, John?"

"The Germans executed 103 Italian officers on Kos yesterday. As soon as you sign off on your interrogation we're going to have our own firing squad. Tell Stephanie to come up with a procedure for selecting the people to be on it."

Brandy said, "I have never heard of an atrocity of that magnitude between civilized combatants in modern times."

Col. Randal said, "Time to quit thinking of the Nazis as civilized."

Brandy said, "I shall take that under advisement. The interview may take a while but you shall get your information. Not in any hurry I hope."

"No, I'm not."

Brandy Seaborn looked like a movie star. Lived for adventure. But she was also a highly skilled MI-5 officer with the ability to throw a switch on an instant's notice and go from being a happy girl to a counterintelligence interrogator able to conduct what is described in polite conversation as a "harsh" interview.

Then go out for an evening of dinner and dancing with friends.

Col. Randal almost felt sorry for the Brandenburger.

The operative word being "almost."

The phone rang. From the desk outside, King said, "Captain Fawcett-Tatum on the horn, Chief."

"Yes, Stephanie?"

"How many people constitute a firing squad?"

"I have no idea."

"The girls are fighting among themselves to be on it. Including me. Do you have any objection to an all-female detail?"

"Ask Jane. No—belay that. Use your own judgment."

"We shall not be issuing the customary blank round."

Col. Randal had a bad feeling the Royal Marines might not be aiming for the heart either.

THE PHONE RANG AFTER EVERYONE HAD LEFT. KING said, "Mandy for you, Chief."

Mandy Paige said, "John, we developed information on a possible location where a Brandenburger may be in hiding. One of our phone callers talked to a woman who thinks she observed something suspicious in a house near where she lives."

"I'll be right down."

When Colonel John Randal walked out Happy was waiting patiently beside the Merc's desk. While he may have been Major the Lady Jane's dog he knew where the action was likely to be.

Happy had the same "on/off" switch as Brandy Seaborn.

When Col. Randal, King, and Happy arrived in the TOC Master Sergeant Mack Beckwith was waiting.

"Sir, all the other patrols are out currently. Capt. Jaxx is resting his dog. Lieutenant Novak has gone to inspect Warthog's Tiger tanks. So, I've organized a scratch patrol for you. Only six men not including the *King Duck's* Fire Control Team and your Command Party.

Col. Randal said, "That should be enough—I'll inform Captain Jaxx to be ready to follow us out with his people if we need them. We won't require his dog."

Mandy said, "Skipper Finley is repositioning the *King Duck* per my request. He should be on station in a few minutes. I can guide you to the location of the house if you like, John."

Structures on Castelrozzo had numbers but no street address because there were not any streets—only cobblestone paths. Most were trails not large enough to merit being called a lane. The house numbers were not all in sequence.

That complicated navigation.

The island was characterized by sheer vertical limestone cliffs dropping off to the water. In most places the slope of the escarpment went straight downhill and plunged into the ocean with no beach. Houses were built from the top all the way down almost to the water's edge.

Prior to the war Castelrozzo had been inhabited by the wealthiest Greeks in the Aegean. The locals had always earned their living as "traders"—meaning they trafficked with smugglers to avoid paying Greek taxes. In days past the traffickers had been pirates.

Since nothing was produced on the island the islanders also imported foodstuffs and goods from various places to sell to each other.

And built big houses hanging off the cliffs over the sea.

A great many of the homes, which could be described as mansions, were carved into the side of the steep incline. Individual residences in some cases were built on zero lot lines like condominiums with little or no space between them. Their wide-angle view of the sea was spectacular. But the occupants had no way to see out the sides or out the rear of their houses because of the steep slope which abutted up against it—though a rare few had back windows.

The good news, from a military standpoint, was that type of construction made it easy to move up on an enemy hiding inside by approaching from the rear or on one or the other flank at a 45° angle. Unless, that is, there was another Nazi hiding in one of the houses above and to the rear enjoying his wide-angle view. Then that was a problem.

Small unit tactics conducted against an armed and hostile enemy lying in wait are a cat and mouse game—though in this case rat might be the better description of the Nazis. You make a slow, careful approach. Then pounce.

It is important to get it right the first time when you go in for the kill. Mistakes can be costly.

Rats have sharp teeth.

Mandy expected her offer to guide the patrol to be refused.

She was surprised when Col. Randal said, "OK, you travel with the Sergeant Major but keep your eyes on me at all times. I stop you stop. I kneel down you kneel down. I go prone you go prone.

"If shots are fired you stay down. No sticking your head up to see what's happening."

"Is that clear?"

"Absolutely!"

"Lead out, Sergeant Major."

"Sir, aren't you going to take the patrol?"

"Negative, I'm the dog handler. You're the patrol leader. Let's go."

MSgt. Beckwith ordered, "King get up there with the Colonel."

As the patrol moved out from ABCHQ, Lieutenant Theodore "The Great Teddy" Hamilton ran outside carrying Col. Randal's

Brixia 45mm shoulder-fired mortar and a pack full of mortar rounds.

"Reporting for duty, sir."

Col. Randal said, "All right then, lets' go find you a target, Lieutenant."

Another surprise.

As the patrol snaked its way out of town, Mandy said, "We are looking for a faded salmon-color house on the second finger east of here. It is located on the third level path down from the top. Fifth house to the right of the lane leading up the escarpment.

The problem with advancing to the target was that while the patrol was en route the troops had no idea if Brandenburgers were hiding in any of the houses they were passing on the way. You have to think about things like that.

Patrolling is painstaking work. It pays to be careful.

No matter how many patrols Col. Randal had gone on in his career he always felt a rush of adrenaline at the start. He clicked on. His senses were heightened and his situational awareness made his vision crystal clear and colors appear more vibrant.

He was in his element—in the zone.

As the patrol traversed parallel along the base of the escarpment en route to the second finger, Happy had to investigate each house as they passed by. It slowed the pace but had to be done. Most likely, knowing they were being hunted, the Brandenburgers would be shifting locations. The fact that one sector had been cleared was only good for that day and possibly not even that long.

Col. Randal signaled Lt. Hamilton to move up and march with him.

"I hear the famous magician, Jasper Maskelyne, claims to have camouflaged the Suez Canal to keep the Germans from bombing it—that true?"

Lt. Hamilton said, "Major Maskelyne comes from a long line of illusionists. He was my idol growing up. I aspired to be like him, sir."

Col. Randal said, "Did he hide the canal?"

"Yes and no, sir. I am afraid Major Maskelyne has turned out to be a bit of a fraud. He takes credit for the work of others and exaggerates the extent of his influence on camouflage projects he is a mere participant in."

Col. Randal said, "You mean Maskelyne doesn't really have an outfit called "The Magic Gang" that won the battle of El Alamein single handed by duping the Desert Fox?"

"No sir, a lot of people did their duty at El Alamein."

"Yes they did."

Lt. Hamilton said, "Camouflage Division did mask the Suez Canal. The trick was to place a series of searchlights aimed skyward at certain locations. A sleight-of-hand on a large scale that creates the illusion the canal has vanished during the only time the Luftwaffe pilots can bomb and hope to make it back home from Egypt without getting shot down—at night, sir."

Col. Randal said, "So can you make the village to include ABCHQ disappear?"

"Actually that would not be all that difficult, sir. Remember the illusion I created at RAF Habbaniya by setting up mock buildings? The Golden Square rebel's artillery targeted them . . . not the real ones."

"I do."

"In this case sir, we relocate the village to some other place on the island by utilizing illusions designed to fool aerial viewers.

Hey, Presto!"

Col. Randal said, "You start working on that the minute we get back from this patrol."

"Yes, sir!"

"I don't want to be watching any more enemy airstrikes from my swimming pool."

"Lady Jane said it was a great show, sir."

"Just make it happen, Lieutenant."

The sky was spectacularly blue and seemed even larger than in the Great Sand Sea. The thick scrub ground cover grew out of the limestone all the way down the escarpment to the water's edge, making the island appear covered in a solid green carpet except for the bare, jagged sides of the fingers. The houses up the slope reminded Col. Randal of the adobe pueblos in Santa Fe. The only difference was the colors—instead of adobe there were faded yellows, faded salmons and white—apparently the only shades permitted on Castelrozzo.

Col. Randal did not see anything out of the ordinary about admiring the beauty of the island while hunting a Nazi he intended to kill. The Brandenburgers sealed their fate when they shot Bentley and executed his Vulnerable Points Wing men after they surrendered. If the Abwehr did in fact have a dossier on him they should have known murdering his people was going to have consequences.

That could not stand.

When the patrol came to the cobblestone path leading to the top of the escarpment it was almost straight up. Steps were carved into the path in places but it was a steep climb. Even Happy found it tough going.

Behind them the *King Duck* was dropping anchor.

The patrol consisted of Col. Randal and Happy on point. King was right behind in the "slack" position with the Lovat

Scouts and Lt. Hamilton providing overwatch, followed by MSgt. Beckwith the patrol leader, with Mandy and the rest of the Rangers behind.

Mandy called out their target when it came into sight in the distance. She did not point. Sergeant Major Beckwith immediately ordered a halt and the patrol went down on one knee while he evaluated the situation.

The purpose of the exercise was to kill or capture the Brandenburger thought to be in the house. Capturing was the preferred outcome. But MSgt. Beckwith was not going to risk casualties to do it.

Besides, a dead Nazi was still a win.

This was the point on a patrol when things started to get interesting. It was not unlike a board game with each move having a reason that was carefully thought out in advance. The trick being to make sure you are not playing checkers while the bad guys are playing chess.

Each member of the patrol had a task to perform. The Rangers behind Mandy were on full alert. Every other one faced out in the opposite direction, weapons up, dialed in. The last man, "Tail End Charlie," was facing backward providing rear security. A patrol was a thing of beauty when executed by soldiers as highly skilled with as much combat experience as these Raiding Forces personnel.

MSgt. Beckwith moved up to discuss the situation with Col. Randal.

"If there's Brandenburgers in that house we're already under observation sir."

"Roger that, Sergeant Major. What's your plan?"

"You're really going to make me do this, Colonel?"

"It's your patrol."

"Follow me then, sir."

They walked back to where the patrol was down on one knee waiting for developments. MSgt. Beckwith moved to the middle of the column and spoke in a normal voice. The men were close enough together that they could hear what he had to say without turning their heads.

No one looked in the direction of the house.

"Listen up, we're getting ready to move out. When we do, don't anybody even glance in the direction of our target. If there's any Nazis inside, they've got us in their sights right now.

"When we get up the trail another fifty yards I'll give the command 'now.' At that time, Mandy, Fenwick and Lieutenant Hamilton will drop off the far side of the finger and take up a prone position in defilade.

"Fenwick, you provide overwatch. If you spot a target you're green lit to engage—understand?"

"Perfectly, Sergeant Major."

"Lieutenant Hamilton, same for you . . . if Fenwick opens fire you immediately go into action with the Colonel's 45mm Brixia—that straight?"

"Yes, sir."

"Don't call me sir, Lieutenant. I work for a living."

"Yes s—. . . Sergeant Major."

"We're going to continue to move on up this path. We'll go past the walkway leading to our target as if we are patrolling up to the top of the escarpment. Then when we're past it up the hill out of the line of sight of anyone in the house we'll loop back around. At that point, the patrol will break down into two teams. I will lead one team . . . King, you take the other. Approaching from the rear, out of sight of the Brandenburgers, the two teams will move into position on either side of the house. My team taking the near side. King you've got the far side. We'll both be making sure to stay well back out of the gun target line from the LCT prior to the *King Duck's* shoot.

"Colonel Randal will approach the target directly from the rear closing up on the house to see if the dog alerts. If Happy does, the Colonel will hurl a smoke grenade on the roof, then retreat. Fire Control Team . . . you see smoke that's your signal to Standby Ready. I'll give it a five count then issue you the order to radio the *King Duck* to commence fire.

"Lieutenant, you and Fenwick stand down as soon as the first tank round detonates on target. The signal for the two assault teams to make entry will be a parachute flare I put up plus the verbal command to execute once I get conformation of "end of mission" from the tankers.

"Any questions? All right then, prepare to move out."

It was a good plan with fail safes built in—not as complicated as it sounded. Unfortunately, as soon as the patrol stood up and started moving a pair of .45 Thompson submachine guns opened fire from the second story of the target. The Brandenburger Sea Raiders hiding in the house apparently realizing their location had been compromised must have decided their best option was to go down fighting.

MSgt. Beckwith shouted, "NOW! Commence fire, Lieutenant—patrol double time MARCH!"

As instructed, Lt. Hamilton, Mandy and Scout Fenwick rolled off the side of the path. The Great Teddy fired the 45mm Brixia as he was diving for cover and proceed to keep launching a stream of the fat little explosive rounds once he hit the ground.

Col. Randal and Happy took off running up the cobblestone path with the rest of the patrol hard on their heels.

The 45mm Brixia rounds were detonating on the front of the house. Scout Fenwick was firing his Westley Richards 7x57 red stag rifle at the muzzle flashes coming from the second story windows—not really having a clear target but hoping to keep the German's heads down. Rangers charging up the path were firing from the hip as they ran.

Back at ABCHQ, Captain Billy Jack Jaxx resting his dog heard the gunfire, "Contact—saddle up, boys.

"Let's roll."

The Thompson submachine gun is a dangerous close-in automatic weapon that fires a big .45 Colt Automatic Pistol (ACP) round. It has serious knockdown power. However, the submachine gun is only effective to approximately seventy-five yards. The patrol, moving hard and fast up the path, was quite a bit farther out than that. The Nazis were not hitting anything. In addition to being hampered by the range factor, firing a submachine gun held up over your head without looking in the "spray and pray" position, as the Nazis were being forced to do by the covering fire from Lt. Hamilton and Scout Fenwick, is not conducive to accuracy.

Nevertheless, the incoming rounds cracking past were a definite motivating factor for the patrol.

No one slowed down.

As Col. Randal and Happy ran up the cobblestone sidewalk past the turnoff to the target to be above and behind the house, King and his team pulled around them and sprinted into the lead. The dog did not much like getting shot at and was moving out smartly so the Merc and his team of Rangers had to really turn on the speed to pass them.

King's men raced straight across the escarpment in back of the target and sliding down the incline proceeded to the far side of the house from where they would set up their block prior to making entry.

To the near side MSgt. Beckwith brought the remainder of the patrol to a halt as soon as they made it to a location out of the line of the Brandenburgers fire he was satisfied with. The pause was only temporary

"On me."

Then the Sergeant Major took off running hard to close the distance to the target keeping in mind the necessity of halting far enough back to be safely out of the gun target line of fire about to be unleashed from the two Tiger tanks onboard the *King Duck.* The four hard-charging Rangers and two Fire Control sailors were right behind him.

The idea was to initially be on the near side of the house in a blocking position in the event the Brandenburgers attempted to bail out and flee in that direction. Then MSgt Beckwith's Rangers would slide into position to make their assault through the front door once the 88's finished working over the target.

Col. Randal paused to allow King and the Sergeant Major's teams to take up their positions. As soon as they were he and Happy approached the house from the back, working his way down the slope until they were level with the top of the roof. At this point looking over it he was staring straight down the barrels of the two Tiger tanks mounted on the bow of the *King Duck*.

Happy alerted by lying down. The signal was redundant everyone already knew there were Germans inside.

Lt. Hamilton was pounding the front of the house non-stop with 45mm Brixia mortar rounds. Col. Randal hoped The Great Teddy did not overshoot the building. If Happy was blown up he was going to be in big trouble.

That possibility had not been taken into consideration in the hasty frag order.

After checking both sides to ensure everyone was in place he lobbed a smoke grenade on the roof. As soon as one is thrown the handle pops off in midflight like any other hand grenade. But unlike fragmentation, concussion or white phosphorous grenades—which have a four-second delay fuse, smoke grenades have an instantaneous fuse. There was a *craaack* as soon as the canister left his hand.

Violet smoke started billowing out.

The second he could determine the grenade was not going to roll off the roof, Col. Randal moved out "smartly", as drill sergeants are prone to say—at a right angle to get as far away from the back of the target as possible before the Tigers opened.

He and Happy hit the dirt.

The two tanks fired as one. *BOOOOOM!*

The report of the cannon came rolling in across the water.

One round went into the second story and detonated inside. The other was a "short round," striking in front of the front door. The shell glanced off the hard ground, slammed through the door, and blew up.

An accident. Pure dumb luck. But both floors of the house simultaneously received a dose of high explosives and red hot shrapnel.

The *King Duck's* tanks continued their fire mission marking the last shell with a smoke round.

The instant the white smoke wafted signifying last round and the Fire Control Team relayed, "End of mission.", MSgt. Beckwith fired the signal flare to launch the attack and shouted loud enough for the teams on both sides of the house and Col. Randal in the rear to hear, "EXECUTE, EXECUTE, EXECUTE!"

The Sergeant Major advanced his team sliding down the wall to close on the front door in order to make entry leaving the Fire Control party to cover the near side of the house. King led half his team around from the far side and across the front to follow the Sergeant Major's team in leaving the other half behind in a blocking position. The idea was to flow in behind the initial entry team to get as many men as possible— force on force, making a dynamic entry through the front of the house while the two sides of the building were covered by fire.

Col. Randal and Happy closed up behind the house and stood fast which was an improvised move not covered by the plan.

Three Brandenburger Commandos wearing U.S. Army uniforms boiled out a second-story window so tangled up together—being in a hurry to exit the house, they landed on top of each other. In the rush to get going, which is a failing of hasty missions, no one had foreseen this development either. There should have been a security man with the dog team.

The only thing that stood in the way of the Brandenburgers living to fight again another day was Col. Randal and Happy.

The Nazis came hard.

Everything seemed to be taking place in slow motion except that was a dangerous illusion. Events were happening fast—lightning fast. Col. Randal was only armed with his pair of 1911 Colt .38 Supers and the 380 Remington M-51 pocket pistol Beverly had given him.

He was the dog handler. Better to have his hands free. Or so he had thought.

Col. Randal had to let go of the leash to draw his pistol. Happy instantly charged the three Nazis who were attempting to regain their feet in order to bring their M 1928 Model .45 Thompson submachine guns into play.

However the Germans were disadvantaged having been concussed from the Tiger tank shelling, the two-story jump to the rock-hard ground, the fact they were downhill while he was uphill, and that they were attempting to shoot and move at the same time. Also, the Nazis had a vicious attack dog streaking toward them with big teeth and evil intent which had to be a distraction.

Nevertheless the Brandenburgers got off the first rounds—that missed.

The Colt 1911 .38 Super was in Col. Randal's hand and up with no conscious thought to make it happen. He blocked out everything around him, including the three Thompsons SMG's being fired at virtual point-blank range, to focus on the gold bead mounted on his pistol's front sight.

Then working left to right he touched the trigger off fast.

BLAAM, BLAAM, BLAAM, BLAAM, BLAAM, BLAAM!

Rapid fire double taps. He did not miss. The .38 Super rounds dropped two of the Nazis instantly DRT—dead right there. Their heads seemed to hit the ground before their feet left it.

In real life men shot dead do not fall anything like the way actors do in the movies.

The third German was reeling from the effects of the pair of high velocity rounds to his chest but was still upright. He was struggling to bring his Thompson submachine gun into action holding down the trigger blazing away but the rounds were impacting harmlessly into the ground in front of him.

Happy launched from six feet out and hit the Brandenburger dead center in his already wounded upper torso knocking him over. The dog had the Nazi on the ground by the throat shaking him like a rag doll. The enemy soldier was screaming—or at least attempting to but making a bad job of it with the animal's jaws clamped down on his vocal cords.

The German was flailing around which seemed to enrage Happy more or maybe only made the game more fun. The fight was over in less than three seconds start to finish except for the dog continuing to work over his victim long after he was dead.

Everything was strangely quiet.

Col. Randal automatically changed magazines without glancing down at his weapon, eyes up to maintain situational awareness, and called off Happy.

The dog trotted back looking pleased with himself.

Col. Randal reached down and scratched him between the ears, "I owe you one."

MSgt. Beckwith leaned out the second-story window. "You OK down there, Colonel?"

"I'm good."

"We're clear in here, sir. One Brandenburger Sea Raider KIA—88's got him or it might have been the Great Teddy. Hard to say."

Lt. Hamilton, Mandy and Scout Fenwick came jogging up from their overwatch position. Capt. Jaxx and his patrol, having double-timed all the way from ABCHQ, were closing in right behind them.

Mandy said, "I have seen you in action before John, but nothing to compare to this . . ."

At RAF Habbaniya she sat next to him on the base's water tower with Golden Square artillery rounds whizzing by calmly spotting targets while he sniped Iraqi rebels outside the wire with a scoped .55 Boys Anti-Tank Rifle.

" . . . what do you think this is the Gunfight at the OK Corral? Have you gone completely crazy!"

Capt. Jaxx said, "You shot it out with three Nazis armed with Tommy guns all by yourself, sir?"

Col. Randal said, "Don't tell Jane."

6
IT'S HARDER IF YOU'RE STUPID

1800 HOURS.

BEVERLY BLACKWELL ANNOUNCED OVER THE intercom, "Prepare for takeoff."

The Supermarine Walrus began its run lifting into another spectacular Aegean sunset. She had her navigator, Corporal Tom Murphy aka "Murph the Surf" sitting next to her in the cockpit. Lieutenant General "Geronimo" Joe McKoy, Major General James "Baldie" Taylor and Colonel John Randal were in the passenger compartment. The two generals may or may not have been real general officers. Lt. Gen. McKoy's rank only applied when he was physically present in the state of Arizona and Maj. Gen. Taylor's was "local"—meaning only in a specific area. The last known place he held it was Abyssinia though he had continued to use the rank in Egypt from time to time.

Nevertheless, both "generals" were in uniform this evening. The idea being to impress the Fortress Leros commander Brigadier Robert Tilney—until recently a lieutenant colonel serving as a battalion commander in 234th Brigade. Col. Randal's party only had one day to be on the island and needed to make sure they got the VIP tour.

What the British officer commanding was going to think about a U.S. Army lieutenant general arriving unannounced and unexpected with long silver gunfighter-style hair hanging out the back of his green Commando beret was an open question.

Maj. Gen. Taylor said, "Leros is ten miles in length and varies in width from one to five miles. That translates to twenty square miles of area with over twenty-five miles of coastline. The terrain is mountainous with hard lava rock, making it almost impossible to dig emplacements without extensive use of explosives. The island is divided into three parts joined by two narrow isthmuses. In the central section lies the town of Leros.

"As you know, Colonel, from your previous visit when you came calling at Portologo aboard a two-man cockleshell, the Italians expended great effort to turn Leros into a major naval base. A flotilla of Regia Marina submarines was stationed in the harbor at one time but there are no subs now. In fact, only a few warships of any class are berthed there at this point—one destroyer from the 4th Destroyer Squadron and eight MAS boats from the 3rd Motor Torpedo Boat Flotilla.

"There are seven CANT Z 501 seaplanes, which may or may not all be serviceable at any given time. We would consider commandeering them for Raiding Forces except for a design flaw. The single forward-facing engine is mounted overhead above the pilot's compartment on the high wing and during rough water landings the propeller has a propensity to crash down into the cockpit."

Lt. Gen. McKoy said, "Pam and Beverly will be glad to hear you canned that plan, Jim."

Col. Randal said, "Roger that."

Maj. Gen. Taylor said, "To defend the base the Italians installed a significant number of naval and antiaircraft guns—twenty-four batteries in all: Three 152mm, two 120mm, four 102mm, one 90mm, fourteen 76mm, and seventeen searchlight batteries. The Italians have approximately eight thousand troops on the island—sixty-five hundred of which are land-based sailors—meaning low-grade soldiers, one battalion of the 10th Infantry Regiment Regia, one Blackshirt Company, and Regia Marina Marine guards for the naval installations.

"Admiral Luigi Mascherpa has command of Italian forces. However, the new Badoglio government that came to power after Mussolini's arrest placed him under Brigadier Tilney's overall command without conditions. That did not sit well with the Admiral.

"The primary British unit is the 234th Brigade most of whom have been sitting on Malta for the last two years being bombed around the clock. It consists of the 1st Battalion Queens Own Royal West Kents, 4th Battalion Royal East Kent Regiment of the Buffs (4 REKR) (-) one company, 2nd Battalion Royal Irish Fusiliers (2 RIF), 1st Battalion King's Own Royal Regiment (1 KORR) . . ."

Col. Randal was surprised to learn the KORR was in the brigade. The First Battalion King's Own Royal Regiment had been flown in from India to reinforce RAF Habbaniya during the siege. He formed Strike Force out of volunteers from it. Captain Roy Kidd, an American with a British mother, had been one of them.

" . . . B Company of the Second Royal West Kent Regiment (2 RWKR), detachments from the LRDG, the SBS, a detachment from the 28th Heavy Anti-Aircraft Battery, and a section of the 3rd Light Anti-Aircraft battery.

"GHQ Cairo is convinced with these troops Leros can be held against any attack by the Germans. Brigadier Tilney has adopted the slogan, 'No enemy shall set foot on this island unless to be a prisoner of war.'"

Lt. Gen. McKoy said, "Bold talk for a man who's spent the last seven hundred days hunkerin' down in a shelter gettin' bombed into the Stone Age."

Maj. Gen. Taylor said, "The 234th Brigade is not better for their time on Malta and the Regia Marina's land-based sailors are barely more than civilians issued rifles. GHQ Cairo is living in a dream state believing these troops are capable of putting up a serious defense against the Wehrmacht."

Col. Randal said, "1 KORR performed well at Habbaniya and the follow-on campaign into Iraq. They're good men. I understand the battalion was involved in heavy fighting at El Alamein."

Lt. Gen. McKoy said, "The KORR wasn't on Malta but they have been sittin' on Cyprus unemployed for the last year or so gettin' soft guardin' Snow White and his acrobat girlfriend Tinker Bell. They ain't the same outfit you used to know, John. Too many losses in the desert, too many green replacements with no combat experience.

"Best officers killed or transferred out."

Col. Randal noted Lt. Gen. McKoy seemed to know quite a bit about the 234th Brigade. He had clearly been doing his enemy *and* friendly forces assessment. Always a step ahead.

Col. Randal said, "How do we play this?"

MAJOR THE EARL LORD GEORGE JELLICOE, DSO, MC, commanding officer of the SBS was waiting on the dock holding a hooded flashlight when Lieutenant General "Geronimo" Joe McKoy, Major General James "Baldie" Taylor and Colonel John Randal deplaned. His presence on Leros was a fairly new development.

Col. Randal said, "So how did you end up on Leros, George?"

Maj. Lord Jellicoe said, "When I discovered SBS had been deployed here I ordered the Italian skipper of the MAS boat I was aboard to make a detour to the island so I could rejoin my command, sir."

Lt. Gen. McKoy said, "I heard you had to hide in a closet while Germans were using the room for an office."

Maj. Lord Jellicoe said, "I shall be delighted to brief you on the entire sordid affair at a later date, General. After hearing my tale one could not be blamed for drawing the conclusion this war is being run by drunken lunatics. You shall not believe a word of it.

"What service may I provide tonight, gentlemen?"

Maj. Gen. Taylor said, "General McKoy requires an escort to Brigadier Tilney's headquarters. I need to see Admiral Mascherpa in Portologo. Then you can take Colonel Randal on a tour of the disposition of your SBS and the LRDG."

Maj. Lord Jellicoe said, "My pleasure, sir. Come with me."

Out in the harbor Beverly Blackwell taxied the Walrus to a place she could begin her takeoff run. The seaplane raced across the water and lifted into the sky. It disappeared into the night.

Col. Randal was clicked on. He disliked being on Leros but did not know why. And he wished he was on the plane with Beverly headed back to Castelrozzo.

Maj. Lord Jellicoe had a jeep. He dropped Lt. Gen. McKoy and Maj. Gen. Taylor off at their destinations. Then he drove to the center of the island where the Special Boat Section had been ordered to set up the Fortress Leros Mobile Counterattack Force.

Col. Randal said, “A joke, right?”

“Negative.”

Col. Randal said, “SBS and LRDG combined have been reduced to less than company strength and you are expected to respond to hotspots everywhere on the entire island—twenty-five square miles with no motor transport?”

Maj. Lord Jellicoe said, “That seems to be the current thinking, Colonel—between the SBS and LRDG we have one hundred three men fit for duty, sir. But there are only twenty-five men in the Mobile Counter Attack Force. The rest are scattered around performing other duties.”

Col. Randal said, “You do realize the 1st Parachute Battalion, Brandenburger Regiment is on Kos about a ten-minute flight away?”

“Brigadier Tilney discounts the possibility of an airborne assault, sir.”

“Lovely.”

Col. Randal and Maj. Lord Jellicoe spent the next day touring Leros. Brigadier Tilney’s defense plan divided the island into three sectors. The north was held by the Buffs, the center by the RIF and B Company RWKR, and the south by the 1 KORR (-) one company held in central reserve. The Long Range Desert Group, or what there was left of it, had been broken into small teams because it was no longer capable of functioning as a unit due to extensive combat losses and the New Zealand squadron having been pulled out by its government. The teams were sent to the principal batteries to “stiffen the morale of the gunners”—

meaning "hold the Italian artillerymen at gunpoint to stand to their guns should it be necessary."

No one really expected much from them.

Brigadier Tilney's Fortress Leros HQ was located in the central sector inside a tunnel bored into Meraviglia Hill.

Maj. Lord Jellicoe said, "The Brigadier seems to enjoy his new cave though I understand it is substantially less spacious than his last one, sir."

The jeep drove past a small house. The place was guarded by Italian sentries. There was zero activity—no one coming or going.

Col. Randal said, "What's that?"

"Colonel Turnbull's Headquarters."

"He's still on the island?"

"Negative he has recently decamped for Cairo with his entire staff. They spent their days here sticking pins in maps and making grandiose plans ignoring the fact no troops are actually available to carry them out. Colonel Prendergast, the former commander of the LRDG currently serving as Colonel Turnbull's deputy, is so disgusted he has requested a transfer back to England, sir."

Col. Randal said, "My understanding is Prendergast has only been on the job for a few weeks."

"Says that was quite enough time, Colonel."

There were three separate air raids as they drove around the island. With no RAF air opposition to worry about, the Luftwaffe, flying Ju-87 Stukas and Ju-88 bombers off the airfield on Kos, was able to take all the time it needed to reduce their targets. The primary points of interest were Port Laki and Portologo Harbor—scene of Col. Randal's last visit to the island with Lieutenant Jackson Taylor, USNR.

Dive sirens could be heard screaming like gigantic man-eating mosquitoes. Lying in a ditch watching a flight of Stukas working over an artillery battery a short distance up the road, Maj. Lord Jellicoe said, "Notice the lack of return antiaircraft fire?"

"Roger that."

"Bloody navy delivered the wrong caliber ammunition to our AA gunners, sir."

Col. Randal said, "Shipped it to Kos."

Maj. Lord Jellicoe said, "You know about that?"

When Col. Randal and Maj. Lord Jellicoe drove up to the battery after the Germans had completed their bombing attack they found Lieutenant Colonel John "Jake" Easonsmith, the new commanding officer of the Long Range Desert Group, at the battery.

Spotting him as the jeep pulled in, Maj. Lord Jellicoe said, "Some say Jake's the finest officer to ever serve in the LRDG, sir."

Col. Randal said, "Good to know."

They found Lt. Col. Easonsmith surveying the damage. There was still the smell of cordite in the air from the bombs. The battery of 76mm guns was out of action. The cannons were turned over and thrown about like toys. This was not indiscriminate bombing. The Luftwaffe had the island plotted. While most of the pilots were focused on the two primary targets, others were methodically working through a secondary target list.

Col. Randal, Lt. Col. Easonsmith and Maj. Lord Jellicoe huddled over the hood of the jeep to conduct a map study and discuss the current state of affairs.

Col. Randal said, "Major Jellicoe has provided me his thoughts on the local situation. Now I'd like your take, Colonel. Don't sugarcoat it."

Lt. Col. Easonsmith said, "Until shortly before the Italian armistice there were Germans stationed here on the island. They know the topography, the layout of the port facilities, and where all our gun emplacements are located. The Nazis are aware of Italian personnel being split almost equally between army, navy and civilian construction contractors. Whatever number you have been provided for Italian defenders divide that by at least two based on their lack of combat power and low state of morale—a conservative estimate of the situation.

"The Italian officers appreciate that their troops are of low quality with poor morale and do not trust them to do their duty. Your average Italian soldier simply wants the war to be over. The men had no idea how they would be expected to fight the Nazis after the armistice. Some Regia Marina officers continue to wear their German Iron Crosses.

"The presence of German agents on the island, or at least sympathizers, is likely if not certain.

"There is virtually no communication between Admiral Mascherpa and Brigadier Tilney. They are barely on speaking terms. The Admiral resents falling under the command of a British officer he feels is junior to him. When they do converse if there is a disagreement the Admiral goes around the Brigadier contacting Cairo GHQ directly.

"More often than not our Plans Division staff tend to side with the Italian who may be a capable sailor but has no concept of how to command ground forces. His staff dine off white table cloth covered tables and drink fine wine with their sumptuous meals while the rest of us barely have enough food to survive.

"The 234th Brigade had to be snuck in piecemeal under cover of darkness aboard Royal Navy destroyers, Greek schooners, and caiques hiding from the Luftwaffe, which did nothing to improve the troops' confidence.

"Our gun emplacements have no overhead cover. Many are located on high points making it easy for the Luftwaffe pilots to identify the batteries from the air. Antiaircraft ammunition is in short supply due to logistical failings.

"We have no wheeled transport.

"Need I go on, Colonel?"

Col. Randal said, "Listen up . . . here's what we're going to do…"

LIEUTENANT GENERAL "GERONIMO" JOE MCKOY, Major General James "Baldie" Taylor and Colonel John Randal boarded the Walrus in the dark after a long day on the island. The three officers were uncommonly quiet. Each was wrapped in his own thoughts. Not much had been said on the short drive to the dock as Major the Earl Lord George Jellicoe drove them to meet the seaplane.

They were barely on board when Beverly Blackwell announced over the intercom, "Prepare for takeoff."

As soon as the plane was airborne Col. Randal moved up to the cockpit. He wanted to get his mind off Leros. Talking to Beverly was like taking a happy pill—he needed one.

Major the Lady Jane Seaborn was in the co-pilot's chair.

Lady Jane said, "I flew out to keep Beverly company. She shall be on her own for the return flight. You and I have a date in the back of the plane for some quality personal time together. The 'do not disturb' sign is in full force and effect.

"Missed you, babe."

Col. Randal said, "I missed you too."

He meant it.

Beverly said, "How was your trip, Johnny?"

"Not good. I need Corporal Murphy to transmit three priority messages for me."

Beverly spoke over the intercom, "Murph the Surf to the cockpit."

The corporal arrived, crawling along the tunnel from his open-air navigation/signals station in the nose of the Walrus.

Col. Randal said, "Contact Admiral Ransom, signal him to begin assembling every MAS, MGB, and PT boat he can lay hands on in the vicinity of Castelrozzo.

"Instruct Captain Hoolihan to place his Royal Marines on Standby Ready Alert.

"Then advise Mrs. Paige and Lieutenant Commander Seligman to report to me as soon as we arrive."

"Yes, sir. Straight away. Anything else, sir?"

"Let me know when you get a response."

The cabin was dark as Col. Randal and Lady Jane made their way down the aisle. The Luftwaffe had a small number of night fighters in their inventory so Beverly had turned off all interior lights. One little flicker was all it would take for a lurking Nazi pilot to spot the plane.

Her father, Major General Sam Houston Blackwell, had drummed a saying into her during her growing up in South Texas: "Life's hard—it's harder if you're stupid."

Beverly was not stupid.

As he and Lady Jane were moving past, Maj. Gen. Taylor said, "Colonel, a word?"

"Yes, sir."

"General McKoy and I have been going over our findings. We want to give you a quick rundown on what we learned along with our initial conclusions. Then we want to hear your takeaway."

Lt. Gen. McKoy ticked off five concise points:

"One. Of the troops on the island only the 234th Brigade can be trusted and they consist of garrison troops not capable of maneuver warfare.

"Two. German command of the air and the immediate proximity of their naval bases to Leros give the Nazis control of the air *and* sea. Since they can sail durin' daylight hours and we can't, their ability to reinforce once the invasion commences is greater than our own.

"Three. The shortage of ammunition, the lack 'a wheeled transport to shift units, the sorry state 'a the troops' trainin' combined with the Italian's low morale, coupled with the German command of the air and sea means once the fight commences the longer the battle for Leros lasts, the greater the Nazi advantage.

"Four. To have any hope of a successful outcome our side needs an early favorable decision—which means aggressive maneuver tactics and superior firepower concentrated at the point of attack.

"Five. Based on everything I've just said that ain't possible."

Lt. Gen. McKoy's typical, laid-back drawl had transitioned to a crisp, rapid-fire, military-style delivery of facts leaving his opinions until the conclusion. It was clear to Col. Randal that his time at the Command & General Staff College and the Army War College—which "Geronimo" Joe tried to downplay—had not been wasted.

Maj. Gen. Taylor said, "Anything else, General?"

Lt. Gen. McKoy said, "Brigadier Tilney is of the opinion that if denied the ability to land on the beaches the Germans won't be able to achieve a forced entry lodgment. His conclusion: the enemy—and this is a direct quote, 'must be destroyed at the water's edge at the earliest possible stage.'"

"To accomplish that he plans to defend every possible landin' site along the entire twenty-five-mile perimeter coastline. Bein' spread out over that much distance will only aggravate an unreliable field communications network and depends on 'a non-existent motorized ability to shift troops."

"What we have is Brigadier Tilney establishin' a defensive posture weak everywhere not strong anywhere—violates every known principle of defense."

Maj. Gen. Taylor said, "Your thoughts, Colonel?"

Col. Randal said, "Leros is a death trap."

LIEUTENANT COMMANDER ADRIAN SELIGMAN, THE commanding officer of the LSF, and Mrs. Veronica Paige (MI-9) were at the dock when the Walrus landed at Castelrozzo.

Col. Randal said, "We have a situation requiring MI-9's immediate attention, Mrs. Paige. The Germans are preparing to invade Leros. The island's defenses are inadequate. It will fall in the near future. When that happens, I want you to bring out the SBS and the LRDG troops. They have priority for evacuation.

"Is that clear?"

"Perfectly."

Col. Randal said, "MI-9 will need to make a reconnaissance. I'd send Sergeant Major Mikkalis if I were you. Determine your pickup points for the SBS and LRDG. Be prepared to have caiques standing by under camouflage at those locations. Also, establish liaison ashore with Colonel Easonsmith and Major Jellicoe to guide their people to the extraction points."

Veronica said, "Consider it done, Colonel."

"Commander, I want you to give Mrs. Paige one hundred percent support until the Leros situation is resolved."

"Aye aye, sir."

Col. Randal said, "The SBS and the LRDG are needed for future operations, so I say again, they have priority. Is that clear?"

Lt. Cdr. Seligman said, "Absolutely, sir."

Veronica said, "Understood."

Col. Randal said, "I know you two are heavily committed to bringing out evaders from Kos. Continue the mission but start planning for the Leros evacuation now. You're going to need caiques in unprecedented numbers and you need to have them pre-positioned ready to go."

Lt. Cdr. Seligman said, "If Admiral Ransom will give the order, we can pull in boats currently tied up supporting the clandestine services, sir."

Col. Randal said, "I'll speak to the Admiral."

Lt. Cdr. Seligman said, "Bear in mind the LSF has boats at sea from here to Yugoslavia, Colonel. Even by diverting them from our other commitments we shall still not have an adequate number for an operation of this magnitude.

"Another consideration is only a handful have been converted to the quiet-running Matilda tank engines at this point. Our only option will be to commandeer additional diesel-powered fishing craft."

Col. Randal said, "I don't care if you use canoes."

"Quite right, sir."

Vice Admiral Sir Randolph "Razor" Ransom, Lieutenant Randy "Hornblower" Seaborn, DSO, OBE, DSC, RN, and Captain Butch "Headhunter" Hoolihan were gathered in the TOC when Col. Randal and Lady Jane arrived. Captain Billy Jack Jaxx, sensing the prospect of an impending mission, was also standing by in the event his services were required.

Lady Jane continued on through the TOC up to the second-floor suite.

Col. Randal said, "Captain Hoolihan, are you prepared to accept a Warning Order?"

It was standard operating procedure for a commander to ask that question in exactly those words prior to issuing a Warning Order. The answer was always, "Yes, sir."

Since the response was always the same some COs dispensed with the question.

Not Col. Randal. He always asked. When it came to issuing orders he was a stickler for protocol.

Capt. Hoolihan said, "Yes, sir."

Col. Randal said, "Situation: the LRDG has a clandestine coast-watching team on Symi, thirty-six miles off Kos. It is only a matter of time before the Germans discover its presence.

"Mission: Extract the coast-watcher team on Symi.

"Execution: Proceed to the island aboard MAS, MGB or PT boats as available. Recover the LRDG operators. Be prepared to make a forced entry landing in the event the Germans have already arrived.

"Concept of the Operation: You develop it, Butch."

That was not how a commander was supposed to do it.

"Yes, sir."

"What are your questions?"

"When, sir?"

"Anytime in the next ten minutes."

"Sir!"

"Take Lieutenant Novak with you."

"Lieutenant Novak?"

"He's the new officer in from the 509th Parachute Infantry Battalion. Jumped on Benevento with us. Jake's been through the Combined Operations Training Center at Inveraray so he knows his way around boats. But he's never gone on an amphibious type mission.

"Show him how's it's done, Captain."

"Yes, sir."

The Headhunter rushed to brief his troops—waiting armed, equipped and prepared to deploy, as stipulated by the Standby Ready Alert Murph the Surf had radioed ahead. In Raiding Forces when a Standby Ready Alert was issued the troops on notice were going on a mission.

There was no if—only when.

Col. Randal said, "Admiral, will you organize the transportation for Capt. Hoolihan, sir?"

VAdm. Ransom said, "How large is the LRDG team?"

"Six men, sir."

VAdm. Ransom said, "We have the two MAS boats, our fastest craft. Best keep the naval component composed of vessels with the same speed differential. We can spread the Marines out evenly between the two so they are all transporting the same weight. It is not possible to reach Symi in the remaining hours of darkness tonight, which dictates laying up under camouflage before proceeding on the mission tomorrow.

"Lieutenant Seaborn, transfer your flag to your mother's boat to act in the capacity of squadron commander."

"Aye aye, sir!"

Capt. Jaxx said, "Need me for anything, Colonel?"

Col. Randal said, “You specifically requested the assignment to hunt down the remaining Brandenburgers, Jack—you’re in charge. Make it happen.”

“Yes, sir. What about you, sir?”

“I’m going with Butch.”

VAdm. Ransom said, “Negative.”

Col. Randal said, “Sir . . .”

“The firm of Hornblower & Headhunter is fully capable of carrying out the Symi assignment, Colonel. You shall be flying out to Alexandria with me tomorrow. I have a dog and pony show laid on you need to attend.”

“Yes, sir.”

Before he went upstairs to grab a couple of hours’ sleep, Col. Randal pulled Veronica aside.

“First Battalion King’s Own Royal Regiment is on Leros.”

“Oh, dear!”

Veronica had been at RAF Habbaniya. She knew the KORR. Specifically Strike Force.

Col. Randal said, “You have your marching orders for priority of extraction. That said, after you pull the SBS and LRDG, try to bring off as many King’s Own men who served on Strike Force as possible.”

“I shall. You can count on it, Colonel. My chance to repay them for valorous service rendered.”

On the way out of the TOC Col. Randal stopped to speak to VAdm. Ransom again.

“Sir, there are eight MAS boats berthed in the harbor at Leros….”

VAdm. Ransom said, “The instant their location came to my attention I requested they be transferred to Small Raids Inc. minus the Italian crews—no joy.

"Brigadier Tilney initially ordered all Regia Marina craft away from the island to be available to fight another day. Admiral Mascherpa went over his head to appeal directly to GHQ Cairo to have the order rescinded. The bloody fools in Plans Division complied and countermanded Tilney's order.

"We can write off those MAS boats."

Col. Randal said, "Randy's been a lieutenant for over three years, sir. Normally the skipper of an MGB holds the rank of lieutenant commander. Now you're planning to use him as a squadron leader. Don't you think it's time he be promoted, Admiral?"

VAdm. Ransom said, "I am unable to put forward my grandson for advancement. It would be perceived as nepotism throughout the navy. Especially at his young age."

"I see, sir." Which meant Col. Randal did not . . . or did not want to.

"On the other hand, you Colonel, acting in your capacity as the commanding officer of Raiding Forces . . ."

Col. Randal said, "I'll have Stephanie initiate the paperwork, sir."

VAdm. Ransom said, "Outstanding! Nothing prohibits me from arranging for endorsements from my well-placed Royal Navy friends. Thank you, Colonel."

Col. Randal said, "Let's keep this between ourselves until it's approved, sir."

He had a history of announcing surprise promotions, the presentation of decorations or qualification badges at unexpected times and places.

VAdm. Ransom said, "Aye aye."

Before Col. Randal made it out of the TOC Doctor Layton Winthrop walked in. The professor was on Castelrozzo conducting archeological digs. Lady Jane had invited him.

"A word, Colonel."

"What can I do for you, Professor?"

"You are likely not aware I am the handler of a small network of SOE agents that run from here to Greece—all archeologists who were conducting excavations prior to the war. Hitler and Himmler both have a keen interest in archeology. They hope to discover the genesis of the Master Race or anything that might support their mad concept of it.

"The Nazis have allowed archeologists to continue working their digs after the war started under the impression they were merely harmless academics."

This was news to Col. Randal.

He said, "And this matters how?"

"I have agents on Symi, Colonel."

"Really?"

"Oh yes, Symi is said to be the birthplace of King Nireus. The second most handsome man in the Trojan War. After Achilles, of course."

Col. Randal said, "What is it you believe your people can do for me, Doctor?"

"Since my agents are hiding in plain sight with freedom of movement they should be able to locate the LRDG Coastwatchers team and escort them to an isolated beach far from any German military interference. From there, in relative safety, Mrs. Paige's MI-9 people can pick them up."

Col. Randal said, "Stand by, Doctor."

He looked across the TOC and made eye contact with Capt. Jaxx who came over immediately. "Jack, get down to the dock—don't let Randy sail yet."

"On the way, sir!"

Col. Randal said, "Professor, do you have anything going on Kos?"

"Why yes I do, actually."

Col. Randal made eye contact with Veronica. She excused herself from a conversation with Captain Stephanie Fawcett-Tatum.

"Yes, Colonel."

"Mrs. Paige, I believe you've met Doctor Winthrop."

"I have."

"In addition to his scholarly pursuits the professor runs a string of SOE operatives. He has agents on Kos and Symi. The professor's volunteered to help our people E&E to safe locations where you can conduct your extractions."

Veronica said, "In that case, Doctor, you are about to become my new best friend."

THE BLACK-PAINTED CONSOLIDATED PATROL bomber (PBY) with the golden eyes of a Siamese cat and "BLACK CAT" painted on its nose took off from Castelrozzo at 0700 hours with Beverly Blackwell at the stick. Normally, she and Captain Pamala Plum-Martin flew together aboard the Catalina. However, the Royal Marine pilot and King had departed on a whirlwind LEAF EATER trip to Morocco to call on the chief of police—their corrupt diamond-buying contact in the protectorate.

The Spaniard had a liking for fit, tanned blonds, which described Capt. Plum-Martin down to the ground.

Today it was just Beverly in the cockpit.

Onboard were Lieutenant General "Geronimo" Joe McKoy, Vice Admiral Sir Randolph "Razor" Ransom, James "Baldie" Taylor—no longer in uniform—Colonel John Randal,

Lieutenant Colonel Sir Terry "Zorro" Stone, Lieutenant Commander Adrian Seligman, Major Clive Adair, Major the Lady Jane Seaborn, Captain Stephanie Fawcett-Tatum, Doctor Layton Winthrop and Waldo Treywick. Captain Billy Jack Jaxx, who had been ordered to take a day off from his Brandenburger hunting, was riding in the cockpit with Beverly.

Brigadier Dudley Clarke and Cuthbert Bowlby, having flown out the night before, would be meeting the plane when it arrived in Alexandria.

Col. Randal wondered why VAdm. Ransom had ordered these particular people to be on the flight. It was an eclectic group for a single briefing even for Raiding Forces. What did they have in common that demanded their presence?

He knew why Lady Jane was there—she and Beverly were going on a shopping safari.

Lady Jane said, "Your dog is disappointed you are leaving again."

Col. Randal said, "He's your dog and only misses me because he hoped I might take him on patrol."

Across the aisle, Waldo had broken out a book. Col. Randal did a double take. He could not recall ever being physically present when the ex-ivory poacher had ever read anything not on the label of a can.

"What're you reading, Mr. Treywick?"

"Dale Carnegie's *How To Win Friends and Influence People*—pretty good stuff, Colonel."

"Really?"

"Yeah, it says so right here on the first page, '*The more you get outta this book the more you'll get outta life—the only book you need to lead you to success.*'"

"I see."

"With all those real estate deals me and Joe—I mean the General—has been makin' lately out in California due to the 'Jap Flap,' I'm thinkin' maybe now might be the time to start workin' on my people skills."

"Where'd you get the book?"

"Rocky gave it to me as a present."

"I'd like to take a look at it when you finish."

"Good idea Colonel bein' as how your favored method 'a influencin' people is at pistol point. As for winnin' friends—that ain't on your list 'a things to do at all."

Lady Jane was sitting next to Col. Randal trying hard not to laugh out loud. When Waldo went back to reading she whispered, "When I hold etiquette classes for the officer candidates for direct commissions do you have any idea who always attends?"

"That would be negative."

"Mr. Treywick and Billy Jack."

"Are you kidding?"

"Waldo is interested in self-improvement. Jack is polishing his social graces to get the girls."

Col. Randal said, "Do you think I need to work on my people skills?"

Lady Jane laughed, "You keep letting your guns do the talking."

A small caravan of khaki-colored Dodge and Chevrolet command cars was waiting when the PBY splashed down. Flanigan was parked nearby having driven up from RFHQ outside Cairo with Lady Jane's Rolls-Royce. Everyone climbed aboard their respective vehicles and rolled out.

After a short drive along the shore to a remote location the little convoy—minus the Rolls which turned off for the exclusive boutiques in Alexandria's shopping district—pulled up at a checkpoint. The senior Military Policeman spoke to VAdm. Ransom briefly then waved them through. The convoy drove down a one-lane road through two more checkpoints to a secluded dock—what was known in intelligence circles as a "black site."

Royal Navy Shore Patrol sailors armed with 9mm Lanchester submachine guns were set up in a semicircle that backed up to the water's edge. A line of Royal Navy Volunteer Reserve (RNVR) sailors were standing on the jetty at parade rest—the submarine's skipper and his crew.

Moored behind them was the pigboat.

Lt. Gen. McKoy said, "Old timey sailors came up with the nickname 'pigboat.' They thought undersea craft looked like porpoises when they surfaced. Porpoises are called 'sea pigs.'"

Waldo said, "I never knew that."

Submarines were not unknown in the Aegean. The 10th Submarine Flotilla operated out of Alexandria from time to time. However, this one seemed smaller than the 10th Flotilla's U-class boats.

It was completely sterile—no markings.

VAdm. Ransom gathered the party around for a briefing.

"What we have here is an off-the-books Holland 602 H-class submarine. It was built during the last war by the British Pacific Construction and Engineering Company at a shipyard in Barnet on the south shore of Burrard Inlet near Vancouver. This boat was one of the subs designed as 'kit boats' intended to be boxed up and shipped to Russia to be reassembled.

"Once in their crates the subs were transported by rail to the United States for shipment overseas. When the U.S. port authorities discovered the contents, being neutral at the time, the kits were seized and stored in a naval warehouse where they sat gathering dust for the next twenty-seven years. Now two of them belong to Small Raids Inc.—actually three.

"FIRE EATER requires Motor Gun Boats of various classes and LSF/MI-9 caiques be at sea all across our AO carrying out tasks for Small Raids Inc. and supporting the various intelligence agencies. Concurrently Raiding Forces has Commando raiding parties traveling to and from distant targets.

"Major Adair has informed me Phantom does not have the capability required to communicate with all these long-range commitments unless we set up relay stations on uninhabited islands. Colonel Randal is dead set against the idea of relay stations on the grounds that once in place they become sitting targets.

"The enemy has excellent direction-finding capabilities—DF. That means the other side would know where our radio stations are located as soon as they send their first transmission. The Germans would not likely ignore them for long.

"Nothing we considered seemed like it would work until we hit upon using submarines as our relay stations. There is a long list of objections to the idea but those can, for the most part, be negated if we develop proper tactics. We are currently in the process of refining those.

"Then what seemed like an insurmountable problem cropped up. The Royal Navy does not have an adequate number of submarines for its own needs. They are not about to provide any of theirs to Small Raids Inc. to support a guerrilla campaign in a backwater theatre of operations.

"When I spoke to my old shipmate, Admiral Cunningham, about assigning us subs he looked at me as if I were a raving lunatic.

"Not only are submarines not available, but trained officers and crew are also at an absolute premium. Since we are old shipmates to humor me, the Admiral did offer to supply the personnel to man them provided I could lay hands on a submarine or two, laughing hysterically at the time.

"Small Raids Inc. conducted a worldwide search in hopes of locating what we needed in some small country we could beg or borrow from. On a parallel course we were developing plans to launch an operation to capture a pair of submarines from the Italians who had a few in service.

"Staff was collecting target data for a raid on the Regia Marina submarine base at Portologo when we heard rumors of H-class kit boats from the last war stored in the U.S. Acting on my request General Donovan put OSS on the case to locate their whereabouts. Not only did Wild Bill find the warehoused subs he managed to solve another of our major problems—spare parts.

"Small Raids Inc. needs two operational subs. One is to be on station while the other is in port being serviced. In that way the boats stay shipshape and the crew can be given shore leave in order to be rested and ready to go back to sea.

"General Donovan shipped out three kits. The third boat will be cannibalized for parts.

"The Royal Navy and the U.S. Navy may have no use for H-class submarines because of their small size and technical obsolescence but at least five are currently still operational in the coastal waters off the U.K. Three are used for training purposes at the Royal Navy 'Perisher' course in Plymouth—so named for its high failure rate of those officers who aspire to be submariners.

"Admiral Cunningham was true to his word. He contacted the commandant of the 'Perisher,' one Lieutenant Commander Edward Young, who by happenstance was a highly successful captain of an H-class sub at the outbreak of this war before taking charge of submarine training. Sympathetic to our needs and aware his H-class sailors had been serving at Perisher for nearly three years and desired more active sea duty, he shipped two complete crews to Small Raids Inc.

"Assembly of our subs was completed by the naval yard here in Alexandria. The crews have arrived. Now it is time to conduct sea trials.

"Still quite a lot of jumps for us to get over before becoming operational but here we are. The Small Raids Inc. submarines are classified TOP SECRET, 'Need to Know' and no one not physically present today has the requisite need until further notice. I hardly need to remind this group of the importance of security.

"You were brought here because of the wide divergence in your job description and/or military experience. In the coming days I shall be interviewing each of you for your ideas on how to best integrate subs into Raiding Forces and other government agency operations.

"I want your best thoughts."

There was a buzz among the people in the group for a wide variety of reasons. Maj. Adair was impressed with the concept of using submarines instead of land-based radio relay stations because fixed transmitting sites were so vulnerable. Cuthbert Bowlby and Jim saw possibilities of utilizing submarines for clandestine insertions/extractions of intelligence operatives on distant targets. Lt. Col. Stone realized submarines would resolve most of his current Command & Control problems. Brig. Clarke's eyes were glittering for reasons he was not prepared to disclose. Dr. Winthrop thought the subs were a means for communicating with his far-flung network of archeologist spies some of whom currently had to rely on long caique commutes to get messages out. Veronica thought the subs might be useful for extracting evaders from islands deep in enemy-infested waters that were difficult for her M-9 caiques to penetrate. Capt. Jaxx thought launching a small-scale raid unannounced and unexpected in the dark of night from a submarine would be a cool delivery method.

Not everyone present was as enthusiastic.

Waldo was feeling light-headed at the sight of the submarine. He was trying not to imagine what it would be like to be onboard the H-class boat when it slipped beneath the "wine-dark" waves.

"Hell no, I won't go!"

Lt. Gen. McKoy said, "Roger that."

Col. Randal said, "Submarine duty is probably an acquired taste."

AS THE SUN WAS BEGINNING TO SINK AND THE Egyptian air was cooling all the Small Raids Inc. and Raiding Forces personnel in Alexandria took whatever transportation available—from Major the Lady Jane Seaborn's white Rolls-Royce to taxi cabs—to the naval air station on the edge of town. Major General Sam Houston Blackwell was inbound with a flight of six C-47 Dakota aircraft returning 575th Ranger Force troops from Italy.

Everyone wanted to be on hand to welcome them back.

Five of the C-47s came in for a landing. The sixth plane piloted by Maj. Gen. Blackwell race tracked over the airfield. Being a hands-on, lead-from-the-front commander, Bronc never missed an opportunity to give his pilots additional training either by doing or observing.

The pilots that landed and their crews had received the benefit of completing a long-distance flight to include navigation—a skill set virtually all USAAF pilots and navigators needed more practice in.

Now they were about to watch a demonstration of aerial delivery. Maj. Gen. Blackwell's plane was loaded with an olive drab painted U.S. Army Indian Model 640 motorcycle on a wooden pallet. It was rigged with three parachutes.

Bronc was going to drop it over the airfield.

U.S. Army Airborne doctrine called for heavy equipment to be landed by gliders. While there was nothing wrong with that model—every army in the world used it—Maj. Gen. Blackwell was of the belief there were going to be times and places where gilder landings would not always be practical. In conjunction with Airborne Command at Fort Benning his Troop Transport Command (TTC) was experimenting with the concept of heavy equipment airdrops—an idea in its infancy.

Bronc was inventing it.

Dropping heavy equipment by parachute is always exciting to watch. However it is a good idea not to be standing on the DZ while doing the watching. A safe distance off to one side being highly recommended.

Sometimes it worked and sometimes it did not.

Ten of the returning 575th Ranger Task Force personnel led by Captain Roy Kidd had volunteered to jump and then be followed out the door by the parachute-rigged motorcycle. The jumpmaster was Lieutenant Windell Mead, Airborne Command, on temporary duty (TDY) to Troop Carrier Command to help develop Maj. Gen. Blackwell's heavy equipment air drop capability. The plan was for the Rangers to exit, then the parachute-rigged motorcycle would be rolled out, followed by Lt. Mead.

Colonel John Randal was sitting on the hood of the Rolls-Royce between Lady Jane and Beverly. He had never witnessed a heavy equipment drop and was interested to see how one worked. Lieutenant General "Geronimo" Joe McKoy, Captain Billy Jack Jaxx and Waldo were standing nearby smoking Waldo's custom-rolled cigars.

As the returning Raiding Forces personnel deplaned they assembled around the Rolls-Royce. Lady Jane had arranged for iced drums containing bottles of Egyptian Saqqara Gold beer for the men. The Rangers were having a good day, drinking cold beer, glad to be back.

There is no feeling in the world to compare with returning from a combat mission.

Overhead at a thousand feet, twice the altitude most Raiding Forces drops took place, Maj. Gen. Blackwell lined up on the runway. Parachutes started blossoming out of the tail looking like swimming octopuses before their main chutes cracked open. Then the motorcycle was rolled out.

It fell nose down with something whirling around behind it—the something was Lt. Mead.

He had put the jumpers out then, with the assistance of two USAAF aircrew, shoved the motorcycle out on a wooden pallet. Unfortunately at that point the handle on the ripcord of his reserve parachute became entangled with the static line of the motorcycle's parachute.

It deployed inside the Dakota.

Lt. Mead was unceremoniously sucked out of the aircraft striking his head on the side of the door as he went, knocking him unconscious. Meanwhile the Indian hit the end of its static line, snapped it, and plunged straight down, plowing into the tarmac about a hundred yards from Lady Jane's car. The bike shattered into a million pieces.

The Ranger's laughing and horseplay ceased.

Waldo said, "The problem ain't gonna be the solution this time."

Capt. Jaxx said, "Look, there's a towed parachutist behind the plane."

Onboard the aircraft in the troop/cargo compartment panic ensued. The two aircrewmen attempted to pull Lt. Mead back into the aircraft. Failed—it was impossible.

The U.S. Army Airborne had an SOP that covered what to do in the event of a towed parachutist. If a jumper was towed and conscious he was to put one or both of his hands on the sides of his helmet. If the paratrooper was able to give the signal standard operating procedure called for the jumpmaster to cut the static line. All jumpmasters were required to carry a jump knife strapped to their ankles for just this eventuality.

However there were problems.

Lt. Mead *was* the jumpmaster and he had his jump knife strapped to his leg per SOP. The aircrew did not have knives. Not that it mattered. There was no signal from the lieutenant because he was unconscious.

In addition, cutting a towed parachutist loose is only possible when the jumper was wearing a reserve parachute. Lt. Mead's reserve chute *had* deployed and become entangled which was why he was being towed. Cutting him free was not an option.

The aircrewmen were still unable to pull Lt. Mead back in even after the copilot came back to help because the canopy of the reserve chute was wrapped around the tail wheel. If that was not enough of a problem Bronc was running out of fuel. He needed to put down. Landing was going to drag the lieutenant to death.

It was probably a good thing the spectators didn't know about the fuel.

Beverly Blackwell said, “On our return flight from Sicily we were flying on fumes when we arrived here.”

So much for ignorance is bliss.

Col. Randal called to Captain Cord Granger who had just walked up carrying his gear slung over one shoulder, sipping a beer. “Did you make a refueling stop?”

“Negative, sir.”

Word spread around the base about what was taking place. People came out to watch. Some were standing on the roofs of buildings. A jeep roared up to the Rolls-Royce. A Royal Navy signals rating was behind the wheel. He was frantic almost to the point of full-blown panic but managed to blurt, “The aircrew is unable to recover the towed parachutist, sir.”

Beverly said, “Hop in the jeep, Johnny—let’s go.”

Col. Randal jumped in the back of the jeep with Beverly in the passenger seat. He had no idea what she had in mind. There was no time to ask.

Before they roared off Col. Randal ordered, “Jack, get the two strongest men you can find. Take a jeep and position it on the far end of the airstrip. When Bronc’s plane comes in for landing try to keep up with it long enough to pull the jumper in and cut the static line.”

There was no way that would work but it was the only option he could think of.

“Yes, sir!”

Parked by the hangers next to the control tower were two of the Small Raids Inc. Special Operations Squadron Walruses. Beverly pointed in their direction and ordered the sailor, “Go—NOW!”

The driver floored it.

On flat ground on a stable surface a jeep has good speed. They were screaming down the tarmac. The driver fishtailed up next to one of the Walruses brakes screeching. Beverly jumped out.

"Come on, Johnny."

Two startled mechanics were standing by the Walrus when Beverly, with Col. Randal following right behind, ran past and jumped onboard. They made their way to the cockpit. Not bothering to strap in, Beverly cranked up the engine and immediately got on the radio to the tower.

"Clear the airspace—green light my flight. I'm out of here, boys."

Col. Randal was pretty sure she was not following correct radio procedure and the transmission had not been a request.

The Walrus taxied out onto the runway before receiving an acknowledgment.

The tower radioed, "You are cleared for takeoff—Godspeed, unknown pilot."

By then Beverly was rolling halfway down the strip.

As the little amphibian bi-plane lifted into the sky she outlined her plan—such as it was.

"OK, you go up in the nose, Johnny. I'm going to fly in behind Daddy's plane and ease up to the towed parachutist. You reach out pull him into the cupola.

"Then cut him free."

Thinking this was the worst plan he had ever heard in a career filled with bad ideas, Col. Randal said, "Can do."

What could possibly go wrong?

Beverly radioed her father, Maj. Gen. Blackwell, to explain what she was about to attempt. He reduced his airspeed to 110 miles per hour to give the Walrus a chance to catch up. Col. Randal crawled along the tunnel to the nose of the aircraft. Standing in the open topped cupola with the wind blowing in his face he could see the paratrooper twisting in the slipstream just below the C-47.

Beverly pulled the Walrus in close behind him. So close Col. Randal could see that twenty-four of the twenty-eight canopy lines had snapped—he counted them. Four lines the size of nylon fishing cord were all that was keeping the towed parachutist from plunging to his death.

Chances were they would snap at any second.

As the gap closed turbulence made it impossible for Beverly to get close enough for Col. Randal to reach out for the parachutist. Even after he had climbed most of the way out of the cubicle onto the nose of the fuselage—without having anything to hold on to. It was a long way down and he, he was not wearing a parachute, and had always been afraid of heights.

One after the other Beverly made five failed approaches.

Maj. Gen. Blackwell radioed he was going to gain altitude to three thousand feet in hopes the higher air might be smoother. He also began giving detailed instructions to his daughter on how to shoot her next approach.

Beverly radioed, "Enough, Daddy. You fly your plane. I'll fly mine."

Maj. Gen. Blackwell responded, "Wilco, be advised I have less than five minutes of fuel left—get it done, baby girl."

Standing up in the open-topped cupola on the nose of the Walrus without a safety line, no parachute, and nothing to hold on to, ready to reach out for a dangling paratrooper who was twisting in the slipstream while the two aircraft struggled not to crash into each other was as terrifying an experience as any Col. Randal could remember.

Except possibly his first basket jump from *Bessie,* the balloon at No.1 Parachute School.

That had been pretty bad.

The idea was for him to grab Lt. Mead and pull him into the cupola—only possible because the Walrus was a pusher-type aircraft. The problem was the opening to the cupola was not wide enough for two people to fit through unless standing up straight. And while reaching out to pull the lieutenant in if the two planes suddenly lurched apart there was the real possibility Col. Randal could be jerked out.

An added complication was he was only carrying his Fairbairn Fighting Knife. It sported a long, elegant, double-edged needle point blade. Perfect for sliding between the ribs of a Nazi sentry but not much good for chopping.

He needed a machete.

Beverly said over the intercom, "Here goes! This one's the charm Johnny."

The plane edged in toward the towed paratrooper. Col. Randal could see blood dripping from his helmet. Was he alive or dead?

Lt. Mead's eyes came open.

When Col. Randal reached out Lt. Mead wrapped his arms around him in a bear hug nearly dragging him out of the cupola. With neither hand free his only hope was to try to brace himself with his knees. Keeping in mind all was lost if he dropped the knife.

Then the Walrus hit an air pocket. The nose smashed into the tail assembly of the C-47 inches in front of Col. Randal causing damage to both airplanes. Horrified, he tried to duck down to get away from the impact but Lt. Mead was hanging on for dear life.

Besides, Col. Randal realized if the amphibian was damaged bad enough to crash what good was ducking going to do?

Lt. Mead slammed down onto the top of the fuselage due to a sudden slack in the static line that occurred when the two aircraft collided. He was lying face down, spread eagle with his legs dangling off the port side. Col. Randal was struggling to keep both of them from falling off. Lt. Mead was desperately clutching on.

There was no way to reach the static line to cut it with his knife.

Aboard the C-47 the copilot found a hatchet in the aircraft's Emergency Survival Kit. He whacked the static line as hard as he could and it parted. On the Walrus, Col. Randal managed to slice the four remaining lines.

Lt. Mead was free now but in danger of sliding off the nose and dragging him along.

Beverly radioed, "OK, Daddy, take it to the barn."

Maj. Gen. Blackwell banked away, turning for the airfield. His fuel gauge was flat lining. As he touched down the C-47's motors cut out one after the other.

Beverly followed him down. Up front on the nose Col. Randal and Lt. Mead were hanging on half in and half out of the cupola with only each other to hold onto. As the Walrus rolled to a stop they were still hanging on to each other as hard as they could. Neither man was about to let go.

After Lt. Mead had been taken away in an ambulance Beverly said, "That was intense."

Col. Randal said, "I liked you better as a bathing beauty bimbo—not the superhero you've turned into."

Beverly laughed, "You thought I was a bimbo?"

"Yes I did—affirmative."

"Epic."

"Cut it out, Beverly."

7
WHAT COULD POSSIBLY GO WRONG?

MAJOR GENERAL SAM HOUSTON BLACKWELL SAID, "I'd like to fly A few of your people down to RFHQ. We've got business, Colonel. And not much time to do it in."

Beverly Blackwell said, "Your plane has a damaged aileron it's not airworthy."

Maj. Gen. Blackwell said, "The one you rammed is the duty aircraft I use. My personal VIP C- 47 will be arriving any minute now. Wait till you see it, baby. I had the cabin designed by the interior decorator who did the Rice Hotel in Houston."

Major the Lady Jane Seaborn said, "You have two military aircraft at your disposal, Bronc?"

Maj. Gen. Blackwell said, "I *am* the CO of the United States Army Air Force's Troop Carrier Command. The one I flew in here is my work plane. Wouldn't do to have the Commanding Officer of TTC winging around the country in a beat-up standard-issue C-47 rigged for dropping paratroops and hauling gliders."

Beverly said, "Your plane is hardly beat up."

Maj. Gen. Blackwell said, "It is now after you got through with it. First impressions are important. Especially for the kind of surprise inspections I like to pull. Arrive unannounced and unexpected like a bolt of lightning out of the clear blue. Shock and awe capitalizing on the element of surprise—with a little showmanship like Johnny taught me."

Lady Jane laughed, "I am certainly impressed, Bronc."

"As am I, Lady Jane. You turned out to be everything Beverly and Jack advertised. Drop-dead gorgeous—fun to talk to. I thought they were blowing smoke."

Lady Jane said, "Beverly and Jack said that about me?"

"Yes, ma'am. Now if your cousin Brandy only lives up to half her advanced billing this could turn out to be the beginning of a great relationship for all of us . . . but it'll have to be brief.

"I'm flying out tonight."

Beverly said, "Sorry, Daddy. Brandy's at sea. Not due back for days."

Lady Jane said, "She will be disappointed to have missed you, General."

Colonel John Randal said, "I was hoping to show you our Advanced Base on Castelrozzo, sir."

Maj. Gen. Blackwell said, "Another time Colonel. I'll explain the hurry on the plane. We've got a lot to talk about.

"Heads up, when I fly out tonight you'll be coming with me."

This was news to Col. Randal.

A gleaming, gloss black Skytrain, the official USAAF designation for the C-47—in actual practice nearly always called a Dakota—flew in and landed. Maj. Gen. Blackwell's bucking bronco logo was painted on the nose white on black underneath a large stenciled "BRONC." There was no doubt who the plane belonged to. He thought the white paint looked better against the black than the red letters on his olive drab duty plane—first impressions being important.

Maj. Gen. Blackwell said, "I've got room for ten PAX on the hop down, we don't crowd in a lot of people on the VIP plane. Every seat is first class. Bring Lady Jane and Beverly along. I'd like 'em to see my flying hotel suite."

Col. Randal said, "Wilco."

He walked away to join Lieutenant Colonel Sir Terry "Zorro" Stone, who was talking with Vice Admiral Sir Randolph "Razor" Ransom and Lieutenant Commander Adrian Seligman.

"Sir, General Blackwell is flying a group of us to RFHQ in the next few minutes. He'll be taking off again later tonight for the States. Apparently, I am expected to travel with him."

VAdm. Ransom said, "Not a good time for you to be away, Colonel."

Col. Randal said, "We need to get Colonel Stone, Veronica, and Stephanie back to Castelrozzo ASAP. Would it be possible for you to have one of the Special Operations duty pilots fly them to the island? Beverly's going to be traveling to RFHQ on Bronc's plane."

Lt. Cdr. Seligman said, "I need to return as well."

VAdm. Ransom said, "Certainly. I shall make the arrangements."

Col. Randal said, "Is there any way possible for you to fly to RFHQ with us, Admiral? I'd like you to be on hand to hear what the General has in mind about this trip to the US? If it's not urgent I need you to intervene to keep me here, sir."

VAdm. Ransom said, "Good thinking, Colonel this is no time for you to be absent from your post."

After consulting with the rest of the group about their plans two seats were still open on Bronc's VIP flight. Col. Randal made eye contact with Captain Billy Jack Jaxx. He was standing with Captain Roy Kidd at the ice barrels drinking beer and swapping war stories with the Rangers.

The two came over.

Col. Randal said, “General Blackwell’s flying people to RFHQ as soon as his plane finishes refueling. You two be on board. We may have an opportunity for a CARD GAME later in Lady Jane’s suite. Roy, first opportunity I want a briefing on your actions following our drop on Benevento.”

Lieutenant General “Geronimo” Joe McKoy, VAdm. Ransom, Brigadier Dudley Clarke, Cuthbert Bowlby, James “Baldie” Taylor, Lady Jane, Waldo Treywick, Capt. Jaxx, Capt. Kidd and Beverly boarded Maj. Gen. Blackwell’s shiny black C-47 for the short hop to RFHQ. The interior of the aircraft was South Texas meets Art Deco at Neiman Marcus.

The result was surprisingly tasteful oozing masculine opulence.

Oversized yellow ostrich leather bucket seats with mahogany armrests, a golden Oriental carpet running the length of the aisle, elegant theater lights along the interior bulkheads and plenty of room. Toward the rear, there was even a conversation area with bench seats.

Absent were steer horns, six shooters for handles on the overhead bins, saddles, lariats or big silver belt buckles. This was cattleman chic, not faux cowboy. There is a difference.

Lady Jane said, “Love your plane, Bronc, in a way it reminds me of my father’s gunroom when I was a little girl—my favorite place.”

Red the Flying Clipper Girl stepped out of the sleeping compartment in the tail of the plane.

This was an unexpected development.

Maj. Gen. Blackwell said, “The two of us met on a commercial Clipper flight outta London. Got to talking and discovered we had mutual friends. I've been trying to recruit Red to join up and be a WAC ever since. I want her to be my senior VIP flight attendant."

Beverly said, "How's that working out?"

"Not having much luck she's a hard bargainer."

Red said, "We worked out an arrangement for me to fly a few long-distance flights aboard his VIP plane on loan from BOAC. A reverse 'Hands Across the Sea.' In a small way."

Col. Randal knew the stunning Clipper Girl was MI-6. He wondered if Maj. Gen. Blackwell did. Was the British Secret Intelligence Service keeping an eye on the USAAF?

Probably.

Maj. Gen. Blackwell said, "Nothing I'd rather do than sit and visit with you, Lady Jane, but I'm going to need some alone time with the Colonel."

Lady Jane flashed one of her heart-attack smiles, "My loss."

Maj. Gen. Blackwell said, "We'll get together in a few, Colonel."

The pilot announced over the intercom, "Prepare for takeoff."

Maj. Gen. Blackwell made his way down the aisle to where Beverly and Capt. Jaxx were sitting. "Go ride with Red in the back, baby. Me and the Captain need to talk some football."

Beverly laughed. "Have fun."

Maj. Gen. Blackwell said, "Whose picture you carrying in your pistol grip these days, Jack?"

Capt. Jaxx drew his 1911 Colt .38 Super from his shoulder holster, spun it over, and presented the handgun to Bronc, butt first. "Round in the chamber, sir—hammer's down."

Jack Cool.

"Roger—that ain't the recommended method of carry, son."

Maj. Gen. Blackwell checked out the more than semi-nude photo of SS Hauptsturmführer Gretchen von Coffenhauser, "Holy Moses..."

Capt. Jaxx said, "Col. Randal shot her."

"You joking?"

"Negative, sir, long story short—in a recent development indications are the Hauptsturmführer may not be dead. There's a possibility Gretchen's behind the Brandenburger raid on Castelrozzo. Some believe she could have sent the Brandenburger Sea Raiders to kidnap Colonel Randal."

"That true?"

"Don't know yet, sir."

Maj. Gen. Blackwell said, "What's Lady Jane have to say about the late, or maybe not so late, Miss von Coffenhauser?"

Capt. Jaxx said, "She's been pretty forgiving of the Colonel's past track record with women. Remind me sometimes I'll show you a bootleg copy of the security report SOE Cairo generated on him when he first came out to Egypt, sir. They ran a boatload of hookers at him to see if he'd talk—great read."

Maj. Gen. Blackwell said, "Make sure you do, Jack—that's an order."

"Wilco."

When the plane reached cruising altitude Maj. Gen. Blackwell moved up to the front to sit with Col. Randal. He and Capt. Jaxx had talked nonstop. But they never made it around to the subject of Texas Longhorns football.

Maj. Gen. Blackwell said, "On the subject of you going to work for me full time, Colonel. You're not interested. I respect that. But I don't give up once I've set my sights on something."

Col. Randal said, "That's what Beverly tells me, sir."

Maj. Gen. Blackwell said, "I've got a new offer I've cleared with General Donovan. I'll appoint you to be my Troop Carrier

Command's Paratroop Advisor. The assignment will be 'on call,' meaning when a parachute drop's pending you come in on TDY.

"You'll be my airborne forced entry architect with worldwide responsibilities. I'm offering you a seat at the big table with the Army's senior war planners. Your job will be to work with the unit or units committed to any parachute operation TTC is tasked to support. You'll assist with the airhead planning to include, but not be limited to, selection of drop zones. Unit commanders will be required to have the Troop Transport Command Paratroop Advisor, meaning you, sign off on their Airborne Landing Plan or I refuse to fly the mission.

"Your work is done once the jump takes place. You'll be released to return to Raiding Forces. I'll fly you back VIP class aboard this plane.

"'Right Man, Right Job.' What's your take, Colonel?"

Col. Randal said, "I can do that, sir."

Maj. Gen. Blackwell said, "All right then. This is going to work good. Here's what you need to know right now, this minute. After the Sicily drop, Eisenhower wrote General Marshall a memo. It said, and this is pretty much a direct quote, 'I do not believe in the airborne division. It is too difficult to control . . . '

"That's a problem since the army already has the 11th, 13th, 17th, 82nd, and 101st airborne divisions.

"The Chief of Staff ordered the Commander of Army Ground Forces, General McNair—the man who authorized the formation of airborne divisions in the first place—to come up with a recommendation on what action to take as a result of Ike's memo."

Col. Randal said, "Do you have any idea what General Marshall's take is, sir?"

Maj. Gen. Blackwell said, "Off the record but made known to me Marshall has privately indicated to McNair he places a great deal of weight on Eisenhower's opinion.

"Now here is where it starts to get interesting. We have a witches' brew of opinions, hurt feelings, reputations, egos, ambitions and high-level military/political gamesmanship. McNair's bitter because Marshall passed him over for Eisenhower's job. He wants to stick it in Ike's eye, and Marshall's too by demonstrating they don't know what they're talking about.

"Which they don't on this subject. Every major power in the world is raising airborne divisions as fast as they can stand 'em up. Why General Eisenhower sees it any different doesn't make much sense. May have something to do with the fact he's never actually commanded so much as a platoon in combat. Who's to say?

"My personal impression of Ike is favorable—all I know is he's off base on this one."

Col. Randal said, "The 82nd's jump on Sicily saved the beachhead from being overrun on the first day, General. It may not have been a parade-ground-perfect exercise but Colonel Gavin's Five-o-Five disrupted the German's counterattack. The drop was so scattered it confused the other side as to our actual intent and gave General Patton time to get established ashore."

Maj. Gen. Blackwell said, "Make sure you say that at the appropriate time."

"Yes, sir."

Maj. Gen. Blackwell said, "You know Eisenhower?"

"Negative, sir."

"Well, he knows you," Maj. Gen. Blackwell said. "I was in a senior command meeting following the 575th Ranger Force jump on Benevento when your name came up. General

Eisenhower said, "Randal . . . isn't he the officer who cut off Smiling Jack's head and mailed it to my secretary in Manila?"

"General Eisenhower said that?"

"Who's Smiling Jack?"

"A Huk bandit."

Maj. Gen. Blackwell said, "You may have yourself a Supreme Allied Forces Commander issue, Johnny."

Col. Randal said, "That going to be a problem for you, sir?"

"Hell no . . . forget Eisenhower. He's got his own troubles—as in a big plateful of egg headed straight at his face."

"Sir?"

Maj. Gen. Blackwell said, "General McNair selected General Swing, the commander of the 11th Airborne Division, to evaluate the concept of airborne division-sized units in response to Ike's memo to Marshall. The idea being to determine if Army Ground Forces should retain them for deployment overseas in their current role, convert them to standard line infantry divisions or break them up to use as individual replacements.

"Swing set up what is called the 'Swing Board.' It's brief, laid out by McNair, is to conduct a review and then a field training exercise to test their findings. Marshall and Eisenhower were blindsided. They expected the Commander of Army Ground Forces to rubber stamp Ike's recommendation—not convene a committee they have no control over."

Col. Randal said, "How does this affect us, sir?"

Maj. Gen. Blackwell said, "Well, without airborne divisions to drop there's not much of a combat role for Troop Transport Command. It will become nothing more than the Army's airline. That's not going to work for me. I'll resign my commission, head back to South Texas, raise beef and watch my oil wells produce.

"Both are reserved occupations so there's nothing the Army or the Draft Board can do to stop me. I'll be 4F."

Col. Randal said, “I can’t see you sitting out the war, sir. What’s your next move?”

Maj. Gen. Blackwell said, “We’re flying to Camp Mackall this very night. Then, starting tomorrow or the next day we’ll both have seats on the Swing Board. At least until we can get our opinions on the official record.”

Col. Randal said, “You believe our input will be enough, sir?”

Maj. Gen. Blackwell said, “Yeah, should be. McNair makes the final decision and he’s not about to admit he made a mistake. Swing’s not going to recommend disbanding his own 11th Airborne Division. Ridgway’s being flown in from Italy to be on the panel—can’t see him standing down the 82nd.

“The other combat arms board members are all airborne division commanders, senior paratroop or glider infantry officers not likely to vote themselves out of a job. The rest are my senior TTC people — votes are in my pocket.

“I’d say we’ve got the deck stacked.”

Col. Randal said, “That does sound like a plan.”

CAPTAIN BUTCH “HEADHUNTER” HOOLIHAN WAS aboard Brandy Seaborn’s MAS boat. It was tied off along the shore of the lightly inhabited Halki Island, population 325. The island was seventy miles from Symi. It was one of the over 1,400 islands in the Aegean and being so small and remote not much was known about the place. With nightfall the netting that had concealed the two boats in the squadron all day was taken down. Lieutenant Theodore “The Great Teddy” Hamilton was along on the mission to supervise the squadron’s camouflage and he had made the MAS boats virtually disappear.

Hey, Presto!

They were preparing to execute the second stage of the operation. Lieutenant Randy "Hornblower" Seaborn was outlining the next evolution. The mission was to extract the Long Range Desert Patrol's six-man S1 Patrol under the command of Captain Alan Redfern. It had been on Symi conducting a Coast Watch mission reporting on Kregsmarine traffic for the last two weeks.

A larger Special Boat Section detachment under the command of Captain Ian "Jock" Lapraik was based in Symi Town at the other end of the twenty-two-square mile island. They were not part of tonight's mission. The SBS had its own transport caiques commandeered from the Italians stationed in the town.

It was not known if Germans were currently present on the island though rumor had it they had sent a reconnaissance element to spy out the state of the Italian defenses. In the event enemy troops were on Symi a fight was a real possibility. The Royal Marines had come prepared for such a contingency.

Capt. Hoolihan was not going home without the LRDG Coastwatchers.

As an added complication it was known that Italian soldiers stationed on Symi prior to the armistice were still there. Italy was no longer an Axis Power and the Nazis were known to be executing Italian officers. They would likely want to be taken off the island.

And that was a problem.

Lt. Seaborn said, "The last thing we want is to be transporting additional passengers back to Castelrozzo, Butch. If you encounter any of our former enemies who attempt to attach themselves to your patrol discourage the idea with all necessary force. When you locate the LRDG Coastwatcher team ashore bring them straight on board as quickly as possible. Maybe we can get away from the island before the Italians realize what is taking place.

"We need to conform to what Colonel Randal always says, with alacrity—'Get the hell out of Dodge.'"

Capt. Hoolihan said, "My favorite part of any mission."

Brandy said, "Our best defense is speed. We want to be able to outrun Kriegsmarine patrol boats if necessary. Try really hard not to overload our MAS boats with extra passengers tonight."

Capt. Hoolihan said, "I hear you loud and clear, Mrs. Seaborn."

Brandy laughed. "One of the reasons I enjoy sailing with you, Butch, you take directions so well."

Capt. Hoolihan was not sure if that was a compliment or not.

Things started going wrong almost immediately. Voice communications with the Coast Watch team could not be established. That could be for any number of reasons. Possibly the operators had disassembled their U.S. manufactured Collins 18M Transmitter/ Receiver Field Set radio to make the trek to the extraction point. Hopefully, that was the case.

Because it was the only scenario with a happy ending.

Tonight was what is described in military terms as a "hasty" mission. On hasty missions unknown variables are the norm. That is why it is critical for the right officer to command the ground element. One who could be depended on to adapt to changing circumstances and not be rattled by surprise developments.

For they would surely come.

Capt. Hoolihan was arguably the most experienced raiding small unit leader in the Royal Marines. He was certainly one of the most decorated. While there is no such thing as business as usual on a high-risk clandestine operation, for the Headhunter tonight was pretty much business as usual.

Dangerous mission. Zero intel. Far behind enemy lines—no support available.

Capt. Hoolihan opted for a Col. Randal quote of his own, "Let's do this."

ONE HOUR AFTER MAJOR GENERAL SAM HOUSTON Blackwell's VIP C-47 touched down at the RAF landing strip near Raiding Forces Headquarters Colonel John Randal called for a CARD GAME. Notified to be present were Lieutenant General "Geronimo" Joe McKoy, Major the Lady Jane Seaborn, Captain Billy Jack Jaxx, Captain Roy Kidd, Beverly Blackwell, and Waldo. The other players were all elsewhere on other business.

Captain Preston Butterfield III was at RFHQ when Col. Randal and his entourage arrived. While a CARD GAME plank holder because of his expertise with diamonds he was not a participant in its strategy sessions serving in more of an advisory capacity. Flanigan, at the security desk outside the door to Lady Jane's third-floor suite, was given a verbal list of attendees.

No one else would be allowed in.

Vice Admiral Sir Randolph "Razor" Ransom and James "Baldie" Taylor were pressed into service to take Maj. Gen. Blackwell to dinner at the Gezira Club in Cairo. Lady Jane had one of her Royal Marines chauffer them in her Rolls-Royce. When he heard about it Cuthbert Bowlby phoned Brigadier Raymond "R. J." Maunsell, and the two decided to join them at the Gezira.

As they were preparing to depart Lady Jane said, "General, I understand you and John are flying to North Carolina later tonight."

"We are."

"Would you mind terribly if Beverly and I came along?"

Maj. Gen. Blackwell said, "Love to have the both of you Lady Jane. Unfortunately, the Carolina Hotel where we have reservations is booked solid. There's a tidal wave of big brass about to descend on Pinehurst for the conference we're attending. Even the BOQ at Camp Mackall is out of rooms and that includes those always set aside for general officers."

Lady Jane said, "If I can arrange hotel accommodations we are welcome then?"

"Yes ma'am, you are but . . ."

Lady Jane laughed. "Enjoy your dinner Bronc. I shall alert Beverly to start packing. What time is wheels up?"

Maj. Gen. Blackwell said, "I'd say as soon as I get back from Cairo. If you need a little longer that's not a problem. The plane takes off when we get there.

"Keep in mind we may end up sleeping out back of the hotel in a tent."

"Perfect."

Maj. Gen. Blackwell said, "Explain to me again why you, the Colonel, and Beverly can't come to dinner tonight?"

Lady Jane laughed. "That is classified I could tell you but then . . ."

Maj. Gen. Blackwell said, "Let me get this straight. Beverly's going to be in a meeting I don't possess clearance for or have the 'Need to Know' to attend?"

"Correct, General."

"I turned my head and that pretty little girl grew up."

"Yes, she did."

"Yeah, well that feels like a kick in the stomach."

CARD GAME convened in Lady Jane's suite at RFHQ at the appointed time.

Col. Randal said, "I'll be flying out for the States later tonight so Jane I'm counting on you to brief Pam, King, Mandy, and the Sergeant Major on everything we cover here."

Lady Jane said, "Beverly and I shall be traveling with you."

Col. Randal said, "In that case General McKoy you fill 'em in."

"Can do, John."

Col. Randal said, "I'll make this short and simple in compliance with our standing orders. The President ordered General McKoy to focus his attention on LEAF EATER. A couple of things to be aware of and they're both significant: First, the President not only has personal knowledge of our diamond interdiction operation he shows a special interest in it. Second, he wants us to give it our full attention—maximum priority.

"That being the case effective immediately General McKoy will be taking charge of LEAF EATER. I'll remain as the chairman of CARD GAME. I'd appreciate it if you keep me advised on developments, General."

Lt. Gen. McKoy said, "Hold on a minute, John . . ."

Col. Randal said, "I have accepted a reoccurring assignment to work for General Blackwell as the Troop Transport Command's Paratroop Advisor. What that means is I'll be away for brief periods at times. On top of our raiding program requiring more and more of my attention that means now's the time for me to hand off LEAF EATER to our most qualified officer.

"Make it happen, General—by order of the President."

Lt. Gen. McKoy said, "This ain't how I want things to go down, John."

Col. Randal said, "Consolidate all LEAF EATER subordinate operations, the Congo, Morocco, The Three and taking down smugglers out of Cairo. Everyone reports to you. All reports and recommendations flow through you.

"Is that clear?"

The CARD GAME members were taken off guard by the development.

"Clear."

It was said good officers do, great officers delegate. Col. Randal was known for his ability to delegate; however, this seemed different. Who would walk away from an assignment the President of the United States was personally monitoring?

The answer was no one interested in advancing their service career.

Col. Randal said, "We have LEAF EATER diamond interdiction and FIRE EATER for operations in the Aegean. They're too much alike. We need a new name for LEAF EATER. Since Waldo's dinosaur is supposed to have a long neck I thought LONG NECK might work—your call, General."

Lt. Gen. McKoy said, "Got a good ring to it. I like it. What do you think, Waldo?"

Waldo said, "Wish I was drinking one."

Capt. Jaxx said, "That's a Rodge."

Col. Randal said, "I've been thinking about LONG NECK. We've all had questions we're never going to get answers for. Where I am on the operation is we've got our marching orders. We need to salute, drive on and continue the mission.

"President Roosevelt's personal interest confirms LONG NECK has national security implications—that's enough for me."

Capt. Jaxx said, "Roger that sir."

Capt. Kidd said, "Affirmative."

Waldo said, “Answers are probably above our pay grade anyway. Still, the whole deal don’t make much sense. Nobody wantin’ us to turn in the diamonds we recover —not that I’m complainin.’”

Lt. Gen. McKoy said, “What part of ‘drive on and continue the mission’ don’t you get, Waldo?”

“I’m just sayin’. . .”

Lt. Gen. McKoy said, “We’ll get the job done, John—count on it.”

Lady Jane laughed. “Bring me the sparklers.”

Beverly said, “Exactly.”

IT WAS PITCH DARK. NO MOON. BRANDY LED THE MAS boats on the run over to Symi at max speed. Lieutenant Randy “Hornblower” Seaborn, standing with her on the bridge, shared his mother’s love for going fast. The two of them held to the theory that the less time spent in the open sea in enemy-controlled waters the less opportunity there was for a chance encounter with the Kriegsmarine.

That concept may or may not have been valid but it sounded good. Many successful small boat commanders preferred a more cautious method . . . traveling at slow speed, not leaving a wake or creating phosphorescence, sneaking in and out of places, taking time. A strategy that placed heavy reliance on patience and stealth.

It was not that Lt. Seaborn shunned surreptitious approaches altogether. They had their place. Just not out in the open sea. Once the squadron was within three miles of Symi he would order a reduction in speed. Then two miles out another with additional decreases as the squadron made landfall.

By the time they closed with the island the boats would almost be idling.

Hornblower had been on more clandestine missions to insert or extract intelligence agents—known in the trade for some reason as "false nose jobs"—than any small boat commander currently serving in the Royal Navy. The same was true for pinprick Commando raiding parties. And he had been a "run and gun" specialist in his MGB 345 shooting up fixed targets ashore or enemy convoys driving along the 1,200-mile Via Balbia coastal road in Libya at night.

The way he was maneuvering the squadron tonight was based on experience not reckless adventurism. Which is what it felt like to Captain Butch "Headhunter" Hoolihan's heavily armed Royal Marines onboard. Screaming across the waves deep in enemy waters in the dark of night aboard a military speed boat pounding toward unknown danger is not for the faint of heart.

Small-scale amphibious Commando raiding is best left to those who can master their fears, live in the moment and do the next right thing whatever that might be. Iron discipline and the ability to function under extreme duress as a part of a team are a must. The ability to shoot straight in limited light is a plus.

The navigating officer said, "Any time, Lieutenant."

Hornblower glanced at his mother. "Skipper."

Brandy rang the signal to reduce speed.

Capt. Hoolihan had limited information at his disposal about the LRDG team he was going ashore to extract. He knew:

- S1 Patrol had been fired on by Italians when they initially landed—a friendly fire incident it was said. The Italian lieutenant in command of the unit doing the shooting apologized. The LRDG had been mistaken for Germans—which may have been true.

- S1 Patrol was billeted in a remote monastery at the invitation of the Greek abbot.
- The LRDG's Collins 18M Transmitter/Receiver radio was set up on top of a mountain a forty-five-minute climb away from the abbey. The choice of location for the radio station gave the operators the ability to observe Symi Town and a distant view of German-occupied Rhodes.

All the LRDG's training at the Mountain Warfare School at Cedars in Lebanon was being put to the test on this mission. The Long Range Desert Group's transition from Road Watch to Coast Watch had been intensive with a high washout rate of the old hands. The operators were required to master new skills like parachuting, mountain climbing and signaling techniques not needed previously.

That said reconnaissance was their game.

No one was better at it.

CAPTAIN BILLY JACK JAXX RODE TO THE AIRFIELD with Colonel John Randal, Major the Lady Jane Seaborn, and Beverly Blackwell in Lady Jane's Rolls-Royce. Major General Sam Houston Blackwell's VIP Dakota was standing by on the flight line. The plane's motors were running.

Col. Randal briefed Capt. Jaxx nonstop for the entire ride.

"Have one of the Special Duties pilots fly you to Castelrozzo as soon as possible. Take Captain Kidd with you. Everyone on the island wants to kill Brandenburgers—that's fine. Keep as many search parties in the field as possible. But what I want is for you and Roy to organize two Quick Reaction Teams to respond to the intelligence Mandy develops."

Capt. Jaxx said, "Wilco."

Col. Randal said, "Work with Mandy—you two try to get along. She provides targets. You and Roy react to them."

Capt. Jaxx said, "What about Captain Chatterhorn and the other teams? They'll want in too, sir."

Col. Randal said, "They're to continue the pattern grid searches. No one needs to know priority of intelligence dissemination other than Colonel Stone. Keep him in the loop at all times.

"Is that clear?"

"Perfectly, sir."

"And Jack, try really hard to capture another walking, talking Brandenburger. We need to develop an idea about the Germans original intentions. I'll have to be away for at least a week so I'm counting on you, stud."

Capt. Jaxx said, "We'll get you a prisoner, Colonel."

Col. Randal said, "Something bothering you?"

"You're not being transferred out of Raiding Forces are you, sir?"

"Negative, but if I was I'd take you with me—you have my word."

Maj. Gen. Blackwell was waiting on the tarmac outside the plane. The passengers' luggage was carried on board. Red was standing by in the cabin to assist everyone. The navigator was waiting beside the door to the flight deck. Once everyone was seated Bronc stuck a finger up in the air and made a circle. The navigator ducked back inside the cockpit to relay the command.

The C-47 started to taxi.

Lady Jane rested her head on Col. Randal's shoulder, "This is fun."

He was always amazed at how little it took to entertain her.

ON SYMI, CAPTAIN ALAN REDFERN, THE commander of the LRDG team, had his hands full. The fifty-man Italian garrison in nearby Panormitis was in a near state of panic ever since news had arrived of the German invasion of Kos, fifty-eight miles away. Word of the Germans executing Italian officers *en masse* was also known which did nothing for his allies' spirits.

Also bad for Italian morale was the fact the Greeks on the island wanted to kill them because of their brutal occupation. Given the chance, they would.

On Rhodes, forty miles away, there was an increase in Luftwaffe air traffic. Enemy planes could be seen patrolling the Rhodes Channel. The activity was a clear indication Nazis would be coming to Symi soon.

The night previous the Italian officers held a farewell dinner for themselves at the monastery. They were not going anywhere. This was more of a "we who are about to die" type of wake in advance of the funeral.

The depressed officers were imagining the worst to come.

In the middle of the meal an alarm was raised that the Germans were in the building. Shots were fired. Panic ensued. Convinced the LRDG was being overrun Capt. Redfern rushed to his room and burned his papers including the names and addresses of all the contacts on Symi and Rhodes.

Then he discovered it was a false alarm.

The next day, knowing that Raiding Forces was sending boats to evacuate his LRDG operators later that night, Capt. Redfern decided to transfer the fifty demoralized Italian soldiers to Symi Town, where preparations were underway for the main defense of the island. He wanted to prevent them from interfering with the extraction of his team. The troops had departed aboard caiques by the time Lieutenant Randy "Hornblower" Seaborn and his two-boat squadron arrived.

Unfortunately Capt. Redfern had been forced to sail with the Italians to give them the courage to go. His plan was to travel to Symi Town, drop off the passengers, then return. The idea was to arrive back in time to be extracted with his LRDG S-1 teammates.

This was as bad as a plan can get for the extraction of a Coast Watch or any other type of team from hostile territory. It was dependent on split-second timing and luck. Separating the leader from the team to be pulled is the worst of all possible ideas.

What could possibly go wrong—everything!

In what had to be a minor military miracle the extraction went like clockwork—almost.

An unhappy Captain Butch "Headhunter" Hoolihan was standing on the beach with the LRDG Coastwatchers team. The operators were reluctant to leave without their team leader. A caique appeared out of the dark with its diesel engine going *bong, bong, bong*—slid into shore and a man stepped out.

Capt. Hoolihan said, "Captain Redfern, I presume?"

"Affirmative."

Capt. Hoolihan said, "We are ready to depart Captain. Your people's gear has been stowed aboard the MAS boats. The men did not want to depart until your return. Not me—we were pulling out in another five minutes with or without you."

Capt. Redfern said, "Sorry it took so long there was no other option but for me to go. On our approach to Symi Town we heard machine gun fire. I put in to obtain information from the local

Greeks. The Nazis have landed and an attack is under way as we speak.

"The Italians were put ashore and placed in the care of a detachment of SBS troops setting up defensive positions outside the village. I only came back here to pick up my team. We shall be going back to help Captain Lapraik. Jock has twenty-six SBS men in Symi Town and I have no intention of leaving them behind to be killed or captured."

Capt. Hoolihan said, "You know Germans have landed. You have no idea in what strength. And you want to stay on Symi and fight it out—sure about that?"

Capt. Redfern said, "Anticipating the likelihood of a German invasion at some point I made arrangements with the local Greeks to set up a series of supply caches down the length of the island in the event a guerrilla campaign in the hills became a necessity.

"We shall stay on as long as it takes to disengage all British troops from Symi Town. Then we can leapfrog back down the mountainous spine of the island carrying out a fighting withdrawal. My plan is to fall back to the caiques we prepositioned at the far uninhabited end of the island for just such a contingency."

Capt. Redfern knew Capt. Hoolihan by reputation. Everyone in the Middle East did. The Headhunter was a legendary Raiding Forces officer. Aware of his experience in the Abyssinian Campaign Capt. Redfern was hoping to appeal to the Headhunter's instinct as guerrilla warfare expert.

Capt. Hoolihan said, "You secreted an adequate number of caiques to bring everyone out at the end of the day?"

"Over twenty."

"Stand by."

Capt. Hoolihan waded out to where Lieutenant Randy "Hornblower" Seaborn's MAS boat was anchored. Once onboard he huddled with his naval counterpart, Lt. Seaborn and Brandy. The two Seaborns did not like what he proposed.

Brandy said, "Have you lost your mind, Butch?"

Lt. Seaborn said, "My orders are to extract the LRDG Coast Watch Team."

Capt. Hoolihan said, "Once at sea naval regulations authorize the officer in command to modify the mission's orders due to exigent circumstances."

Brandy Seaborn said, "No, Randy . . ."

Lt. Seaborn said, "Ditch Redfern's caique. Load his LRDG people aboard this boat. We shall patrol down the coastline to Symi Town in order to investigate the report of a German landing to pass on to Small Raids Inc. Once there in the event you choose to put your Royal Marines ashore that is your decision.

"Understand if you do Butch this squadron shall be returning to Castelrozzo at flank speed the instant they disembark. At that point you will be on your own.

"No one is coming back here anytime soon."

"Fair enough."

Brandy said, "Speaking strictly as your mother, Randy, you are a total idiot."

MAJOR THE LADY JANE SEABORN, BEVERLY Blackwell and Red the Flying Clipper Girl were playing cards in the conversation area at the back of the VIP Dakota. Major General Sam Houston Blackwell and Colonel John Randal were sitting together talking—for hours.

Maj. Gen. Blackwell requested a complete top-to-bottom briefing on Raiding Forces activities from the first Keystone Cops Commando raid two weeks after the British Expeditionary Force's return from Dunkirk to the latest news on the Brandenburger raid on Castelrozzo. Mostly he listened. But from time to time Bronc asked short penetrating questions indicating a deep professional interest in all things military—and in particular concerning the evolution of Raiding Forces.

There were a couple of reasons for his line of inquiry.

The United States Army had zero Special Operations capability. No one knew how to conduct them or how to integrate Special Forces into conventional operations. And no one seemed inclined to learn. The 1st Ranger Battalion had been raised to be the U.S. version of British Commandos—temporarily. The plan was then, after gaining experience, the unit would be disbanded. The Rangers were to be scattered around conventional units arriving in the UK from the States to share their newly acquired skills in order to bring up the standard of training.

That had not happened but now the 1st Ranger Battalion was fighting in Italy being misused as light infantry by senior commanders who did not understand how to take advantage of the Rangers unique skill sets.

The War Department's primary concern was to raise large conventional units. A lot of them fast—100 divisions. With such rapid expansion undreamed-of promotions were in reach for officers who had spent the inter-war years stuck in grade.

Big was in.

Small, as in Ranger Battalions, independent parachute infantry battalions or regiments, meant no promotion past the rank of colonel. So there was not a great deal of motivation to study the concept of Special Operations since there were no general's stars to be had.

But Bronc saw possibilities.

Maj. Gen. Blackwell said, "You've got a large Area of Operations with anywhere from twelve hundred to fifteen hundred islands to raid—no one seems to be sure of the exact number. There's no U.S. support and only limited backing from Great Britain. All up with the SAS, LRDG, and GSS you say Raiding Forces only has slightly over six hundred men. The majority of those, consisting of the 575th Parachute Infantry Regiment and the 10th Ranger Battalion—styled, "Ranger Force", are still behind the lines in Italy fighting their way out.

"The numbers don't work—at least I can't see it, even if all your men make it back, which they won't.

"What's your plan, Johnny?"

Col. Randal said, "After conferring with General McKoy and Waldo Treywick the consensus was we …meaning I—needed to turn a lemon into lemonade, sir."

Maj. Gen. Blackwell said, "So, how do you intend to do that, exactly?"

Col. Randal said, "The Constant Pressure Concept . . ."

LIEUTENANT RANDY "HORNBLOWER" SEABORN, sailing in the lead MAS boat, heard machine gun fire the same as Captain Alan Redfern had on his first approach to Symi Town. As his little squadron continued on he spotted a caique in the Symi Channel—it made off.

As he was about to order the second MAS boat to break formation and give chase another larger caique appeared from behind a small island and bore down on the squadron firing a 20mm cannon.

Brandy Seaborn ordered, "Guns!"

The Thunderbolt on her boat was already trained on the caique awaiting the orders. Guns pressed the butterfly trigger. Four 20mm cannons and six .50 caliber machine guns roared to life.

No wooden vessel can stand up to that kind of concentrated fire.

Guns swept the caique from left to right utilizing his signature paint brush stroke. In seconds it was dead in the water. The enemy craft turned to kindling in a heartbeat. It started burning.

There were no signs of life onboard.

Lt. Seaborn said to his mother, “Nicely done, Skipper.”

The other smaller caique that had run away came about and pulled alongside. It was the LS7 belonging to Levant Schooner Flotilla Greek Sacred Squadron Commander Andreas Londos. After a hurried discussion, Captain Butch “Headhunter” Hoolihan, the remainder of his men, Capt. Redfern and his eight LRDG operators transferred to LS7, leaving ten Royal Marines behind on the MAS boats as security.

The two MAS boats came about kicking up rooster tails of water in their wake as they headed for the open sea and home. LS7 continued toward Symi Town. Capt. Redfern and Capt. Butch Hoolihan pumped Cdr. Londos for information relating to the invasion but he did not have much to tell.

Capt. Redfern said, “Put me ashore short of the port with one of my people. We can move overland to reconnoiter the village. Wait here Headhunter until I send for you. Best to find out what we are facing before going in.”

Capt. Hoolihan said, “Time spent on reconnaissance is rarely wasted.”

Capt. Redfern said, “We tend to say that quite a lot ourselves in the LRDG.”

LS7 made its way to shore. Capt. Redfern and one of his operators disembarked. Minutes later as they were making their way along the beach they were spotted by a passing SBS caique. Fortunately, the boat's crew recognized them as British instead of opening fire.

The caique took the two LRDG operators aboard and transported them the rest of the way to Symi Town to confer with Captain Ian "Jock" Lapraik, the SBS's commanding officer. Capt. Redfern was pleased to find his counterpart in high spirits even though the Germans were ashore in force.

In force being a relative term—it was a tiny battle.

Capt. Lapraik said, "The Nazis arrived in Perdi Bay aboard a German-flagged Greek schooner this morning. Initially no one fired on them because we believed they were ours. Then as the landing developed Italian Fascists loyal to Hitler moved ahead of the main body with loudspeakers calling on our Italian troops not to fire.

"Naturally we shot them all down—the fools."

The only thing clear at this point was the situation in the waters and onshore around Symi Town was in a stalemate. The Germans occupied a ridge overlooking the town but they were not doing much and did not seem disposed to move out of their position. Three SBS emplacements had their position triangulated and were firing on them.

Capt. Redfern sent the SBS caique back to bring LS7 to their location.

As soon as it arrived Capt. Hoolihan led his troops ashore. At this stage of the battle twenty additional Royal Marines Commandos plus the eight LRDG operators were a major reinforcement. They were immediately inserted into the battle line.

Capt. Hoolihan took in the situation at a glance. Symi was one of the most picturesque islands in the Dodecanese chain—rugged terrain. The Germans had established themselves on the crest of the ridge above the village. Not the military crest which was a mistake an experienced commander would not make—worth noting.

The SBS, LRDG, the Italians, and now his Royal Marines held the port itself. While the Nazis occupied the high ground they could not accomplish their mission unless they came down and took the town. Taking the high ground is usually a tactically sound maneuver. However in this case the high ground was a bald ridge in full sight of the Symi Town defenders.

Knowing only the basics about tactics is dangerous.

The Germans were being picked off one by one.

The only option the Nazis had was to infiltrate patrols into the town. They were too weak in numbers—approximately ninety men before the sniping began, to conduct a full-scale assault of the built-up area.

That plan was not without risks.

The Royal Marines, SBS, LRDG and Italians blocked every street and every alley forcing the Nazis to fight to make entry. And, they would have to come down across open ground in broad daylight to reach the village in order to try to fight their way in.

Civilians in the area were posting alerts every time a German patrol moved off the ridge. The Greeks would hang white flags out a window on the far friendly side of the home or building they were occupying directly opposite of where the enemy was sighted to signal their approach.

White flags generally indicate a willingness to surrender. Normal rules of engagement stipulate they should not be misused. However in the Aegean no one was adhering to the Geneva Convention.

Besides, white pillowcases were all the locals had to make flags with.

Once a flag went up indicating a target, all guns engaged delivering massive firepower—.50 caliber machine guns, Italian manned 20mm, and 40mm antiaircraft cannons lowered to be employed in the ground defense mode.

After having an opportunity to evaluate the situation Capt. Hoolihan pulled his Royal Marines out of the fighting line to create a Reaction Force under his personal command. Now, as soon as a white flag went up, he rushed his team to the location and put in a counterattack.

The Royal Marines had the advantage in this kind of fighting over the German invaders who seemed incapable of establishing a coordinated base of fire.

The Marines were heavily armed with automatic weapons. They were highly experienced in conducting brief intense engagements at close range where establishing fire superiority was key. Capt. Hoolihan assigned two .30 caliber AN/M2 (aircraft) Browning Light Machine Gun "Stingers,"—purpose-built to U.S. Marine Corp 1st Para-Marine Battalion specs, to the Reaction Force. The rest of the Royal Marines on the team were armed with in theatre, armory modified to Colt Monitor specifications, .30 BARs, aka Baby BARS, or the submachine gun of their choice.

Following one firefight with a German patrol Capt. Hoolihan amused his Marines by lighting a cigarette off the red hot barrel of his .45 M1928 Thompson submachine gun—the Headhunter's long-service individual weapon from his first day in Raiding Forces.

The battle raged all morning. As time went by Symi Town's defenders began to gain confidence. The Royal Marines mouse-trapped from house to house to get at the Nazis who came down off the ridge and made it into the village, moving through holes they knocked in the walls with sledgehammers—demolitions being in short supply.

Momentum shifted away from the numerically superior Germans.

Street fighting was not something the Royal Marine Commandos, LRDG or SBS had much experience with. But they were picking up on it fast. Fighting in daylight was also taking some getting used to.

For the last two years their raids had all been at night.

The Italians manned the heavy weapons, primarily antiaircraft guns employed in the ground defense role. There was a large stockpile of ammunition and they were expending it liberally. The gunners were fighting hard to good effect.

For their part, the Germans did not seem well led, nor did they fight with their usual aggressiveness. And they were not counterattacking when the opportunity presented itself as called for by Wehrmacht doctrine. A prisoner revealed the Nazi occupation troops, consisting of a company(-) from the 999th Light Division—criminals released from prison and given limited military training, had not expected to encounter resistance.

The Germans had intended to walk in unopposed, occupy the island, shoot the Italian officers, rape a few women…

It was not working out that way. By the middle of the afternoon, the 999th had enough. The decision was made to break contact, pull back, re-embark and go home. Three Stuka dive bombers arrived overhead from Rhodes to provide air cover for their withdrawal.

The planes rolled in with their dive sirens screaming almost vertical coming straight down on their attack run not aiming at any specific target. The dive bombers targeted the middle of the village carrying out a typical Nazi aerial terror attack.

Everyone with a weapon opened fire at the planes. Tracers vectored in on the lead Stuka. The Royal Marines, LRDG, SBS and Italians—some standing up out in the open for a better shot, blazed away.

They nailed the lead JU-87.

It came down and crashed head first exploding in a massive fireball.

The follow on two Stukas, each armed with a 1,000lb bomb and four 110lb bombs—a bombload that could only be achieved by leaving the rear gunner/radio operator back at base, continued the attack pickling their entire load on the first pass. The bombs slammed into the village creating violent explosions. Several buildings crashed down trapping hapless Greek townspeople in the rubble. The dive bombers pulled up, came around, and flew out of sight.

There was no doubt in anyone's mind the Luftwaffe would be back.

A frantic emergency rescue operation headed up by the local volunteer fire department commenced. Taking advantage of the opportunity, the Germans pulled back over the ridge and retreated to their schooner. They left behind sixteen men KIA and six POWs while carrying with them thirty wounded—the last being an estimate that did not include ambulatory.

British casualties were one KIA and one WIA. Italian losses: two KIA and seven WIA. The number of Greek civilians killed, wounded or injured was not yet known because people were still buried in the rubble.

Intermittent air raids continued for the remainder of the day hindering rescue operations, but for the moment the invasion of Symi was over.

At 1800 hours as the sun was going down Capt. Hoolihan, Capt. Redfern and Capt. Lapraik loaded the Long Range Desert Group, Special Boat Section, the Royal Marines and the exuberant Italian soldiers who had fought well against the Germans this day, on the approximately fifty caiques that had begun assembling at Symi Town when the Germans made clear their intentions of pulling out. When everyone was onboard the little armada sailed.

The SBS and LRDG were ordered to rejoin their units on Leros. The Italians, knowing they were not welcome on Greek islands no matter how much fighting they had done, went with them. The Royal Marines and the rest of the fleet of fishing boats made for Castelrozzo.

The battle of Symi, at least the first one—the Germans would be back—was a victory but no one felt much like celebrating. Capt. Redfern, ever the consummate observer, noted in the journal he maintained on Coast Watch missions: " . . . petrol dumps all destroyed, all other stores loaded into caiques. Left behind were some forty-five hundred unfortunate people, terrified, homeless, and foodless. The town gutted, on fire, and beginning to smell of the dead bodies buried in the wreckage from the constant aerial bombardment . . ."

Capt. Hoolihan said, "Let's get the hell out of Dodge."

"Headhunter," Capt. Lapraik said, "you have been spending far too much time with the bloody Yanks."

8
LIKE THE DEAL YOU AND LADY JANE HAVE GOING. MINUS THE JAPS

COLONEL JOHN RANDAL WAS SITTING NEXT TO Major the Lady Jane Seaborn on Major General Sam Houston Blackwell's VIP C-47 Dakota. She had her arm looped over his shoulder and her scarlet nails splayed on his chest. He was looking through a U.S. Army Field Manual Bronc had given him—*FM 31–30 Tactics and Techniques of Air-Borne Troops*.

It was stamped *RESTRICTED.*

Two things immediately came to his attention. One, this must have been written prewar as no one hyphenated "Airborne" today—not even the British who loved hyphens. And two, he had no idea what the classification "Restricted" meant.

Strolling up the aisle to visit his pilots on the flight deck Maj. Gen. Blackwell glanced down and noticed Col. Randal studying the field manual.

"James Gavin the commander of the 505th Parachute Infantry Regiment wrote that when he was a captain or major before the

U.S. entered the war. Ever want to know what 'Jumping Jim' knows about Airborne Operations?

"Well, he wrote the book."

Col. Randal said, "Some say his Five-O-Five is the best regiment in the army, sir."

Maj. Gen. Blackwell said, "I have heard that myself. You weren't in the States when our parachute units were being organized. I thought you might get a kick out of seeing what airborne doctrine looked like prior to our people before having any actual experience to base it on."

Col. Randal said, "A detailed FM, sir—impressive in its depth."

Maj. Gen. Blackwell said, "Give me a report when you're done."

"Wilco."

Thirty minutes later when Maj. Gen. Blackwell came out of the cockpit Col. Randal was still flipping through *FM 31–30*. The manual was well-written and included every aspect of a battalion or regimental-sized parachute unit's organization, training and preparation for an airborne operation. Missing was anything on division-sized units. That meant it must have been written before there were any airborne divisions—making the depth of Col. Gavin's insight on the subject even more remarkable.

Maj. Gen. Blackwell said, "Anything jump out at you so far?"

Col. Randal said, "Paragraph 99: Flight Formation. It's under Tactical Employment of Parachute Units—'*Responsibility for the flight formation on the jump rests with the parachute commander.*'

"Sounded a little vague until I skipped down a few sentences and found where Colonel Gavin states '*he'*—meaning the parachute unit commander—'*decides on the formation the air transports should fly during the jump.*'"

Maj. Gen. Blackwell said, "We can safely say that ain't ever going to happen on my watch—go straight to it, don't you Johnny?"

Lady Jane laughed. "Yes he does—always."

Col. Randal said, "I didn't believe it would, General."

Maj. Gen. Blackwell said, "All those other tasks Paragraph 99 stipulates the parachute commander makes the call on—not doing them either. Those are your responsibilities, Colonel. The unit commander recommends. You approve. I sign off on."

Col. Randal said, "On every combat jump I've made except for Dieppe the troop transports weren't flying any known formation by the time the planes arrived over the DZ, sir."

"Now that's the kind of detail I'm counting on from you," Maj. Gen. Blackwell said. "How'd that Dieppe drop work out?"

"They shot down my plane."

0500 HOURS

MANDY PAIGE TAPPED ON THE DOOR OF CAPTAIN Billy Jack Jaxx's Room. He had recently arrived on the duty plane from a night on the town in Cairo. Jack Cool had been hoping to catch a few more Zs before continuing his anti-Brandenburger patrolling.

"Open up, Jack."

"Keep it down Mandy be a little more discreet. Try scratching with your nails like the other girls. We don't want everybody to know you're dropping by this early to jump my bones."

"In your dreams. We have a tip on the possible location of one of the Nazis. Get dressed, meet me in the TOC in five minutes."

"Alert my people. I'll be right down."

"They are assembling now."

By the time Capt. Jaxx arrived in the Tactical Operations Center Master Sergeant Mack Beckwith was there with six SOG operators and the Lovat Scouts, armed and equipped, ready to roll. Four of his SOG people present had returned from the Benevento jump only yesterday.

Mandy and the Sergeant Major were standing by a wall map of the built-up area of Castelrozzo with Capt. Jaxx's patrol gathered behind them. The residences in the target area, most of them abandoned or closed up, were scattered up the side of the escarpment concentrated in a tight pattern due to the steepness of the slope.

Mandy said, "We received a phone tip from a woman who saw what she believes to be one of the Brandenburgers going through her garbage scrounging for food. She watched him take what he found into an empty house and phoned in the location.

"I have contacted Captain Finley. The *King Duck* is in the process of being repositioned to provide fire support. He will need to wait until BMNT in approximately forty-five minutes for line-of-sight target acquisition.

"Corporal Billingslea is standing by with his dog. And I have one of the local policemen, Officer Diakos, to act as your guide. Ball's in your court, Jack."

Capt. Jaxx said, "Sergeant Major, how're we doing on Number 69 stun grenades?"

"One each per man, sir."

"Grappling lines?"

"We have four, Captain."

"Composition C?"

"One pound per, sir."

Way overkill. Properly placed it was enough explosives to bring down Hoover Dam. The "P for Plenty" formula was in full force and effect for this patrol.

That was fine with Capt. Jaxx.

"Colonel Randal wants a POW. I promised him a walking, talking Brandenburger. Listen up boys don't kill this one."

The troops laughed but it had a hard-edged quality.

Capt. Jaxx said, "Capture a prisoner and I'll give you a forty-eight-hour pass you can spend enjoying the entertainment in lovely downtown Castelrozzo Village."

This time the men laughed for real. There was no entertainment in downtown Castelrozzo Village. Lady Jane had not had a chance to open the small bistros, bars and nightclubs she was planning.

Mandy said, "I want to accompany you, Jack."

"Negative."

Lieutenant Colonel Sir Terry "Zorro" Stone arrived from his suite upstairs having been alerted an operation was about to take place. While he was the Deputy Commander of Raiding Forces and temporarily in command with Colonel John Randal away he did not attempt to insert himself into the planning. He observed and was on hand to be consulted if needed.

Mandy said, "Terry, may . . ."

"Captain Jaxx is the officer in charge. Make your request to him. You know the drill."

If looks could kill Lt. Col. Stone and Capt. Jaxx would be DRT—dead right there.

Capt. Jaxx said to the SOG operator serving as his radio operator (RTO), "You in contact with Captain Finley?"

"Yes, sir, five by—loud and clear."

"Colonel Stone, anything, sir?"

"Do what you do best, Jack—make that your second best."

"Sergeant Major?"

"Good to go, sir."

"OK boys, let's rock."

Jack Cool.

MAJOR THE EARL LORD GEORGE JELLICOE WAS IN A slit trench on Leros sweating out another of the increasingly more frequent Luftwaffe air raids. Not only were more attacks being put in but there were more Junkers Ju-87 aka Stuka dive bombers in each flight and now Ju-88s were added to the mix. He was wondering how it had all gone wrong.

Life had sailed straight downhill ever since the night a little over a week previous when his dinner at the exclusive Hotel St. Georges in Azzib with a ravishing Greek refugee—who had the face of an A-list movie star and the body of a Kit-Kat dancer—had been interrupted by a military policeman bearing a message instructing him to report to the local SOE office forthwith.

Upon arriving Maj. Lord Jellicoe was ordered to fly to GHQ Cairo immediately. Right then that night. A plane was standing by.

When it landed a staff car waiting at the airfield rushed him to Grey Pillars.

Once there he found a Plans Division staff meeting in progress.

Even though Maj. Lord Jellicoe arrived late no one bothered to recap what he had missed. Knowing what he knew now, the SBS commander would describe the lack of effort to fill in a key player, about a special mission of national strategic importance he was expected to conduct, as military malfeasance.

It was certainly stupid.

Eventually he was able to discern the plan under discussion was for Colonel Douglas Turnbull to leave Egypt by sea with a small party and proceed via Castelrozzo to Rhodes eighty miles west of ABC. The idea was for the Colonel to land secretly from an MGB at Trianda some ten miles southwest of Rhodes Town. His mission was to contact the Italian Military Governor of the Dodecanese Islands, Admiral Inigo Campioni, to ensure the Italians intended to take over the island from the Germans stationed there and hold it until British forces could arrive.

Rhodes, with its airfields, was the key to the Aegean.

Col. Turnbull was also to remind the Italians they were expected to honor their commitments to surrender their weapons to the Allies at the appropriate time, to release all POWs, to not allow them to fall into German hands and to turn over all Italian-held territories in the Dodecanese to the Allies for the continued prosecution of the war.

Military diplomatic missions in a given AO do not get much more important than that.

While Col. Turnbull was to be the officer in charge of the mission to Rhodes, he was not present at the conference. Apparently, Plans Division did not feel it necessary to brief him in person. They were simply going to issue him his orders.

Maj. Lord Jellicoe thought at the time it seemed odd to plan an operation to negotiate the takeover of the most strategically significant piece of real estate in the entire Aegean with no input from the senior officer of the team charged with the responsibility of doing the negotiating. However, nothing the Plans Division could do would surprise him.

From that point on everything that could go wrong did.

Later that night Maj. Lord Jellicoe parachuted onto Rhodes with an SBS radio operator and an interpreter who had exaggerated his parachuting skills. He was making his first-ever parachute jump without the benefit of any training. He paid the price.

Col. Turnbull's party never made it to the island.

That left Maj. Lord Jellicoe as the senior British officer on the mission. He had no option other than to conduct negotiations on behalf of His Majesty's Government having only heard a few sentences about what was to be agreed on. With no real experience in politics and no interpreter—his being in hospital victim of a mangled PLF, it was a lot to expect.

Negotiations did not go well possibly because of his junior rank. Admiral Campioni was indecisive—demanding assurances and refusing to act. Even though his troops outnumbered the Germans something like seven to one.

The Nazis did not hesitate. They promptly seized control of the island. Despite the odds.

Rhodes being lost or more accurately squandered, Maj. Lord Jellicoe was forced to run for his life, escaping by sea and ending up on Leros where the bulk of his Special Boat Section troops were ensconced in defensive positions. Why his small-scale amphibious raiding unit was on the island he never understood.

Lightly armed, specialist, SBS raiders had no business being used as line infantry.

One thing was clear. The war in this part of the world was spiraling out of control. It did not require military genius to understand what was about to happen next.

The Germans were coming.

Maj. Lord Jellicoe's only hope was for Colonel John Randal to carry out the plan he outlined on the inspection tour after SBS was attached to Raiding Forces. Admiral-of-the-Fleet John Rushworth Jellicoe, 1st Earl—his father, had been one of the most famous fighting sailors in the history of the British Empire. Lord George was beginning to wonder if it had been a mistake not to follow in his father's footsteps and go into the Royal Navy.

The Stukas kept bombing.

CAPTAIN BUTCH "HEADHUNTER" HOOLIHAN WAS onboard Commander Andreas Londos' Levant Schooner Flotilla's Greek Sacred Squadron caique L7. The Commander led the way for an armada of fifty-one caiques filled with military stores brought off Symi, plus elements of the Long Range Desert Patrol and Special Boat Section, Italian personnel and his Royal Marines—destination Castelrozzo with a stop off at Leros scheduled for some of the boats.

No one had ever envisioned having this many Greek fishing boats in one fleet. The caiques were a big fat target for the Luftwaffe which dictated Cdr. Londos only sail at night. As the crow flies it was 102 miles to Castelrozzo.

Capt. Hoolihan said, "How long will it take to reach ABC?"

Cdr. Londos said, "In fair weather—eight or nine days, maybe longer. We have to skirt German-held islands then travel down the Turkish coastline. No way possible for us to sail straight to Castelrozzo."

A crow could get there faster.

Cdr. Londos showed Capt. Hoolihan around the L7. From any distance the boat looked innocent enough but it was heavily armed. Collapsible mounts were installed so a 20mm Solothurn antitank rifle, two .50 caliber Browning HMGs and a pair of .303 caliber Vickers K (twin barreled) LMGs—all concealed under tarps or fishing nets, could be pulled up and locked into firing position within seconds.

Cdr. Londos said, "Each LSF boat is fitted out with two cases of hand grenades. My crew are all equipped with a revolver of their choice and a 9mm Lanchester submachine gun. We have thousands of rounds of ammunition stowed below."

Capt. Hoolihan was familiar with the Lanchester. It was the Royal Navy's standard issue submachine. His friend, Captain Roy Kidd, Raiding Forces' acknowledged expert on all things military small arms related, had provided him the back story on the weapon.

Prior to the war the British military system had blinders on when it came to submachine guns on the grounds, "Gentlemen do not employ gangster weapons." When the Nazis—not being gentlemen—invaded France there was not a single submachine gun in the British Expeditionary Force but the Germans had a lot of them.

Belatedly the Royal Navy realized they needed submachine guns to issue to boarding parties, other land-based sailors and for the Royal Marines. None were to be had. With no submachine gun of its own the Royal Armories took the path of least resistance and performed an evaluation of the Nazis' Bergmann 9mm MP-28 with the idea of copying it. The weapon chosen was a strange choice.

The MP-28 was not even the best SMG in the German inventory.

It was already an obsolete design but the Royal Armory adopted the weapon anyway calling their version "Lanchester" after the director of the Sterling Armaments Company who was going to produce them.

Capt. Hoolihan's Marines refused to carry them.

The Royal Armories' thinking on weapons was rooted in days long past. When the order was placed for Lanchester Mark I's—the British nomenclature for the German MP-28—Sterling was instructed to add a bayonet lug.

Cdr. Londos noticed Capt. Hoolihan eyeing the device on the muzzle of the Lanchester he had slung over his shoulder. "We do not have a single bayonet in our stores, Butch."

Capt. Hoolihan said, "Advanced thinking, Commander."

"The attachment gives us something to laugh about. My lads do not tend to see themselves as bayonet fighters."

Capt. Hoolihan said, "Tell me, how do you intend to conceal all these boats come daylight?"

"That is a good question. Your lad, The Great Teddy, came to LSF Mosquito Base on Cyprus to indoctrinate the Greek Sacred Squadron caique crew on the mysteries of camouflage. He attached great importance to making our caiques appear to be a rock or clump of bushes.

Capt. Hoolihan said, "Teddy loves his work."

"The crew despises it," Cdr. Londos said.

"Why?"

"All the paraphernalia, the nets, the poles, the pole caps, and grapnels take up an enormous amount of space below. Everyone hates the job of hauling them up, installing the nets for a few hours only to take it all down and stow below later. The process also involves the tricky business of raising and lowering the mast—on Teddy's orders specially modified by shortening—to allow the stick to be pivoted down in order to lie flat on top of the cabin to make it easier to camouflage.

“The ends of the nets are attached to rocks on the shore and weighted down with lead then thrown over the side into the water on the other side to anchor them. The netting taut. That means bamboo poles have to be put in place on deck to prop it up in order to give my sailors freedom of movement topside.

“When properly installed, the L7 vanishes—‘Hey, Presto’ . . . like The Great Teddy says. But it is hard work!”

Capt. Hoolihan said, “Lieutenant Hamilton is a magician.”

Cdr. Londos said, “Not even he could hide all these boats.”

“Why not?”

“Except for the handful of LSF craft the L7 is the only caique in this entire ragtag fleet equipped with camouflage gear . . . all the rest are fishing boats.”

MAJOR GENERAL SAM HOUSTON BLACKWELL AND Colonel John Randal were sitting in the front of the VIP C-47 with Waldo’s custom-rolled cigars stuck in their teeth. The cigars were unlit in deference to Major the Lady Jane Seaborn’s well-known dislike of smoke in an enclosed space.

Bronc was laughing, “So you boys would just stroll up to the counter at some departure airfield, whisper ‘Frogspawn’ and they’d bump someone off the manifest to let you on the flight—just like that?”

Col. Randal said, “Yes, sir.”

“You got any more tricks up your sleeve?”

Col. Randal reached into the inside pocket of his uniform and produced the pigskin case containing his credentials. “Our ‘get out of jail free cards,’ sir.”

Maj. Gen. Blackwell said, “Are these things authentic?”

Col. Randal replied, "Did President Roosevelt or Prime Minister Churchill actually sign them? How would anyone know sir? Who do you call to confirm something like that?"

Maj. Gen. Blackwell said, "Yeah, it's brilliant Colonel. I need more 'a that kinda' thinkin' in Troop Transport Command. But from here on out you ain't gonna have to depend on maybe or maybe not counterfeit credentials to hop a USAAF airplane. I'll have my office cut priority orders for you over my signature.

"Anyone who flies transports worldwide will recognize it—you're golden, son."

"Works for me, General."

Maj. Gen. Blackwell said, "I understand Lady Jane's husband has gone missing, presumed dead, that right?"

Col. Randal said, "His ship was sunk en route to the CBI. The navy doesn't have any reports of survivors. In those waters, sir, the possibility of being rescued by the Japanese is highly unlikely. And the chance of survival is not good even if he was. There are reports of shipwreck survivors picked up by Japanese submarines being executed on deck with samurai swords.

"Rescue is no guarantee."

Maj. Gen. Blackwell said, "From what intel I've seen, on the Bataan Death March and the slave labor camps the Japs are holding our POWs in, I'd say getting captured might be worse than drowning.

"How's Lady Jane taking it?"

Col. Randal said, "They were not on good terms, sir."

Maj. Gen. Blackwell said, "How in the world did you ever hook up with a woman like Lady Jane?"

Col. Randal said, "I have no idea General."

"You out kicked your coverage on that one, son—I ever mention I met the husband?"

"Negative."

"At least once a year I like to go on safari in Africa. Before the war I had a running buddy in Nairobi—a half-broke Lord named Joss Hay—the Earl of Errol. Wasn't much on big game hunting, didn't drink a lot or do drugs, but he chased women full time, all the time nonstop. Nicknamed himself 'The World's Greatest Pouncer.'

"He lived outside of town in a place called Happy Valley with a buncha' expatriates all running away from something or someone.

"Joss belonged to the exclusive Muthaiga Country Club in Nairobi where wife swapping is the in-house sport. He would invite me to go when I was back from the bush. Those expats are a bunch of practicing sex maniacs.

"Between us that scene's not really my style. Takes the fun outta chasing women if there's no challenge to it. But when in Rome . . .

"Anyway, we ran into Commander Seaborn at the club a couple of times when his destroyer was in port—wild man."

Col. Randal said, "Really?"

Maj. Gen. Blackwell said, "Yeah, well, me and Joss won't be partying at the Muthaiga anymore. The World's Greatest Pouncer got hisself gunned down by his fiancée's husband. Crazy as it sounds the happy couple had only been married to each other about six weeks when the wife and Joss became engaged—sorta like the deal you and Lady Jane have going—minus the Japs.

"Ever cross paths with the Earl in Nairobi?"

"Not that I recall," Col. Randal lied.

CAPTAIN BILLY JACK JAXX WAS WORKING THROUGH his hastily improvised plan as his patrol traveled up the escarpment. It was not optimum for a patrol leader to be developing his "Concept of the Operation" while conducting a movement to contact. Being focused on the task at hand, not distracted and working through options for his "Actions on the Objective" being all important.

But time was of the essence.

The need to hit the target before sunrise left him no time to analyze the mission, issue a Patrol Order, conduct a rehearsal, test fire weapons or anything else prior to moving out.

The men in the patrol were some of his SOG operators who had trickled back to friendly lines following the Benevento drop. They had been flown to RFHQ then on to ABC. SOG believed themselves to be the best of the best . . . and maybe they were. The problem was these were random operators out of the thirty-man Small Operations Group Capt. Jaxx commanded. The unit was composed of three teams, each led by a lieutenant. Only one of his three officers had made it back at this point and these men were from all three of the teams.

Not an overwhelming concern but again not optimal.

Knowing it was vital to reach the target under cover of darkness to avoid detection, Officer Diakos was leading the patrol up the escarpment to their ORP at a rapid clip. The Greek was moving fast for a fifty-year-old with a beer belly. Corporal Sid Billingslea and his dog were right behind him. They were followed by Capt. Jaxx who was worried the VPW dog team might be a problem. The Brandenburgers had executed six Vulnerable Points Wing security specialists in cold blood.

VPW personnel were looking for payback and the dog, sensing his handler's emotions, would likely want in on it as well.

As they traveled Capt. Jaxx was running through his list of options following the Rules for Raiding which called for him to 'Plan Missions Backward.' He needed a prisoner. There was a Brandenburger reported to be in the house they had targeted. If so he would be armed. The question was how to get an elite Sea Raider, highly skilled in the use of firearms, extensively trained in hand-to-hand combat and with a strong desire not to be captured, into detention.

They could not just walk up to the door and knock—or maybe they could.

Depending on the definition of knock.

Most houses on Castelrozzo were at least two stories. Mandy had advised this was the case with his target. The houses usually abutted the steep slope of the escarpment in the rear and rarely had back doors or rear windows—but not *never* as Colonel John Randal and Happy had discovered.

Mandy had advised the house had six points of entry. Two front windows upstairs, two windows downstairs, and a ground-level front door. There was a second-story balcony.

The balcony was something he could work with.

Capt. Jaxx made a note to do something special for Mandy if her information proved out. He had no doubt it would as she had a talent for asking all the right questions. Now it was up to him to formulate his plan of action based on the answers she extracted.

Then execute it.

At this point Capt. Jaxx had a preliminary idea of who and what concerning his patrols "Actions On the Objective." The trick was to tailor each man's individual strength to each task to be accomplished. This was "Right Man, Right Job" planning as also laid out in the Rules for Raiding.

Being able to craft a simple plan that works with all the variables and unknowns inherent in any operation is why tactics are an art—not a science. The ability to conduct mission planning on the move while closing on the objective is small-unit leadership elevated to its highest form.

Capt. Jaxx's primary plan was simple. The patrol would make entry to the house and capture the Brandenburger hiding inside—with the intent of keeping him alive to be interrogated.

His Fallback Plan aka Plan B, as called for in the Rules for Raiding, was for Acting Provisional Lieutenant Skipper Warthog Finley to level the place. If at all possible Warthog's services would not be called for. Requesting fire support from the *King Duck* would be an admission of failure—at least on one level.

It meant he would not be bringing in a prisoner—but then again a dead Nazi is always a win.

Officer Diakos had been trotting up the path. Now he slowed to a walk. The sky was still pitch dark but it would be sunrise soon.

The policeman came to a halt.

Capt. Jaxx moved up. "We there?"

"Your target is the third house, Captain."

When the column stopped the men knelt down on one knee every other man facing in the opposite direction with weapons at the ready. Master Sergeant Mack Beckwith moved up from the rear of the column, where the assistant patrol leader traditionally travels, to the front of the file to be available to confer.

Movement to the ORP had been swift and silent. Nothing unusual about that. SOG was meticulous in their execution of basic infantry skills. What makes special operators special is doing what every conventional infantry soldier is trained to do only doing it a hundred times better. There is no magic involved. The secret is in having the discipline and patience to execute each individual personal action with precision. Every detail, like placement of a hand or setting a foot, all carefully thought out in advance. To an observer a SOG patrol in movement would seem choreographed.

Slow is smooth. Smooth is fast. Force on force.

The Small Operations Group took pride in its patrolling skills. There was heavy peer pressure for every man to perform at his highest level. No slack, no do-overs, no mistakes, all the time every time—professional.

It was almost impossible to be selected for the Small Operations Group and *becoming* a member of the unit was easier than *staying* in it. Those not able to perform at the level SOG demanded 100% of the time were reassigned elsewhere in Raiding Forces without prejudice.

Jack Cool may have been a playboy but he was a superb troop commander.

Capt. Jaxx silently signaled MSgt. Beckwith to have the patrol set up a perimeter formation. Now it was time to conduct his "Leader's Recon." He needed to place eyes on the target to see it for himself.

Leader Recons can be tricky. The patrol leader needs—or at least likes—to take one last look before executing the mission. He may or may not choose to have his subordinate element leaders accompany him in order to let them observe what it is they are going up against. It is always a good idea to verify that the objective looks the same on the ground as it does on a map or as intelligence described prior to the mission.

The problem, as Capt. Jaxx knew, was there would be no one left to lead an attack if all the leaders moved up to check out the objective and were killed or captured. How to configure his Leader's Recon was one more point on the list of items Capt. Jaxx was still working through.

The men were ordered to pull in tight down on one knee. Capt. Jaxx was kneeling in the center of the patrol formation. He wanted everyone to be able to hear what was about to be said even though he was whispering.

"Hansen and I are going to move up and conduct a brief Leaders Recon. If we are not back in fifteen minutes, Sergeant Major, you hit the target. Is that clear?"

"Clear, sir."

Private First Class Norvel "Horn Dog" Hansen had been working with Lieutenant Jake Novak's patrol as a team leader because of his natural leadership skills. Due to his status as a longtime SOG member MSgt. Beckwith had pulled him in to load out with his old outfit for this morning's mission. PFC Hansen was not acting as a team leader but that was about to change.

Capt. Jaxx had an assignment for him.

The SOG operators silently returned to the prone position with their weapons facing out. Capt. Jaxx and PFC Hansen slipped into the dark. The two moved up the cobblestone path to the nearest house. Flattening out with their backs to the front wall they slowly and carefully inched their way across the length of the residence.

Then came to a narrow side yard.

Capt. Jaxx signaled PFC Hansen to cover him. Moving fast but not running, he made his way across to the next house. Anyone watching might believe his silhouette was a shadow caused by a cloud passing across the moon. Upon reaching the side of the second house Capt. Jaxx slapped the stock of his .30 Baby BAR with the palm of his hand.

PFC Hansen immediately closed up.

The two worked their way along the front wall again. At the far corner Capt. Jaxx froze. Only a few feet away was their objective. The two-story structure was exactly as advertised. Except from this position there was no way to verify the report of no rear windows or back door.

He would have to live with that.

Capt. Jaxx reached back and grabbed a fistful of PFC Hansen's jump jacket and pulled him up close.

"You're my second-story entry team leader, Hansen. I want you to take Masterson and Berkowitz—work your way around behind the house. Get up on the roof. Then ease your way over the top to the front leading edge.

"You drop down alone onto the deck and place a breaching charge on the door. Then lower a second charge over the rail by its electrical cord and retreat to the far end of the deck on this side toward me. The Sergeant Major will have one of his people waiting below to attach the charge you send down to the front door. The explosives will be configured into a ring main system that detonates both charges simultaneously—you're my designated demo man.

"I'll be right here with the Lovat Scouts and the dog team. Flash your red filtered flashlight three times to let me know when you're good to go. When I respond with a series of flashes that's the signal for you to crank the handle on the blasting machine and light off the charges.

"Execute on my first flash. Have Masterson and Berkowitz rappel down to the balcony as soon as the charge blows. You three effect second-level entry. The rest of the patrol will be hitting the door on the ground floor.

"Take it to 'em hard and I mean bring it! But remember put a stun grenade in prior to entry. Every room, Hansen. Grenade, then go.

"Don't kill my Brandenburger."

"Yes, sir, Captain"

"I mean it, Horn Dog."

CAPTAIN BUTCH "HEADHUNTER" HOOLIHAN STOOD on the bow of L7 and watched as the sun went down in a spectacular blaze of colors. They had taken the risk of sailing all day to put as much sea room as possible between the fleet of caiques and Symi. It was hoped the Nazis would be tied up extracting their troops from the island and not pay attention to civilian fishing vessels fleeing the battle area.

The wind was strong at their back but dead-on course to Castelrozzo which was over a week away according to Commander Andreas Londos. Capt. Hoolihan was not pleased about how long the voyage was going to take. He had been in almost nonstop action for most of the last four years. A long voyage at sea moving at tooth-grinding speed did not much appeal to him—at least not at first.

On reflection he was beginning to rethink as he was standing there unwinding from the intense firefight of the morning while listening to the waves slapping against the wooden hull of the L7. It could turn out to be a nice development—a pleasure cruise. In his world of small-scale, high-speed, amphibious, pinprick raiding, most unexpected developments were neither nice nor pleasurable.

Capt. Hoolihan's tranquility did not last long.

The wind increased. The sky turned menacing and gray. L7 began dipping and rising in a steady, undulating motion. The sea became rougher and the waves higher. From time to time one or another of the caiques in the fleet would appear ghostlike out of the darkness and then disappear again as if swallowed up.

At low speed the L7's Matilda tank engine was almost silent but at the rate she was presently traveling it was loud enough. When one of the other caiques came into sight the motor drowned out the *bon, bon, bon* sounds of the fishermen's diesel engines adding to the eeriness. Capt. Hoolihan retreated to the boat's cockpit to get away from the steadily increasing spray as the caique rose and fell. From there, with Cdr. Londos who had taken over the helm, he had a catbird's seat view of the rise and fall of the black water.

A giant wave ahead was looming. It had a foaming white top and appeared to be charging them. To Capt. Hoolihan the wave looked like it was going to crash down and bury the caique under millions of gallons of seawater.

At the last instant the swell went under the L7 lifting it higher and higher like a roller coaster—not a comforting feeling—before racing down the far side into the trough then up again on another wave.

It was a wild ride.

One wave passed only to be replaced by another and another with no end in sight.

Capt. Hoolihan was an experienced sailor. At least he thought of himself as one. But he had never experienced anything like this.

It did not do Headhunter's morale any good to see Cdr. Londos' hands gripping the wooden wheel so hard that he appeared to be in danger of breaking it off.

With every roll the mainsails boom dipped into the sea. From below came the sounds of men cursing as they were thrown about. The heaving and tossing went on for hours. It seemed like it was never going to end.

At first light Cdr. Londos steered for the nearest island to lay up. The crew fell to, broke out their camouflage paraphernalia and had the L7 swathed in netting within a few minutes. From their sheltered position of concealment they watched as caiques from their fleet straggled past in ones and twos looking for their own safe harbor.

Cdr. Londos said, “Enjoy your first night at sea in a motorized sailboat, Captain?”

Capt. Hoolihan said, “So much for my hopes of an idyllic cruise through the idyllic Greek Islands.”

“Cheer up, Headhunter, you only have six or seven more nights left.”

“Most of my time at sea these last two years has been reasonably close inshore,” Capt. Hoolihan said. “We had rough weather but never anything like last night. Is it always so stormy?”

Cdr. Londos said, “The Aegean can be mercurial. You acquitted yourself well, Captain. My crew are impressed.”

Capt. Hoolihan said, “I was scared stiff.”

He was wondering how Cdr. Londos intended to assemble the caiques for the next night of sailing.

The answer was he was not even going to try.

CAPTAIN BILLY JACK JAXX ISSUED A WHISPERED frag order to his troops who had pulled in tight again. The plan was as outlined to Private First Class Norvel “Horn Dog” Hansen but he had to give Master Sergeant Mack Beckwith and Corporal Sid Billingslea their marching orders. And the rest of the men needed to hear the entire plan.

“Sergeant Major you’ll conduct the assault phase. Take up a position on the near side of the target. Designate one of your people to move up to the front door and standby for Hansen to lower a breaching charge over the balcony. Once it comes down, have your ground level demo man attach it. Then he's to withdraw back to your staging position around the side of the house.

"Once that's accomplished and you're satisfied your team is good to go, signal me with your red filtered light—two long flashes. Horn Dog's going to signal me from the balcony when he's ready. I should get his signal before your man's back from placing the breaching charge.

"The instant I have an up from both of you, I'll signal the order to execute. Hansen's going to initiate the charges on my first flash—*boom*—and then you go.

"Remember, I want a live, fully functional prisoner. After you breach, make sure to throw a stun grenade into each room to clear it before entering. I'll remain outside with Corporal Billingslea, the Lovat Scouts and the Fire Control team—we'll constitute the reserve element.

"Corporal, you keep your dog under tight control. Only release him on my orders—is that clear?"

"Clear, sir."

"Questions?"

There were none. SOG never stopped training for situations such as this. To the uninitiated, Capt. Jaxx's frag order might have sounded like something you would hear from kids playing army. Not the case.

In fact the plan was a highly sophisticated tactical blueprint reduced to sounding Short and Simple, per Raiding Forces Rules, the mark it was crafted by a true professional.

Every operator knew what he was supposed to do and what every other man was supposed to do. This was important in the event anyone went down—someone else would step in and continue the mission. The troops were quite at home with the hurried nature of the operation not giving it a second thought.

SOG had unquestioned confidence in their commander, in themselves and in the other operators in the patrol.

MSgt. Beckwith only had to designate the individual in his team who would place the charge on the front door, assign the order of entry and the SOG patrol would be ready to launch.

Typically the Sergeant Major designated himself Number 1 through the front door.

Capt. Jaxx gave MSgt. Beckwith and PFC Hansen a brief interval to go over last-minute details with the men in their teams.

"All right, saddle up boys—let's go."

PFC Hansen's team was first out, traveling straight up the side of the escarpment in order to be able to loop around and approach the target from behind. Capt. Jaxx gave him a five-minute head start then led MSgt. Beckwith's team to the second house on the cobblestone pathway—next door to the target. Once in position he paused to let the Sergeant Major take charge.

MSgt. Beckwith made a quick head check around the corner. He reached back, grabbed a handful of the jump jacket of the SOG operator behind him, pulled him close and whispered *GO*. When the first man was in position the Sergeant Major continued an individual tap out until everyone was across in place crouched along the near side wall of the target.

Then he went.

After working his way up the slope and coming in on the back of the house PFC Hansen discovered getting up on the roof was going to be more difficult than he had hoped. At a lot of the residences that backed up to the steep escarpment it was possible to simply step off the ground onto the roof.

Not this house. The edge of the roof was over their head. No problem. Grappling hooks were tossed up and hooked in the gutter. PFC Hansen and his men hand-over-handed their way up the ropes.

When all three operators were on top they carefully low-crawled across not making a sound. At the edge of the roof on the front side Private Donny Masterson grabbed one of PFC Hansen's hands. Private Tommy Berkowitz took the other.

Then they lowered him down to the deck very carefully.

Once he was on the balcony PFC Hansen peeled off the backing on the block of Composition C that was going to be used to breach. Underneath was adhesive designed to be sticky enough for the explosive to be held in place when laid against a flat surface. He pressed the block to the second-story door leading out onto the balcony.

The Composition C was glued solid.

Based on Mandy's intelligence about the doors, MSgt. Beckwith had assembled a two-charge ring main system prior to departing ABCHQ. However, the blasting caps remained to be attached to the end of the 30-foot electrical cord and molded it into the Composition C on the door—this was a safety measure. No thinking demo man wanted to end up like the dummies in the cartoons.

There are several ways to initiate explosives. The methods typically used are: 1) a fuse that burns at a timed rate the demolitions man determines by trial and error clocking it prior to the mission; or 2) an electrical blasting machine.

A ring main system is an ignition technique that allows multiple charges to be detonated in different places at the same time. For simultaneous detonation ring main systems require the use of an electrical blasting machine. Tonight PFC Hansen was equipped with a U.S. Army 10 Cap blasting machine. The nomenclature indicated it was capable of setting off up to ten blasting caps/explosive charges at the same time.

He only needed two. One up on the balcony. The other on ground level at the front door.

In cartoons any character placing explosives almost always experiences a premature detonation because the handle of their blasting machine somehow manages to be pushed down at the wrong time—usually when the character is in the act of standing over a big bundle of dynamite. The U.S. Army and British Army were cognizant of those cartoons. Aware their ranks are filled with troops equally as accident prone as the cartoon characters, if not worse, they both adopted the same handheld 10 Cap blasting machine.

Which it was hoped was idiot proof.

To initiate an electrical charge all the demo man had to do was pull the handle up from the machine about three inches. Then—arm held at a 45-degree angle, fingers extended and joined, palm cupped around the charging handle—twist vigorously.

There was no way to push the handle down eliminating most problems encountered in the cartoons. But not all of them. The prudent demo man did not hook up the detonating cord to the blasting machine prior to crimping the blasting cap and placing his explosives.

And kept the 10 Cap initiating device on his person at all times.

When PFC Hansen was finished placing the charge on the door he lowered the ground floor charger over the edge of the balcony. Then he lay down on the deck and low-crawled under the window to the end nearest where Capt. Jaxx and his party were crouched across the side yard. He connected the electrical wire to the blasting machine and pulled up the charging handle—

realizing too late he probably should have waited on pulling up the handle.

Then PFC Hansen leaned over the balcony and flashed his red filtered light three times.

Before he got the second flash off Capt. Jaxx's signal to execute came back.

Startled at how fast it happened—the downstairs demo man had been quick about attaching his charge. PFC Hansen dropped his flashlight and twisted the handle on the blasting machine as hard as he could.

KAAAABOOOOOOM!

The result was a blinding flash explosion that nearly blew him off the balcony.

Masterson and Berkowitz jumped down from the roof. Rocked by the violence of the detonation, night vision destroyed, and ears ringing PFC Hansen staggered past them to the destroyed door and lurched in. He was pretty sure he did not need a Number 69 Grenade to help stun anyone inside the first room.

Down below MSgt. Beckwith led the charge on the front door through a thick cloud of dust and smoke. Like PFC Hansen he did not bother with a stun grenade on the initial entry. His team was not as affected by the explosion because they had been around the side of the house shielded from the blast.

Throughout the house stun grenades flashed and thundered as the SOG operators flowed from room to room dealing controlled violence in a tightly enclosed space as quickly as possible under tight team discipline.

The No. 69 stun grenade was a British design. There was no U.S. counterpart. The outer shell of the grenade was composed entirely of hard plastic Bakelite. When the No. 69 exploded it did not produce shrapnel like an iron fragmentation grenade—its purpose was to stun the opposition temporarily.

Deploying the No. 69 was relatively simple. The cap was unscrewed, dropped and the grenade thrown—no pin to pull. As the grenade sailed through the air a linen tape with a curved lead weight on the end unraveled in flight freeing a ball bearing inside the fuse. This armed the "All Ways" action and the grenade was primed to explode on impact.

The term "All Ways" referred to the design feature that guaranteed all of the possible ways the grenade could strike a target—upside down, sideways, at an angle etc.—would trigger instantaneous detonation.

A lot of thought had gone into idiot proofing the No. 69.

Unscrew, throw, bang. No pin to pull. No waiting for a timed fuse to cook off—which a hyped-up frag grenade thrower eager to get at the opposition could easily time wrong with unhappy results.

The No. 69 stun grenade was about perfect for clearing buildings.

Capt. Jaxx closed up on the house with the Lovat Scouts and the dog team. He did not follow the Sergeant Major inside, which was possibly a first for him, being that leading from the front was his signature leadership style. It required a great deal of personal discipline not to rush in and take charge.

He was pacing back and forth with his RTO at his heels as the No. 69 stun grenades were going *WHOOMPH, WHOOMPH, WHOOMPH.* Today he was acting as a commander not the assault team leader. Unwritten SOP, meaning accepted practice in Raiding Forces, dictated Capt. Jaxx stand by in a central location readily available to make an immediate command decision should one be required.

Lugging his highly modified .30 Baby BAR as he marked time waiting for a report, Capt. Jaxx was beginning to think he had brought too much gun. There was no possible chance the automatic rifle was going to be used. In the future if he was going to be playing the role of commander rather than assault team leader other options for his primary weapon might need to be considered.

His old 9mm Beretta MAB-38 submachine gun or maybe a .30 M1 carbine would be more suitable—something to consider.

The longer the take-down went on the more impatient Capt. Jaxx became. Col. Randal had once confided how he hated waiting on the sideline while an operation was in progress half hoping he would not be needed—half hoping he would be.

Now Jack Cool understood the feeling.

MAJOR GENERAL SAM HOUSTON BLACKWELL'S VIP C-47 touched down at the civil aviation airport in Pinehurst, North Carolina. When his party, consisting of Colonel John Randal, Major the Lady Jane Seaborn, Beverly Blackwell and Red the Flying Clipper Girl deplaned there was a command car with a red plate and two silver stars on the front bumper denoting the car belonged to a major general waiting for Bronc.

There was also a limousine.

Maj. Gen. Blackwell said, "Wonder who that's for?"

The chauffeur, dressed in what appeared to be a Confederate cavalryman's uniform, walked over. "Lady Seaborn, the manager of the Carolina Hotel sends his compliments, ma'am. If your entourage will come with me, please."

Noting his nameplate, Lady Jane said, "Thank you, Perkins."

Maj. Gen. Blackwell said, "You've got to be putting me on."

Beverly laughed, "You're about to discover travel with Lady Jane takes first class to a new level, Daddy—even for a rich South Texas major general like you."

"I can see that."

A USAAF lieutenant walked over and saluted, "Sir, I have orders to escort you to the Carolina Hotel."

Maj. Gen. Blackwell returned the salute, "Follow the limo, Lieutenant. I'll be riding with the rest of the party."

"Yes, sir."

As they were loading into the hotel's limousine, Maj. Gen. Blackwell asked Col. Randal, "Is it always like this with her?"

"Pretty much, General."

"So how did she manage to get rooms? The Carolina's sold out—there's a war on?"

"I have no idea, sir."

The Carolina was a beautiful antebellum hotel built to resemble an enormous plantation house. It was framed by a long column of ancient moss-covered oak trees that created what the staff called "Oak Ally." Outside of the hotel was parked a fleet of military command cars, many sporting red plates and stars that indicated the rank of the general officer they belonged to. The enlisted drivers were standing in a modified position of parade rest beside their vehicles in crisp khaki uniforms most wearing spit-shined brown Corcoran jump boots.

There was also a line of horse-drawn carriages to take the hotel's guests on a tour of the property.

When they arrived a squad of Confederate soldiers stormed the limousine to unload the luggage. Inside the lobby was as magnificent as the entry hall of the fictional Tara in *Gone with the Wind*—only fifty times bigger. It was teeming with senior officers who turned to stare when their party walked in.

The staff of the hotel formed up in a receiving line. This caused a stir because they had not accorded any other guests such an honor. More than a few of the high-ranking guests took note, wondering what could have merited the tribute, feeling somewhat slighted.

The hotel manager in a CSA officer's uniform—it said so on his belt buckle, festooned with gold braid, introduced himself as "Colonel" Longmore. He escorted Lady Jane, followed by the rest of her party, down the receiving line introducing her to the staff. She took her time speaking to every person.

Then with no pretense of checking in they were whisked up to the top floor in a private elevator. On the way up Col. Longmore said, "Lady Seaborn, you'll be occupying the Jefferson Davis suite. General Blackwell, you suh, will be in the Robert E. Lee suite. And you other two lovely ladies share the General Albert Sidney Johnston—there's two bedrooms."

Maj. Gen. Blackwell said, "Sounds like I got an upgrade."

As they were getting off the elevator, Lady Jane whispered, "Jefferson Davis?"

Col. Randal said, "President of the Confederacy."

The sparkle in her sea green eyes told him Lady Jane was trying hard not to giggle.

Clearly, the Carolina Hotel did not know the Civil War was over or that the South had lost.

Maj. Gen. Blackwell said, "We should have brought your two slave girls, Johnny—fit right in."

Walking down the corridor to their suites, Col. Longmore said, "The Carolina is thrilled to be accorded the opportunity to establish a relationship with the Bradford, ma'am."

Lady Jane's hotel in London. Her manager had reached out.

A steward in a starched white jacket was standing outside the Jefferson Davis suite holding a silver tray with a white envelope on it.

"Telegram for you, Colonel Randal, suh."

Once inside the suite Col. Randal opened the envelope.

WALKING TALKING SLIGHTLY DAMAGED

Jack Cool.

9
WE DON'T HAVE ANY ELEPHANTS

MAJOR GENERAL SAM HOUSTON BLACKWELL AND Colonel John Randal arrived at the location on Camp Mackall designated as the host site for the Swing Board, one of the five movie theaters on the base. The camp was the Headquarters of the U.S. Army Airborne Command and home to the 11th, 13th and 17th Airborne Divisions. The 101st had trained there prior to moving to Fort Benning.

Tables had been placed on the raised stage below the movie screen for the board members to conduct their business.

The theater seats normally occupied by the movie audience were filled with less stellar attendees, such as parachute and glider infantry regimental commanders from the three airborne divisions stationed on base, visiting field grade officers from Fort Bragg and Fort Benning, various airborne staff types, pilots—both powered and glider—and a platoon of general's aides.

The senior officers present were all plank holders of what was known as the "Airborne Mafia": Major General Joseph

Swing, CG of the 11th Airborne Division—Chairman of the Board, Major General Matthew Ridgway in from Italy where his 82nd Airborne Division was fighting, Major General George Griner, CG 13th Airborne Division, Major General William Miley, CG 17th Airborne Division, Major General William Lee, CG 101st Airborne Division and Major General Elbridge Chapman, Airborne Command.

Also, Colonel P. Ernest Gabel, USAAF Transport Command—a different organization from Maj. Gen. Blackwell's Troop Transport Command though there was some overlap in their duties.

Most of the general officers had brought a deputy to sit in for their boss at most of the board meetings. The generals had other commitments. They would personally attend when time permitted, a specific subject under discussion piqued their interest or a matter before the board required their input. If and when an eminent light like Lieutenant General Lesley McNair decided to visit for a day then all the generals would flock back except Maj. Gen. Ridgway who needed to return to his division in Italy sometime in the next week.

Col. Randal wondered why with the 82nd Airborne engaged in combat Colonel James Gavin had not attended in his place. After all, "Jumping Jim" was the author of *FM- 31–30 Tactics and Techniques of Air-Borne Troops.* He had commanded the 505th PIR on the Sicily and Salerno jumps, which would seem to make him 'Right Man, Right Job.'

Besides, Maj. Gen. Ridgway was a "straight leg" or "leg" for short. Both were derisive terms applied by paratroopers to anyone who was not a paratrooper. It derived from what takes place when a parachutist is coming in to make a PLF. Prior to hitting the ground a jumper unlocks and bends his knees to absorb the shock. The bent knees mark him as "airborne" as opposed to being a "straight leg."

The distinction can get complicated. "Glider riders" are "airborne" but they are also "legs." Unless they have been to Jump School. In that case the individual jump qualified glidermen is a paratrooper serving in a "leg" outfit.

Col. Randal was opposed to having elites within elites as current doctrine allowed to exist in airborne divisions made up of paratroopers and glidermen. The distinction was a source of resentment and friction. He did not see how that could possibly be beneficial for morale.

And he was not in agreement with the existing military policy that allowed a general to command an airborne division without being parachute qualified. Paratroopers consider themselves a cut above. They are disdainful of those who do not jump out of airplanes.

Paratroops can be tricky to command if you are not one of them.

Behind his back, Gen. Ridgway was called "The Non-Jumping General" by the "All Americans" in his 504th and 505th Parachute Infantry Regiments even though those same men held him in high esteem as a combat commander.

Currently airborne division commanders had no reason to be jump qualified because airborne doctrine called for them to land by glider along with their staff. After they jump out of their airplanes paratroopers are light infantry soldiers as are glidermen once they link up on the ground. At that point it is of no importance who landed by parachute and who landed in a glider.

Still, Col. Randal was a proponent of leading by example. He believed the Commanding General of a cavalry division needed to know how to drive an armored car, the CG of an armored division needed to know how to drive a tank and the CG of an airborne division needed to jump with his men—or at least go to the trouble to be airborne qualified even if he did choose to land by glider on a combat operation.

It was a view he thought best kept to himself based entirely on his personal concept of leadership. There were a number of officers present who would not agree with him. Nevertheless, Col. Randal noted Maj. Gen. Ridgway was the only division commander at the table who was not wearing Jump Wings. Apparently his belief in leading by example was shared by the majority of the senior board members—even Bronc was sporting parachute wings.

Good to know.

Maj. Gen. Swing called the meeting to order. The first item on the agenda was to introduce the primary members of the board. This was a mere formality. With the exception of Maj. Gen. Blackwell and Col. Randal the other officers knew each other.

Some had been classmates at West Point.

All of them were new at being generals—not one had held rank higher than lieutenant colonel eighteen months previous.

Maj. Gen. Swing said, "I would like to introduce General Blackwell. He tells me his friends call him Bronc. Get acquainted with the General he has Troop Transport Command. Bronc drops your parachutists and tows your gliders.

"Good man to know—you're not going into battle without him."

Everyone at the table laughed. It did not escape their notice the key player in the room was a reservist. With the exception of Maj. Gen. Ridgway none of the other generals had ever met him. However, most of them had been at an informal meet and greet in the lobby of the Carolina Hotel when Bronc's entourage arrived last night.

It had made an impression.

Maj. Gen. Blackwell said, "This is my Paratroop Advisor, Colonel Randal."

Not much of an introduction. No one seemed interested. Advisors came and went. But a few sets of senior grade eyes locked in on the four gold stars signifying combat jumps on his U.S. Parachute Wings—the only decoration Col. Randal was wearing.

As Maj. Gen. Swing made his opening remarks outlining the purpose of the board, Col. Randal studied the group of the officers at the U-shaped table. The board could best be described as a case study in military political gamesmanship. Not one man present had any motivation to question the validity of retaining airborne divisions on the army list.

Before even getting started the attitude of the Board was clearly "nothing to see here". The future of the airborne division was assured unless something went wrong when the field test was conducted. And that could be a problem.

Sometimes the Aggressor Forces win.

The board adjourned at noon. Most of the members had tee times later that afternoon. Everyone would reconvene the next morning at 0900 hours. As the meeting was breaking up Col. Randal wondered why Bronc had gone to the trouble of flying him to the States to sit on a board that had already decided the question. He had only known Maj. Gen. Blackwell for a short time but it was long enough to realize Bronc had a motive for everything.

There must be a reason he was here.

No one invited Col. Randal to play golf.

LIEUTENANT GENERAL "GERONIMO" JOE MCKOY and Waldo Treywick were flying over a camel caravan east of Cairo in a Raiding Forces Special Operations Walrus piloted by Captain Pamala Plum-Martin. Down below King was at the wheel of a gun jeep with one of Captain Preston Butterfield III's ex-Foreign Legion soldiers in the back manning the pedestal mounted twin .303 Vickers K machine guns. The Merc and Capt. Plum-Martin had been pressed into service when they returned from a whirlwind trip to coordinate their LONG NECK diamond buying activities with the Police Chief in Morocco. Today the plan was to go after a caravan known to be carrying a stash of contraband stones. The smugglers were headed overland to Turkey where the gems would be sold to Nazi agents.

Just over the horizon Capt. Butterfield's gun jeep patrol was shadowing the column of camels.

Lt. Gen. McKoy said, "What do you think, Waldo?"

"I'd say about any time now."

The caravan was approximately a hundred miles east of Cairo. It was passing through hard scrabble desert not the rolling sand dunes of the Great Sand Sea. There were unlimited places where Capt. Plum-Martin could set down once Capt. Butterfield stopped the camels.

The crime lords, known as The Three, who were wholly controlled by Waldo aka Mr. Big, did not sell these particular diamonds to the smugglers. They were rogue traffickers who had gone around The Three which was a mistake. Major A. W. "Sammy" Sansom had confidential informants (CI's) saturating Cairo's underworld who knew to the last carat the weight of the stones on those camels.

It was a big parcel.

While the traffickers were transporting a large consignment of diamonds the caravan itself was small. Only eight animals.

The smugglers wanted to travel light and fast. Even so, camels are slow plodding creatures which made for a long 1,200-mile journey. Based on information provided by The Three, who had their own sources—the names of the smugglers; the number, quality, and weight of the stones; the date and time of departure; the final destination; and the names of the German agents waiting in Turkey to buy the diamonds—Capt. Butterfield and his band of ex-Foreign Legionnaires had monitored the caravan's progress from the time it pulled out of Cairo's city limits.

There was no way the traffickers could escape; however it never hurts not to be overconfident.

Lt. Gen. McKoy said, "Pam?"

Capt. Plum-Martin said, "We should stay airborne until Preston has the caravan halted in the event they try to scatter. Once the melodrama stops I shall radio King to mark a place for us to put down."

Lt. Gen. McKoy said, "Tell Preston to let 'er buck."

On receiving the signal to execute, Capt. Butterfield went into action immediately. His six gun jeeps, including the one driven by King, appeared over the crest of a sand dune and drove straight toward the caravan at high speed kicking up tall plumes of dust.

Down below the caravan halted as the traffickers tried to decide what to do next. It did not take them long to reach a decision. The camels exploded out in all directions making a run for it—every man for himself.

Waldo, an ex-ivory smuggler of much experience said, "Probably have a rendezvous set up to meet at later—a rally point just like our patrols use."

Lt. Gen. McKoy said, "Good luck with that."

Capt. Butterfield's gun jeeps closed the distance. The Legionnaires went into action firing short bursts from their .303 Vickers K machine guns to convince the traffickers of the wisdom of halting. The gunners were not trying to hit anything.

Their reason for aiming wide had nothing to do with them being humanitarians. The Legionnaires were allowed to sell the camels and split the money. They needed the animals in good shape not shot full of holes.

The tactical situation was this. The gun jeeps had speed and firepower. The smugglers had two more camels than Capt. Butterfield had jeeps. On the flat surface of the desert with Capt. Plum-Martin orbiting overhead the traffickers should not be able to exploit the gun jeeps' disadvantage in one-on-one numbers.

She provided eyes in the sky.

Down below Capt. Butterfield signaled the gun jeeps to break formation with each jeep going after an individual camel rider. This was not one of those situations where the bad guys were going to stop and throw up their hands. The traffickers had an idea of what was in store for them if captured.

The situation on the ground was developing fast. Within minutes each of the gun jeeps had run down a rider. The Legionnaires were holding them at gunpoint but two had broken away with the smugglers giving their animals the whip. Capt. Butterfield spotted one of the runners. He dropped off a man to hold the trafficker he had captured then raced in pursuit.

After a short chase Capt. Butterfield ran down his second camel rider.

From overhead in the Walrus it was a great show.

There was no way anyone could escape, but out of the cloud of dust kicked up by all camels and the gun jeeps wheeling and turning, one trafficker emerged going wide open headed into the great unknown. And he was getting away.

Lt. Gen. McKoy said, “How fast can a camel run?”

Waldo said, “I’ve heard it claimed forty miles per.”

Lt. Gen. McKoy said, “Almost as fast as a Quarter Horse. Look at that rascal go.”

Capt. Plum-Martin said, “I am speaking with King. The dust is obscuring the view. From the ground he is unable to see anyone making a break for it.”

Waldo said, “What you wanna bet that crook’s the one’s got all the rocks?”

Lt. Gen. McKoy said, “Count on it, Waldo.”

Capt. Plum-Martin said, “I gave King an azimuth.”

Waldo said, “He’s gonna have a hard time catching up before that bandit has a chance to stash our sparklers behind some rock.”

Lt. Gen. McKoy said, “You up for this, Pam?”

“You know I am, General.”

“Lock and load, Waldo we’re goin’ in. Get the left window. Take it to him, Pam.”

Capt. Plum-Martin did not need a second invitation. She immediately slipped left banking into a turning dive. The obsolete Walrus was a notoriously slow aircraft but it could outrun a camel.

Since this was an observer mission over friendly territory no one onboard was armed with anything other than their sidearms. The Walrus was capable of carrying machine guns in the navigator’s cupola over the nose and small bombs under the wings. But none were onboard today.

Lt. Gen. McKoy said, “Come in from behind and make a low-level pass over his head.”

“Stand by.”

“How many rounds do you have for that Fitz Special ’a yours, Waldo?”

"One reload. I wasn't expectin' to get in a firefight."

For personal carry, Lt. Gen. McKoy was a Colt man. Today he was armed with his two favorite ivory-stocked .45 Colt Single Action Army aka Peacemaker revolvers w/.45 ACP cylinders. He had not expected a shootout either . . . but he enjoyed carrying the Peacemakers. And being well dressed meant a 1911 Colt .38 Super in a Mexican slide holster around in back and a .380 Colt 1908 Hammerless pocket pistol in his boot.

Like Waldo, he did not have much spare ammunition.

The good news was the Walrus was a pusher-type aircraft so there was no risk of accidentally hitting the propeller firing out the windows. Capt. Plum-Martin lined up directly behind the runaway camel. She was skimming above the desert floor.

Breaking out his custom Smith & Wesson 38–40 Triple Lock Fitz Special, Waldo said, "We aim for the camel or the rider?"

Lt. Gen. McKoy said, "Go for the camel jockey. Our pistols probably don't have enough knockdown power to drop an animal 'a that size with one shot."

Capt. Plum-Martin locked in behind the trafficker. Even though the Walrus was slow and she had reduced airspeed nearly to the stalling point the ground was screaming past below. The smuggler looked back over his shoulder. He pulled out a big, long-barreled 7.63mm Mauser C-96 pistol and started shooting at the plane.

Hanging out the right-side window, Lt. Gen. McKoy shouted, "Lead him short, Waldo!"

Then both men were firing their revolvers as fast as they could. Lt. Gen. McKoy managed three aimed shots with his Single Action Army. Waldo got off four with his S&W Fitz Special—it having the advantage of being double action. There was no visible sign either shooter accomplished anything other than to motivate the camel to kick it into a higher gear.

The plane flashed past. Lt. Gen. McKoy and Waldo hurriedly began reloading. Their empties were rattling around on the deck under their seats as they were ejected.

"You hit anything, Joe?"

"Negative. You?"

"Nope."

Capt. Plum-Martin poured on the power, stood the Walrus on one wing which was a hair-raising maneuver at low altitude, and came around to make another run. She was throwing the obsolete biplane around like a stunt pilot performing aerobatics.

"Where you holdin', Joe?"

"On the camel's tail. Let's give it a little daylight on this pass, we're probably shootin' long."

When firing from a moving vehicle or airplane you do the exact opposite of a skeet shooter or bird hunter. Wing shooters lead their target putting the bead out in front of it. And, maintaining their swing they imagine placing a pie plate out in front of the target as they continue to swing through it—pull the trigger with the barrel still moving, and let whatever they are shooting at fly into the shot pattern.

Hey, Presto!

Today the idea was to aim *behind* the camel—leading it short, so the speed of the Walrus's travel would cause the bullet, which is a lot smaller than a pie plate, to impact on the runaway diamond trafficker.

Shooting a moving target with a handgun from a car or airplane is harder than it sounds.

King could be seen in hot pursuit. However, he was only maintaining pace not noticeably catching up to the camel. He could have ended it right then with his pedestal-mounted machine gun except, like Capt. Butterfield, he had dropped off his gunner to secure the first smuggler he apprehended.

There was no way to drive and fire the .303 Vickers Ks in the back of the jeep.

The Walrus' wild gyrations made reloading the revolvers difficult. Waldo fumbled his shells. They bounced around under his boots out of reach. He managed to get his pistol fully recharged but was going to be left with only three rounds after he expended the bullets in his pistol's cylinder.

Capt. Plum-Martin had brought the Walrus back around and was lined up on the camel again.

Lt. Gen. McKoy said, "Get it done, Waldo—Power River let 'er buck!"

Then the two began blasting away at the smuggler. As they flew directly over the camel Lt. Gen. McKoy hung way out the window firing almost straight down. It should have been a chip shot for a skilled exhibition-class shootist like him.

No joy.

Lt. Gen. McKoy said, "If I'd 'a had my lariat I coulda' roped him."

Waldo said, "I'm down to my last three beans."

Capt. Plum-Martin said, "Take my pistol."

Lt. Gen. McKoy was thinking about the idea of roping the smuggler. Not having a rope was pretty much a kill card for that game. However, if he *did* have a rope he would have had to move up into the open-topped cupola on the nose to make the throw.

"I'm headin' to the navigator's station to get a better angle."

Working his way down the narrow crawl space to reach the cupola while Capt. Plum-Martin was throwing the Walrus around the sky like a high-performance fighter was a nightmare experience. Once again she had it standing up on one wing coming back around for another pass.

Lt. Gen. McKoy made it to the end of the tunnel only slightly dinged up from banging into the sides and all the wild gyrations.

Straight ahead the Walrus was fast approaching the galloping camel. Capt. Plum-Martin was down so low on this pass she was almost at the point of scraping the desert floor. Lt. Gen. McKoy elected to go with his 1911 Colt .38 Super on this pass because it held more rounds and could be fired faster. He held the pistol out in both hands, rested his forearms straight out in front of him on the edge of the cupola, acquired a sight picture and waited.

When the Walrus was almost on top of the trafficker the man turned, raised his Mauser C-96, and begin firing wildly over his shoulder again.

Ignoring the incoming rounds, taking his time, going slow in a hurry, Lt. Gen. McKoy placed the gold bead on the front post of his sight at the point where the man's *mahawi*—saddle—met the camel's back just behind the hump. He held fire until the range closed to virtual point-blank. Then when everything felt right, touched it off—three times fast.

BLAM BLAM BLAM!

The shots sounded almost like one.

As the plane flashed over the rider he pitched off the side, hit the ground and bounced. King raced by the dead smuggler in hot pursuit of the panicked camel in case the gems were in its saddle bags. Sooner or later the animal had to get tired.

Lt. Gen. McKoy said, "By orders of the President—eradicate any and all diamond traffickers."

Waldo said, "You eradicated him."

CAPTAIN BUTCH "HEADHUNTER" HOOLIHAN WAS dozing in a hammock on the deck of L7 under camouflage netting waiting for the sun to go down. The caique was tied off on a remote stretch of Kalymnos Island. At least they thought it was remote.

"Ahoy."

Capt. Hoolihan rolled out of the hammock and grabbed his .45 Thompson submachine gun.

"Ahoy LSF caique."

Commander Andreas Londos rushed up on deck and crouched down next to him. There was not supposed to be any British troops on Kalymnos much less U.S., and the voice had a distinctly American twang. Through the netting they could see a slim bearded man wearing khaki battledress standing on the shore.

"Permission to come aboard?"

Capt. Hoolihan looked at Cdr. Londos. The Greek nodded approval. Neither of them was thrilled by this unexpected development. There was no way to know who or what the stranger was. He could be a Nazi agent or a member of a German coast watch team—that seemed more likely.

Capt. Hoolihan ordered, "Advance and be recognized."

The stranger moved to the water's edge.

Capt. Hoolihan said, "Who goes there?"

"Lieutenant Jackson Taylor, United States Navy."

Capt. Hoolihan whispered to Cdr. Londos, "No way. Taylor's dead."

Cdr. Londos pulled his .38 Webly revolver, "Are you certain?"

"Colonel Randal brought back his personal effects after the OSS Martine Unit raid on Portologo," Capt. Hoolihan whispered. "Taylor drowned. We held a service for him at Advanced Base Castelrozzo."

Cdr. Londos whispered, "Order the man to demonstrate his identity."

Capt. Hoolihan said, "Do you have any proof you are who you say you are?"

"Just my dog tag."

Cdr. Londos whispered, "A Nazi could have taken it off Lieutenant Taylor's body."

Capt. Hoolihan said, "Who is the last American you spoke to?"

"Colonel John Randal, Raiding Forces."

Cdr. Londos said, "Permission granted. Come aboard."

LtJG Taylor climbed on L7. He could not help but notice all the 9mm Lanchester submachine guns pointed at him. The Greek sailors doing the pointing looked a lot like pirates. In fact that is what they were.

"Boy am I glad to see you, Headhunter!"

Capt. Hoolihan said, "I failed to recognize you with the beard, Jackson, you are supposed to be dead."

LtJG Taylor said, "Colonel Randal and I washed ashore not far from here after our kayak broke up in the surf. The Colonel apparently tried to give me artificial respiration but I must not have responded. Probably due to being concussed when the waves crashed my head against the rocks."

Capt. Hoolihan said, "Colonel Randal believed you drowned."

"A group of nuns conducting a search for one of their girls who had gone missing found me. They thought the same thing. Sent for a priest instead of a doctor."

Capt. Hoolihan said, "Lady Jane's Royal Marines cried at your funeral."

LtJG Taylor, the playboy Hollywood dentist to the stars, said, "I was knocking on heaven's door, that's for sure. Concussion, hypothermia, cracked ribs—Colonel Randal must have been overenthusiastic attempting to perform artificial respiration."

Capt. Hoolihan said, "What have you been doing all this time?"

"The nuns took me to their convent to recover. Been there ever since. Still not a hundred percent. I hit those rocks pretty hard." LtJG Taylor said.

"Drank half the Aegean."

Capt. Hoolihan said, "Any German troops on the island?"

LtJG Taylor said, "There's a small Italian garrison. Since the armistice they've restricted themselves to barracks. Don't venture out much . . . worried about what might happen if the Greeks decide to rise up—lot of bad blood on this island.

"The Nazis are expected to arrive at any minute."

Cdr. Londos said, "How did you know where to find us?"

LtJG Taylor said, "One of the local boys was walking along the shore. He noticed an unusual lump at the edge of the water, claimed he nearly tripped over it. I came down to check things out and recognized The Great Teddy's camouflage technique.

"There have been reports of other uncamouflaged caiques that appeared overnight farther down the coastline."

Capt. Hoolihan said, "You ready to go home, Doctor?"

LtJG Taylor said, "Roger that. The girls cried, huh?"

"They had been counting on you to whiten their teeth."

JAMES "BALDIE" TAYLOR ARRIVED AT Castelrozzo aboard the Raiding Forces' Hudson. Major General Sam Houston Blackwell had provided floats for the transport to be converted into a seaplane which is different from an amphibian that can put down on land or sea. With the floats mounted the Hudson could only make water landings. But that was all Raiding Forces needed for the flight between RFHQ and ABC.

The Hudson flew approximately 50 mph faster than the Black Cat—cutting down on the commute time.

Jim immediately went into conference with Brandy Seaborn. The golden-tanned MAS boat skipper with hair the color of wheat had arrived back on the island in time to see Captain Billy Jack Jaxx bring in his Brandenburger prisoner. She took charge of the interrogation.

Unhampered by the need to adhere to the Geneva Convention—enemy troops caught out of uniform were not protected by the Accords, Brandy used every trick in the book to extract information from the Nazi.

The problem was, her subject did not know much of intelligence value.

The German gave up everything about the Brandenburgers raid team organization, planning, training, sea and overland movement to the target, execution of the assault, and what occurred once the Nazis realized their mission had failed. He did not provide any information on who or what was behind the raid. The Brandenburger Regiment believed in compartmentalization and the need to know. Personnel involved in any given operation were told only the details they needed to carry out the mission.

Brandy was able to confirm that Colonel John Randal had been the primary target. The Nazi claimed he had never met SS-Hauptsturmführer Gretchen von Coffenhauser though he recognized her name. He did not know if she was dead, alive or involved in the mission in any way.

Jim said, “You are confident you mined all the information the man has to give?”

Brandy said, “I am. We can go back in and reinterrogate him if you like. Say the word, James.”

Jim said, “General McKoy likes to say, ‘Why take a chance?’”

Brandy said, “Nothing ventured nothing gained.”

Two hours later they emerged from the basement of ABCHQ without having obtained any other information of significant value. Lieutenant Colonel Sir Terry “Zorro” Stone, Capt. Billy Jack Jaxx and Mandy Paige were waiting in the TOC to hear a report.

Brandy stopped to brief them while Jim went in search of Veronica Paige.

“There were thirty-three Brandenburgers on the raid. Nineteen have been killed so far. You have your work cut out hunting down the rest, Jack.”

Lt. Col. Stone said, “Tell me what you require to achieve a resolution, Captain. We cannot allow any of those Nazis to remain on the loose.”

Capt. Jaxx said, “Let me get with Roy Kidd, sir. We need to rethink our strategy. One thing’s for sure . . . Mandy’s intel has been dead on.

“I need more of it.”

Mandy said, “We can increase the reward for information. That might help. Fliers are being printed to be delivered to every house by local postmen. The phone bank will continue calling the list of numbers we obtained from the Castelrozzo Telephone Company.

“Other than that I am wide open to suggestions.”

Major Zargo came into the TOC. "You asked for me?"

Brandy handed him a slip of paper. "This is the name of the Brandenburger contact on Castelrozzo. Not only did the woman provide local intelligence she sheltered a two-man reconnaissance party that landed on the island a week prior to the raid. I thought you would be the appropriate person to decide the appropriate action to take with her."

Major Zargo had known Brandy since Habbaniya. Those who had been on the RAF base during the siege tended to share a bond. He appreciated her allowing him the opportunity to handle the disposition of a Greek traitor.

It showed respect.

Maj. Zargo said, "With permission I shall resolve this matter for you."

Lt. Col. Stone said, "Granted."

As they were leaving to have a late breakfast, Mandy said, "Major Zargo is not a man to cross."

Capt. Jaxx said, "Roger that, he's what they had in mind when they invented the word 'hardcase.'"

Captain Lionel Chatterhorn passed them with four stone-faced VPW men coming to take charge of the prisoner. The Nazi was able to walk, was not bleeding and had no visible signs of broken bones or of otherwise being tortured. But he had clearly had a bad day.

It was about to get worse.

Mandy said, "Serves him right. Never should have murdered our men. Poor Bentley."

The war in the Aegean had passed the tipping point. It was spiraling out of control. The two sides hated each other.

Rikke "Rocky" Runborg was sitting alone at a table in the mess that was almost empty at this time of the morning. They joined her. The Norwegian, who Waldo called "The Human

Heatwave," liked to tease Capt. Jaxx the way Brandy teased Colonel John Randal.

When Rocky pronounced his name with her accent it sounded like "Bill Lee."

He thought it was sexy as hell.

Mandy said, "Rocky, you are a highly trained intelligence operative. You have experience working undercover. What were you taught about avoiding detection in a village like Castelrozzo?"

Rocky said, "Beware the children."

Capt. Jaxx said, "Yeah, kids go everywhere, see everything, keep secrets and don't always tell adults —I know I didn't."

Mandy said, "I shall have Major Adair instruct Mayor Stephanopoulos to organize a town hall meeting of all the Greek children immediately. Jack, you would be perfect to speak to them."

Capt. Jaxx said, "I don't know, Mandy. I've never talked to a group of kids. One of 'em might ask me how many people I've killed."

Mandy said, "I shall take that as a yes."

JAMES "BALDIE" TAYLOR MET WITH VERONICA Paige, the head of MI-9 in the Aegean. Escape was an unwanted organization originally assigned to Middle East Command then attached to Brigadier Dudley Clarke's A-Force under the cover name "N Section' before being handed off to Raiding Forces for lack of any other place to put it. Colonel John Randal did not have a spare officer to assign to a job that was large in scope but with no assets or support, so he did the unthinkable—placed a female in charge.

That was simply "not done."

Veronica turned out to be an inspired choice conforming to Raiding Forces Rule 'Right Man, Right Job'—only in this case, Right Woman. MI-9 was initially tasked to provide training in Escape and Evasion techniques to RAF aircrew. She organized mobile teams of handpicked FANYs to travel from base to base putting on the E&E classes.

The pretty girls kept the men's attention while teaching a subject they should have been highly motivated to learn but generally were not—getting captured was something that was going to happen to someone else. From time to time Lieutenant General "Geronimo" Joe McKoy and/or Lieutenant Theodore Hamilton traveled with the mobile training teams putting on shooting exhibitions and magic shows.

Veronica's plan worked to perfection. In short order MI-9 had a backlog of RAF and USAAF airbases requesting a return visit while others were inquiring as to when she could schedule her mobile team of instructors for an initial class.

Unknown to those without a Need to Know there was a TOP SECRET component to the MI-9 training. Certain select aircrew, both enlisted and officers were provided private training in clandestine techniques for sending and receiving secret messages from inside a POW camp.

Brig. Clarke of A-Force was an officer with an enviable track record for his ability to create an organization and then turn it loose, stand back and watch it flourish—one of his creations being Raiding Forces. Only he could never completely resist the temptation to dabble in their business when the mood struck.

For example, Brig. Clarke organized a pair of escape lines for Veronica anchored on the west coast of Turkey then on to

Castelrozzo and up the Aegean to Greece. Working with Brig. Clarke, two Royal Navy officers who had been appointed counsels in Turkey, Commander V. Wolfson and Lieutenant Commander Noel Rees, built up a clandestine naval base in Turkey near Cesme opposite Chios on the peninsula west of Izmir.

Somehow Brig. Clarke persuaded the local governor to declare the peninsula where the base was located a prohibited zone. No one in or out. Except for Raiding Forces, LSF or MI-9.

The end of the escape line—or the beginning, depending on whether you were operating the line or an evader traveling down it to safety—was Greece via Skiathos, Skopelos, and Skyros. There was also a hidden advance caique base farther south at Antiparos which was going to have to be supplied by Vice Admiral Sir Randolph "Razor" Ransom's two H-class submarines.

MI-9 was proving so effective in bringing evaders home the RAF joked any aircrew known to be down and on the run in Greece for as long as a month should be posted as Absent Without Leave (AWOL). Veronica was very popular with men who E&E'd from enemy territory and made it back safe.

More than a few volunteered to work for her in MI-9 willing to go back in harm's way to help other soldiers, sailors and airmen in need of being rescued. Firsthand experience made the former evaders some of the best Escape operatives. On her watch MI-9 had gone from being a one-woman shop to having escape lines—aka rat lines—from Greece to Castelrozzo, a clandestine base in neutral Turkey, a small army of operatives and its own fleet of caiques.

A lot of what Veronica did was classified TOP SECRET with a tightly restricted "Need to Know" list.

Even Col. Randal was not cleared for all the details.

Jim said, "My reason for flying out was to have a chance for us to talk privately, Veronica. Events are evolving rapidly in this part of the world even though it has become a military backwater. As you are aware out here every agency has to perform certain other tasks unrelated to their primary function.

"Escape is going to be expected to do so as well. On occasion you will be required to carry out assignments unrelated to assisting escapers and evaders."

Veronica said, "Such as?"

Jim said, "You are aware I serve as an intelligence liaison officer between MI-6 and SOE. I am also the MI-6/SOE liaison to OSS. At least that is how my role is described on paper. You are not cleared to know all the details of my activities but from time to time I shall come to you with a request and you will carry it out."

Veronica said, "John put me in charge of MI-9 after GHQ Cairo and A-Force demonstrated little interest in spending money, assets or time on the program. Then as soon as we began to enjoy modest success MI-9 in London sent out an officer to replace me and take over. Colonel Randal sent him packing.

"Are you attempting to stage a coup as well?"

Jim said, "*Fait accompli.* You work for me, Veronica and always have. That is strictly 'Need to Know' and no one other than the two of us possess the need. The chain of command runs from MI-6 through A-Force to you in MI-9 here in Raiding Forces.

"You likely noted GHQ Cairo and SOE were not on the list. That said, from time to time they can be expected to show up with requests for you to perform certain undertakings. You will not accept those assignments until and unless you clear them through me first."

"Do you have any documentation to confirm what you say, Jim?"

"Not a scrap."

"Am I permitted to ask John for verification?"

"Negative."

Veronica said, "What would happen if I chose not to agree to your terms?"

Jim said, "You will be on the next boat back to England."

Veronica said, "What is it you expect of me?"

"Continue the mission," Jim said. "You are still the chief of agency. I have no intention of interfering with your day-to-day operations. On occasion I shall ask for MI-9 to perform a task you will be perfectly willing to accommodate.

"In the event GHQ Cairo, SOE, or any organization other than Raiding Forces or A-Force request you to use MI-9 resources for operations of their own design, contact me immediately. The two of us will jointly decide whether you comply or not.

"I will shield you from any repercussions in the event we elect to refuse."

Veronica said, "What kind of assignments should I be expecting?"

Jim said, "Primarily inserting or extracting agents from some remote location or the other. SOE will be requesting MI-9 to run guns to guerrilla organizations throughout the Aegean—you comply after consulting with me. Randal should like that mission. He might even handle it for you.

"Professor Winthrop has an intelligence network of anthropologists stretching from here to Greece. When he comes to you for assistance consider him one of ours. The Professor is under the impression he works for SOE but between us that is not exactly the case."

"Understood."

Jim said, "I want you to view me as your patron and protector. If you are in need of something do not hesitate to ask. If at all possible to accede to your request, it will be done."

Veronica said, "I shall hold you to that."

Jim said, "Beverly is listed as the OSS Escape officer. Originally she was merely a placeholder on the Americans' TO&E to justify her existence and still is to some extent. Make her feel a part of MI-9. We want Beverly to report to Donovan that she is actively engaged in Escape in the Aegean, which means he is. It is in our best interest for OSS to believe they are involved in something significant out here.

"General Donovan is an empire builder. We can count on him to leap at the chance to take credit for MI-9 operations in the Aegean. Working through Beverly I want you to give him plenty of success stories he can use to talk up OSS in Washington."

Veronica said, "I can stage manage that."

"Keep Donovan invested in your work," Jim said, "and we may be able to tap into OSS for material assistance we are not able to lay hands on from any other source."

Veronica said, "Consider it done."

CAPTAIN BILLY JACK JAXX AND CAPTAIN ROY KIDD huddled in a corner of the Tactical Operations Center. The purpose of the meeting was to discuss new ways to kill or capture the remaining Brandenburger Commandos still at large on Castelrozzo. Searching house to house was continuing with additional new patrols out; however, the process could take weeks or even months.

Capt. Jaxx said, "What we're doing is working. But we need to step it up. Got any ideas Roy?"

"Beaters."

"Beaters?"

"In India when I was on loan from my regiment to hunt problem tigers I would get the village chief to organize beaters. The natives would march through the jungle online banging drums, blowing whistles, and shaking rattles hoping to drive the man-eater out into the open where I could shoot it. Sometimes the local maharaja would provide elephants we could use to ride behind the line of beaters to use as a mobile shooting platform.

"That's what we need to do here, Jack."

"We don't have any elephants."

"Yeah, but we do have beefed-up security on the island—2nd Battalion, Cyprus Regiment."

Capt. Jaxx said, "Break it down for me."

Capt. Kidd said, "We set up a grid to search utilizing the Cyprus Regiment battalion and provide overwatch for the infantry by positioning snipers on top of buildings that provide our shooters interlocking fields of fire with no dead ground between them. We'll have the troops sweep through taking their time putting on a show of force—not necessarily checking each house in detail. The goal is for the Brandenburgers to spot the beaters coming and abandon the place where they're hiding to move to new shelter out of the line of march.

"When they do, the snipers light 'em up."

Capt. Jaxx said, "I like it."

Capt. Kidd said, "I can set up on one building with my scoped .55 Boy's Rifle. From the right location it should have enough range to cover the entire search area. The Lovats can each recruit a spotter, so that makes three teams. And there's a new man out from the States I want to try—Sergeant Volkmann.

"He's from OSS assigned to be the Raiding Forces armorer. The outfit sent him to the Marine Corps Scout Sniper School because the U.S. Army doesn't have a sniper school.

"In addition the Sergeant was a member of the President's Hundred before the war."

"President's Hundred?"

"The top one hundred scoring shooters, both military and civilian, in the annual National President's Rifle and Pistol matches. Sergeant Volkmann qualified with the rifle using an '03 A-1 Springfield. We can marry him up with a spotter to make a fourth sniper team."

Capt. Jaxx said, "That going to be enough shooters?"

"It's what we have. Raiding Forces is full of expert marksmen but they're not trained snipers or match-grade riflemen. We only want the best."

"All right then let's set it up for tomorrow," Capt. Jaxx said. "I'll coordinate with Colonel Stone to authorize me the Cyprus Regiment's beaters. You handle the snipers."

Capt. Kidd said, "Can do."

Capt. Jaxx said, "How do you want me to organize the drive?"

"Lay out a series of grids on an overlay of the map of Castelrozzo," Capt. Kidd said. "Starting on the east side of the village make each one five hundred yards wide running all the way to the top of the escarpment.

"We'll clear one grid per day."

"Got it."

Capt. Kidd said, "I'll take the shooters out later today to conduct a reconnaissance to identify our overwatch positions. We need to be in place an hour before BMNT. You start your drive at full daylight.

"Remember no early start, we need the Brandenburgers to see us coming and we need to be able to see them when they move."

Capt. Jaxx said, "You want my people to work up the escarpment or down?"

"Doesn't matter to me."

"We'll drive uphill then. Push the Germans back onto the plateau. I can have an ambush up there waiting if any Nazis make it that far."

"Good idea, Jack."

COLONEL JOHN RANDAL WAS SPRAWLED ON A couch in the living area of the Jefferson Davis suite at the Carolina Hotel. He was reading a field manual, *Raid Operations Department of the Navy, USMC*. On page 1 paragraph 1 under "Purpose" it stated:

> Raid Operations explains the doctrine, tactics, techniques and procedure for raid operations conducted by Marine Air-Ground Task Forces. It highlights the advantages, disadvantages and other critical factors a commander and staff member must consider during the planning and execution of a raid operation.

That sounded pretty good—the U.S. Marines Corps did like detailed planning.

Beverly Blackwell breezed into the suite without knocking. She was wearing a white sheath-type evening dress that left nothing to the imagination concerning the state of her physical fitness as a result of Rocky Runborg's daily training regime.

"Lady Jane?"

Col. Randal looked up and said, "Bedroom."

The blond Texas beauty queen breezed past and disappeared inside. Apparently, she and Major the Lady Jane Seaborn had a last-minute wardrobe crisis to attend to. The cocktail party Lady Jane was hosting for the Swing Board was about to begin in the main ballroom downstairs so they were working against a hard deadline.

He went back to his reading, "Paragraph 2. Scope. This MCMP is intended for the use by commanders and their staffs, planning guidance, and execution principles apply to amphibious and non-amphibious raids."

Hmmm. No mention of airborne raids that might be carried out by the USMC's Paramarine 1st Parachute Battalion. It was said the U.S. Marine Corp did not embrace the concept of dropping paratroops ahead of an amphibious landing. Col. Randal wondered why?

Red arrived. "Hello John . . ."

The Flying Clipper Girl was stunning in her hunter-green sheath. Col. Randal was of the opinion all redheads should wear green. He pointed to the bedroom.

Looking at Chapter 1 "Raid Design" he was surprised to see a quote from Brigadier Orde Charles Wingate, Burma 1943. "Nothing is so devastating as to pounce upon the enemy in the dark, smite him hip and thigh, and vanish silent into the night."

The U.S. Marine Corps quoting "Wingnut." How did that happen? The Brigadier was currently in the CBI in command of a brigade he called "Chindits" carrying out long-range penetration raids deep in the jungle, far inside Japanese controlled territory, in "columns" of approximate battalion size.

Sounded good, especially to the local press who had nothing much to write about in a remote theatre where the British banished their generals who did not perform up to expectations elsewhere.

If the Aegean was the "war that never was" Burma was the "forgotten war."

The problem, according to Jim Taylor, was the Chindits accomplished little more than being an irritant to the Japanese. The columns marched, fought and died under extremely harsh jungle conditions suffering staggering casualties. Almost no one walked out fit to return to duty.

Battalions that were irreplaceable in that remote war zone were decimated. The number of Chindits killed in action was not great, but it was shocking how many sick and wounded troops were intentionally left behind in the jungle because they would slow down the march. Survivors who made it out were riddled by disease with little to show for their valiant effort.

Jim claimed Wingate's operations were of questionable military value except as public relations stunts.

Chindits made good press.

Col. Randal studied the Table of Contents. There was an Appendix titled "Considerations for Amphibious Raids" and one styled "Considerations for Special Boat Raids." He wondered what the difference might be.

Flipping over to Appendix C—Amphibious Raids under "Principals," he read, "Plans must be as simple as possible." The Marines were also advocates of "Keep it Short and Simple"—good.

Col. Randal wondered if the USMC had ever heard of Occam's razor?

Skipping down, "The raid force must be as small as possible. Do not send 100 Marines to conduct a raid 15 Marines can accomplish."

A worthy concept. Marines were known for doing more with less. On the other hand you can overdo it.

In Col. Randal's opinion there was no such thing as overkill—Lieutenant General "Geronimo" Joe McKoy was an advocate of the concept, "Too much ain't enough."

Over in Appendix F—"Considerations for Special Boat Raids"—he found, "Small surface craft maximize the advantage of surprise through stealth as the relative signature of small raiding parties embarked aboard small boats is minimal."

This FM was going to require closer study—almost sounded like the Marines were describing the LSF's caiques.

Lady Jane came out of the bedroom adjusting one of the diamond ear studs he had given her and wearing a black evening dress that fit like a snakeskin—drop-dead gorgeous.

She had his U.S. Army "Pinks and Greens" uniform blouse draped over one arm.

"Time to go, babe."

He stood up and Lady Jane helped him into the tailor-made jacket smoothing it across the back. All of his decorations were in place to include U.S. and British parachute wings. Before Col. Randal could protest, Lady Jane said, "Bronc's orders."

Beverly and Red joined them.

"Wow, Johnny you look beautiful!"

"That's enough out of you, Beverly."

Major General Sam Houston Blackwell knocked on the door. They went out into the hall and moved to the elevator. Bronc punched the button for the second floor.

Lady Jane said, "We are going to the lobby, General."

“Yes we are, but the plan is to walk down the stairs to get there. Never waste a grand entrance.”

Col. Randal noted Maj. Gen. Blackwell had lost most of his good ol’ boy Texas drawl since their arrival at Camp Mackall. He was all business every move calculated. As they descended the massive spiral staircase people gathered in the lobby turned to stare.

Flashy arrival—check.

Seized the moment—check.

Impressions are important—check.

Col. Randal wondered what game the General was playing tonight. Low key at the board meeting. High profile at the cocktail party.

Brigadier General William “Wild Bill” Donovan was waiting to greet them at the foot of the staircase. He had flown in from Washington for Lady Jane’s event. Wild Bill did not have any real need to be there other than he and Maj. Gen. Blackwell were longtime friends.

The fate of the airborne division was of no importance to the Office of Strategic Services.

Col. Randal wondered about that too.

The antebellum main ballroom was large enough to accommodate the Swing Board and all of the officers who had been sitting in the theater seats at the morning meeting. Lady Jane was the hostess, but she was throwing the party for Maj. Gen. Blackwell. Typically the least known member of a military board would not be holding the initial social event.

But Bronc was doing it by proxy.

It was Lady Jane’s cocktail party thrown at his request—a fact not being advertised.

There was no official receiving line this being an informal gathering. However, when Maj. Gen. Blackwell’s entourage walked in a line quickly formed. Col. Randal thought the generals might want the chance to introduce themselves to Bronc or Wild Bill, but he was fairly sure everyone else was in it for Lady Jane, Beverly and Red—who would blame them?

Not him.

Col. Randal did not feel any real sense of connection to the people present. He was an outsider. Tonight his role was to be a cardboard pop-up consort for Lady Jane. Wear the Pinks and Greens. Full decorations. Don't talk—well, maybe a few words.

He could do that.

Maj. Gen. Blackwell's aide rushed over to stand at the beginning of the impromptu line. Protocol for military receiving lines dictated each person introduce himself to the aide when they came to him even if they had known each other for years. The aide then turned and introduced that person to the senior officer standing first in the line—in this case, Bronc, who would, in turn, introduce them to Beverly who was standing with her father.

Brig. Gen. Donovan and Red were next in line which meant Col. Randal, being junior, and Lady Jane were on the end.

As the officers arrived in front of Col. Randal to shake hands few of them made eye contact. They were staring at the decorations on his chest. Almost none had been in combat yet and were impressed by bits of ribbon.

Col. Randal was reminded again of how green the U.S. Army was at this point in the war.

Once decorum had been satisfied Brig. Gen. Donovan pulled Col. Randal aside.

"You are aware General McKoy met with the President when he was in Washington recently."

"Yes, sir."

Brig. Gen. Donovan said, "Did the old scout mention the President ordered him to exterminate diamond traffickers posthaste? FDR wants those who engage in the illicit trade of diamonds terminated with extreme prejudice. When I'm in Washington I have to brief him daily on Raiding Forces' progress in that endeavor.

"You need to keep me posted with information to report."

Col. Randal said, "General McKoy informed me the President ordered him to go back to Egypt and monitor LONG NECK—the term used for the traffickers was 'eradicate, sir.'"

Brig. Donovan said, "The President said *exterminate.* I was in the room. I know you have questions about the motive for the order.

"Don't ask again the answer would be the kiss of death. In fact if you were to discover even so much as the code name of the TOP SECRET project behind the national security need for LONG NECK—not the details just the name—I would have to pull you out of Raiding Forces and assign you to be the army recruiting officer in some place like Butte, Montana."

"I understand, sir."

"No, I don't think you do."

"Sir, my people . . ."

"Let me help you out, Colonel. Tell them two things: One, industrial diamonds power the German war machine—that is true. Two, the United States has a desire to put an end to DeBeers' worldwide monopoly on diamonds —which is not the case.

"They'll believe the second reason even if it isn't true."

Col. Randal said, "Breaking up the diamond cartel's monopoly so U.S. jewelers can buy stones from whoever they please is an openly discussed . . ."

Brig. Gen Donovan said, “Pure propaganda put out by DeBeers’ public relations department to CYA the company for turning a blind eye to their diamonds being sold to Nazi Germany through third parties. Since there is not a single commercial diamond mine in production anywhere in the U.S. why would our government care who has a monopoly on marketing them?

“The answer is, it doesn’t.”

Col. Randal said, “Based on General McKoy’s report of his conversation with the President I consolidated all LONG NECK ancillary operations and put him in charge. He’s running the show.

The General will report directly to you, sir.

Brig. Donovan said, “Good plan. However, it’s my understanding he is not entirely pleased with being assigned as the LONG NECK case officer. Let me make this perfectly clear, Colonel—diamond traffickers pose a direct threat to the national security of the United States.

“Do you understand?”

“Yes, sir.” Col. Randal noticed he said “traffickers” were the threat—not diamonds.

“You need to have your people get with the program.”

Brig. Gen. Donovan was aware Raiding Forces personnel tasked with carrying out LONG NECK were unenthusiastic about taking the assignment on blind faith. He had information certain of Col. Randal’s people were continuing to question *why* stopping diamond trafficking was important. And he knew some were not comfortable with the order to eliminate the smugglers.

Meaning kill them out of hand—DRT as Captain Billy Jack Jaxx liked to say—dead right there.

Col. Randal was less than thrilled Wild Bill seemed to know so much about what was going on inside Raiding Forces. Did he have a mole in the unit? Who might it be?

Brig. Gen. Donovan said, “Colonel, I’m a lawyer and like to believe a good one. Here is my legal opinion—anyone who traffics with the enemy is classified as a collaborator. Under the Geneva Accords collaborators can be shot precipitously with no violation of international law, no harm no foul.

“Is that clear?”

Col. Randal said, “Crystal.”

“Do your job.”

Now Col. Randal understood why the Chief of OSS had flown down tonight. He was there to tighten him up. Wild Bill was not paying a social call.

“Yes, sir.”

Major General Matthew Ridgway came over, “Your Benevento drop was an eye-opener for me, Colonel. Something to factor in when future 82nd Airborne missions are in the development stage. I’d like you to brief me on the details when we have the opportunity.”

“My pleasure, sir.”

“We will be reorganizing the 82nd in the near future and I’m going to be needing a couple of battalion commanders. Any chance you have capable officers in Raiding Forces you would care to recommend? Promotion goes with the assignment.”

Col. Randal said, “I do, sir. Let me check with them first. If there’s any interest I’ll have my people report to your headquarters for an interview.”

Maj. Gen. Ridgway said, “I don’t believe we have a complete grasp yet on what to expect from airborne operations—specifically parachute drops. It’s still all new to us at this stage. I can use battle-experienced battalion commanders with an unconventional mindset.”

“The officers I have in mind can provide that, sir.”

Maj. Gen. Ridgway said, “Fresh ideas are always welcome in the 82nd.”

After he left, Major General William “Bill” Lee walked over, “I bet Matt was soliciting you for potential battalion commanders?”

“Yes, sir . . . that is a fact.”

“My One-O-One will be deploying to Europe shortly. None of my battalion COs have ever heard a shot fired in anger. Due to the Airborne’s rapid expansion we’ve promoted people far past their competence level. If you have qualified candidates I need battalion commanders with airborne combat experience under their belt a lot worse than General Ridgway does.”

Col. Randal said, “Sir, I have three majors who would make outstanding battalion commanders. If any or all of them express interest we can request General Blackwell fly them to Fort Benning for you to meet with.”

Maj. Gen. Lee said, “Whether it works out or not you just made a friend in the 101st, Colonel.”

There was a reason the Screaming Eagles worshipped their commanding general—a man the troops referred to as “The Father of the Airborne.”

Maj. Gen. Blackwell tapped a wine glass with a knife for everyone’s attention. “Colonel Randal, front and center.”

Having no idea what this was about Col. Randal moved to the front of the room. Bronc’s aide produced a sheet of paper and read. “Attention to orders! The President of the United States is pleased to present Colonel John Randal a second oak leaf cluster to his Distinguished Service Cross signifying a third award for actions in and around Benevento, Italy, on or about…”

As Lady Jane came forward to pin the medal on his blouse she lit off one of her best grade heart-attack smiles. Col. Randal had to remember to breathe. She had that effect on him.

Lady Jane laughed, "You are beautiful John."

A photographer for the local newspaper the *Southern Pines Pilot* was on hand to take photos.

Since the decoration was completely unexpected, Col. Randal was wondering if Bronc had orchestrated it as an opportunity to direct attention to himself. Why not? He had stage-managed everything else since arriving at Camp Mackall. If so it was artfully done. In record-breaking time Maj. Gen. Blackwell had established himself as a power player in the Airborne community.

The commander of Troop Transport Command was emerging as a force to be reckoned with.

MANDY PAIGE WASTED NO TIME IN HAVING THE children of Castelrozzo assembled at ABCHQ. They were broken down into three age groups. The six- to ten-year-olds were given an ice cream party. Captain Billy Jack Jaxx came in and spoke to them about the importance of keeping their eyes open for Germans hiding on the island. The youngsters were impressed because he talked to them like they were adults.

No one had ever done that before.

He made hunting for Nazis sound like fun.

Capt. Jaxx said, "If you see anything suspicious, any man you don't know, anyone who looks like they're sneaking around, see where they go then come straight here and report to Mandy—we pay ice cream for information."

An army of tiny counterintelligence operatives was about to be unleashed on Castelrozzo.

Eleven- to fourteen-year-olds were next. Capt. Jaxx spoke to them like grown-ups too, which got the children's attention. Their marching orders were to "look, listen, and report."

It went well.

The last group, ages fifteen to nineteen, consisted mostly of girls. Nearly all of the boys had left the island as they approached military age. The teenage girls liked Capt. Jaxx—a lot.

He stood in front of the room leaning back against a desk looking out over the top of his Ray-Ban aviator glasses. He was wearing his pistols and a Fairbairn Fighting Knife—Jack Cool to the max.

"Questions?"

The older girls went wild waving their hands to be recognized. Naturally he called on the best-looking one first. Her question, asking for his phone number, was in Greek so he turned to Mandy for a translation.

"She wants to know if you have a younger brother."

10
ICE CREAM LOTTERY

CAPTAIN ROY KIDD MET WITH HIS THREE designated snipers, Tech Sergeant Luke Volkmann, Lovat Scout Lionel Fenwick and Lovat Scout Munro Ferguson. Each shooter would have a spotter. To cut down on the patrol's size, so as to not draw unwanted attention, the spotters would not be accompanying the patrol to select locations for the sniper's overwatch positions to.

In the event they were observed by a Brandenburger in hiding Capt. Kidd did not want to tip his hand as to what was being planned. No scoped rifles were being carried on the recon. TSgt. Volkmann had a .45 Thompson submachine gun, the Lovats were armed with .30 M1 Garand rifles. Capt. Kidd was sporting his newest favorite individual weapon, the Owen Carbine—a made-in-Australia 9mm submachine gun nicknamed the "Diggers Darling." The submachine gun featured a magazine on *top* of the receiver and had a reputation for extreme reliability.

No Brandenburger with eyes on this group of soldiers would have reason to suspect they were anything more than another of the many patrols crisscrossing the village. Capt. Kidd was hiding his intentions in plain sight. That allowed the patrol to be able to move around openly without giving anything away.

Long-range marksmanship and sniping in particular are skills that require detailed planning, patience, careful camouflage, knowledge of ballistics and skill with the rifle/ammunition being used. In addition are all the other elements that go into precision shooting, including but not limited to estimating range, doping windage, sight picture, hold, breathing and trigger control.

Everything has to come together perfectly for the sniper to deliver the rifle round on target. One shot one kill being the purpose of the exercise. It is not easy.

Capt. Kidd was meticulous in his planning. He never took anything for granted. Never made an assumption or left anything to chance. Prior to moving out from ABCHQ he issued a brief Sniper Order which is quite a bit different from a standard Patrol Order.

The Sniper Order utilizes the acronym METT-TC as taught by the Lovat Scout cadre at the Commando Depot's Sniper School in Achnacarry, Scotland.

"Mission: Neutralize Brandenburger Commandos known to be hiding in abandoned houses in Castelrozzo Village. A drive will be conducted by elements of the 2nd Battalion, Cyprus Regiment to flush the Nazis out of their places of concealment. Four Raiding Forces sniper teams will be in overwatch positions to engage Nazis driven out into the open.

"Enemy: Fourteen Brandenburger Commandos are known to be at large somewhere in Castelrozzo Village or elsewhere on the island. These are highly trained individuals, dangerous men with nothing to lose. Do *not*—I say again—do not underestimate their capabilities.

"Terrain: Urban terrain primarily single-family residences, a few spread out on large individual plots, but the majority with zero lot lines meaning small to no side yards in some places and no back yards because of the steep slope of the escarpment. Due to the nature of the neighborhood and the extreme angle of the incline Brandenburgers who do come out of concealment seeking to avoid being caught up in the Cyprus Regiment's sweep will be channelized making them easier to spot.

"Troops Available: A Company, 2nd Battalion, Cyprus Regiment conducting a sweep up the escarpment and three Raiding Forces ambushes located on the military crest at the top.

"Time: All four teams will ingress their hide positions individually under cover of darkness and RON. Be in place by 0500 hours—an hour prior to BMNT. As briefed previously, after sunrise provides full light an infantry company of the 2nd Battalion, Cyprus Regiment will move out online working their way up the escarpment to conduct their sweep of the grid being searched.

"Civilian Concerns: Exercise extreme care identifying your target. There are civilians in the area. None of them will be in uniform. None of them will be armed. The Brandenburgers are dressed in U.S. Army style khaki unless they have changed into stolen clothes.

"In the event an armed civilian is observed you are green-lighted to take the shot.

"Questions?"

There were none.

Capt. Kidd said, "No anti-sniper threat is anticipated. But if you can see them, they can see you. Same goes for range . . . if they're in range, you are too.

"Let's make this happen people."

COLONEL JOHN RANDAL WAS AT THE TABLE ON stage in the theater hosting the Swing Board. Today the discussion covered the origin of the airborne division, its TO&E and the types of missions one could be expected to perform. The history of the evolution of the airborne in the U.S. Army was told by officers who had lived it. True military visionaries. They had been working from a blank page until Colonel James Gavin sat down and wrote *FM 31–30*.

He was enjoying the briefing.

The story began with the Test Platoon, an experimental unit composed of crazy pioneers—volunteer paratroopers who jumped wearing helmets borrowed from the post football team for headgear, not knowing the standard infantry helmet would work fine with some minor modifications to the chin strap. The men had no idea what they were doing. Some had never flown in an airplane prior to volunteering and could legitimately claim to have never landed in one.

Soon independent airborne battalions were formed. Eventually some of these were grouped into independent airborne regiments. At approximately the same time the 82nd Infantry Division and the 101st Infantry division were notified they had been selected to become the U.S. Army's first two airborne divisions. This entailed each division transferring out one of their line infantry regiments to be replaced by one of the independent parachute regiments and converting the remaining two infantry regiments in the division to glider regiments.

The Great Teddy would have said, "Hey, Presto!"

Col. Randal noted the glider troops were not volunteers.

The 82nd Airborne Division was tapped to deploy overseas first. It's TO&E was the one parachute and two glider infantry regiment configuration. Prior to embarking a second parachute regiment was attached—the 504th PIR under Colonel Reuben Tucker.

At that time it was decided to reconfigure airborne divisions. The new TO&E called for two parachute regiments and one glider regiment though it had not been implemented in most of the divisions at this time. It was believed the new model division would be the pattern U.S. Airborne troops went to war in.

Col. Randal thought the officers on the Swing Board and from the audience who made presentations were highly motivated, hardworking, can-do innovators. Men he would be proud to serve with.

Those in command slots that is—parachute or glider.

He was not as favorably impressed with the field grade staff officers. Most were not jump qualified for the simple reason staff intended to land by glider. This violated Col. Randal's personal concept of leadership. Staff officers would be making life-and-death decisions for the division parachute troops without ever having jumped from an aircraft in flight.

Which meant in his opinion the staff could not possibly understand all of the nuances of a combat parachute drop—period.

For the most part the staff officers who made presentations struck him as egotistical men—who did not know what they did not know but had an answer for everything. When asked a question by a member of the board not one ever said, "I don't know, sir, I'll have to get back to you."

The staff officers reminded him of the Plans Division at GHQ Cairo.

The paratrooper versus leg issue was an easy fix. All the division CG and the staff officers had to do was make the effort to take minimal jump training and make their five qualifying jumps.

After that they could go back to glider riding to their heart's content wearing Jump Wings which would signal the paratroopers in the division they were working for officers who knew what they were doing. Why the staff did not realize that was a mystery.

Was it arrogance or fear?

And there was one other thing. If anyone on the staff did not want to jump out of airplanes they could transfer to a line infantry division. Problem solved.

It became clear to Col. Randal the men in the audience and on the Swing Board did not actually know much about airborne operations other than the mechanics of how to load out, fly to a drop zone, release the gliders and/or drop paratroopers.

With the exception of Major General Matthew Ridgway and Major General Joseph Swing, not one person present had ever been involved with so much as observing an actual airborne combat operation. The commander of the 11th Airborne Division had been dispatched to England on TDY to serve as Lieutenant General Dwight D. Eisenhower's Airborne Advisor for the 509th Parachute Infantry Battalion's jump on North Africa. Everything on that operation had gone wrong. With the exception that the paratroopers had gone into action fighting when and where they landed and performed brilliantly, even regrouping, loading out and making an additional improvised drop to secure the enemy airfield they had missed on the initial drop.

Lack of combat experience was not the staff officers' fault. Col. Randal did not hold it against them. But he knew all the staff studies, sand table exercises and field training in the world could not prepare anyone for the experience of jumping out of an aircraft in flight, in the dark of night behind enemy lines, having missed the drop zone by miles because the pilots failed to locate it.

The same would apply to a forced-entry landing in a glider—which is at best a controlled crash.

Col. Randal was shocked to learn the TO&E of the U.S. Army airborne division had not been developed after a detailed study of how the British, Russians, Germans or even the Italians—countries that had been at war for years—structured theirs. The U.S. model was a Frankenstein design of glider and parachute regiments cobbled together because it was the most convenient way to start from zero and end up with something.

"Hey, Presto!"

"Colonel Randal . . ."

As if reading his mind, Major General Sam Houston Blackwell said, "What is your opinion of the new proposed two parachute, one glider regiment model Table of Organization?"

It was a trick question. Bronc already knew the answer. They had discussed it at length aboard the VIP plane on the flight over.

"Sir, I don't care for it."

This statement caused a stir in the room. Speakers knew not to go off script. No one was supposed to offer up any opinion that might be interpreted as criticism of the airborne division.

Not if they valued their career.

Maj. Gen. Swing said, "Why is that, Colonel?"

"I'm against the idea of elites within elites, sir. The concept of having paratroopers and glidermen in the same unit means volunteers serving alongside non-volunteers. The result is a class system.

"Can't be good for morale or unit cohesion."

Maj. Gen. Swing said, "Elaborate if you would, Colonel, that system exists now in line infantry divisions between draftees and regulars."

Col. Randal said, "Paratroopers wear Jump Wings, blouse their pants into their jump boots and are paid hazardous duty money. Glidermen are not authorized any of those perks. They're thought of as second-class citizens by the paratroopers even though landing by glider is arguably more dangerous.

"In Raiding Forces, to avoid any semblance of the problem even the female Royal Marines who perform our rear echelon duties are all jump…"

Maj. Gen. Blackwell interrupted, “Including Lady Jane and my daughter Beverly who you’ve all met. One of the girls in the Colonel’s outfit claims parachuting is better than sex. I don’t know about that but it might be a selling point for recruiters.”

Everyone in the theater laughed but it was short-lived. An uncomfortable silence fell over the meeting. Col. Randal had touched a raw nerve.

Paratrooper-vs-Leg class warfare was the pink elephant in the room.

Paratroopers were the darlings. The glory boys. Those not parachute qualified had to know they were looked down on by those who were—but no one, meaning officers field grade and above, dared acknowledge it. Why? Because in the officer ranks most of the top-tier staff, and in the case of the 82nd Airborne Division, its commanding general, were not jump qualified.

And the non-jumpers were in full-blown denial.

Major General William Lee said, “If you could make a structural change, Colonel, what would that look like?”

“An all-parachute division, sir—three PIRs.”

Major General Matthew Ridgway said, “You don’t believe there’s a place for glider regiments in an airborne division?”

“No sir, not permanently assigned. My recommendation would be to have a pool of independent glider regiments. Then once a combat drop is in the planning stage the division commander would have the ability to indent for one or more GIRs as needed to fit the mission profile.

“Might even be more flexible to have slimmed-down airborne divisions of only two parachute regiments in anticipation of glider regiments being attached for combat operations as needed.”

Maj. Gen. Ridgway said, “Don’t you feel there is merit in having the division staff go in by glider in order to land neatly assembled in one place ready to open for business immediately as we do now?"

Col. Randal said, "Sir, if the staff of an airborne division is aboard a glider that breaks free of the tow rope en route to the landing zone, gets shot down or is destroyed in a crash on the landing zone, the CG has a major command and control problem on his hands before the ground tactical phase of his operation ever gets started."

Maj. Gen. Blackwell said, "That, gentlemen, is why he's my Paratroop Advisor."

PROFESSOR LAYTON WINTHROP WAS GIVING A lecture in one of the rooms on the ground floor of Advanced Base Castelrozzo Headquarters titled "The Cyclades and their Mysterious Society Lost in Time." There were about twenty Royal Marines, WRENs and FANYs listening raptly along with Brandy Seaborn, Veronica Paige, and Rikke "Rocky" Runborg. Lieutenant Colonel Sir Terry "Zorro" Stone and Captain Hawthorne Merryweather, Political Warfare Executive (PWE), were the only men in the audience.

Captain Billy Jack Jaxx was standing in the back. He and Dr. Winthrop had struck up a friendship. He liked history.

Dr. Winthrop thought of Jack Cool as a modern-day Billy the Kid.

"The Cyclades are a group of over two hundred and twenty-five islands located southeast of Greece. The word 'Cyclades' refers to the islands forming a circle. Greek mythology tells that the God of the Sea, Poseidon, became angry at the Cyclades' nymphs and turned them into islands."

Capt. Jaxx wondered what it was the nymphs might have done to deserve that.

"Today the Cyclades people are best remembered for the mysterious, flat-faced marble figurines that have survived down through the . . ."

Mandy Paige stuck her head in the door and saw Capt. Jaxx. She walked in and whispered, "Jack, your presence is required in the TOC."

As he exited the room, Capt. Jaxx said, "We were just getting to the good part."

Mandy said, "You interested in archaeology—really?"

Capt. Jaxx said, "I've always liked to hunt for arrowheads."

Mandy said, "Two of the children from your talk this morning claim to have seen a Nazi."

"No kidding?"

"They requested to speak to Captain Jack. You promised ice cream. They are expecting you to deliver."

"Tell GG to break it out."

As they were walking toward the TOC, Mandy said, "I heard the part about the nymphs. Most likely you were wondering if they were the origin of the word nymphomaniac."

"The thought may have crossed my mind."

"You are so predictable."

In the TOC, two boys in short pants were waiting. Nikolas and Christos, who appeared to be about six or seven years old, were chatting with Captain Stephanie Fawcett-Tatum. The boys wore dead-serious expressions.

The two perked up when Capt. Jaxx walked in.

"Well, men, I understand you have something to report."

"Yes, sir, Captain Jack, we found a Nazi!"

"Follow me then. Let's walk over to the chow hall. Mandy's got ice cream waiting. You can brief me while you polish it off."

While both boys spoke basic English, they had no idea what "chow" meant or how to "polish" ice cream.

Over heaping bowls of homemade vanilla the boys laid out their tale. They had been playing soccer on the pathway leading past their parents' homes while keeping their eyes peeled for Germans. A number of the houses in their immediate neighborhood were abandoned and boarded up—a good place for a Nazi to hide.

The boys claimed to have seen a strange man walk past a window on the ground floor of one of the empty houses.

Capt. Jaxx said, "What did he look like?"

"Happened too fast, Captain Jack."

The two were not able to give any description other than "... a man walked by an open window."

Capt. Jaxx was not sure if he believed them. Making a false statement to obtain a reward—like ice cream—was not unknown to him from his law enforcement days as an unpaid reserve deputy for his grandfather, Sheriff Marlboro Jaxx. On the other hand he and Mandy had asked the island's children to report suspicious activity—this was a report.

And a boarded-up house should not have any open windows.

Capt. Jaxx said, "Can you two studs show me where you saw your Nazi?"

Neither one of the boys knew what a stud was but they chorused, "Yes, sir!"

CAPTAIN ROY KIDD LED HIS SNIPERS OUT ON A recon patrol to select their overwatch positions for the next morning's sweep. The idea was to identify four mutually supporting hide positions with good visibility and interlocking fields of fire. The terrain was straight uphill with a near forty-degree angle of slope. The "Uphill and Downhill Rule" was in full force and effect. It stipulated when shooters fired uphill *or* downhill they would need to aim lower than the typical hold on level ground because the trajectory of the round was flatter, which would cause the strike of the bullet to be higher.

Not a problem for the snipers working for Capt. Kidd. Today the degree of bullet rise would be measured in inches.

The grid to be swept was a rectangle approximately 500 x 750 yards. The length of the distance up the escarpment was pushing the normally accepted maximum effective range of Tech Sergeant Luke Volkmann's M1903A1 Rifle, Sniper, w/telescope, Sighting Unertl 8X in U.S. Marine Corp nomenclature, and the two Lovat Scouts' scoped 7X57 Westley Richards rifles. Even so all three shooters were capable of making one thousand-yard shots.

Captain Billy Jack Jaxx would be establishing a series of three small ambushes along the military crest of the escarpment at the far end of the grid. Any Nazi spotted moving within 250 yards would be in their kill zone and taken under fire.

Any Brandenburger attempting to avoid the line of march of the beaters would have to break cover. The terrain dictated that when they did they would be channelized into an open area at some point. That was going to make it easier to spot them.

While this was a relatively small-scale operation the preparation Capt. Kidd put into organizing it was meticulous. A lot of prior planning is needed for a successful sniper mission. The skill of the shooters has to be blended with the advantages the terrain offers.

He did not hurry the snipers as they selected their positions. The patrol worked from left to right along the bottom of the grid. All four shooters went inside and up to the top floor or roof of each of the houses being evaluated. This gave them all a chance to observe the field of fire from each firing position providing the shooters with a complete perspective of the entire grid and an idea of what the other snipers would be seeing from their hide.

If there was anything the sniper who was to occupy a potential site did not like, anything at all, Capt. Kidd backtracked, took everyone downstairs, and went in search of another location. There was no debate. No making do. He believed it was crucial for each shooter to have a firing position he was completely satisfied with—100%.

Once a position was chosen each sniper made notes that would be used later to create a range card.

Capt. Kidd paid a great deal of care to the sequence the snipers would be placed across the grid. He put TSgt. Luke Volkmann, on his first combat mission, to the far left in the No.1 position. No. 2 would be for his No. 32 Mk.1 scope sighted, tripod-mounted, Boys .55 Anti-Tank Rifle modified for sniping—enough range to cover the entire grid. No. 3 would be Lovat Scout Lionel Fenwick and No. 4 for Lovat Scout Munro Ferguson.

He had “Right Man, Right Job” in mind for the placements except for the Lovat Scouts—they were interchangeable.

When everyone had their assignment the patrol made its way back to ABCHQ. Once there they linked up with their spotters. Each sniper produced the range card for his position from the notes he had taken. Then he briefed his No. 2 individually on what had occurred on the patrol to include detailed specifics of their field of fire. For the remainder of the day the sniper and spotter would stay together until line of departure (LD) time around 2400 hours.

Anticipation was high. The men were looking forward to the mission. They were professional marksmen and this was an opportunity for them to use their skills.

MANDY PAIGE WAS SHOUTING AT CAPTAIN BILLY Jack Jaxx as he was preparing to go check out the Nazi Nikolas and Christos claimed to have spotted.

"You asked my *mother* to pose for a picture to put in your pistol grip!"

Capt. Jaxx was dressed in traditional Greek fisherman's garb. Short-billed black hat. Black shirt. Long thigh-length vest and baggy pants. The plan was for him to do a walk-by of the house where the boys claimed they had seen a "strange man."

His suppressed .22 Colt Woodsman and a 1911 Colt 38 Super were in shoulder holsters under the vest. Capt. Jaxx alternated between the Colt Woodsman .22, a handgun he had grown up shooting, and a High Standard Military Model D .22. He liked them both giving the Woodsman a slight edge because of muscle memory developed from all his years shooting jackrabbits with one.

"How could you?"

"Brandy did a photo shoot, so did Legs Parker. They're about the same age as Veronica. Besides, your mom's pretty hot."

"What did my mother say?"

"That she'd think about it."

"Jack, you are incorrigible!"

"I don't know what that means."

Walking downstairs when they arrived in the TOC Mandy had a pickup team waiting consisting of the only people at ABCHQ immediately available to accompany Capt. Jaxx and the boys. The patrol included Lieutenant Colonel Sir Terry "Zorro" Stone, Lieutenant Dan Bonham, recently returned from Italy,

Master Sergeant Mack Beckwith and Private First Class Norvel "Horn Dog" Hansen.

Currently Raiding Forces personnel were thin on the ground. Men were spread from Italy to Cyprus, on LSF schooners all along the Turkish coast or at sea on caiques going on or returning from a mission. Here on the island, most of the troops were out on patrols searching for Brandenburgers.

The only reason PFC Hansen was at ABCHQ today instead of out with Lieutenant Jake Novak was MSgt. Beckwith had ordered Horn Dog report there to provide him the benefit of nonjudicial individual "counseling." The session was compulsory. It was universally agreed no one in their right mind would offer themselves up voluntarily to be counseled by the Sergeant Major.

He could bring smoke.

MSgt. Beckwith's sessions started out, "Listen up troop, you Goldbrick . . ." and proceeded downhill from there. The Sergeant Major did not view his job as a popularity contest but he was well-liked by the men. Getting your heels locked by the Top had become a rite of passage in Raiding Forces.

Those who had experienced them liked to brag his "ass chewings" were "Purple Heart quality."

As soon as he had his patrol assembled Capt. Jaxx issued a Frag Order allowing the two Greek boys to listen in making them feel like a part of the team.

"We have an intel report about an individual in an abandoned home who should not be there. When we move out I will depart first with my two junior secret agents, Nikolas and Christos. Colonel Stone will be in command of the patrol. Sir, you will follow me out maintaining a visual on my party a hundred yards or so back. When the boys reach a place they can surreptitiously indicate the house we will pause to give you time to catch up and establish an Objective Rally Point.

"At that time, the boys will return to their home go inside and await developments. I'll do a walk-by to determine if an assault is warranted. Then come back to the ORP.

"On my return, I'll provide a target brief then Colonel Stone, sir, you'll lay out our plan of action.

"No indirect fires are available. The *King Duck* is supporting the patrols operating up the coast—we're on our own."

Lt. Col. Stone said, "You are more current, Captain. I want you to plan the actions on the objective. Lead the patrol."

Right man, Right Job regardless of rank.

"Can do, sir—questions?"

There was not enough information for anyone to have any.

As the patrol was getting ready to move out, Mandy said, "I'm coming with you Jack."

"Negative."

"You need me there to interpret."

"The boys speak English."

"You are worse than Colonel Randal."

"You're not getting shot on my watch, Mandy."

Capt. Jaxx said to the boys, "All right, men, let's go."

Mandy thought it curious he called the boys men and the men boys—they seemed to like it.

Capt. Jaxx, Nikolas and Christos started along the path leading up the escarpment from ABCHQ. The boys did not live far away. Which went to underscore the need for clearing the island of all the Brandenburgers. They could be hiding anywhere.

No one on Castelrozzo would be safe until all the Nazis had been killed or captured.

The boys traveled at a fast clip. They bounded up the escarpment like mountain goats. It did not take long to reach another cobblestone path that traversed the slope to a row of houses.

Capt. Jaxx said, "Which one is it? Don't point."

"The peachy one."

"Go home. Stay inside. I'll check on you later."

The boys scampered off. Capt. Jaxx watched as they disappeared into a house catty-cornered across the path from the target. Nothing was stirring. The island was on lockdown none of the locals were outside.

Waiting for Lt. Col. Stone to catch up with the patrol before starting his walk-by Capt. Jaxx was struck by how it seemed such a normal day on Castelrozzo. After the war the island would be the perfect getaway vacation paradise. Now those in residence lived with the constant threat of an air raid and cold-blooded Nazi killers lurking around the village.

The potential for violence at any moment on such a beautiful day felt surreal—a word he had learned in an English Lit class at UT but never had much use for before in his world of girls, football and war.

It seemed appropriate today.

The target was boarded up. Like the boys said, the ground floor windows were open. That was a tell. With them closed it would be suffocating inside. Whoever was in there or had been in there wanted to catch the breeze blowing in off the sea.

The boys claimed the windows had been shut the day before.

Lt. Col. Stone arrived with the patrol. The men silently dropped to the ground out of line of sight of the target. This position was now the ORP.

Capt. Jaxx began his walk-by inspection strolling casually along the path the boys had taken to their parents' house. He made it a point not to stare at the faded peach-colored target or even look in that direction. It required effort.

Houses on Castelrozzo were faded pink, faded peach, faded cantaloupe yellow, or snow white. This one, like the majority of others on the island, was vacant . . . abandoned by the owners three years earlier. When the Italians first occupied the island anyone who could flee did so with more continuing to do so over the years.

There were no buyers for the vacant properties.

Capt. Jaxx did not believe in the occult, séances, chanting at little crystals or having his cards read. But he was aware he possessed a heightened sense of perception at times like this. He could not explain it and never tried. But sometimes on operations he knew things there was no rational reason for him to know—like right now he knew he was under observation, no question about it.

Not a good feeling.

It required a great deal of self-discipline to resist the impulse to turn back for the ORP.

The target was on his immediate left and the boys were in the house off to the right. Capt. Jaxx could see the two kids peeking out an upstairs window with their chins resting on their crossed forearms. As he walked past studying the objective out of his peripheral vision, not turning his head, nothing other than the open windows gave an indication of anyone inside.

He knew there was.

The two boys screamed, "WATCH OUT!"

Capt. Jaxx reacted immediately. He whirled around instinctively drawing his Colt .38 Super and pointing it at the giant dressed in U.S. Army khaki, at least six feet six, 250 pounds, all muscle, charging at him full speed. The Nazi clutched a dagger the size of a butcher knife in one massive fist fixated on making a silent kill. Were his intentions to murder a Greek or had he somehow divined the man walking past was a Raiding Forces operator?

Not that it mattered.

Capt. Jaxx's grandfather, the Sheriff, had hammered the "twenty-one feet knife rule" into him for as long as he could remember: "At twenty-one feet it takes 1.5 seconds for a mature unimpaired man armed with a knife to close the distance."

About the amount of time it takes the average person to draw a sidearm and fire two rapid shots. There is no guarantee two pistol rounds will stop an outraged attacker inside that distance. And the operative word was "*unimpaired*." He knew Brandenburgers were routinely issued pharmaceutical-grade Pervitin—aka speed—to help keep them awake, alert and improve their battle performance.

This Nazi was not unimpaired.

Events were unfolding in slow motion but there was no stopping them or putting the genie back in the bottle. The knife looked razor sharp and it was big — more like a short sword.

Adhering to his personal favorite Raiding Forces Rule, "It Never Hurts To Cheat," Capt. Jaxx had taken the precaution of drawing his Colt .38 Super and holding it down flat against his right leg the instant he felt the tingle alerting him he was being watched.

It was good he did.

The German was on him fast and there was nothing to be done about it. As the distance closed Capt. Jaxx could see the pupils in the man's gleaming blue eyes were the size of pinpoints. He was that close and the enormous Nazi was that high on amphetamines.

The situation was officially not good and deteriorating fast.

Instinctively he brought his elbow in tight against his side, assumed a bent-kneed crouch and commenced firing from the hip like gunfighters do in the movies. Capt. Jaxx knew this was never a good idea in real life no matter what some experts claim or that the FBI taught the stance to their agents.

Capt. Jaxx was also aware it's not how fast you get off your shots that counts it's how quick you connect and where.

BALAAM-BALAAM-BALAAM-BALAAM!

The string of shots was fast, very fast—Capt. Jaxx was not the "average" shooter. The last round was muffled because the barrel of his pistol was pressed against the Brandenburger's stomach just above his U.S. Army issue belt buckle when he touched it off.

The German was dead he just did not know it yet.

Then the giant was on him. They fell to the ground grappling for the knife. Hyped up on Pervitin, adrenaline and rage, in addition to being a Jumbo-sized monster, the Brandenburger Sea Raider exhibited superhuman strength.

Capt. Jaxx never stood a chance.

BALAAM!

The Nazi stopped fighting. He pitched forward. Dead.

Trying to push the German off, Capt. Jaxx struggled to see around the huge body pinning him to the ground. Mandy was standing three feet away holding one of the .32 Sauer 38H pistols Colonel John Randal had given her. She had both hands held out straight in a perfect shooting stance having fired a single round into the base of the Brandenburger's skull.

Fight-ending shot placement.

"I ordered you to stay home."

"I don't work for you, Jack. Besides, you never said not to go for a walk."

"Yeah, well try walking over here and helping drag King Kong off me."

Mandy said, "Almost hated to put a stop to it I was having so much fun watching him mop up the ground with you—wish I had a camera."

Capt. Jaxx said, "What are you talking about I had this bad guy right where I wanted him."

"So, when exactly were you planning on letting him in on that?"

Lt. Col. Stone and the patrol, along with Mandy's VPW security guard, who was mortified his charge had given him the slip when she raced off to save Capt. Jaxx—came double timing along the path.

Seeing the fight was over they turned and rushed the house.

In a matter of minutes, "Clears" were coming from inside. PFC Hansen came out carrying the German's .30 M1 Carbine and U.S. Army issue load-bearing gear, "Webbing '37." There was an empty knife sheath dangling from the belt.

"Next time you need to try picking on someone your own size, sir."

The boys ran over from where they had been watching the action. "Are you all right, Captain Jack?"

"Roger that men—you two studs just won the Raiding Forces ice cream lottery."

Jack Cool.

Nikolas and Christos thought he was.

COLONEL JOHN RANDAL WAS BACK AT THE TABLE on stage in the Fort Mackall Theater for another meeting. The discussion was back on track. Major General Joseph Swing's Operation Officer from his 11th Airborne Division aka the "Angels" was giving a presentation on the types of missions an airborne division might expect to be assigned.

"Airhead: An airborne division may be dropped by parachute/air landed by glider deep in the enemy's rear to set up an airhead where follow on line infantry and artillery reinforcements can be flown in behind them and landed to build up a corp or even army-sized force. Capturing an airfield is typically associated with this type of mission. However if that is not possible plans for an improvised airstrip must be included in the plan. The concept of the operation is to leap over the hardened outer ring of enemy defenses to set up a base of operations from which to continue the offensive. This type of operation is designed to avoid the casualties associated with a forced entry amphibious assault on a heavily defended enemy shore, to avoid having to breach an enemy defensive line, and/or to speed up the pace of an offensive by leapfrogging ahead on the axis of attack deep in the enemy's rear."

Col. Randal glanced at Major General Sam Houston Blackwell. Bronc's lips tightened into an almost imperceptible smile. The idea was pure fantasy but it had been around as long as there had been parachutes in the army. Both men knew a mission like the one being described was first proposed as far back as WWI—to drop the 1st Infantry division by parachute behind the German trench line.

Luckily for the Big Red One the war ended before the operation could make it out of the planning stage. Paratroopers dropped behind enemy lines with a seize and hold type mission need to be relieved by ground troops within forty-eight to seventy-two hours—twenty-four hours is better. No one could have possibly believed in the last war the Allies were going to punch through the German main line of resistance (MLR) and link up with the 1st ID in that amount of time. Trench warfare had been going on for four years at that point in the war and the Allies had never been able to do it yet.

There was also the problem that even today the USAAF and the RAF combined did not have the airlift capability to fly in the supplies necessary to sustain an airhead of the magnitude being briefed. That was a problem. This was the perfect example of a concept dreamed up by armchair strategists who had no idea what a night jump looked like when the sun came up the next morning or any concept of the logistics required to support an airborne operation.

An airhead was never going to happen as briefed though on a smaller scale it was a viable use of airborne forces.

"Key Terrain: an airborne division may be tasked with dropping in ahead of an overland attack to seize key pieces of terrain such as an enemy transportation hub, a town, a key road junction or mountain pass. The purpose of the exercise would be to capture a strategic piece of terrain to prevent the Nazis from rushing reinforcements toward a beachhead lodgment, impede a counterattack, speed up an offensive or for any other tactical opportunity that might present itself that could be exploited by a drop on the enemy's axis of advance.

"The recent drop by the 503rd Parachute Infantry Regiment, reinforced by the Australian 2/4 Field Regiment artillery—the Diggers having virtually no parachute training whatsoever, on the small airfield located at Nadzab, New Guinea is a perfect example. Australian pioneer troops marching overland arrived quickly to improve the landing strip. The first plane ferrying in infantry troops landed the next day allowing them to make a movement to contact and attack the Japanese coastal defenses from the rear."

Col. Randal thought . . . *A small-scale Key Terrain Operation with a limited objective—quickly relieved by ground forces within twenty-four hours or less. Planned to exploit a tactical opportunity. That sounded good.*

However the Nadzab drop was not an airborne division sized operation. It was not a representative example for the Swing Board to use. No one seemed to notice.

Col. Randal glanced at Maj. Gen. Blackwell who stared back—Bronc did.

"Strategic Reinforcement: An airborne division may be used to provide instant reinforcements at a decisive point in an ongoing operation either during the critical beachhead lodgment phase like the 82nd's drop at Salerno or to plug a hole in the line or strengthen an ongoing attack."

Col. Randal thought . . . *Salerno a perfect example of an airborne mission that worked as intended and contributed significantly to the success of the overall operation.*

"Lastly, the Airborne Carpet: When a major offensive is preparing to kick off, an airborne division/or multiple airborne divisions can be dropped along the axis of attack far in advance of the line of departure to seize and hold bridges or other key terrain features like road junctions etc. to prevent them from being blown up by the enemy in an effort to impede the attack. The concept of the operation is for an airborne carpet to be laid down followed by a lightning riposte of armor and mechanized infantry—our ground forces race down the airborne carpet and slam into the enemy deep into their unprotected rear.

"The Airborne Carpet requires split-second timing, precision drops and/or surgical glider landings, and the armored tip leading the charge must be aggressively led adhering strictly to the operations timetable. Laying down an airborne carpet paves the way for exploitation by a powerful combined arms force of paratroopers/glidermen, tankers, mobile artillery, and mechanized infantry. Surprise, speed, and a sledgehammer blow delivered at the end of the carpet are a must."

Col. Randal saw possibilities. The idea was one he had never considered. However, the concept had a lot of moving parts which is never desirable for a military operation and did not even remotely conform to Raiding Forces Rule, "Keep it Short and Simple". Overall success was wholly dependent on all units involved carrying out their individual assignments and did not take into consideration what the German might have to say about the incursion.

He decided to study the concept in more detail. Maj. Gen. Blackwell made eye contact with him. Col. Randal gave a slight nod.

They were on the same page.

"Gentlemen, that concludes my presentation."

Major General Matthew B. Ridgway said, "I, for one, would like to hear more about the Nadzab drop."

Maj. Gen. Swing said, "Noted, I shall have someone in to brief us—any other comments?"

No one had anything else to add. The senior officers on the board realized how crucial the Nadzab jump by the 503rd PIR was to the final Swing Committee findings. It was being billed as the "first successful airborne operation of WWII."

Not true but then truth is the first casualty of war.

And the Board still seemed to be overlooking the inconvenient fact that the mission had not been carried out by an airborne division.

Maj. Gen. Blackwell said, "I'd like to hear what Colonel Randal has to say on the subject of airborne missions. He's been conducting classified parachute operations nobody has ever heard of for the last four years. Hollywood's getting ready to make a movie about one of 'em.

"Sound off, Colonel."

Col. Randal could have cheerfully throttled Major General Sam Houston "friends call me Bronc" Blackwell.

Maj. Gen. Swing said, "Do you have anything to add, Colonel?"

Col. Randal said, "Only this, sir. Division-sized airborne operations are in their infancy. Our side has never actually conducted one—not with an entire division. From everything I've heard today our planners are using standard infantry tactics as the basis for the majority of the missions being proposed.

"I believe that's shortchanging what an airborne division brings to the fight."

There was a stir in the audience—this time of interest.

Maj. Gen. Blackwell stuck one of Waldo's custom-rolled cigars in his teeth and leaned back in his chair. The reaction of the rest of the officers on the Commission was the exact opposite. They leaned forward interested to hear the response to the follow-through question they all knew would be coming.

Maj. Gen. Swing said, "Please enlighten us, Colonel?"

Col. Randal said, "The highest and best use of airborne troops is to be dropped in ahead of a seaborne invasion to shield it during the critical initial amphibious assault landing phase. The idea being to buy enough time for the follow-on buildup of artillery, armored fighting vehicles, supplies and the like to be established ashore.

"From what I heard today the tendency by planners when faced with such a mission is to assign our airborne units conventional infantry tasks once they have been inserted such as to capture a town, a road junction, or a bridge. The seize and hold until relieved concept starts to fall apart when the troop transports fail to find the drop zone, high winds scatter the paratroopers, when the gliders are shot down or crash on landing.

"Long distance night airborne combat operations are not parade ground exercises but that's OK—even desirable in certain instances. What no one here seems to be appreciating is the effect thousands of highly motivated, heavily armed, teenage paratroopers or glidermen, taught to use their initiative, licensed to kill with orders they seem to remember as 'when in doubt march to the sound of the guns' or something like that, roving around inside their lines in the dark of the night, have on the enemy commander. The airborne troops ambush wheeled vehicles, cut power lines, blow up targets of opportunity, shoot at anything that moves then move on somewhere else and do it again.

"The local German commander tasked with responding is paralyzed into inaction by a blizzard of enemy reports pouring into his HQ. When plotted on his map the actions don't make any sense. Are there a thousand paratroopers at large or a million? What's their intent?

"How to counter 'em?

"I believe there's a need for another mission profile to be developed specifically for the airborne division—'Disruptive Operations Incidental to an Airborne Assault.'

"Strategic chaos—you can sell that one, sir."

There was dead silence in the theater.

Maj. Gen. Blackwell said, "I have in my possession intercepted German intelligence analyzing the Sicily drop. It was provided to me on my recent trip to Cairo by the British Secret Intelligence Service, MI-6. Who, by the way doesn't have a dog in this fight about the future of U.S. airborne divisions.

"It states Field Marshal Rommel and General Student, the commander of German Airborne Forces, have both independently come to the conclusion in their official after-action reports that the drop by Gavin's 505th, Tucker's 504th, and Randal's 575th Parachute Infantry Regiments on Sicily was the only thing that prevented an immediate German counterattack against the Allied beachhead.

"During the time it took the Nazis to cut through the fog of war created by widespread misdropped paratroopers, seeming to be everywhere to no definable purpose, Patton's amphibious forces established a foothold ashore. By the time the Nazis sorted it out the buildup was in full swing and the lodgment too strong for the Germans to destroy.

"Rommel and Student both make the case that had a timely counterattack taken place the Allies would have been driven back into the sea on the first day—destroyed at the water's edge. And that, gentlemen, is the assessment of the other side about an airborne operation the Supreme Allied Forces Commander Europe and others in high places view as a failure.

"Ike's dead right about one thing though, an airborne division's not easy to control—not in the hours immediately following a night combat jump. But like Colonel Randal pointed out, that's a good thing. It's in our nation's best interest for this committee to factor in the positive effect of chaos, confusion and disruption when planning airborne missions—because they will surely happen."

Maj. Gen. Ridgway said, "Can I see the intelligence you described, General?"

"I'll have copies made available to the entire Board—understand the report is classified."

Maj. Gen. Swing said, "That would be greatly appreciated, General."

Maj. Gen. Blackwell said, "An administrative announcement if I may, gentlemen. I'm having a private dinner at the Carolina tonight for the division commanders in the Robert E. Lee suite—take the private elevator. Lady Jane and my daughter Beverly will be hosting another reception downstairs. A commander's call for all airborne battalion and regimental commanders stationed on, TDY, or visiting Camp Mackall.

"Red will be there as well so anyone would have to be an idiot not to attend."

Maj. Gen. Swing said, "What time, General?"

"Immediately following a demonstration I understand is laid on for later this afternoon. We can repair straight to the hotel afterwards. Cocktails then dinner."

The receptions were news to Col. Randal.

Maj. Gen. Swing said, "I'll instruct my staff to prepare a paper preliminarily styled 'Disruptive Effects Ancillary To A

Forced Entry Airborne Assault.' I would like you to make yourself available to them, Colonel. There will be questions."

"Yes, sir."

COLONEL JOHN RANDAL AND MAJOR THE LADY Jane Seaborn were lying out by the Olympic-sized pool at the Carolina Hotel. They were enjoying being able to spend time together without the threat of some life-or-death emergency hanging over their head. A lazy stress-free afternoon.

Col. Randal was dozing.

Lady Jane was watching the men around the pool watching her.

Beverly Blackwell and Red the Flying Clipper Girl were playing tennis.

It did not get much better than this.

A steward in a starched white jacket arrived carrying a silver tray with an envelope on it emblazoned with the Carolina's logo.

"Colonel Randal, suh . . ."

Since he did not have his wallet with him Lady Jane took money out of her purse for a tip.

"Thank you Miss Lady Seaborn, ma'am."

Col. Randal opened the envelope. "Mackall Army Airfield in one hour with the women. Wear fatigues. Bronc."

So much for a laid-back afternoon.

Lady Jane stood up and wrapped a fluffy white beach towel around herself much to the regret of the male admirers. She signaled to one of the teenage pool boys.

"Shaun, run this note over to Beverly and Red on the tennis court."

"Yes ma'am, Lady Seaborn."

Col. Randal said, "He knows them?"

Lady Jane laughed, "Every man on this property over the age of twelve knows Beverly and Red."

"Right, what could I have been thinking?"

Inside the lobby on the way to the elevator they stopped by the concierge's desk.

Col. Randal said, "We'll need transportation for four to Mackall Army Airfield as soon as we can shower and come back downstairs."

"Yes suh, Colonel. Your driver will be waiting outside. Is there anything else the hotel can do for you?"

"We're good, thanks."

Beverly and Red caught up to them at the elevator.

Col. Randal said, "We'll meet you in the lobby in thirty minutes."

Red said, "Any idea what this is about?"

"Not a clue."

Beverly said, "Daddy shouldn't have been so cryptic. He's having way too much fun being a general."

CAPTAIN BILLY JACK JAXX BRIEFED CAPTAIN Oliver Fernsby, the commanding officer of C Company 2nd Battalion, Cyprus Regiment on his assignment to sweep the grid to be searched tomorrow. The Cyprus Regiment was a typical locally raised Commonwealth unit composed of the Greek Cypriot, Turkish Cypriot, Armenian, Maronite, and Latin inhabitants of Cyprus. The officers and senior NCOs were British.

The 2nd Battalion had been rushed to Castelrozzo to beef up security following the Brandenburger raid. Because of the high percentage of Greek speakers it was an ideal choice for garrison duties on the island. The local women, starved for male companionship, were glad to see so many men were being stationed there on a semi-permanent basis even though most of the village area was off limits to the Cyprus Regiment after normal duty hours.

Capt. Jaxx said, "This is a Warning Order. Are you prepared to copy?"

It was not a question.

"I am."

"Situation: Brandenburger Commandos are in hiding on the island following a failed raid on ABCHQ. They're stranded with no way to escape and probably running out of food. Have to be desperate at this point—exercise extreme caution.

"Mission: To sweep a 500 x 750-yard grid in an effort to kill, capture, or flush the Nazis out into the open so Raiding Forces' sniper teams can take them under fire or drive them into a series of ambushes stationed along the top of the escarpment.

"Execution: Thirty minutes after BMNT tomorrow morning B Company, 2nd Battalion, Cyprus Regiment—meaning you, will conduct a sweep of the grid.

"Concept of the Operation: B Company will move in a company formation, platoons online, squads online up the escarpment. In the event any element of the company encounters or is fired on by one or more of the Nazis believed to be in the grid the entire line will pause while the enemy position is taken under attack and reduced.

"In the event gunshots are heard coming from one or more of the sniper hides B Company will ignore them and continue to march.

"B Company will go end of mission one hundred yards from the top of the escarpment. At that point you will stand by for further orders.

"Prisoners are a priority. You bring me a POW to interrogate. I'll see you get a Mention in Dispatches.

"Command & Control: I'll take you and your officers on a leader's recon of the start line at 1600 hours.

"Questions?"

Capt. Fernsby said, "What can you tell me about the Brandenburgers?"

Capt. Jaxx said, "They arrived wearing U.S. Army khaki uniforms. They may be in civilian dress now. In the event your troops see a local bearing arms they are cleared to engage.

"Any other questions?"

"Negative."

"Bring me a prisoner."

Captain Jaxx then went in search of his ambush team leaders Lieutenant Dan Bonham, Master Sergeant Mack Beckwith, and Private First Class Norvel "Horn Dog" Hansen. It was time to take them on their leader's recon. He was so pressed for Raiding Forces leaders he was reduced to using a private as an ambush team leader—one currently under a cloud with the Sergeant Major for some unspecified infraction.

Capt. Jaxx had also been forced to reduce the number of planned ambushes from four to three. And he had to reduce the number of people in the ambushes from four men to three.

Improvise, adapt and make do—the situation was less than ideal.

Capt. Jaxx had offered a reward for information. He had patrols out all over the island going house to house. Dog teams were working the area with the VPW security specialists. He and Mandy Paige had recruited the children, to include teenagers, of Castelrozzo to report any suspicious activity. Now he was in the process of setting up a grid search with beaters, snipers and ambushes in an attempt to drive the Nazis out of hiding into the open where they could be engaged.

In addition he was planning to request Lieutenant Colonel Sir Terry "Zorro" Stone put up a Walrus filled with spotters to racetrack over the Cyprus Regiment sweep tomorrow in order to maintain constant aerial surveillance.

Capt. Jaxx had promised to hunt down the Nazis. He was attempting to make good on his word. Taking a prisoner able to provide actionable intelligence—that was not working out yet.

THE CAROLINA HOTEL LIMOUSINE ARRIVED AT THE Military Police Station at the entrance of the Mackall Army Airfield. The barrier pole was down. An MP sergeant spoke to the driver.

"Follow that jeep. It's the escort for Colonel Randal."

When they arrived at their destination a flight of six C-47s were parked in trail on the airstrip. Behind each plane was a tow rope attached to a CG-4A Waco—pronounced Wack-O, glider.

Major General Sam Houston Blackwell was standing on the airstrip next to the lead ship with a Troop Carrier Command USAAF lieutenant—his junior military aide, and another paratroop lieutenant in fatigues and jump boots.

"Hop out, Colonel. We're getting ready to make airborne history. You too, Beverly."

Colonel John Randal clicked on. He had no idea why. But he did.

The General's aide climbed into the limousine and drove off with Major the Lady Jane Seaborn and Red the Flying Clipper Girl.

Maj. Gen. Blackwell said, "We're getting ready to put on a demonstration for the big brass. RAF Air Chief Marshal Tedder—claims he knows you Colonel—is here to observe. As is Lieutenant General Lesley McNair, Commanding General Army Ground Forces, Major General Chapman, Commanding General Airborne Command, and a bunch 'a other generals and politicians I've never met.

"I'm flying lead. Beverly, you're co-pilot of the Waco I'll be towing. And Colonel, you'll be in the stick—one of the first paratroopers to jump a glider."

Col. Randal felt the old familiar icicle-being-jabbed-through-his-heart sensation. Based on previous experience it was a surefire portent that whatever was about to happen next stood a good chance of not ending well for him.

Maj. Gen. Blackwell said, "Airborne Command has decided to evaluate the suitability of the CG-4A as a delivery platform for paratroopers."

Col. Randal said, "I can answer that . . ."

Maj. Gen. Blackwell said, "The thinking is if we can drop jumpers from towed gliders at the same time we put them out of the C-47 tow planes we can double the number of paratroopers a powered aircraft can deliver to the drop zone—maybe triple it with a double-tow."

"This is Lieutenant Mascuch of the 551st Parachute Infantry Battalion. He's your escort officer, Colonel. He'll brief you on what's about to take place. Claims the 551st trained with your 575th boys down in Panama.

"You two have something in common."

Beverly Blackwell said, "Daddy, this is insane!"

Maj. Gen. Blackwell said, "Baby, we're talking history being made and we'll be the ones making it."

Beverly said, "Probably what Travis said when he drew that line in the sand at the Alamo—see where that got him."

Col. Randal thought but did not say . . . *Roger that.*

Lieutenant Ricky Mascuch walked Col. Randal to the glider. As he was helping him strap on a U.S. Army T-4 parachute, the young officer explained, "We didn't know you were coming, sir. I can let you lead the stick if you prefer—or be the last man out—tail end Charlie."

Col. Randal said, "It's the 551st's drop Lieutenant. Your jumpmaster should have the privilege of the number one slot. I'll push the stick."

"Yes, sir—in that case you will follow me out the door."

Once chuted up they boarded the Waco. The idea of an airplane with no propeller—meaning no visible means of support, was not heartening. The glider was made of canvas—a *canvass* airplane, with wooden reinforcing struts. The floor was plywood.

Col. Randal was afraid he might put a boot through it.

The interior of the glider was tiny. There were six seats crammed in along each side occupied by paratroopers from the 551 Parachute Infantry Battalion (PIB) sporting grim expressions. The Waco CG-4A did nothing to instill confidence in the people about to take off in it.

All the ambience of a flying coffin.

Lt. Mascuch said, "The men of the 551st PIB are called GOYA-birds by our battalion commander Colonel Joerg—in case you hear someone using it, sir."

Col. Randal said, "What does GOYA stand for?"

Lt. Mascuch said, "Get Off Your Ass—the Colonel's favorite saying, sir. In polite company, we tell people it means, 'Great Outstanding Young Americans.'"

Col. Randal looked around the cramped interior of the canvas cabin. He was concerned about the anchor cable for the static lines. The flimsy structure of the glider did not give him reason to have much conviction the cable would hold once the jumpers started to exit and the static lines began to deploy.

But then . . . what did he know?

Both doors had been removed. That should have made for a quick exit. Unfortunately Waco CG-4A gliders were not designed for paratroopers. The doorways were small. A jumper making his exit would have to duck down in order to squeeze out and there was the distinct possibility his parachute pack might hang up on the door frame.

Suddenly there was a jerk that threw all the paratroopers backward hard against their safety belts. The glider began to roll. There was a long takeoff run. Then a sickening swoop and they were airborne.

Paratroopers usually gave cattle calls and Rebel yells when their plane takes off. Not today. Everyone was dead silent. It did not take a crystal ball reader to know what was going through the men's minds: *What have we gotten ourselves into*?

Including Col. Randal who would have much preferred to still be out by the pool with Lady Jane.

This was his first flight in a glider and it was worse than expected. Major Baltimore "Mongo" Farquhar had said they were 'bloody horrible.' He had not exaggerated the experience.

Lt. Mascuch said, "I'm supposed to brief you on the jump and what happens after, sir. What we're about to do is a demonstration to determine the validity of parachuting from gliders. It's also an initial test to see how quickly paratroopers can assemble on the drop zone."

Col. Randal said, "Is there a ground tactical problem following the jump?"

"Negative, sir. Drop and assemble."

"That's it?"

"Not exactly, Colonel. The whole airborne Milky Way plus a lot of other big brass down from Washington is observing today. We have to get it right. The dignitaries' bleachers have been strategically located in a place where a grove of trees obstructs the actual view of the jumpers touching down making their PLFs."

Col. Randal said, "Why might that be?"

Lt. Mascuch said, "Because the 551st has another company of GOYAs hiding in concealment among the trees, sir. When you recover from your PLF, drop your chute and take up a prone position on the silk. Stay there sir, don't get up until I arrive and give the word—smoke 'em if you've got 'em."

Col. Randal said, "You want me to remain in place on the ground where I land—not move to the assembly point?"

Lt. Mascuch said, "Yes, sir, that's the idea. We need to give the troops waiting in the trees time to run out into the open in a compact tactical formation to show the observers the assembly was a success.

"After that trucks will be waiting to transport us back to the airfield—you have a cocktail party to attend, sir, I understand."

Captain Billy Jack Jaxx had been known to say, "If you ain't cheatin' you ain't tryin' and if you get caught you ain't tryin' hard enough." Today's rigged demonstration might be a stretch even for Jack Cool. However "It Never Hurts to Cheat" had always been one of Raiding Forces Rules.

Col. Randal decided his was not to reason why.

Lt. Mascuch said, "How's it feel to be making airborne history, sir?"

Col. Randal said, "You volunteer for this jump like General Blackwell claims all the 551st troopers onboard today, Lieutenant?"

"Hell no, sir. Colonel Joerg said, 'Get off your ass, Mascuch. You're on the manifest.'"

That was pretty much the end of conversation. Everyone on board was busy thinking their own thoughts. Col. Randal had been on combat jumps when the troops had been more relaxed than these paratroopers were today.

Thankfully the flight to the DZ did not take long.

The experience did not have much to recommend it. The Waco danced around on the end of its tow rope. Canvas flapped and crackled giving the paratroopers something to think about.

Col. Randal had the distinct feeling the glider might fall apart at any moment.

It was a relief when the jumpmaster stood up, stomped his jump boot—but not very hard—held out his fingers and shouted, "SIX MINUTES!"

Col. Randal was ready to go.

What seemed way too long later came the command, "STAND UP AND HOOK UP!"

The jumpers struggled to their feet. This was a simulated combat jump so everyone except Col. Randal was carrying a full basic load of weapons and equipment. The sudden movement caused the weight distribution in the CG-4A to shift and the glider nosedived rocking violently, throwing the jumpers backward, crashing into Col. Randal who was last man.

He went down.

When he landed Col. Randal was within inches of being in Beverly's lap—the cockpit not being a compartment sealed off from the rest of the glider.

She and the pilot were struggling to muscle the controls back and keep the trim tab adjusted to prevent the plane from snapping the tow rope. The University of Texas beauty queen was at least as unhappy with this mission as Col. Randal, and maybe more so. It was probably a good thing he was not aware Beverly was concerned the Waco's wings might snap off any second from the rocking.

Finally, the pilots managed to regain control and brought the glider back to flying somewhat level slightly above the tow plane where it was supposed to be.

Col. Randal was able to shove Lt. Mascuch back up on his feet. Then he managed to muscle himself up while trying not to break anything or put an elbow through the canvass skin of the fuselage. With the stick now standing ready for the jump commands to resume, the cramped passenger/cargo space in the Waco was claustrophobic.

"CHECK STATIC LINES."

The sound of metal rasping on metal filled the compartment. Again, Col. Randal wondered about the anchor line. Counting their parachutes the men were carrying close to a hundred pounds of equipment. The steel cable was going to get a workout—would it hold?

"CHECK YOUR EQUIPMENT"

Col. Randal ran his hands over his reserve it seemed fine. Then, with his right hand he traced Lt. Mascuch's yellow static line from the snap link all the way down into the parachute pack on his back. It was good to go.

He turned around barely keeping his balance and the lieutenant inspected his. Not that it mattered. Col. Randal was going to jump.

He wanted off this glider.

"SOUND OFF FOR EQUIPMENT CHECK!"

Col. Randal shouted, "OK!"

Lt. Mascuch shouted "OK!"

"OKs" rippled up the stick like a string of dominoes.

"ONE MINUTE!"

That sounded way too long to have to wait.

Finally, "STAND IN THE DOOR!"

"GO!"

The jumpmaster led out as was his prerogative, exiting the left door. This was a mistake. Only no one knew it was going to be a problem, this being the first-ever glider drop.

As the paratroopers in the stick were learning by on-the-job training (OJT) jumping a glider was not like jumping a powered aircraft. What was needed was for the jumpmaster and the assistant jumpmaster to stand on both sides of the aircraft and perform synchronized individual tap-outs with the parachutists going out simultaneously from opposite doors to keep the weight from shifting with each exit.

Since no one had ever jumped a glider before the jumpmasters did not know that and this being a training exercise would not have led the stick out the door.

As soon as a paratrooper arrived at the door he turned left or right, slapped his hands outside for leverage the way he did when jumping a C-47 then leaped out. Since the exits were not synchronized, the sudden change of weight caused the glider to be thrown off balance as each man went out the door.

With each exit the Waco would heel over on one wing or the other.

Up front the pilots were fighting to maintain level flight. The CG-4A gave every indication of wanting to roll over, spiral out of control and crash. There was the distinct possibility it would break free of the tow rope.

Having logged considerably more hours flying a glider than the USAAF pilot Beverly knew the most immediate threat was the Waco breaking up in flight. The rapid back and forth motion when the glider's wings dipped as each of the paratroopers went out the door on opposite sides was creating a violent seesaw effect.

Initially, because they were packed in tight, Col. Randal was able to retain his balance by bending his knees and riding with it. Then as the stick started moving forward toward the doors he no longer had the relative luxury of being crammed in like a sardine and was thrown to the plywood floor banging into the back of the two pilots' seats.

Beverly shouted over her shoulder, "You OK, Johnny?"

The stick ahead of him was staggering toward the doors like a bunch of drunks and disappearing. The glider was making wild gyrations it was never intended to perform. Unable to regain his footing and with no one to help him Col. Randal had no option but to low-crawl down the aisle.

As the weight dynamic continued to change with each exit, the Waco was not only winging over side-to-side but dipping and rising. It was a wild roller coaster ride. And for such a tiny cabin the door still seemed like it was a mile away.

Col. Randal was desperate to get out. Immediately in front of him Lt. Mascuch did a right face and attempted to move into the right door. The glider dipped a wing. He was thrown across the aisle and out the *left* door—airborne history in the making.

Col. Randal was reasonably certain a backward static line exit had never been done before.

Then the glider was empty except for Col. Randal and the pilots. He slithered to the door and launched himself out headfirst from the prone position. That was a mistake and may also have been a first-of-its-kind exit itself.

Because the glider did not have a propeller to create prop blast to help deploy the parachutes the 551st was jumping from a higher-than-normal altitude today. This worked in Col. Randal's favor. When the T-4's canopy was pulled out of his parachute pack by the static line before it could crack open he sailed through the lines headfirst like Superman—minus the cape.

That is not supposed to be possible.

Naturally, this resulted in a major malfunction of his main chute.

All the training kicked in automatically. Col. Randal slapped both hands on the ends of his reserve and got his feet and knees together in the tuck position he should have exited from the Waco in the first place. Then he leaned back in midair, placed his right hand on the metal reserve handle, and ripped it out with every fiber of strength he had in his body.

The handle came off in his hand.

Sheer terror, the icicle jabbed through his chest again—this time it felt like a legitimate this is no drill heart attack. A malfunction was the worst nightmare a jumper can imagine and the impression was he had just experienced *two* of them. It took an unhappy couple of seconds to realize the reserve's handle coming free of the chute was how it was designed to work.

He was supposed to drop it. Col. Randal should have known that. This was not the first time he ever had to hit his reserve.

The white silk spilled out, fell down and wrapped around his legs exactly like in the paratrooper song *Blood On The Risers* with its cheerful refrain "*. . . and he ain't gonna jump no more.*"

Not good.

Col. Randal reached down and tore at the reserve canopy. It pulled free. The training kicked in again. He gathered the chute to his chest and attempted to throw it out away from his body to catch air so it would deploy.

The silk blew back in his face.

One more try—it popped open.

Experiencing an incredible sense of relief, he looked down to see the other jumpers' parachutes floating in to the drop zone and collapsing silently as they landed. As per the plan the GOYAs remained in the prone position out of sight of the dignitaries in the bleachers.

Then, because a reserve has a lot smaller canopy than a T-4's main chute, Col. Randal burned in hot and pancaked hitting all four points of contact more or less at the same time. Definitely not the approved school solution parachute landing fall, however PLFs are pass/fail—the standard being any jump you walk away from is a good one.

Col. Randal was not complaining.

As per the plan he stayed on the ground. Laying there waiting to be notified it was time to move out to the trucks Col. Randal decided this was his worst jump ever. The thing was he had thought that before. Reaching in his pocket to take out his old U.S. 26th Cavalry Regiment Zippo to light a cigarette he encountered a problem.

The reserve chute's aluminum handle was still in his hand.

11

MR. CONGENIALITY

CASTELROZZO 2100 HOURS

CAPTAIN OLIVER FERNSBY ISSUED C COMPANY, 2nd Battalion, Cyprus Regiment its Operation Order. They moved out to their start line for the next morning's sweep at 2100 hours. Capt. Fernsby called for them to travel in a company file, platoons in file, squads in file formation. This configuration is difficult to maneuver except when moving straight ahead and results in a serious lack of firepower in the direction of march. A file works best in the jungle, heavy forest or other restricted terrain not found on Castelrozzo. But it was the perfect formation to move beaters in position along a lane to be ready to sweep the grid on line at BMNT.

All C Company had to do was follow the cobblestone path, stop where Capt. Fernsby had posted a guide to mark the far boundary, make a right face and take up position where they stood. C Company would remain overnight (RON) sleeping on the ground on 25% alert and be ready to move out straight ahead up the escarpment thirty minutes after daylight.

Captain Billy Jack Jaxx arrived an hour later walking along the lane in the dark exactly the way he thought the Colonel would have done if he were here. He linked up with Capt. Fernsby arriving out of the dark at his Command Post (CP) alone, unannounced and unexpected. The two officers proceeded to troop the line.

As they carried out their inspection, Capt. Jaxx took one last opportunity to hit the high points of what was expected of C Company, even though he had covered it all previously. The Colonel had taught him there was "no such thing as too much repetition when preparing troops for an operation," rarely saying the word repetition only once.

It was always, "repetition, repetition, repetition."

While the two officers were the same rank Capt. Jaxx was clearly in charge. Capt. Fernsby was impressed to be working with someone of his reputation on his first combat operation. Jack Cool—everyone in Middle East Command knew about his exploits.

Capt. Jaxx said, "In the morning your company will move out on your sweep on my command. The signal's a red flare fired from a Walrus orbiting overhead. I'll be aboard observing.

"As briefed, there won't be any Raiding Forces or attached personnel on the ground in your AO other than our snipers. No locals in uniform of any kind—postman, policeman, fireman, dogcatcher, whatever. If your troops encounter anyone in a khaki uniform or see an armed civilian they are cleared to engage.

"That said, priority goes to taking a prisoner.

"Questions?"

"Negative."

"The four sniper teams will be moving into their hides to your front beginning at 2400 hours. Your men won't see them tonight or tomorrow. In the event they engage a target the snipers will remain in deep concealment until the drive is complete.

"You are *not*, I say again *NOT* cleared to fire your weapons until daylight. If anyone attempts to exfiltrate through your position during the hours of darkness, it's cold steel only—bayonets or rifle butts. Is that clear?"

"Understood, Captain."

"Get me my prisoner."

CAROLINA HOTEL

COLONEL JOHN RANDAL, MAJOR THE LADY JANE Seaborn, Beverly Blackwell and Red the Flying Clipper Girl were at the reception Lady Jane was hosting for the battalion and regimental commanders of airborne units on Camp Mackall. Approximately forty officers were in the room ranging in grade from major to full colonel. Except for the members of the 11th Airborne Division—on orders for the Pacific—these officers were the men who would be leading Airborne Forces against the Third Reich.

They represented the best field grade commanders the United States Army had to offer.

Maj. Gen. Blackwell pulled Col. Randal aside before going upstairs to his suite to host his private dinner for the five airborne division commanders. "I know it's not your style, Johnny, but you need to mingle. These boys are the troop command level decision-makers we're going to be working with for the rest of the war. Get to know 'em.

"They surely want to know you."

"Yes, sir."

Air Chief Marshal Sir Arthur Tedder, DSO, OBE, DFC, stopped by the cocktail party to speak to Col. Randal. "I shall be flying out to Washington directly. Wanted to pop in and say I thoroughly enjoyed your parachuting demonstration this afternoon, Colonel. Was the experience as ghastly as it appeared?"

Col. Randal said, "Ghastly doesn't do that glider jump justice, sir."

ACM Tedder said, "In time of national emergency one must experiment with new techniques. Not always pleasant playing the guinea pig. Still, it must be done."

"Sir, don't let anyone ever try to sell you on the idea of dropping paratroops out of gliders—not even in training."

"Point taken. Nice to see you again, Colonel. Give my regards to Mr. King."

"Yes, sir."

Lady Jane came over to say hello to the Air Marshal. She walked him to the door as he was leaving. With no excuse he could think of to get out of it, Col. Randal decided now was as good a time as any to comply with Bronc's orders—he mingled.

It was not that bad.

Every officer in the room was a battalion or regimental commander. Very important men with big responsibilities. They would be making life and death decisions daily as soon as their units entered combat. Between them Lady Jane's guests commanded tens of thousands of paratroopers or glidermen. To a man they wanted to be done with training, deploy overseas and get in the fight. The monotony of training, training and more training, waiting and wondering had reached the point of being almost unbearable.

Getting to the war was taking a long time.

Despite what Bronc said Col. Randal was surprised the guests were so interested in talking to him about his combat experiences. For once Lady Jane, Beverly, and Red were not the center of attention. These officers wanted to know what he knew.

They wanted to *be* him—a decorated combat veteran back from the war zone willing to answer questions about "Lessons Learned" from those who had not been yet.

It started out with him talking to the commander of the 507th Parachute Infantry Regiment. Gradually a crowd started to gather around to listen in. Soon everyone in the room was there to hear. The officers were peppering him rapid-fire.

The atmosphere was deadly serious.

Except from time to time when he described an event like when Pyro Percy blew up the lighthouse or how the navy accidentally dropped the intelligence-filled safe into the ocean (which Raiding Forces had specifically carried out a raid to capture).

Officers who know they are slated to command in combat but who have never been in a battle have a lot of issues on their mind. Primarily: *What's it like?* With the underlying, *how will I perform under fire?*

The great unknowns.

Col. Randal took every question head-on. His answers were not always what anyone wanted to hear because they did not conform to what they hoped or expected he would say. How anyone took what he said was irrelevant to him. The group picked up on that immediately. And paid even more attention.

They could see he was not trying to impress anyone.

The colonel commanding the 513th PIR said, "If you could give us one piece of advice what would it be?"

Col. Randal said, "Train tactically at all times. Little details are important. Have your men carry their weapons everywhere they go. Eliminate close order drill, marching, singing, and any administrative activity. Priority to night exercises with emphasis on small unit tactics and patrolling, stressing individual initiative. Every troop movement, every problem, even activities like feeding your troops all need to be conducted as if you're in immediate proximity to the enemy.

"You will be soon enough and you'll fight like you train."

Major General Joseph Swing walked in on his way upstairs to the division commander's dinner. He came over to speak to Col. Randal. The two of them moved off to a corner of the room.

"You got my attention this morning, Colonel. Brought up a subject that's been in the back of my mind for some time but you made it impossible to ignore any longer. There's no excuse for the inequity between paratroopers and glidermen. We know better than that—we're better officers.

"My 11th Airborne Division has the one parachute / two glider regiment configuration. We're on orders for the Pacific so it's probably too late at this stage to do anything to change our TO&E. Still, I'm determined to have every man in my division be parachute-qualified before we deploy overseas.

"We'll fight as equals."

Col. Randal said, "Good plan, sir."

Maj. Gen. Swing said, "Airborne Command at Fort Benning has informed me it can't accommodate two regiments of students on such short notice. I'm going to have to organize my own parachute training. Any suggestions on how to go about it?"

Col. Randal said, "Captain Roy "Mad Dog" Reupart, sir. He was my instructor when Raiding Forces went through No.1 Parachute School at RAF Ringway. He's been with us ever since. Recently I've had him on TDY running No. 4 Middle East Training Center—a jump school in the Suez.

"I'll be glad to loan him to you, General."

"Mad Dog sounds like just the man I need."

Col. Randal said, "He'll be here by the end of the week. All you'll have to do is supply Captain Reupart a few parachute-qualified NCOs to act as instructors and schedule the men time to train. He'll make it happen for you, sir."

Maj. Gen. Swing said, "Outstanding, now all I have to do is convince the USAAF to dedicate the aircraft we need."

Col. Randal said, "General Blackwell is always looking for realistic training exercises for his Troop Transport Command aircrews, sir. Dropping paratroops on training jumps is as real as it gets."

Maj. Gen. Swing said, "I'll get with Bronc. Thanks, Colonel."

Col. Randal said, "I'll send Captain Reupart a TWX tonight sir.

Maj. Gen. Blackwell's aide appeared with Lady Jane. "The General sends his compliments, sir. He requests the pleasure of your presence in the Robert E. Lee suite post with."

Col. Randal said, "What's this about?"

"His guests expressed their desire to have you brief them on your Benevento drop before dinner is served, sir."

Lady Jane said, "You are popular tonight."

Col. Randal said, "I'm not sure that's what it is."

CASTELROZZO 2400 HOURS

CAPTAIN ROY KIDD, HIS SPOTTER AND TECH Sergeant Luke Volkmann departed Advance Base Castelrozzo to travel to their hides. Capt. Kidd was escorting TSgt. Volkmann to his position because this was his first actual mission. The sergeant was not familiar with the island having only recently arrived.

Lovat Scouts Munro Ferguson and Lionel Fenwick's two teams would follow them out at fifteen-minute intervals.

The night was pitch dark. No moon out. The village was on full blackout which meant heavy drapes over all windows with no lights showing. Not that it mattered . . . the townspeople were all mostly asleep by now. With the men gone since the war started there was not much nightlife for the locals.

On this shoot the snipers and their spotters were not wearing their ghillie suits. All of the hides would be on rooftops and that called for a different method of concealment. Each man was carrying a rolled-up canvas tarp to place over himself. While it was not perfect camouflage tarps on rooftops to plug leaks were not unknown.

The steepness of the escarpment posed a challenge for the sniper teams. The radical slope made it possible for anyone uphill to see the rooftops of the houses below. Taking up a position on a roof was a tradeoff. Setting up inside to shoot from a second-story window would offer better concealment but would restrict the range of their lateral vision, and the snipers needed the widest possible field of fire.

Each of the shooters was armed with his weapon of choice. Capt. Kidd was lugging his 31-pound .55 caliber Boys Anti-Tank Rifle with its metal No. 32 scope. His spotter was carrying the 14-pound M1919 A4 light machine gun tripod mount modified to accept the Boys Anti-Tank Rifle. TSgt. Volkmann, a graduate of the United States Marine Corps Scout Sniper School, was armed with a USMC Springfield, U.S. Rifle caliber .30 M1903A1 (Sniper) w/8X Unertl scope. The Lovat Scouts had their trusty 7x57 Westley Richards rifles w/detachable private purchase 6X Zeiss scopes—their scopes were not private purchase—they had been captured by their Lovat Scout fathers in the last war.

In WWI the goal for a sniper was 100 kills—in a single day.

The practical maximum effective range of the shoulder-fired rifles was 500 yards. However, hits could be achieved at double that distance. The fact was, in reality, most shots by snipers in combat are taken at relatively close range. Since the grid to be swept was 750 yards in depth, Capt. Kidd had his snipers select hides 300 yards in advance of the C Company start line. The four teams would initially be facing the beaters when they moved out. Then as the line of troops swept past, the sniper teams would shift their position 180 degrees.

The clearing operation was going to be small in scale but complex in execution. There was no guarantee a Nazi was hiding in the search grid. It might all be a waste of time.

But it might not be and that is what made sniping so interesting.

CAPT. BILLY JACK JAXX RETURNED TO ABCHQ. HE linked up with the ambush team leaders, Lieutenant Dan Bonham, Master Sergeant Mack Beckwith, and Private First Class Norvel "Horn Dog" Hansen. Capt. Jaxx had initially planned to travel with them tomorrow to be in a position to observe C Company's advance up the escarpment and to be in overall command. That all changed when Captain Pamala Plum-Martin flew to Castelrozzo in response to a message from Lieutenant Colonel Sir Terry "Zorro" Stone advising her services were required for an anti-Brandenburger operation.

Lieutenant General "Geronimo" Joe McKoy, Waldo Treywick and King arrived with her.

Now Capt. Jaxx was to be onboard the Walrus. He was thinking about taking his .30 Baby BAR along in hopes of getting a shot if a Nazi exposed himself. Watching and waiting while someone else did not conform to his idea of leadership. He believed his troops needed to see him up front on the firing line engaging with his individual weapon at every possible opportunity.

Before nightfall Capt. Jaxx had led the three team leaders on a quick reconnaissance of their ambush locations at the top of the escarpment. Ambushes fall into two primary categories—"Near" and "Far" with an unlimited number of subcategories limited only by the imagination that denote complexity. These were going to be "near linear ambushes" meaning the "killing zones" were close-range with the troops positioned on line. The idea was to have maximum firepower to the front.

All three locations were mutually supporting—ambush sites did not get any better than this.

The operation Capt. Jaxx had designed was a classic "hammer and anvil."

C Company would be the "hammer." It would drive the Nazis onto the "anvil," meaning the ambushes. Weapons in each site consisted of one each .30 Stinger LMG, .30 Baby BAR and .30 M1 Garand rifle.

It was a lot of firepower.

Captain Roy Kidd's snipers were thought to be the primary shooters. Possibly Capt. Jaxx orbiting overhead in the Walrus with his .30 Baby BAR might take down any Nazis shifting their positions to avoid the beaters. If things went according to plan any German flushed out of hiding would never make it as far as the ambushes killing zones.

Still nothing was being left to chance.

Outside ABCHQ he had all nine people gather round in the dark before the ambush teams departed. The men were professionals. Even so everyone was hyped up. You could feel the excitement. Capt. Jaxx wanted to go over the details one last time.

Repetition, repetition, repetition.

"You men all know your jobs. Move into your ambush sites, take up your positions and stand by ready. Thirty minutes after sunrise the signal for the beaters to begin their drive will be a red flare I fire from the Walrus race tracking overhead—you won't be able to miss it.

"No friendlies will be in the AO other than the beaters who will be in British BDUs and the snipers on rooftops. Any armed individual, whether they be wearing U.S. Army khaki or civilian clothes, is to be considered an enemy combatant. On command from your ambush team leader, take them under fire.

"Is that clear?"

In laid-back conversational level voices that belied their impatience to get the last-minute administrative details over with and get going, the nine men responded, "Clear, sir."

No melodrama—the troops knew this briefing was of the category Raiding Forces jokingly liked to refer to as the "last and final, final briefing,—absolutely", was more for Capt. Jaxx's benefit than their own.

"Priority is to take a prisoner. Bring me one. Is that clear?"

"Clear, sir."

Capt. Jaxx knew he was wasting his breath. Any Brandenburger showing himself tomorrow was a dead man. Guaranteed.

CAROLINA HOTEL

COLONEL JOHN RANDAL WRAPPED UP HIS BRIEFING on the Benevento drop to the five airborne division commanders. The group, to include Major General Sam Houston Blackwell, was the most impressive group of officers he had ever addressed. They were arguably the finest major generals in the United States Army.

The division commanders wanted to hear his reasoning behind changing the Concept of the Operation only minutes before wheels up for the jump. Their primary interest was in how he had known to convert the traditional forced-entry seize-and-hold parachute assault he had been briefed to conduct into a hit-and-run guerrilla campaign.

The fact Col. Randal had essentially disobeyed orders and reconfigured his mission profile without permission or informing anyone other than the men of the 575th Ranger Task Force was of little concern to any of them. What they wanted to understand was the *rationale* for his last-minute switch to a new plan—besides the fact the plan ordered by Fifth Army was suicide.

The generals were particularly interested to hear his account of what it had been like on the ground in the minutes immediately following a night combat jump so scattered some of his Rangers missed the DZ in excess of a hundred miles.

Col. Randal walked them through the operation step by step.

Major General Matthew Ridgway said, "How do you recommend we bring order out of the chaos on the scale you describe following a division sized airborne insertion, Colonel?"

Col. Randal said, "By accepting that confusion is inherent in night combat drops, planning for it in advance and turning the disorder you are unable prevent to your advantage, sir."

Major General Swing said, "I believe we may have hit upon the key element for our response to General Eisenhower's assertion that airborne divisions are 'difficult to control.'"

Major General William Lee said, "I concur. We can work with that concept. Quite frankly I never considered the impact *our* confusion might have on the other side."

The generals had follow-up questions. Col. Randal answered with, "my thinking was . . ." or "this is what was happening at…"

The idea of not having a clearly defined initial objective—authorizing their paratroopers to attack targets of opportunity rather than race to an assembly area to organize for an attack on a point-type target, was a novel concept. It did not conform to current doctrine.

The idea did not sit well with everyone.

While Col. Randal's belief that scattered drops produced good outcomes because they resulted in confusion to the enemy might be true it was still a radical concept. The division commanders wanted to command large formations attacking places with names—fight battles that would make the history books—not have little bands of paratroopers roaming the countryside creating havoc.

Maj. Gen. Swing said, "Anything you would have done differently?"

Col. Randal said, "Issued my Rangers more demolitions, sir."

Maj. Gen. Ridgway followed Col. Randal out into the hall when he departed to return to the reception downstairs.

"Colonel, a word if I might?"

"Yes, sir."

"I'll be promoting Jim Gavin to assistant division commander of my 82nd Airborne Division in the next month or so. That means a vacancy opening up for command of the 505th PIR. I've been impressed with the way you handled yourself the last few days and your combat record speaks for itself.

"Would you have any interest in being Gavin's replacement?"

Col. Randal said, "Sir, that is a very attractive offer but I'm involved with classified national-level operations that prohibit my leaving Raiding Forces."

Maj. Gen. Ridgway said, "If circumstances should change get in contact with me. And don't forget our conversation about the battalion commanders. I only want the best."

Col. Randal said, "I'll be talking to my officers, sir."

"That's what I hoped to hear."

As Col. Randal turned away Maj. Gen. Ridgway said, "For the record I'm not entirely on board with all of your recommendations but you certainly give compelling arguments to back them up. I've noticed you have not exactly been volunteering the information.

"In the future don't make Bronc drag it out of you. The Swing Board needs healthy debate. We should be more than a rubber stamp."

"Yes, sir."

Maj. Gen. Ridgway said, "Between the two of us I took bad advice. When the 82nd's next mission comes up I'll be jumping with my paratroopers. Heard you on that one, Colonel.

"Loud and clear."

CASTELROZZO

CAPTAIN ROY KIDD AND TECHNICAL SERGEANT Luke Volkmann's two sniper teams were on the move traveling to their hide positions. It was a dark night. Nevertheless, the movement through the village was not difficult. All they had to do was patrol down the cobblestone path to the house Capt. Kidd's team was going to occupy. He left his .55 Boys Rifle with his spotter—he dropped the term Anti-Tank from its nomenclature there being virtually no German tanks anywhere in the Aegean—and continued on with TSgt. Volkmann's team to their position.

Then Capt. Kidd doubled back and led his spotter inside to the attic where they climbed out onto the roof. As per the plan they initially set up facing the start line of C Company. However, he placed the .55 Boys Rifle on the opposite side of the roof pointed up the escarpment.

C Company would only be 300 yards away when the infantry troops commenced their drive. If a Brandenburger was flushed out anywhere in that distance Capt. Kidd planned to use his spotter's .30 M1 Garand to make the shot. Then as the beaters swept past they would transition to the other side of the roof where the .55 Boys Rifle was set up on its tripod.

Capt. Kidd knew they would not be fooling any Brandenburger who saw the silhouette of the weapon under the tarp. Not that it mattered. By then the line of infantry would be on the move leaving any Nazis in hiding with only two options—remain in place and be trapped or make a run for it.

Capt. Kidd had to hand it to Jack Cool. He had this operation wired tight.

At his location TSgt. Volkmann and his spotter were set up ready for something to happen. All they had to do was wait. It was four hours to BMNT. When he looked at his watch he thought it must be broken.

Time seemed to have ground to a standstill—first missions are like that.

TSgt. Volkmann was armed with an armory-built USMC precision sniper rifle. When he attended the USMC Scout Sniper School the Marines liked to say, "We do more with less." Which was true. Their annual military budget was so tight the Corps could only afford hand-me-down surplus weapons and equipment purchased from the Army.

The .30 M1903 Springfield in all its variations was substitute standard — the military's way of saying obsolete. By the time Pearl Harbor was bombed, the bolt action weapon had been replaced by the semiautomatic .30 M1 Garand. The latest model developed during the inter-war years was the .30 M1903 Springfield A4—only Springfield never actually manufactured any M-1903 "Springfields" in any of their variations. They were made by Remington Arms and Smith Corona, the typewriter company.

Unfortunately there were not enough Garands produced at this point to meet the needs of the Army so the Marines had to make do with .30 M 1903 A1s left over from the last war until production met demand.

Not a problem for the Devil Dogs. Corps-level armorers at the Philadelphia Naval Yard handpicked 1,500 .30 M1903A1 Springfields out of the stock of National Match rifle team competition rifles from years past. Then they tore them apart and completely rebuilt them by hand. Each weapon was detail disassembled, miked to ensure absolutely perfect tolerances then all moving parts were polished until they functioned buttery smooth. A unique serial number was stamped on each of the sniper rifle's major parts before it was reassembled to guarantee the same parts stayed with the same rifle. The result was a precision long-range weapon—arguably the best fielded by any nation on either side of the conflict—one rifle built by one USMC armorer issued to one Marine sniper.

"Sniper" was stamped on the Unertl 8X scope.

To the Marines rifle marksmanship was a religion—the cult of the rifleman. From day one in boot camp drill instructors relentlessly instilled in their recruits the creed, "The most dangerous weapon in the world is a United States Marine and his rifle."

That said the Marine Corps tended to march to their own drum when it came to marksmanship. The civilian Unertl 8X scope was adopted for issue to their snipers. The choice was a long skinny—twenty-four inches in length, somewhat fragile, free floating telescopic sight. The tube slid forward in its mount after every round was fired. The Unertl had a spring which automatically slammed the scope back into battery. The system worked perfectly.

The Marines removed the spring.

That meant after every shot a Marine sniper had to reset his scope by hand. It was slow. And the extra movement increased the risk of giving away the shooter's position.

TSgt. Volkmann was a member of the Presidents One Hundred making him one of the best rifle marksmen, military or civilian, in America. He had helped organize a Sniper Course for the Infantry School at Fort Benning based on his training with the Marines. In addition, he was the 511 Armorer for the Fort Benning Rifle Team prior to being recruited by the OSS.

TSgt. Volkmann was not a Marine.

He put the spring back in.

Back along the path in the two hides nearest ABCHQ Lovat Scouts Lionel Fenwick and Munro Ferguson were in their positions. Sniping was what they lived for as it had been for their fathers in France during the last war. Unfortunately, as the two saw it, they had not been called on to do much long-range work lately except for the Benevento jump—then they had done a lot. Tonight both Scouts were partnered with a Raiding Forces operator to act as their spotter. Not that either man required one.

The Lovats would have been content to go it alone.

CAROLINA HOTEL

MAJOR GENERAL SAM HOUSTON BLACKWELL AND Beverly Blackwell were having a nightcap in Colonel John Randal and Major the Lady Jane Seaborn's Jefferson Davis suite. Bronc was in rare form.

"What the hell, Colonel? Joe Swing wants me to support parachute training for the 11th Airborne so he can get all his troops jump-qualified based on your recommendation. No sooner do I agree when Bud Miley hits me up to do the same thing for his boys in the 17th Airborne.

"Wood Joerg, the 551st Parachute Infantry Battalion commander, cornered me in the lobby and asked me to use my influence to get his battalion assigned to Raiding Forces.

"Then if that wasn't enough for one night, Matt Ridgway informs me he wants you released from your current duties to command his 505th Parachute Infantry Regiment in about a month."

Col. Randal said, "Sir, I . . ."

Maj. Gen. Blackwell said, "Poach my Paratroop Advisor… I'm getting on the horn to Donovan. Wild Bill's not going to like the idea of you transferring out of Raiding Forces. Not one little bit."

Col. Randal said, "General . . ."

"What kind of charm offensive have you been running anyway?"

Beverly said, "Daddy, you told Johnny to mingle."

Maj. Gen. Blackwell said, "I said get to know people, not run for Mr. Congeniality."

Lady Jane laughed, "Considering John is about as social as a wounded cape buffalo he can count on my vote. He shall need it."

Beverly said, "Exactly—mine too."

ADVANCE BASE CASTELROZZO

CAPTAIN STEPHANIE FAWCETT-TATUM WAS tearing a strip off Captain Billy Jack Jaxx in the ABC Tactical Operations Center.

"I am not your personal dating service, Jack."

Capt. Jaxx said, "What are you talking about?"

Capt. Fawcett-Tatum said, "Our phones have been ringing off the wall. Teenage girls calling for you at all hours. Ever since you spoke to their group about the Brandenburgers."

Capt. Jaxx said, "Don't blame me. That was Mandy's idea."

"What did you say to them?"

"All I said was if they had information that might lead to the apprehension of any of the Nazis at large on the island to call ABCHQ and make a report—that's it."

Capt. Fawcett-Tatum said, "Those girls want to come make their statements to you, Romeo—in person. Castelrozzo does not issue ID cards. There is no way to verify age and I do not recommend you take the girls' word."

"Not a problem, Stephanie, you know I'm only in to experienced women."

Jack Cool.

SOMEWHERE AT SEA OFF RHODES

VICE ADMIRAL SIR RANDOLPH "RAZOR" RANSOM and Lieutenant Theodore Hamilton were onboard Brandy Seaborn's MAS boat hove to approximately eighty miles from Castelrozzo. Visibility was limited with no moon out and for once, as Homer famously wrote, the sea actually was "wine dark." The high-speed former Regia Marina torpedo boat was idling in the middle of the channel.

There were three Luftwaffe airfields located on Rhodes. The bombers flying off them posed a direct threat to Castelrozzo eighty air miles away. Lt. Hamilton had devised a plan to distract German pilots.

The Great Teddy was at the stern of the boat inspecting a strange-looking device he had built. VAdm. Ransom was watching him work. The Razor was not sure if they were engaged in a boy's prank or a legitimate operation of the war.

He had come along tonight to find out.

Scattered about the deck were a half dozen not very impressive pieces of equipment Lt. Hamilton had grandly designated the Royal Navy Submarine Deception Device (RNSDD) Mark 1 (Flotation).

The RNSDD Mk 1 consisted of three empty brandy bottles and a broomstick painted black. The bottles were securely wired to one end of the stick. There was a small weight at the bottom.

Lt. Hamilton said, "Standing by to launch one each RNSDD Mk1 on your command, sir."

VAdm. Ransom said, "Anchors away, Lieutenant."

The Great Teddy tossed the device overboard. The weight at the bottom pulled the bottles under but did not sink the RNSDD Mk 1. The broomstick popped up with almost four feet of handle sticking out of the water.

It looked remarkably like the periscope of a submarine.

VAdm. Ransom studied the result through a pair of Royal Navy-issue night glasses. No Luftwaffe pilot would be able to resist attacking one of the RNSDD Mk 1s. A bomb dropped on a broomstick was a bomb not dropped on ABC.

"Bloody genius."

CASTELROZZO OFF LIMITS AREA

IT WAS NOT ACCURATE TO SAY THERE WAS NO nightlife in Castelrozzo. You just had to know where to find it. Private First Class Norvel "Horn Dog" Hansen had built-in radar when it came to knowing where the action was. It was said you could drop him blindfolded in any city in the world and he would head straight as an arrow to the seediest bar in town.

PFC Hansen thought of it as a gift.

Horn Dog's team's line of departure (LD) time to move out to their ambush position was 0400 hours. Being the kind of leader who placed a great deal of importance on the morale of his troops PFC Hansen saw no reason why his men should not have a little rest and relaxation prior to. He took them to a recently opened underground bar in the area of the island Lieutenant Theodore Hamilton had used to simulate Castelrozzo Village in hopes of tricking Luftwaffe pilots into bombing the wrong place.

Just like he had done at RAF Habbaniya with the Golden Square's artillery.

Acting on Colonel John Randal's orders The Great Teddy turned a group of abandoned warehouses outside of the central business district into what would appear, to a German aviator from the air at night, as the center of the town. The place was lit up like a Mexican fiesta.

Searchlights crisscrossed the sky.

Major the Lady Jane Seaborn's plan to develop the waterfront area of Castelrozzo into quaint bistros and eateries had not yet to come to fruition. Besides she did not intend to have strip clubs or brothels. It is a long-established economic principle that business abhors a vacuum.

One local entrepreneur saw an opportunity.

He moved into an abandoned warehouse in the middle of Lt. Hamilton's phony village and turned it into what was arguably the raunchiest strip club in the Dodecanese—there were three whorehouses.

The main drawback to the underground club scene/red light district, besides it being off limits, was the very real possibility of being bombed by the Luftwaffe. That prospect did not seem to have a desultory effect on clientele. Business was booming.

While the strip club had no name, the area was called "The Beaten Zone."

PFC Hansen and his two teammates were sitting at a table next to the stage drinking Egyptian beer and having a great time. One of the worst bands in the history of organized music, heavy on drums and cymbal crashes, was blaring. On stage a nasty-looking Armenian stripper was working to whistles and cat calls from the audience.

A big Canadian Special Operations pilot, wearing a trademark Hawaiian shirt, stood up and pointed at PFC Hansen's table. "Hold the noise down over there, Horn Dog. We're trying to enjoy the show!"

PFC Hansen shouted back, "Shut up, redneck. Since when did you need peace and quiet to watch a naked woman?"

Master Sergeant Mack Beckwith walked in.

He was not there to party.

CASTELROZZO LINE OF DEPARTURE TIME

AS THE SUN CAME UP THE WALRUS, PILOTED BY Captain Pamala Plum-Martin, was circling over the grid to be searched. Onboard were Lieutenant General "Geronimo" Joe

McKoy, Captain Billy Jack Jaxx, Waldo Treywick and King. Mandy Paige was on the plane as well having begged Jack Cool to let her come along to observe. Considering there was plenty of space available and she had probably—make that she had saved his life the day before—he agreed to let her. Down below C Company, 2nd Battalion, Cyprus Regiment having stood to at dawn was in their start position. The troops were geared up ready to cross the line of departure.

Aboard the Walrus they could see the troops at the start line. They could see the three ambush teams at the top of the escarpment. They could see Acting Provisional Lieutenant Warthog Finley in the *King Duck* on station offshore. They could not see the four sniper teams.

Or any Brandenburgers.

Lt. Gen. McKoy and Capt. Jaxx were up front in the open-topped navigator's cupola on the nose of the Walrus. Both men had binoculars and their personal sidearms. And Jack Cool had brought his .30 Baby Bar—just in case.

The sun was a golden globe rising out of the turquoise Aegean Sea.

When it was light enough to drive away any shadows that might conceal a Nazi attempting to slip away Capt. Jaxx fired the red signal flare for the troops to step off across the LD. Down below the line of infantry moved out smartly sweeping up the escarpment. Almost as soon as the troops began their advance the parade ground formation began to disintegrate as the soldiers became channelized having to pass through tiny side yards and go around residences that were built like duplexes and triplexes.

In military terms the terrain was constricted.

The troops attempted to re-form after they flowed around a structure but the line never regained its precision. And that was all right. The idea was to force out the Brandenburgers.

Not to conduct a parade.

Watching the operation unfold from overhead was a great show. The troops were working their way up the escarpment. The officers and NCOs were traveling along behind trying to keep the line dressed right as much as possible making sure there were no gaps.

Lt. Gen. McKoy said, "Lookin' good, Jack."

Capt. Jaxx said, "I don't think the Nazis will hang around to shoot it out."

Lt. Gen. McKoy said, "They'll run. If any of 'em are in there we'll get 'em. You got yourself a plan workin,' here young Captain."

In the four sniper hides the shooters and their spotters were on high alert surreptitiously observing developments as they unfolded. Since the line of advance stretched completely across the base of the search grid something could occur anywhere, anytime. With no warning.

The snipers had to be ready.

Technical Sergeant Luke Volkmann was scanning his field of fire through the 8 power Unertl scope on his purpose built .30 M1903 A1 (Sniper) rifle. It provided excellent magnification and clarity. On the initial part of the drive if a Nazi exposed himself it would be a chip shot.

TSgt. Volkmann was surprised to discover this mission seemed much the same as a high-stakes rifle match. He had imagined it would feel different to be scanning the terrain through his scope, cocked, locked, and greenlit to engage a live enemy combatant for the first time. While he was conscious of a heightened sense of awareness his emotions were flat-lined, no adrenaline rush, no jitters, no drama. He had a task to perform and he was prepared to fulfill it in a precise, methodical, military manner the way the Marines had taught him at Scout Sniper School.

For today's operation, TSgt. Volkmann was classic "Right Man, Right Job" in accordance with Raiding Forces Rules.

The next hide position over was Captain Roy Kidd's—Raiding Forces Chief of Snipers. Through his binoculars he was carefully studying the houses the line of infantry beaters was advancing on. The troops were moving slowly checking out the residences as they came to them.

The climb was steep but C Company was advancing.

Capt. Kidd was a skilled hunter. He had been involved in a lot of drives like this when he was in India eliminating man-eating leopards and tigers that were terrorizing local villages. The technique almost always worked. The trick was to never let whatever was being driven know the real threat was not the line of beaters.

When hunting dangerous game, patience is a virtue. That is exactly what this was today. A manhunt.

Up on the top of the escarpment Lieutenant Dan Bonham, Master Sergeant Mack Beckwith and Private First Class Norvel "Horn Dog" Hansen—whose tail feathers were still smoldering from his latest run-in with the Sergeant Major in the Beaten Zone—were ready in their ambush positions.

They were watching developments down the slope. Not much was going on. Typical of ambushes.

Boring!

Until the bad guys show up.

The thing is sometimes they do. Sometimes they don't. You never know.

Overhead in the Walrus Lt. Gen. McKoy was staring through a pair of the much-traveled 7x50 Swarovski binoculars he had commandeered while serving with a Light Car Company in Egypt during the last war. He elbowed Capt. Jaxx to get his attention without taking the glasses down from his eyes. Something was moving.

"Nine o'clock sharp, Jack."

Capt. Jaxx slid around next to where Lt. Gen. McKoy was standing. He raised the Leica 8x50 field glasses Colonel John Randal had given him when they were together in Ranger Patrol shortly after he first arrived in Raiding Forces—the Colonel carried a pair of Zeiss 7x50s he'd captured with Swamp Fox Force at Calais.

Anyone who could get their hands on German glass did.

Down below Capt. Jaxx spotted a khaki-clad figure moving between houses two cobblestone paths up the escarpment ahead of the C Company line of beaters. He grabbed for his Baby BAR.

Lt. Gen. McKoy spoke into his headset. King leaned across Capt. Plum-Martin from the right-hand seat. He looked out her window through his pair of 7X50 Seiner binoculars and spotted the Brandenburger.

He pointed.

Capt. Plum-Martin brought the Walrus around.

In the seats behind her, Mandy crawled over Waldo who was looking out his window and leaned over his shoulder. After searching for a moment she saw the Nazi. Her immediate reaction was regret for having only brought her pair of .32 Sauer 38H pistols.

Mandy wanted to shoot him.

In his hide TSgt. Volkmann's spotter saw the German.

"Bogie, two o'clock."

TSgt. Volkmann shifted in the direction indicated. He acquired the target. When he did the 8x Unertl brought the Nazi in so close he could see the man had not shaved in several days.

The range was less than one hundred yards. More like seventy-five. Through the scope the Brandenburger appeared to look TSgt. Volkmann straight in the eyes. He placed the crosshairs on the man's heart then dropped them down a couple of inches because he was shooting downhill and the round would strike slightly higher than the aiming point.

Not a big deal at this range.

The spotter said, "Send it."

TSgt. Volkmann took up the slack in the two-stage military trigger. It came back until it hit the wall of the second stage and firmed up. He took a deep breath and held it.

Most shooters are taught to take a breath, let out half of it, squeeze the trigger and be surprised when the weapon discharges. TSgt. Volkmann did not do it that way.

He took the breath, held it and pressed the trigger through the second stage making sure the weight against his finger was evenly distributed. No surprises. He knew exactly when the rifle was going to go bang.

BOOOOOM!

The sound of the shot was unnaturally loud in the early morning air. A distinct *whap* followed—the sound of the round striking the Brandenburger. The man's head hit the ground before his feet left it.

In the movies when someone gets shot it never looks like that—total body collapse.

There was no celebration in the hide. TSgt. Volkmann and his spotter remained in position ready for the next target. He had his first kill.

What did it feel like? Nothing. Not a thing.

Onboard the Walrus there was a different reaction. Capt. Jaxx had his Baby BAR halfway to his shoulder when TSgt. Volkmann fired. Lt. Gen. McKoy slapped him on the back. "Yeah, good job, Jack—well designed, perfectly executed. That's what I call a plan."

In the cockpit, Mandy said, "Excellent!"

No brotherly (or sisterly) love for the Nazis who arrived in the night and murdered Raiding Forces personnel in cold blood.

Down below C Company kept advancing up the escarpment.

SOMEWHERE AT SEA

COMMANDER ANDREAS LONDOS SAID, "FROM Mosquito base on Cyprus we first sail to Castelrozzo, then along the Turkish coast to our hunting ground where we perform any number of missions—transporting raiding parties, delivering LRDG Coastwatcher teams, attacking enemy flagged caiques. By the time we return we have usually traveled at least two thousand miles."

Captain Butch "Headhunter" Hoolihan said, "Long way in a small boat—impressive."

For the last eighteen months or so Capt. Hoolihan had been carrying out high-speed pinprick raids aboard one or another of Lieutenant Randy "Hornblower" Seaborn's MGBs or PT boats. Initially he was impatient to get back to Castelrozzo to pick back up where he had left off. However as time went on he was beginning to get into the rhythm of life at sea aboard a sailing craft that looked like it could have seen service in the Trojan War.

The sky, the sea, the waves thumping against the hull, the wind whistling through the rigging, the halyard banging against the mast, and the never-ending singing of the wireless as Sparks listened to incoming signals produced a hypnotic effect.

In the British military system, which influenced the Greeks in the LSF, nicknames are an obsession. Some are colorful to denote a character trait. Most are standard issue boilerplate—a redhead is called "Ginger," "Buck" if a man's last name is Rogers, "Foggy" for the intellectually challenged, short people are called "Lofty," as are tall people—the list is endless.

Radio operators are called "Sparks." The radioman was a popular sailor on Cdr. Londos' boat. He delivered the news. Everyone wanted to hear the reports. Lately, they were all bad. A Royal Navy destroyer sunk, Leros experiencing heavy air raids, reports of German atrocities as they occupied one or another of the islands previously held by the Italians.

While the pendulum was gradually beginning to swing in the Allies' favor elsewhere, here in the Aegean it was all Germany all the time.

As they sailed Lieutenant George Paspati, a new member of the Levant Schooner Flotilla, Anglo-Hellenic Squadron was entertaining Lt. Hoolihan and Lieutenant Junior Grade Jackson Taylor with the tale of how he had escaped from Greece, been captured and thrown into an Italian prison, made his escape and worked his way to Egypt where he was recruited by an intelligence organization so secret he was not cleared to know its name.

Lt. Hoolihan glanced at LtJG Taylor. They knew its name. Special Operations Executive.

Lt. Paspati said, "The name of the section I was assigned to was called Experimental Detachment G3. There were only two of us in it. Our subunit was so hush-hush we were ordered not to reveal our real names to each other.

"We were put through an intensive high-speed telegraph transmissions course. High speed is essential because of the need to transmit messages fast when behind German lines to avoid radio detection. We did not want their radio goniometers to have time to pinpoint our location.

The plan was for us to be dropped into Greece one at a time on different assignments.

"We drew lots to decide who would have the honor of going first—I lost.

"A few days later the instructor who had trained us on radio procedure quietly advised me in confidence he was worried. My friend failed to make his first radio check. Then a few days later the captain informed me the Germans knew our agent was coming and captured him the minute his parachute touched ground.

"The Nazis had infiltrated our organization. All Experimental Detachment G3 projects were canceled. Shortly after that is when I had a chance encounter with Commander Londos. He had need of officers with sailing experience. I was an amateur yachtsman and he recruited me for the Greek Squadron of the Levant Schooner Flotilla.

"This is my shakedown cruise with the LSF. As soon as we complete this voyage, provided Commander Londos gives me a favorable report, I shall be outfitting my own caique. Possibly we will sail together again someday."

Capt. Hoolihan did not say anything but Lt. Paspati's story squared with what Baldie had always claimed about SOE Cairo. The organization was so unprofessional it posed a threat to the men and women who worked for it. Acting on his advice Raiding Forces made it a practice to avoid them as much as possible.

The sun was up and they were still at sea in violation of LSF policy that called for skippers to sail at night and lay up during the day under camouflage. Cdr. Londos had been weaving in and out of the small islands that dotted the Aegean for the last eight hours. He was not covering as much of the distance to Castelrozzo as he would have liked and had pushed on wanting to travel a little farther before stopping.

A three-engine Bréguet 521 long-range reconnaissance flying boat came over at low altitude. The Bréguet 521 was built by France prior to the war. When the Nazis invaded France and installed the Vichy French government the Armee d l'Air seaplanes had been pressed into German service.

The aircraft's wingspan was three times the length of Capt. Londos' caique. It carried a crew of eight, was armed with five 7.92mm machine guns, and a complement of bombs. The plane was large enough to transport a squad of soldiers.

So much for an idyllic Aegean cruise. The men onboard the LS7 watched mesmerized as the plane come around making a big circle. Coming straight for them.

It seemed to be flying in slow motion.

Cdr. Londos ordered, "Anyone not dressed as a fisherman go below now."

On deck the crew remained calm but one or two drifted toward the Vickers K machine gun on the stern and the 20mm on the bow. The rest of the Greek sailors had their 9mm Lanchester submachine guns stashed nearby out of sight.

Capt. Hoolihan crouched on the steps leading to the cabin below peeking out to keep an eye on developments. His men were closed up behind him with their weapons at the ready. He was not sure what to expect next.

The Bréguet 521 completed its lazy circle and came in to land. It taxied to within fifty yards of the LS7. The airplane looked like an oversized Walrus except instead of being a pusher-type there were three giant engines mounted side-by-side directly over the pilot's compartment facing forward. While the aircraft was armed with five 7.92mm machine guns spaced out in the nose, both sides of the waist and in the tail, only the nose and one of the waist guns could be brought to bear on LS7.

The seaplane's props made a terrific racket.

A door opened and a figure appeared and tossed an inflatable raft into the water. Three more men climbed out on the float and boarded it. They started paddling toward the caique.

Cdr. Londos was chewing on the stem of his pipe sizing up the situation. When the raft was halfway there he barked the command to fire in Greek, "Twpa!" (Now!)

The fish nets over the Vickers K and the Oerlikon 20mm automatic cannon were pulled back. Sailors reached for their 9mm Lanchester submachine guns. And Capt. Hoolihan led his Marines up on deck.

In response to Cmdr. Londos' command firing broke out but got off to a slightly ragged start. Soon all weapons aboard the caique were roaring in unison. The Vickers K gunner took out the Luftwaffe machinegun bubble in the waist while the Oerlikon gunner shot up the Bréguet's nose gun—neither German weapon got off more than a few wild rounds. The sailors blazed away at the fuselage of the seaplane with their Lanchester SMGs.

Capt. Hoolihan's Royal Marines concentrated their fire on the raft.

A storm of furious small arms rounds was dancing around it splashing the water, slicing into the sides, and striking the occupants in a hail of fire long after the Nazis aboard were shot to pieces.

Then the Marines turned their weapon on the big flying boat.

Tracers vectored in. The side of the airplane was pockmarked so fast it was as if The Great Teddy had swept the fuselage with his magician's wand performing one of his illusions leaving behind hundreds of bullet holes. Suddenly they were just there.

Hey, Presto!

Burning aviation fuel began spewing out from a ruptured fuel tank. Aircrew, two of them on fire, attempted to abandon ship only to be shot dead. Then the Bréguet 521 exploded.

It was all over in less than a minute.

Cdr. Londos ordered the caique to get underway. Everyone stood silently and watched astern as they continued on their journey more than a little shaken by the suddenness of the turn of events capped off by the blast. All that remained of the Luftwaffe float plane was the shell of the fuselage burning down to water level along its entire length.

Capt. Hoolihan said, “Blew up a destroyer, left for dead on an enemy-occupied island and attacked by a giant flying boat. What’s next for you, Jackson?”

LtJG Taylor said, “I don’t want to think about it.”

CASTELROZZO

C COMPANY, 2ND BATTALION, CYPRUS REGIMENT continued pushing through the houses up the escarpment. After Tech Sergeant Luke Volkmann’s single gunshot no other enemy contact resulted from the sweep. The troops came to the dead Brandenburger, searched him for documents, collected his weapons and continued on.

Overhead in the Walrus everyone onboard scanned the ground looking for movement. Except for the C Company soldiers, nothing. Captain Billy Jack Jaxx was disappointed. He wanted more results.

Standing next to him Lieutenant General “Geronimo” Joe McKoy was pleased with the morning’s progress. He had spent most of his adult life hunting down fugitives with the U.S. Marshal’s Service. Long experience taught him wrinkling out the Germans was going to be a long, tedious, time-consuming process.

Any progress was good progress.

By now the Nazis situation was desperate. They had to know there was no hope of getting off the island. But the Sea Raiders would not go down easily.

Capture meant death.

King said, "There—eleven o'clock."

At the back of the last row of houses a figure darted out into the open heading up the escarpment moving fast toward the castle at the top.

Master Sergeant Mack Beckwith spotted the Brandenburger from his ambush site at the same time as Private First Class Norvel "Horn Dog" Hansen from his. The Sergeant Major got off the command to fire a split second faster than PFC Hansen. Two Stinger light machine guns, two Baby BARS, and two M1 Garand rifles opened putting out crisp, controlled, bursts of concentrated, grazing fire from Raiding Forces operators who had been waiting their chance.

Since both sites were categorized as "near" ambushes the range was almost point-blank—twenty-five yards. The Brandenburger went down.

Then it was over.

CAROLINA HOTEL

COLONEL JOHN RANDAL AND MAJOR THE LADY Jane Seaborn were asleep in the Robert E. Lee suite at the Carolina Hotel. Lady Jane liked to keep one tawny leg wrapped over him while she slept. He liked that too.

The phone rang.

"Colonel Randal."

"Colonel, this is the front desk. Sorry to disturb you, sir. One of our staff is on the way to your room with a telegraph marked 'urgent for immediate delivery.'"

Col. Randal grabbed the monogrammed hotel robe at the foot of the bed and went to the door.

The steward arrived carrying a silver tray with an envelope on it. Col. Randal clicked on. Unexpected messages at 0200 hours are never good.

GROUND ATTACK ON LEROS IMMINENT STOP
YOUR IMMEDIATE RETURN REQUESTED STOP
SIGNED
RANSOM,
VICE ADMIRAL
ROYAL NAVY

12
THAT WOULD BE A FLUNK

THE HUDSON FLOAT PLANE CAME IN FOR A LANDING off Castelrozzo. Onboard were Colonel John Randal, Major the Lady Jane Seaborn, Beverly Blackwell, and Lieutenant Ricky Mascuch, formerly of the 551 Parachute Infantry Battalion—the GOYAs. Col. Randal always kept an eye out for talented junior officers.

He recruited the lieutenant for Raiding Forces.

When Col. Randal had awakened Major General Sam Houston Blackwell to show him the telegram concerning Leros, Bronc rang Mackall Army Airfield and ordered his VIP Dakota prepared for immediate departure. The General rode with them to the airbase in the Carolina Hotel's limousine to make sure all preparations for the flight went smoothly.

Bronc was remaining at Camp Mackall.

Red the Flying Clipper Girl had stayed behind at the hotel since she would be working a flight out of Washington D.C. to the U.K. later in the week.

After a long flight, the VIP Dakota landed at an RAF airfield not far from Raiding Forces Headquarters. Col. Randal and his entourage transferred to the Hudson for the second leg of the trip to ABC. He was not able to get an update on the situation on Leros before they took off.

As they stepped onto the dock at Castelrozzo Col. Randal could see a line of infantry advancing up the escarpment off to his right. A Walrus was circling overhead. The *King Duck* was anchored offshore with its two Tiger tanks on the bow pointed in the direction of the troops.

Lieutenant Colonel Sir Terry "Zorro" Stone and James "Baldie" Taylor were there to meet them.

"What's going on, Terry?"

"Capt. Jaxx has an anti-Brandenburger operation in progress. He has been conducting company-sized clearing operations these last three days to force the Germans out of hiding. Captain Kidd has sniper teams stationed on rooftops providing overwatch for the search grid and there are blocking positions in waiting at the top of the escarpment should any Nazi try to make a break for it."

Col. Randal said, "How's that working?"

"Fairly well actually. Jack's people have killed five Brandenburgers. Slowly but surely we are running the Germans to ground."

Jim said, "How was your trip to the States?"

Col. Randal said, "It had its moments."

When the party arrived at ABCHQ, Col. Randal was surprised to see a group of young boys hanging around outside.

"What's this about?"

Col. Stone said, "The boys are waiting for Jack to return. He and Mandy unleashed a wave of junior counterintelligence operatives on the Brandenburgers. They offer ice cream for intelligence."

"Really?"

"Jack Cool is the Pied Piper of Castelrozzo. Local hero and teenage heartthrob. Stephanie gives out his room number to the

Greek girls who are clogging up her switchboard—he never gets any sleep.

"We call the boys who follow him around, 'Jack's Pack.'"

Col. Randal said, "How did that happen?"

Lt. Col. Stone said, "Rocky advised us children pose the biggest single threat to anyone attempting to remain undercover. Kids are inquisitive and know everything that takes place in their neighborhood. Mandy arranged to have Jack speak to all the students on the island and the rest is history."

Col. Randal said, "Provide any useful information?"

"Yes and no. The Brandenburgers are finding it difficult to make a move without one of the youngsters spotting them. We keep a Ready Reaction Team on standby round the clock to respond. The boys lead us straight to where the Germans are hiding.

"The teenage girls—they only want to meet Jack."

Col. Randal said, "Good for him."

Lt. Col. Stone said, "I would not have thought it possible to enjoy as much success against the Brandenburgers as quickly as we have. We believe there are only six remaining at large. Jack has been relentless in hunting them down."

In the distance a single rifle shot rang out.

"Make that five, old stick."

THE TACTICAL OPERATIONS CENTER SEEMED EMPTY. normally the TOC was bustling with Special Operations types from one unit or the other passing through coming from or going on one mission or another. However, today only Major the Lady Jane Seaborn's Royal Marines were present. The bulk of the 575th Ranger Task Force had still not returned from the

Benevento jump. Other Raiding Forces personnel who had not deployed to Italy and Major Zargo's Greek Sacred Squadron personnel were scattered along the Turkish coastline in remote bays aboard Levant Schooner Flotilla boats. They were living on barracks ships—schooners—conducting small-scale raids on distant islands utilizing caiques to carry out Colonel John Randal's Constant Pressure Concept.

Most of the Special Boat Section and Long Range Desert Group troops were on Leros with a half-dozen LRDG Coastwatcher teams scattered about the Aegean on uninhabited islands observing Kriegsmarine naval activity.

The TOC may have had fewer people than normal but it was a busy place. . . . phones ringing and radios breaking squelch. Raiding Forces had commitments from Italy to the Congo and they all needed something all the time and the local teenage girls kept calling for Capt. Jaxx.

Vice Admiral Sir Randolph "Razor" Ransom was in his office on the phone. He waved at Col. Randal through the open door when he came in. The Razor got off the call and walked out.

"Glad you are back, Colonel. No time for pleasantries. We can do your briefing right here, straight away if that is agreeable."

"Yes, sir."

Captain Stephanie Fawcett-Tatum ordered two of the Royal Marines to set up canvas folding chairs in front of the large wall map depicting the Aegean Area of Operations. Lady Jane and Beverly Blackwell decided to sit in. Col. Randal made eye contact with Lieutenant Ricky Mascuch and pointed to a chair.

Brandy Seaborn arrived with Captain Penelope "Legs" Honeycutt-Parker. Right behind them came Lieutenant General "Geronimo" Joe McKoy, Captain Billy Jack Jaxx, Captain Pamala Plum-Martin, King, Mandy Paige, and Waldo Treywick.

They had seen the Hudson land and cut short their aerial observation to return to the TOC.

VAdm. Ransom briefed, "Time is short but it is necessary to start from the beginning to make sure we all have an understanding of what got us here before bringing everyone up to speed on the current state of affairs.

"When the Italians signed the armistice Prime Minister Churchill sent out a missive that advised, 'Now is the time to play high and dare.' Jumbo Wilson was slow to act and missed his main chance by failing to take advantage of the opportunity to occupy Rhodes. So in his mind he did the next best thing—reinforced Leros, even though the Germans have achieved control of the air and the Royal Navy is currently only committing token support to the Aegean because it cannot afford to squander capital ships in what has become a military sideshow.

"Churchill was shocked by Wilson's failure to act and realized significant operations in the Aegean were a forlorn hope without Rhodes. He sent a follow-up cable authorizing the General to scale back on the play high and dare instructions. To no avail.

"Jumbo saw Leros as a way to redeem his reputation and he continued to march.

"The 234th Brigade under General Brittorous was raised on Malta for service in the Dodecanese. The brigade consists of the 1st Battalion Queens Own Royal West Kents, 4th Battalion Royal East Kent Regiment of the Buffs (-) one company, 2nd Battalion Royal Irish Fusiliers, and 1st Battalion King's Own Royal Regiment, B Company of the Second Royal West Kent Regiment, detachments from the LRDG, the SBS, a detachment from the 28th Heavy Anti-Aircraft Battery and a section of the 3rd Light Anti-Aircraft battery. It has been made clear to General Headquarters Cairo these are all the ground troops it is ever going to receive due to the drawdown of combat units for the campaign in Italy.

"General Wilson posted the 234th to Leros betting all his chips on one roll of the dice. The brigade's commander, General Brittorous, proved ineffectual and was removed from his post. He was replaced by Brigadier Tilney.

"A poor choice because of his lack of infantry experience which is proving painfully obvious.

"What we have is an island that we cannot adequately defend, manned mostly by troops who have spent the last eighteen months to two years sitting idle on Malta while being bombed daily, commanded by an inexperienced, less than qualified brigade commander.

"The 234th is in an untenable situation. The German's recent capture of Kos provided them an airfield only thirty miles away from Leros and for once the Royal Navy does not rule the waves.

"Jim, what do you have on enemy and friendly air?"

Baldie said, "The Luftwaffe has in excess of twelve hundred planes capable of striking Leros. Some targets on the island, for example Portologo, are being hit by air raids multiple times per day. Attacks continue around the clock.

"British air consists of a handful of squadrons flying off Cyprus three hundred eighty-five miles from Leros. The island is faced with a telling disparity in the time/distance continuum the Luftwaffe enjoy. Our pilots have less than thirty minutes loiter time on station once they arrive over the island—the Germans can keep up a continuous round-robin flying off Kos."

VAdm. Ransom said, "Jim, are you able to provide any details on the Luftwaffe's new Wonder Weapon squadron reported to have arrived in theatre?"

Col. Randal had never heard of a Wonder Weapon squadron.

Jim said, "The 1/KG100, a Dornier-217K squadron equipped with HS-293 antishipping guided missiles—the only unit of its kind in history, arrived a week ago. Two days later 1/KG100 scored its first kill—the destroyer *Rockwood.* As you can imagine the Navy is not pleased with this development and even less inclined to support the war in this part of the world.

"The Aegean has suddenly become much more dangerous for surface ships."

VAdm. Ransom said, "Anything else you would care to add?"

Jim said, "The RAF can only muster a half squadron of long-range Spitfire fighters, a squadron (-) of Hurricane long-range fighters, three squadrons of Beaufighters, and four squadrons of Wellington light bombers.

"The USAAF provided a group of P-38 fighters for a few days that were extremely effective but has since withdrawn them. As the situation stands the Luftwaffe has achieved air superiority over Leros—a prerequisite for invasion which the Germans have styled OPERATION LEOPARD.

VAdm. Ransom said, "Two days ago Signals Intelligence indicated the Germans had completed preparations to launch OPERATION LEOPARD. Then day before yesterday the Luftwaffe's air attacks intensified which was a signal landings were imminent. This morning, following a fifty-day non-stop aerial bombardment of the island, the German's amphibious assault began at dawn.

"Details of the invasion are conflicting as to be expected. First reports from the battlefield are never accurate. There are no reinforcements to send and the Royal Navy does not have the bottoms to conduct a contested evacuation of the magnitude necessary to transport the 234th and other supporting units, which in any event would be suicidal without sufficient air cover.

"What say you, Colonel?"

Col. Randal said, "We have to get our people off the island."

COLONEL JOHN RANDAL CALLED FOR A MEETING TO be held in fifteen minutes in the suite he shared with Major the Lady Jane Seaborn. He wanted to get everyone away from the distractions of the phones and radios in the Tactical Operations Center. And he wanted a few minutes to think through what to do next.

The decisions he was about to make now were going to be life or death for some very good men.

Walking out the door he ordered Lieutenant Colonel Sir Terry "Zorro" Stone, "Dispatch someone to bring in Captain Kidd, Captain Stirling, and the Sergeant Major—now."

Lt. Col. Stone said, "On the way."

Col. Randal added, "Stephanie, I want to see a current list of all the Raiding Forces officers and NCOs currently on ABC fit for duty."

Captain Stephanie Fawcett-Tatum said, "I shall bring it up straight away."

Col. Randal made eye contact with Mandy Paige. She walked upstairs with him, Lady Jane and Beverly Blackwell. At the landing to their suite Flanigan was sitting at his desk having taken up his station the moment he learned Col. Randal was back on Castelrozzo.

Lady Jane went straight inside.

Beverly broke off to go to her room to freshen up before the briefing.

Col. Randal said, "Flanigan, as soon as people start arriving hold everyone here. I need to speak to Mandy privately. No one in until I give you the word."

"Sir!"

Col. Randal waited until Mandy closed the door, "Everyone but me seems to be aware General McKoy is not pleased about being put in charge of LONG NECK. You're my counterintelligence officer—I need some counterintelligence."

Mandy said, "What is your specific question?"

"How does the head of OSS in Washington have information about CARD GAME I don't?"

"I have no idea, John."

"What's the story about the General being unhappy?"

"News to me. I heard what you heard. He protested when you gave him the assignment."

"Find out."

"I shall."

"Bring in the General and Waldo."

As soon as they came in Col. Randal said to the three of them, "Donovan flew down to Camp Mackall to give me an attitude adjustment about LONG NECK. So now I'm telling you what he told me. No more questions about *why,* just go and do.

"For the last time is that clear?"

Lieutenant General "Geronimo" Joe McKoy said, "Ain't that many questions bein' raised, John. I'll snuff out any more that come up. You take a bunch 'a bright people with a lotta experience, give 'em a mission—they sorta like things to make sense."

Col. Randal said, "Now it does—we are simply following orders. Mandy, everyone in."

As the group filed in, Col. Randal pulled Captain Roy Kidd aside. "Captain Jaxx is about to be pulled away on another assignment. Can you take over his anti-Brandenburger duties temporarily?"

It was not really a question.

"Yes, sir."

"I won't be requiring you for this briefing. Get back to work. Word is you and Jack have been doing an outstanding job."

In a unit where top performance was expected at all times it was high praise.

“Thank you, sir—Jack’s been all over going after the bad guys.”

Col. Randal surveyed the people taking their seats in the small map area off the living room. “Mandy, where’s your mother?”

“Before leaving you ordered MI-9 caiques to the Leros area to stand by awaiting developments. She went on the *Santa Claus* with Sergeant Major Mikkalis.”

Col. Randal said, “Not my intent.”

“Apparently you failed to make that clear.”

Capt. Fawcett-Tatum handed him the list of officers and NCOs who had returned from Italy. It was a short list.

Col. Randal said, “Stick around, Stephanie, I want you wired in on this.”

When Jim came in Col. Randal said, “What can you tell me about Patmos Island?”

Jim said, “It is a small key located a little over thirty miles off Leros on the opposite from Kos. That is the sum total of what I know.”

Col. Randal made eye contact with Capt. Fawcett-Tatum. She came over immediately. “Is Professor Winthrop in the building?”

“He is.”

“I need him.”

Col. Randal stepped up to the front of the room, “The Nazis have begun their final assault on Leros. When I toured the island Lord Jellicoe informed me it could not be defended with the resources available. Since that time his Special Boat Section and the Long Range Desert Group have both been attached to Raiding Forces. That makes the SBS and LRDG our men. We are going to bring them off. I would have done so earlier had I been given authorization—which still has not been forthcoming.

“Now we’re just going to do it.”

Capt. Fawcett-Tatum came in with Dr. Layton Winthrop and they took seats.

Col. Randal said, "Some claim a fighting withdrawal is the most difficult of all military operations. That may be true. We're about to find out.

"Dr. Winthrop sir, have you ever been to Patmos?"

"I have."

"Come up here and give us a briefing on the island."

Dr. Winthrop said, "Patmos is a thirteen-square-mile island located thirty-one miles off Leros with a population of approximately three thousand. In ancient times it was known as the 'beginning of the end of the world.' Saint John wrote the Book of Revelation there. Ever since, the place has been known as 'The Island of the Apocalypse' . . ."

Col. Randal said, "Doctor, could you fast forward to modern days?"

Dr. Winthrop said, "Certainly, the village of Patmos is the capital. It is built around the Monastery of St. John which is located on the highest feature on the island. Beautiful, white-washed mansions of the wealthy islanders ring the imposing sixteenth-century structure.

"Skala, the main port, is the largest town. Seaward there is a narrow entrance. It makes a dogleg into the anchorage past steep hills standing like guard posts on both sides of the channel at the mouth. A quarter mile inside the harbor the bay widens out and forms the perfect safe harbor.

"All roads on the island lead to Skala."

Col. Randal said, "Is there a place suitable for a drop zone?"

"Immediately behind Skala are the only sheep pastures on the island. They are quite extensive."

Col. Randal said, "Thank you, Doctor. Any chance you have a contact on Patmos?"

"Unfortunately, no."

Col. Randal said, "Jim, do you have a report about enemy forces on the island?"

"Intelligence indicates an element of the 999th Light Division in unknown strength occupied it recently. No additional information is available. Based on past performance the Germans should not be in greater than company strength."

Col. Randal said, "Admiral, can the *King Duck* reach Patmos before sunrise tomorrow?"

"If Warthog were to steam within the hour."

Col. Randal said, "Stephanie, phone down to the TOC and have the duty officer alert Captain Finley to stand by for sailing orders.

"Is Lieutenant Hamilton on Castelrozzo?"

"Capt. Jaxx said, "Sir, he's with C Company observing their sweep."

Col. Randal said, "While you're at it Stephanie send a runner to have Teddy report to me as well."

"Straight away, Colonel."

The atmosphere in the room was tense. A mission to Leros was imminent. No one knew what it was going to entail. What was perfectly clear was Raiding Forces would be going in with almost zero intelligence and no authorization to carry out the operation.

Failure meant capture or death—success could result in court martial.

Col. Randal said, "Brandy, how many fast movers do we have available to press into service?"

"Only Penelope's and my MAS boats. She is still working up her crew. Randy's at sea. We may be able to radio him to rendezvous with us."

Col. Randal said, "Parker, any reason you can't exercise your crew on a cruise to Patmos?"

"None."

"Admiral Ransom, can I count on you to coordinate our naval assets, sir?"

"With pleasure, Colonel."

For once Col. Randal skipped the traditional, "Are you prepared to accept a Warning Order" opening statement.

"Situation: Elements of Raiding Forces are on Leros. The Germans are invading. The Luftwaffe has control of the air.

"Mission: Rescue our people trapped on the island.

"Execution/Concept of the Operation: Under cover of darkness tonight at a time to be worked out in coordination with Admiral Ransom, I will conduct a parachute assault on Patmos Island with Captain Jaxx and a twenty-man team. Priorities are to capture and secure Skala Harbor. Once the harbor is secure, Brandy and Captain Honeycutt-Parker will enter and offload an additional twenty-man team led by Captain Stirling. With any luck Lieutenant Seaborn will be able to rendezvous prior to the landing of troops to provide additional naval support.

"Once the harbor area is under our control Captain Jaxx will march on Patmos Village and secure it.

"As soon as Brandy and Captain Honeycutt-Parker have landed their Raiding Forces personnel ashore the MAS boats will depart for Leros where I'll land with a small party to link up with Lord Jellicoe and Lieutenant Colonel Easonsmith.

"The two MAS boats will load any of the troops immediately available designated to be extracted then return to Patmos which will serve as our staging base for the evacuation. Every LSF caique at sea will be ordered to make for Skala. The *King Duck* will arrive before dawn and stand by ready to assist in transporting our SBS and LRDG people back to ABC.

"The following night the MAS boats, LSF caiques and Mrs. Paige's MI-9 boats will return to Leros to begin the exfil of the SBS, LRDG and certain elements of the 1st Battalion, King's Own Royal Regiment. We will continue the withdrawal until all our people are brought out or the island is overrun and the garrison captured. After that Mrs. Paige will continue the MI-9 rescue operation for as long as evaders on Leros are trying to escape."

"Administration and Logistics/Command and Signal: We'll be working out those details between now and the time the MAS boats depart for Patmos.

"Anyone with questions see me privately—let's do this people."

Lieutenant Ricky Mascuch, sitting next to Capt. Jaxx said, "It would take a week and fifty staff meetings to conduct a training exercise of this complexity at Camp Mackall. Ever since I met Colonel Randal it's like I've been strapped to the nose of one of those German V-1 buzz bombs and blasted through space.

"Is it always like this around here?"

Capt. Jaxx said, "Negative, you got here on a slow day—welcome to Raiding Forces, Lieutenant."

Jack Cool.

COLONEL JOHN RANDAL SAID, "BEVERLY, STAND FAST."

As people were filing out Jim stopped for a word. "I shall be going with you, Colonel. You could very well run into trouble from some of the local commanders when you start pulling out troops. My general's rank might prove useful, even if it is only local—they have no way of knowing that."

Col. Randal said, "Offer accepted, General."

Lieutenant General "Geronimo" Joe McKoy strolled by.

Col. Randal said, "Hang on, I'd like to speak to you in private."

As Mandy Paige came past she said, "Do you absolutely have to do this, John? Invading Patmos with a mere platoon against an enemy occupier of unknown strength is bad enough. Landing on Leros while a full-scale German invasion is in progress is the worse idea I have ever heard."

"They're my men."

"You will be rescuing people who may not be aware of that fact and some, like the LRDG, do not even want to be a part of Raiding Forces."

"We'll work that out later."

Capt. Jaxx walked over, "Will you be selecting the airborne assault team personnel, sir?"

"That's your prerogative, Captain."

"Yes, sir. Where will you be?"

"Dropping in with you."

Beverly Blackwell walked up.

Col. Randal said, "Develop the air plan for me. Keep in mind the Luftwaffe has night-fighter capability. You're not flying this one."

Beverly said, "In case you failed to notice Johnny, our Hudson was the only aircraft in the bay when we landed. Pam's Walrus was race tracking over the island. We're the only two pilots you have available—I'm flying."

Col. Randal said. "All right then a single pass, low-level drop, then run for ABC—are we clear?"

Beverly laughed, "Seriously, you sound like Mandy when she's trying to keep *you* out of trouble."

Col. Randal ordered, "One pass and gone—let me hear you say it."

"Clear."

When the room was empty, Lt. Gen. McKoy said, "What's goin' on, John?"

"I need an on-ground commander at Patmos when I depart for Leros—you available for the assignment?"

Lt. Gen. McKoy said, "You know I am—Coordinatin' operations?"

Col. Randal said, "The entire island – military and civilian – things may get complicated."

Lt. Gen. McKoy said, "How do you want me to get to there?"

"Your call, if it were me I'd go in aboard one of the MAS boats."

"Anything else I need to know, John?"

"Waldo stays here. I can't have our two key LONG NECK players on a mission as high risk as this. You tell him or I will, General."

"He ain't gonna' like it."

"Well, think of something. You're good at that."

Flanigan stuck his head in the door. "The Great Teddy, sir."

"Send him in."

"Lieutenant Hamilton reports, sir."

"Stow your gear aboard the *King Duck.* It sails within the hour. We're evacuating the SBS and LRDG from Leros using Patmos Island as a staging base. Your mission is to camouflage the LCT, MAS boats, LSF caiques and any other boat that may arrive."

"Sir!"

"You work for General McKoy. He'll brief you prior to your departure."

"Aye aye, sir!"

Lt. Gen. McKoy said, "Consider yourself briefed Lieutenant. I don't have any information—nada."

COLONEL JOHN RANDAL MET WITH THE TEAM leaders who would be landing on Patmos Island. Captain Billy Jack Jaxx and Captain "Pyro" Percy Stirling, DSO, MC, who had only returned to Castelrozzo from Italy the day before. He had not enjoyed the benefit of the initial briefing.

Lieutenant General "Geronimo" Joe McKoy sat in.

Col. Randal said, "Captain Jaxx, you will jump on Skala with a twenty-man party, eliminate any/all German troops in the harbor area and then you will be released to march on Patmos Village.

"Captain Stirling, you will land ashore with a twenty-man party from the MAS boats skippered by Brandy and Parker. You will affect liaison with Captain Jaxx and assist him in securing Skala. When he moves out to Patmos Village your team will remain behind and secure the harbor for follow-on naval traffic. Standby to go to Captain Jaxx's assistance in the event he should request it.

"I'll jump in with Captain Jaxx and be in overall command until such time as he moves out on his secondary mission to Patmos Village. At that point I'll hand off command to General McKoy. He will be the on-scene ground commander of the island for the duration of the evacuation operation.

"There's no intelligence on enemy forces on Patmos other than they're likely 999th Light Division troops. No map of the island. No Greek speakers are immediately available to act as interpreters other than Lady Jane, Mandy, or Cat—none of whom will be participating in this operation.

Lt. Gen. McKoy said, "I've got an idea on that."

Col. Randal said, "Good, you're going to need assistance with the locals."

Capt. Jaxx said, "If we scrape together every Raiding Forces operator on ABC we may not have enough people available to make up two twenty-man teams, sir."

Col. Randal said, "If that's the case, Captain Stirling, you can fill in your team with volunteers from the Cyprus Regiment."

Capt. Stirling said, "Rather hope it does not come to that, sir."

Col. Randal said, "There's no Plan B. If we get in trouble no one's coming to bail us out. Don't come in understrength because you don't like the quality of the troops, Captain."

"Yes, sir."

Capt. Jaxx said, "You said I could have anyone on the list. I'd like Lieutenant Hays, Lieutenant Novak, the Sergeant Major, and King—that leaves a few good people for Roy to work with here, sir."

Col. Randal said, "Negative on King."

COLONEL JOHN RANDAL MET WITH VICE ADMIRAL Sir "Razor" Ransom and Beverly Blackwell to discuss the Time On Target (TOT). Formerly an artillery term now adopted by the Airborne as well it meant the exact time the first paratrooper or the first piece of equipment is to be dropped on a DZ. The TOT needed to be coordinated to coincide with the MAS boat's arrival.

VAdm. Ransom said, "Approximately one hundred twenty-five nautical miles to Patmos. Brandy and Penelope can travel that distance in six hours with no undue strain."

Beverly said, "The Hudson can make it in an hour."

VAdm. Ransom said, "What time do you want to drop, Colonel?"

"We'll jump at midnight."

CAPTAIN BILLY JACK JAXX ASSEMBLED HIS TEAM for the drop on Patmos. The troops were SOG, 1/575th Parachute Infantry Regiment, 10th Ranger Battalion, and two were old hands from the American Volunteer Group—a tough battle-hardened group of men. For officers he had, Lieutenant Clint Hays, Lieutenant Jake Novak aka "Jake the Snake," and Lieutenant Ricky Mascuch, who would be making his first combat jump.

Lt. Mascuch was being brought along for the experience and as a spare officer. Master Sergeant Mack Beckwith was the senior NCO.

The Warning Order Capt. Jaxx gave was even sketchier than the one Colonel John Randal had issued. The men, only recently returned from heavy combat following the Benevento jump, did not appear to notice . . . or maybe they did not care.

"Situation: We drop on Patmos Island at 2400 hours.

"Mission: Secure the island.

"Execution/Concept of the Operation: "Jump in—kill everybody not wearing the same uniform we are.

"Command & Signal: I'm in command—follow my lead.

"I'll get back to you later on all the other paragraphs I skipped."

Jack Cool.

CAPTAIN "PYRO" PERCY STIRLING, WITH Lieutenant Dan Bonham as his second in command, was able to recruit twenty mostly fit 575th Ranger Task Force men for his team although some of them had been dinged up on the Benevento drop and subsequent hit and run fighting. He gathered them together to issue his Operations Order. The Rangers had no reservations about serving under a British officer. Capt. Stirling was a living legend in Raiding Forces. In days past he had struck terror in many a heart—more than a few belonging to his own people. Troops who worked with him were always cognizant of what might be about to blow up next. While the Rangers liked his style the team was somewhat relieved to learn no specific demolition targets were laid on for the Patmos mission.

Once Capt. Stirling completed his briefing he led his people down to the dock and they began loading on the two MAS boats. Ahead lay a long run through enemy-controlled waters in a high-speed powerboat followed by the unknown of landing ashore against a hostile force they had no intelligence regarding. The prospect did not seem to overly concern anyone.

The Rangers moved onboard, stowed their gear and racked out.

SNATCHES OF WHAT WAS TAKING PLACE ON LEROS came in all Afternoon. The information was confusing and often contradictory. There is a truism about combat that can be counted on 100% of the time—first reports from the battlefield are always inaccurate. Colonel John Randal stayed in the TOC glued to the bank of radios. He did not learn much in the way of details.

What did become apparent to him was the German strategy.

There were a pair of isthmuses cutting Leros into thirds. Major the Earl Lord George Jellicoe had his CP near the one on the north central end of the island. Paratroops from the 22nd Air Landing Division had made a drop on it. Elements of the LRDG were stationed on the south end where another drop occurred.

The Nazis were attempting to cut the island into three pieces.

Then defeat the 234th Brigade in detail.

Col. Randal realized the German airborne phase of the invasion was going to complicate the extraction mission. The boats and caiques used to evacuate the SBS and LRDG would not only have to avoid the Kriegsmarine amphibious assault craft landing troops and naval patrol boats patrolling off the beach, the Raiding Forces teams going ashore to guide the troops to the extraction points would also have to contend with German paratroopers at large roaming the interior of the island.

And the British defenders were going to be trigger happy. Another given—friendly fire is not friendly.

Major the Lady Jane Seaborn and Happy came down to the TOC to sit with him. She did not say much. There was no need to. Her tightly drawn razor-sharp cheekbones and the absence of any sign of the heart-attack smile said it all.

The dog lay down, rested his head on his paws, and watched.

The tension in the Tactical Operations Center was palpable. A disaster was in progress. And there was nothing anybody could do but listen in.

Meanwhile elements of Raiding Forces were preparing to sail straight into the heart of the action.

Captain Billy Jack Jaxx arrived to check on the latest news. He had broken his team into patrols under Lieutenant Clint Hays and Lieutenant Jake Novak. Parachutes were drawn. Additional .30 Stinger LMGs and .30 Baby BARs were distributed to those who wanted them. Every man was issued a double basic load of ammunition and grenades.

Then the waiting began.

Captain Stephanie Fawcett-Tatum said, "One of your boys is out front, Jack. He says he knows where a Brandenburger is in hiding."

Col. Randal said, "Let's go talk to him."

Anything to get away from the radio.

When they walked outside the boy said, “Captain Jack, I can show you a Nazi hideout.”

Capt. Jaxx said, “Bad timing, Lucas.”

Col. Randal said, “Why don’t the two of us go check it out, Jack?”

Capt. Jaxx said, “Roger that sir, I’m not doing anything but marking time here listening to bad news.”

“Exactly.”

The waiting was always the worst part. Listening to a battle on the radio you were about to join is not for the faint of heart. No matter how many times you have done it before.

Col. Randal went back inside. “Stephanie, have Captain Fernsby send over a rifle squad ASAP to assist us.”

“Wilco.”

“Need to borrow your dog for a minute. I’ll be right back. This won’t take long.”

He gave the hand signal to heel. Happy jumped up so fast he nearly hurt himself.

Outside Lucas was waiting. The boy was excited. They started off up the escarpment with two of the Vulnerable Points Wing security men following. The VPW would drop off one at a time to serve as guides for the Cyprus Regiment squad that would be following them.

Neither Col. Randal nor Capt. Jaxx was armed with anything other than their sidearms. This was a simple visual reconnaissance. They had no intention of approaching the target.

Capt. Jaxx said, “What flavor ice cream are you going to want, Lucas?”

“Strawberry.”

“Show me the color of your money.”

Lucas had no idea what that meant.

They marched for fifteen minutes leaving a VPW trooper to point the way as they went. Happy kept pace with Lucas, brushing up against the boy's legs, being friendly. It did not take long until they left the residential section of that part of the village. A small abandoned single-story building came into sight.

Lucas pointed, "There, Captain Jack."

A single shot rang out, struck the boy in the head and he fell down spurting a geyser of blood.

Normally a highly disciplined dog Happy streaked toward the building like he had been shot out of a cannon. He dived through the open window where the shot had come from. Col. Randal and Capt. Jaxx were stunned. Both were known for lightning-fast reactions, but Lucas' death was a shock.

Shooting the boy was intentional. He was targeted. The Nazi could have fired at either of them.

Capt. Jaxx knelt down to check on Lucas. Col. Randal took off after Happy at a run. Another shot rang out. Then he crashed through the front door with his Colt. .38 Super at the ready.

Inside the enraged dog had the Nazi down on the ground by the throat and was shaking him viciously. The Brandenburger was screaming but what was coming out did not sound much like a scream. Happy was snarling but it sounded exactly like what it was—something out of your worst nightmare.

The animal had gone berserk.

Col. Randal holstered his weapon. He was not in any hurry taking the time to take out a cigarette and light it before calling Happy off. Then he grabbed the Nazi by the collar and drug him outside. The man's screams were louder now without the dog's jaws clamped on his throat though they still did not quite sound human.

Unable to restrain himself Happy attacked the German's legs as he was being pulled. The Brandenburger's high-pitched squealing intensified. Col. Randal called the dog off for the second time but did not really care if the animal obeyed the command or not.

The squad from C Company arrived.

Capt. Jaxx walked over, looked down at the mangled Brandenburger then emptied his Colt .38 Super into him point blank. When Jack Cool ran out of ammunition Col. Randal emptied his pistol into the Nazi—slow, timed shots until his handgun was empty. The man's body shuddered with every round. All ten of them.

So much for needing a prisoner.

The Cyprus Regiment men stood watching . . . transfixed.

Capt. Jaxx said, "We're probably setting a really bad example for the troops, sir."

Col. Randal said, "Yes we are."

After changing magazines he shot the Brandenburger one more time.

THE NEWS THAT LUCAS HAD BEEN KILLED combined with the hysterical radio traffic pouring in from Leros cast a pall over the Tactical Operations Center. Colonel John Randal found Mandy Paige sobbing in a side office.

He was not good with crying women especially ones he cared for.

Col. Randal tried to console her. "Mandy, sometimes bad things . . ."

That was a swing and a miss.

Mandy sobbed, "I mobilized the children to look for the Brandenburgers—it's all my fault."

Col. Randal said, "Actually it's mine. We were taken by surprise. I'm not supposed to let that happen—Jack thinks he's responsible."

A little better that time.

Mandy said, "I hate the way everything is turning out."

"Try hating the Nazi. He murdered the boy."

"We are fighting monsters, John."

"That is a fact."

Walking back out into the main room he spotted Beverly Blackwell wiping away a tear—the final straw.

Col. Randal went in search of Major the Lady Jane Seaborn and found her all alone in one of the empty rooms down the hall standing in front of a giant gild-edged mirror. She was repairing her makeup attempting to regain her composure. Women of her class were taught from birth to never show any emotion in public other than joy—and not too much of that.

"Round up your dog and follow me. Let's go check on the troops."

He needed out of the TOC and he wanted her company.

The first stop was the vacant building Captain Billy Jack Jaxx had designated as his team's assembly area. Twelve Raiding Forces operators were sprawled out on the floor resting on their parachutes. The remainder of the twenty-man party would consist of Col. Randal, Capt. Jaxx, Lieutenant Clint Hays, Lieutenant Jake Novak, Lieutenant Ricky Mascuch, Master Sergeant Mack Beckwith and King.

Jim would be attached in his role as a major general.

When Col. Randal and Lady Jane walked in the Sergeant Major barked, "ATTENTION!"

Instantly Col. Randal ordered, "As you were."

Capt. Jaxx appeared and escorted them as they went around and visited with the men. Col. Randal took his time. Being with the troops was the part of his job he enjoyed the most.

Lady Jane knew every man on the team by name.

Before they departed Col. Randal had the men gather around. "Earlier today a Nazi shot and killed a ten-year-old boy who was guiding Capt. Jaxx and me to his hiding place. When we jump in tonight there's no reason to be gentle with the 999th on my behalf.

"Clear?"

"CLEAR SIR!"

Capt. Jaxx and MSgt. Beckwith accompanied Col. Randal and Lady Jane to the dock where the two MAS boats were preparing to depart for Patmos. Lady Jane and Happy went aboard to visit Brandy Seaborn. MSgt. Beckwith boarded Captain Penelope "Legs" Honeycutt-Parker's boat to inspect Captain "Pyro" Percy Stirling's Rangers traveling with her.

Col. Randal and Capt. Jaxx stood on the dock talking before boarding to check on the troops.

Capt. Jaxx said, "Sir, we're willing to jump into hell with you but there's no getting around it—this Patmos mission is pretty shaky. I don't have any idea what our initial objective is going to look like once we're on the ground or even where it's located.

"As for my follow-on target there's not even a map."

Col. Randal said, "Try not to mention that to Lady Jane."

Capt. Jaxx said, "You think she doesn't know, sir?"

Lieutenant General "Geronimo" Joe McKoy and Dr. Layton Winthrop arrived.

"The Professor's goin' with us, John. He speaks good Greek."

Capt. Jaxx said, "Too bad you can't jump in with my team Doctor—I could use an interpreter."

Dr. Winthrop said, "Maybe next time, Jack. After I take up parachuting."

PIER AT CASTELROZZO

THE FILE OF TROOPS MOVED DOWN TO THE DOCK TO load onboard the black-painted Catalina for the flight to Patmos Island. Captain Pamala Plum-Martin and Beverly Blackwell were the pilots. Corporal Tom Murphy, Beverly's longtime navigator she liked to call "Murph the Surf," would be charged with finding the thirteen-square-mile island. No small task. If they overshot, the *Black Cat* would be over Leros subject to being shot down by both the British defenders and the German invaders.

Major the Lady Jane Seaborn, Mandy Paige and Happy, accompanied by two Vulnerable Points Wing bodyguards, were on hand to see them off.

Colonel John Randal strapped on his parachute. Captain Billy Jack Jaxx assisted, passing him his leg straps, then he conducted a thorough jumpmaster's inspection. It did not matter that it was the middle of the night with no lights. Jumpmasters perform their inspection like Braille readers. It's all by touch starting at the back of the helmet feeling for sharp edges, around and down the chin strap on both sides, back to the front, then palms under the shoulder then the leg straps, checking the safety clip on the quick release, then tracing the static line over the shoulder into the parachute pack, running palms under the harness, shoulder and the back of the leg straps—the purpose of the exercise being that nothing be twisted or out of place.

Capt. Jaxx said, "Recover."

No need to inspect the reserve. Col. Randal was not wearing one. The jump was at 500 feet.

There would not be time to deploy it.

Waldo Treywick arrived to see them off. First thing, he stuffed a handful of his long thin custom-rolled cigars in the inside pocket of Col. Randal's new olive drab M-1942 Jump Jacket. "You might need a spare or two, Colonel."

Col. Randal said, "I'm putting you in charge of seeing to it Mandy doesn't go Nazi hunting while I'm gone, Mr. Treywick.

Waldo said, "How am I supposed to guarantee that?"

Col. Randal said, "If she attempts to follow up on a report of a Brandenburger's location after you order her not to, shoot her in some non-lethal place where it won't leave a visible scar."

Mandy said, "I heard that."

Lady Jane said, "You need an interpreter, John. I speak Greek fluently. There is still time to bump one of the Rangers."

Col. Randal said, "Not tonight, babe."

One of the engines on the Catalina wheezed, backfired, kicked over running rough, then smoothed out to a full roar. Then the other propeller turned over. The jump was a go—once those motors cranked up the worst part of the waiting was over.

Col. Randal followed Capt. Jaxx onboard turning in the door at the last second to salute Lady Jane.

There was a full moon rising off in the distance. It was a picturesque night to be taking off on such a desperate mission. Beverly was the pilot with Capt. Plum-Martin as her copilot. She began taxiing out of the harbor.

When the *Black Cat* was in open water Beverly immediately commenced her take-off run. The people on the dock watched it fly across the moon. Was that a good sign?

On board in the dark the Rangers were sitting quietly thinking their own thoughts. It was not a long flight—only an hour. However, with the Luftwaffe having night fighter capability the getting there was iffy.

Among other things that was on everyone's mind.

Capt. Jaxx was the Jumpmaster but he would not lead the stick out the door tonight. That was Col. Randal's prerogative.

Jack Cool would be last man out the way jumpmasters did it on training jumps.

Once on the DZ Col. Randal would drop his X-type parachute and stand fast marking the assembly point (AP). Capt. Jaxx would land, drop his chute then roll up the stick. If everything went according to plan the result would be a nice, neat formation armed, equipped and ready to fight. Airborne operations rarely go according to plan but hope springs eternal for men who jump out of perfectly good airplanes behind enemy lines in the dark of night.

It could happen.

In the tail of the *Black Cat* sitting on the very end of the long canvas bench seat running the length of the troop compartment, Capt. Jaxx turned to Col. Randal, "OK, sir. So what's the plan?"

Col. Randal said, "We fly low and fast, jump under cover of darkness, develop the situation on the ground, and take out the 999th personnel when and where we find them."

Capt. Jaxx said, "If you were an instructor on a graded training exercise and one of your students came up with *our* Concept of the Operation tonight how would you grade it, sir?"

Col. Randal said, "That would be a straight-out flunk."

STEAMING FOR PATMOS

ACTING PROVISIONAL LIEUTENANT WARTHOG Finley was on the bridge of the *King Duck*. From only a short distance no one would have been able to tell it was a Landing Craft Tank (LCT). Lieutenant Theodore Hamilton had erected false smoke stacks and altered the shape of the blunt-nosed bow with plywood so it looked like one of the many tramp steamers that plied their trade between Turkey, Cyprus and Egypt.

Skipper Finley and The Great Teddy were friends. The tough, hard-drinking, two-fisted sailor recognized the young officer for what he was—brilliant, which he respected. Lt. Hamilton was teaching Warthog card tricks that were probably going to get him in trouble someday in one of the poker games he played in from time to time in the backrooms of dives no person in their right mind would frequent—no matter how heavily armed.

The *King Duck* had been steaming for thirteen hours. Now it was within ten miles of Patmos Island. The LCT may have been ugly, not particularly seaworthy and an uncomfortable ship in even mild weather… but she was reliable.

Colonel John Randal had requested the two Tiger tanks be left onboard the *King Duck* in the event direct fire support was needed at Patmos. That created an additional camouflage problem. Lt. Hamilton was up to the challenge. The Great Teddy had become an enthusiastic proponent of the principle of Occam's razor once he heard Professor Winthrop describe it in a briefing: "The simplest solution is the best solution."

He threw tarps over the two German tanks.

Now they looked like deck cargo—sort of.

Hey, Presto!

CHANGE OF MISSION

LIEUTENANT RANDY "HORNBLOWER" SEABORN WAS aboard his U.S. Navy Lend Lease PT boat pounding toward Patmos Island at flank speed. Normally he commanded the Motor Gun Boat 345, but it was in dry dock. The MGB had a long, tough war behind it and was in need of a complete maintenance overhaul.

Lt. Seaborn was responding to a radio transmission ordering a change of mission from his grandfather Vice Admiral Sir Randolph "Razor" Ransom. He was to be on station off the island by 2300 hours. Other than to link up with his mother, Brandy Seaborn, and Captain Penelope "Legs" Honeycutt-Parker in their MAS boats there was no indication in the signal as to why or what.

For the last week after dropping off Captain Butch "Headhunter" Hoolihan and his Marines, Lt. Seaborn and his crew had been laying up under camouflage by day and patrolling independently at night looking for targets of opportunity. There were hundreds of German chartered caiques at sea transporting supplies to distant Axis garrisons on small islands throughout the Aegean.

Lt. Seaborn was making his best effort to sink them all. Four German-flagged caiques had been destroyed and two more taken as prizes and sent back to Castelrozzo. He was enjoying an exceptionally successful war patrol.

Normally a PT carried four torpedo tubes but Lt. Seaborn had removed two of them in the interest of cutting weight to wring every bit of speed out of the boat. Still, with the pair of 21-inch Mark 8 torpedoes armed with a 466-pound charge of TNT in their warheads, Hornblower was hoping to catch a larger enemy vessel some dark night.

For most of the war he had been operating with Commandos which was dangerous close inshore work requiring extraordinary seamanship, a cool head in an emergency situation and bold executive action when needed.

But it was not ship vs ship naval war.

Now Lt. Seaborn was being given a free hand to operate independently—a bold sea rover playing at being a pirate. At least he had been. There was no telling what this change of mission might portend.

The waters off Patmos were some of the most dangerous in his patrol area.

CHANGE OF MISSION II

COMMANDER ANDREAS LONDOS HAD ALREADY sailed past Leros en route to Castelrozzo steering as far clear of the place as sea space would allow when Sparks informed him of the radio signal from Vice Admiral Sir Randolph "Razor" Ransom ordering him to join up with Veronica Paige of MI-9 off Patmos Island. There was no explanation.

He immediately came about.

Captain Butch "Headhunter" Hoolihan was sleeping in a hammock on deck. Having lived by his wits for so long he was a light sleeper. The change in course brought him awake instantly.

Cdr. Londos, seeing the Royal Marine officer was alert, said, "New sailing orders, Headhunter."

Lieutenant Jackson Taylor came up from below, "Why the change of course, Skipper?"

Cdr. Londos said, "No explanation other than to link up with MI-9 caiques off Patmos."

Capt. Hoolihan said, "Where might that be?"

Lt. Taylor said, "It's a small island thirty miles off Leros.

Everyone on board had been listening to the radio. The crew had an understanding of events taking place. Any island in the vicinity of Leros was not likely to be a healthy place to be.

Capt. Hoolihan had a half dozen of his Royal Marines on the LS7. The rest were scattered around on the privately-owned Greek-skippered caiques fleeing to Castelrozzo. There was no way to contact them because their boats did not have radios.

He did not see how his six Marines could be of much use.

Lt. Taylor said, "If we're going to end up on Leros I might as well have drowned and gotten it over with. Wasn't all that bad an experience actually… now that I think about it."

DESTINATION PATMOS

BRANDY SEABORN AND CAPTAIN PENELOPE "LEGS" Honeycutt-Parker were making the high-speed run to Patmos. They had no navigational charts showing the channels or the rocks, shoals and wrecks to be encountered along the way. Or the minefields. At one point the channel between Rhodes and the Turkish coast, which they had to pass by, narrowed to approximately seven miles. This was a dangerous stretch. If the Kriegsmarine was on the ball they would have patrols out to intercept the Coastal Forces MGB/PT boats and the LSF craft infiltrating the Aegean.

None were met.

In the best tradition of their sister organization, the LSF, Brandy and Capt. Honeycutt-Parker stood boldly on.

They had made this run once before. The next marker was the lighthouse on Cape Krio jutting out on the point from Turkey. The light was turned on. While it verified dead reckoning, it also lit them up which was not comforting.

The MAS boats sped on.

Passing through the strait between Kos and Turkey they set a course for the narrow channel between Kalymnos and Leros. This stretch of water was shallow and mined. Continuing through unscathed they pulled up off Patmos with thirty minutes to spare.

The full moon illuminated Veronica's three MI-9 caiques and Commander Andreas Londos' LS7. A quick exchange of signals completed the link-up. Now all that remained was to wait.

Lieutenant General "Geronimo" Joe McKoy said, "Nicely done, Brandy."

Dr. Layton Winthrop said, "I second that."

The Catalina flew over.

.

13
TOO MUCH AIN'T ENOUGH

CAPTAIN BILLY JACK JAXX WAS WEDGED SPREAD-eagle in the door of the Catalina hanging outside performing his jumpmaster checks. In the moonlight he could see the island of Patmos coming up ahead. He swung back inside and shouted at the stick of paratroopers standing hooked up ready to jump. "ONE MINUTE!"

Then he arched himself back outside for another check mentally ticking off the seconds so he would know when to have Colonel John Randal stand in the door. Down below a cluster of boats flashed by. Capt. Jaxx hoped they belonged to Brandy and Veronica. Normally a jumpmaster has predesignated checkpoints on the ground—usually linear, like a road or a river to orient himself by but that does not happen over a large body of water.

Up ahead Skala Village came into sight—the Initial Point (IP).

Capt. Jaxx swung back inside and shouted the combined commands, "CLOSE ON THE DOOR—STAND IN THE DOOR!"

Each man in the stick shuffled forward, pressing up tight against the parachute pack of the jumper in front of him. Col.

Randal did a right face, slid into the door, reached outside the aircraft arms angled down, and slapped his palms flat against the skin of the fuselage. The left leading toe of his lightweight, canvas-topped raiding boot was out over the edge of the cargo deck. He had his knees flexed.

All automatic.

Capt. Jaxx's arm was braced across the exit door holding him back as the stick crowded forward in accordance with his command to close up. He did not want the second jumper, King, to be shoved into Col. Randal giving him a false signal to exit.

The verbal command "GO" is accompanied by a slap on the leg of the first jumper to eliminate any doubt it's time to exit the aircraft. Due to all the equipment the men were carrying, the crowding, the plane bobbing and weaving, all the noise plus the fact a jumpmaster has a lot on his mind at that point and is not looking when he swings the blow—it could land anywhere.

Premature exits were not unknown.

Why take a chance?

Looking out over Col. Randal's shoulder Capt. Jaxx could see the far edge of town down below—made easier because every house on the island was whitewashed.

Ahead was the start of the pasture—the Final Point (FP)—which indicated the DZ was coming up fast.

When the last house flashed past under his left boot, Col. Randal crouched, ready to make his exit. He pressed down even harder with his palms against the outside of the fuselage for leverage, eyes on the horizon. He knew they had passed the FP—which is almost never an actual point but a linear terrain feature.

Tonight it was the leading edge of the pasture.

At the same time Capt. Jaxx pulled his arm back and slapped Col. Randal, aiming for the back of his leg and hitting him on the side of his parachute pack.

"GO!"

Col. Randal launched out of the airplane as hard as he could hitting the prop blast in a tight school approved solution tuck position. He began spinning around like he was in an invisible whirlpool. The stick of troopers behind him came charging the exit like a runaway freight train. Even so, to Capt. Jaxx it seemed like they were shuffling forward in slow motion. He grabbed the last jumper's static line and shoved it—throwing it—down the cable toward Corporal Tom Murphy who was doing double duty tonight as the navigator and loadmaster. After making a quick head check for a towed paratrooper—a reflex because nothing could be done about it if there was—Jack Cool was out the door.

Jumping with no reserve Col. Randal knew there was no need to count "One thousand, two thousand . . ." but his mind ran through the drill anyway—screaming the numbers. On "three thousand," one second before he would need to hit the reserve chute—if he had been wearing one—the toes of his boots touched the ground.

And he was not dead. A good sign. He never checked his canopy because he had never reached the count of "four thousand" where he was conditioned to make the check. In all the excitement he did not feel the opening shock of the X-type parachute—something he would not have believed possible until it happened to him.

Col. Randal came in backward, knees loose, automatically twisting to his right to get into position for his parachute landing fall, hitting on the balls of his feet—feet and knees together, elbows in tight—*really* tight, chin down on his chest, then falling on the right side of his calf, thigh, buttocks and small of his back. All five points of contact in the correct sequence fast.

WHAAAAAM!

Not a bad PLF—he was conscious, no obvious broken bones and no visible blood—all good signs.

Wanting to get the stick down in a tight formation Beverly must have dropped lower than 500 feet.

Then Col. Randal was up, pulling the safety clip off the chest-mounted quick release while simultaneously turning the dial on the device until the flat section was facing up. He hammered it with his fist to disengage the shoulder and leg straps allowing them to fall free.

The British X-type parachute harness and backpack dropped to the ground.

As always Col. Randal jumped with his 9mm Beretta MAB-38 submachine gun exposed. All that was necessary was to chamber a round and he was armed and ready. Major General James "Baldie" Taylor and King, who jumped in the two and three position behind him, walked over. They took a knee with their weapons pointed out to wait.

A sheep was staring at them.

LIEUTENANT GENERAL "GERONIMO" JOE MCKOY watched the Catalina fly over from the deck of Brandy Seaborn's MAS boat. In the moonlight he could see the parachutes spill out the back. The canopies, as usual, looked like swimming octopuses until they fully deployed.

The plan, such as it was, called for Colonel John Randal and Captain Billy Jack Jaxx's men to sweep through Skala to the bay. Lt. Gen. McKoy was to use his discretion as to when to land Captain "Pyro" Percy Stirling's troops ashore. Now they were reinforced by Captain Butch "Headhunter" Hoolihan's six-man contingent of Royal Marines, the LS-7 being on station.

Lt. Gen. McKoy's initial task was to set up a blocking force seaside of the built-up area. Since the element of surprise still seemed to be intact he decided now was as good a time as any.

"Run us in, Skipper."

Brandy Seaborn said, "Aye aye, sir!"

Captain Penelope "Legs" Honeycutt-Parker followed aboard her MAS boat with her contingent of Rangers.

There was no intelligence available on the docking facilities except for Dr. Layton Winthrop's recollection from his last visit, which had been pre-war. Things could have changed.

In making his decision to land now Lt. Gen. McKoy was taking into consideration the fact the garrison troops occupying Patmos were from the 999th Light Division—a penal unit composed of convicts, not front-line stormtroopers. They did not have a reputation for putting out sentries or patrolling after dark.

The 999th Light Division consisted of German prison inmates who were released to serve for the duration—violent offenders being the most desired. There was a possibility of a pardon on a case-by-case basis should anyone distinguish himself in combat . . . but no guarantee.

For the majority, the war was nothing more than a temporary work release program. The convicts made the most of their opportunity. Rape was the number one division sport. In second place on the 999th's list of favorite pastime sports—random murder—the more random the better.

The Nazis kept score.

The unintended consequence of the atrocities was that 999th personnel were not safe out at night unless they traveled in large groups. Troops had to RON in barracks after dark or restrict their drinking to a single establishment until sunrise—no bar hopping.

Drunk 999th Division soldiers who did venture out alone at night were found the next morning in the street with their throats slit. Historically Greeks and Germans are natural enemies.

Recent Nazi behavior on Patmos had done nothing to change the islander's attitude, and harsh reprisals by the occupiers were no deterrent.

The Greeks were being killed anyway.

Prior to Mussolini's overthrow Patmos had been garrisoned by Italian troops for almost three years. The Italian's behavior toward the locals was only marginally better than the Germans'. The island's women refused to have anything to do with them so prostitutes were imported from Rome. When the armistice was announced the Italians shipped out to Leros.

Without the hookers.

The 999th liked to party, they liked women and were not much interested in having their throats cut. So they requisitioned a large bar for their personal use and stocked it with the unemployed Italian working girls. The Germans had come up with a simple solution to their entertainment needs but in doing so they made themselves predictable.

Occam's razor has its downside when applied to certain military situations.

Based on what Raiding Forces had found on other islands Lt. Gen. McKoy and Col. Randal had reason to believe most of the 999th troops would be concentrated in their barracks or at a bar somewhere drinking themselves senseless. It was not a good thing for the Germans when those two had that kind of advanced understanding of their tendencies.

Faced with the task of securing Patmos the two senior Raiding Forces officers knew where to go calling.

Capt. Hoolihan said, "What are my orders, sir?"

Lt. Gen. McKoy said, "You tell me, Butch. I'm designatin' you to be my Operations Officer. You got yourself about three minutes to come up with somethin' before we hit the beach."

Shades of their mule cavalry days in Abyssinia.

THE *KING DUCK* CAME STEAMING INTO THE protected anchorage at Patmos. Acting Provisional Lieutenant Warthog Finley had two primary tasks to perform. First, he was to be on call to provide fire support during the elimination of the German 999th Light Division forces in the Skala harbor area. Second, he was to stand by to take onboard SBS and LRDG personnel in addition to certain elements of the 1st Battalion, King's Own Royal Regiment, who would be evacuated to Patmos from Leros in the days ahead, for transport to Castelrozzo.

Lieutenant Theodore Hamilton was on the LCT to supervise its camouflage. During the night's voyage he and Skipper Finley discussed various ideas. The Germans enjoyed air superiority which meant the primary concern was to make the LCT invisible from the air. There was netting onboard to accomplish that.

The problem was the possibility that the *King Duck* might have to remain on call for fire missions well after BMNT. The Tiger's 88s could not be hampered by netting. They needed to be able to traverse.

Lt. Hamilton came up with an elegant solution that would have made Occam blush.

Since he had already altered the *King Duck* to make it resemble a tramp steamer The Great Teddy suggested Skipper Finley hoist a German flag. Luftwaffe pilots were not likely to bomb their own ship.

Hey, Presto!

The idea probably broke several international maritime regulations but Raiding Forces Rule #1 stipulated "The First Rule Is There Ain't No Rules." This was the Aegean—no one was going by the book.

Besides Raiding Forces also had another rule that applied: "It Never Hurts To Cheat".

The Great Teddy was an illusionist. They always cheat. He was a professional trickster.

Camouflage mission accomplished acting without orders on his own recognizance Lt. Hamilton had himself run ashore to join Lieutenant General "Geronimo" Joe McKoy. He had brought Colonel John Randal's 45mm Brixia shoulder-fired mortar with him on the voyage out from Castelrozzo. The Colonel might need it when Captain "Pyro" Percy Stirling's team effected a link-up with Captain Billy Jack Jaxx and cornered the Nazis.

At least that was his excuse.

CAPTAIN BILLY JACK JAXX BEGAN ROLLING UP THE stick. The moon was out full. It cast enough light that visibility was not a problem. All jumpers were assembled in under five minutes.

Colonel John Randal whispered the order, "Let's go—move out."

The stick shook itself out and transitioned into a patrol. King was on point. Master Sergeant Mack Beckwith was second in the file in the slack position followed by Col. Randal. The idea was to infiltrate Skala, move through it and develop the situation.

Meaning "see what happens." Specifically Col. Randal wanted to locate the 999th's bar and their barracks.

The Germans would have imposed a curfew on the population after dark so no one should be out and about. From past experience on other islands Col. Randal knew the 999th rarely enforced it. There was almost no way they could. The islanders were spread out over a wide area, they outnumbered the Nazis and they had a nighttime home court advantage.

Knowing that meant the Rangers could not simply shoot anyone they encountered—rules of engagement that complicated the mission.

The patrol worked its way into the village. Everything was quiet, too quiet . . . or so it seemed. Moving through a strange place in the dark of night when you are sure people inside their homes are aware you are outside is always a spooky experience.

The men were on a high state of alert.

Col. Randal had studied the village while standing in the door of the Catalina as it flew over. He estimated from the start of the built-up area located at the leading edge of the DZ to the waterfront to be a quarter mile or so. The problem was the layout of the town was crescent-shaped around the edge of the bay and over a mile in length, making it shallow and wide.

Somewhere in that area the two elements of Raiding Forces had to link up with each other, locate a platoon of the 999th, fix the Germans in place and kill them.

It would have been a lot simpler if Col. Randal had an interpreter. Then he could have knocked on the door of the first house they came to and commandeered a local guide.

King halted and went down on one knee. MSgt. Beckwith did the same. Col. Randal knelt too. A domino effect rippled down the column as the rest of the patrol followed suit, every other man facing out left and right weapons at the ready, last man pulling rear security. Capt. Jaxx made his way forward.

"What have we got, sir?"

"Not sure."

Then King was moving again. Patrolling is start–stop work. Slow is smooth, smooth is fast. When executed by professionals a patrol flows like a ballet with hostile intent.

Leading a patrol is more art than science. Not every officer or NCO is good at it. Even though they are quite capable at other aspects of their job.

Col. Randal let the men work giving very few orders. Tonight he was experiencing the old familiar sensation he never discussed with anyone. That of looking down and watching developments as they unfolded.

He never felt so invigorated as when leading a patrol.

Decisions came as easy as daydreams.

King halted.

MSgt. Beckwith turned and whispered, “Movement to our front, sir.”

The Merc disappeared up ahead. MSgt. Beckwith went with him. That left Col. Randal on point.

Capt. Jaxx arrived silently having moved up the length of the halted column again.

After what seemed a long time but in fact was only a matter of minutes King and MSgt. Beckwith returned. They had a Greek man with them. The islander was clearly rattled by the unexpected turn of events.

Who was this individual and what was he doing out at this time of night?

Maj. Gen. James “Baldie” Taylor whispered, “Let me try him in Italian.”

A reasonable enough suggestion considering Patmos had been occupied by the Italian Army for nearly three years.

After a brief exchange Maj. Gen. Taylor whispered, “He says he was walking his dog.”

Col. Randal whispered, “Anybody see a dog?”

King whispered, “Negative.”

“Tell him we need a guide.”

This time the conversation took longer. It did not require a skilled linguist to understand the Greek was not eager to get involved. In the short time the 999th had been on the island it had succeeded in cowing the population with its wholesale reign of terror—the islander had every reason to be reluctant.

What was being requested was a death sentence for him and his family if the Germans found out.

Maj. Gen. Taylor whispered, “This gentleman would respectfully like to decline your request, Colonel.”

Col. Randal said, “Explain we’re not exactly asking.”

King stuck the tip of his Fairbairn Fighting Knife in the local’s ear. It must have hurt. He started jabbering rapid fire.

Col. Randal whispered, “What’s he saying now?”

“Follow me.”

THE TWO MAS BOATS WARBLED UP TO THE DOCK. the troops remained on board. Lieutenant General “Geronimo” Joe McKoy and Captain Butch “Headhunter” Hoolihan stepped onto the wooden planking. The two had a lot of history working together.

They walked toward a sandbagged position clearly visible at the end of the pier. The post was manned by four bored troopers of the 999th Light Division. The sentries were the only Germans pulling guard duty on the entire island that night.

The men must have really annoyed someone in their chain of command to be so lucky.

Lt. Gen. McKoy had his sidearms, a Colt 1911 .38 Super around back in a Mexican slide holster, a .22 High Standard Military Model D w/silencer in his hand held behind him, and his favorite 4 ¾-inch barrel ivory stocked Colt Single Action Army w/.45 ACP cylinder at his waist. Capt. Hoolihan had his .45 Thompson submachine gun slung over his shoulder around back out of sight and was also armed with a 1911 Colt 38 Super and a .22 High Standard Military Model D w/silencer.

The two did not appear in any way threatening.

The guards in the post saw the MAS boats arrive. The problem for them to sort out was after the armistice some of the Italians had gone over to fight with the Allies, some stacked arms and refused to participate in the war at all, and others, particularly the Regia Marina, continued fighting with the Germans. Lack of clarity may have been the reason the four sentries allowed two complete strangers to walk up to their position unchallenged.

There was the possibility the sentries' naval identification skills were so lacking they could not tell one boat from another. Or, it might have been the monotony of guard duty. Nothing ever happened at the dock at night. Either way not challenging was a violation of standard operating procedure for standing guard duty in any army worldwide from the beginning of organized warfare—challenges are a must friend or foe.

Lt. Gen. McKoy leaned over the top of the waist-high sandbagged berm and shot all four Germans with his suppressed .22 High Standard Military Model D.

WHIIIIICH WHIIIIICH WHIIIIICH WHIIIIICH

Lightning fast, the sound of the four stuttering silenced rounds ran together. So fast Capt. Hoolihan never had the opportunity to bring his silenced .22 High Standard Military Model D out from behind his back where he had also been carrying his pistol in hand.

Then Lt. Gen. McKoy shot all four Nazis once more—headshots, to make sure.

Capt. Hoolihan used his hook-nosed flashlight to signal the MAS boats waiting at the end of the dock. Raiding Forces personnel disembarked. Captain "Pyro" Percy Stirling led them up to the checkpoint.

Doctor Layton Winthrop came with them.

"Allow me a few minutes to go into the town, General."

Lt. Gen. McKoy ordered, "Stay with him, Butch."

While Capt. Stirling deployed the troops in a defensive position on the beach Dr. Winthrop did what Colonel John Randal had wished he could. He walked into the village and knocked on the door of the first single-family residence he came to.

A portly Greek wearing a nightshirt and slippers answered apprehensively. Loud knocking on your door in the middle of the night was always cause for alarm. Especially on Patmos.

The homeowner was less than enchanted when Dr. Winthrop stated his business.

Capt. Hoolihan quieted his protests by the simple expedient of pressing the Cutts Compensator on the barrel of his .45 Thompson submachine gun against the man's belly. A universal nonverbal persuader—worked like a charm.

Now the seaborne element of Raiding Forces had a guide.

The three returned to the dock. Lt. Gen. McKoy took out his Fairbairn Fighting Knife and drew in the sand. "Professor, tell him this is the pier—where in relation to it is the bar the bad guys hang out in? And where's their barracks?"

Dr. Winthrop translated. The Greek took the knife out of Lt. Gen. McKoy's hand and scraped two Xs. One was straight ahead off the end of the wharf. The other was some distance to the right.

Lt. Gen. McKoy said, "Which one is which?"

"The bar is less than two blocks away—straight ahead."

"How far's the barracks?"

Dr. Winthrop asked the Greek.

"Approximately a quarter mile that direction located on the edge of the shore."

Lt. Gen. McKoy called a leaders' conference consisting of Capt. Hoolihan, Capt. Stirling, Lieutenant Clint Hays and Lieutenant Theodore Hamilton.

"Butch and me are goin' to do a sneak and peek to check out the 999th's bar. Percy, you take your leaders, the Professor, the

Greek and one of the Fire Control Teams and go recon the barracks—no contact. Radio back and let us know what it looks like down there."

"Yes, sir."

"I'm going to want to take down both our targets at the same time, so make a plan, Captain."

"Understood, sir."

"Lieutenant Hays, you take charge here. Wait for Captain Stirling's radio call and stand by for my return."

"Wilco."

Lt. Hamilton said, "Where do you want me, sir?"

"You can come with me and Butch, but don't be shootin' off that cannon you're carryin', Lieutenant."

"Sir!"

"All right then. Get 'er done boys."

Lt. Gen. McKoy led out in the direction of the bar. Capt. Hoolihan was next. Lt. Hamilton brought up the rear. Now that they had an idea where they were going finding the only open establishment in town should not be all that difficult. They had barely made it off the beach before the sound of music could be heard to their front.

Sounded like a party was in progress.

Moving up the two blocks slowly and carefully Lt. Gen. McKoy halted in the shadow of a building across the street from the 999th's private club. Raucous music blared. People were laughing, men shouting, women shrieking.

The fools had not posted security.

There was one German out front around the side of the building throwing up.

Lt. Gen. McKoy recognized immediately this target was going to pose a problem. There were a lot of Nazis in the bar and even if they were all drunk they could not all be discounted. The nightclub was screened from the anchorage by other buildings which meant the *King Duck* would not be able to engage it with the 88s mounted on its deck.

While tank guns can be fired in the indirect role like artillery, the *Duck's* gunners were not trained in the procedure. Nor could the Thunderbolt gun mounts on the MAS boats be brought to bear. They were line-of-sight direct fire weapons as well.

Lt. Gen. McKoy was taking his time working out his estimation of the situation when he noticed King standing a few feet away. The Merc simply materialized. Surprises like that were not supposed to happen to him.

"Where did you come from, King—get misdropped?"

"The Chief is three blocks up the street, General. When we heard the music he sent me ahead to pinpoint the nightclub before moving up. We have not located the troop barracks yet."

Lt. Gen. McKoy said, "No problem. Pyro Percy's down the beach about four hundred yards or so east 'a here checkin' out the barracks right now. He's got a radio with him so we can get 'a report as soon as we pull back to the dock.

"Go round up the Colonel and the rest 'a your people and bring 'em on here pronto."

King disappeared the way he came—seeming to vanish into thin air. One second there. The next gone.

Capt. Hoolihan said, "How does he do that?"

Lt. Hamilton said, "Hey, Presto!"

Even The Great Teddy was impressed.

TAKING A CIRCUITOUS ROUTE, KING GUIDED Colonel John Randal's patrol to where Lieutenant General "Geronimo" Joe McKoy's party waited across the street from the 999th's club. The action inside had not abated.

The bar was rocking.

Col. Randal stood with Lt. Gen. McKoy, Captain Billy Jack Jaxx and Captain Butch "Headhunter" Hoolihan in the shadow of a building with the troops strung out behind lined up against the wall awaiting developments. He had experience shooting up enemy bars going back to the earliest days of the war starting with what was known in Raiding Forces legend as the "Gunfight at the Blue Duck."

In military terms an enemy nightclub is a soft target. Drinking spots everywhere all share one thing in common. Regulars feel a false sense of security the minute they walk through the front door.

As they watched, one of the 999th's soldiers stumbled out into the street. Apparently drunk and disoriented he staggered across, zig-zagging straight toward them. The Nazi came within a foot of where the command party was standing without seeing them.

Col. Randal said, "King."

The Merc stepped out from the shadow and slit the man's throat. Master Sergeant Mack Beckwith and Private First Class Norvel "Horn Dog" Hansen dragged the dead Nazi into the alley behind the building where patrol had gathered. In the unlikely event anyone discovered the body the death would be attributed to the local Greeks.

It had happened before.

Whispering so low he was barely audible, Lt. Gen. McKoy said, "John, don't be thinkin' about walkin' in and orderin' yourself a Blackstrap tonight this ain't the time for any fancy gunfightin'."

Col. Randal said, "My plan, which isn't working out, was to jump in, patrol through the village, develop intel on our targets so Captain Jaxx could take 'em down. Then link up with Brandy and let her run my party over to Leros to locate Lord Jellicoe."

Lt. Gen. McKoy said, “Why don’t you stick around and honcho the show? It’s what you’re good at. That way when you head out to Leros you’ll know everything’s under control back here.”

Col. Randal said, “All right then—Captain Jaxx, develop a scheme of maneuver and be prepared to reduce the objective directly to your front on my command.”

“Roger that, sir.”

“Your assault will need to be coordinated to go off simultaneously with Captain Stirling’s attack on the troop barracks. I’ll work that detail out for you—clear?”

“That’s a Rodge, sir.”

“Remain here with your element leaders to work out the plan. Headhunter’s going back with me. I’m taking the rest of the people to the pier. We’ll reorganize and stand by for you to complete your reconnaissance.

“Be there in the next twenty minutes prepared to issue your order.”

“Yes, sir.”

Capt. Jaxx moved back to where his troops were waiting.

“Lieutenant Hays, Lieutenant Novak, Lieutenant Mascuch and you Sergeant Major—on me. The rest of you people are moving out with the colonel. Stand by on the beach prepared to receive an order the minute I return.”

As Col. Randal came past with the command party, Capt. Jaxx said, “Can I have King for the take down, sir?”

“Affirmative.”

The combined two patrols moved out with Lt. Gen. McKoy leading the way. Capt. Jaxx and his party moved up to observe the target. He discovered one extra person in the group, Lieutenant Theodore Hamilton.

The Great Teddy had attached himself to the leader’s reconnaissance.

Capt. Jaxx pulled the four officers, the Sergeant Major and King in tight. “Normally I’d like to conduct a walk-around inspection of the objective but we don’t have the luxury. Lieutenant Hays, I want you to take a team of six men and work your way behind the building and set up a blocking position. Check the left side as you go past. If there’s a window drop off a man to cover it.

“Is that clear?

“Clear, sir.”

“Lieutenant Mascuch, you’ll remain here with me. Set up a base of fire with the remaining men. Deploy your Stingers in pairs covering the front door of the building—BARs on the flanks. Send Private Hansen around the right side to determine if there is a window. If so he’s to remain in place there and cover it.

“Is that clear?

“Yes, sir.”

“Lieutenant Novak you will initially travel with Lieutenant Hays’ party. Upon reaching the back you and King will scale the building. Move to the chimney and stand by with a half dozen frag grenades each. King, give me three dots with your flashlight when you’re in position.

“Is that clear?”

“Affirmative.”

“Lieutenant Hamilton, you’re on me. When I give the word start pumping 45mm rounds through the front windows of the bar as fast as you can with the Colonel’s Brixia.

“Is that clear?”

“Roger, sir.”

“Is Colonel Randal aware you remained behind here?’

“Probably not, sir.”

“All right then, Lieutenant—you work for me now.”

“Outstanding, sir!”

Capt. Jaxx said, "Lieutenant Novak when you hear Lieutenant Hamilton's first round detonate inside the bar, you and King start dropping grenades down the chimney. Lieutenant Mascuch that first 45mm round is your signal to give the command to commence fire.

"We're going to shoot this place up. We will not assault through the objective. Depending on what happens we may or may not enter the building to inspect our results after the check fire.

"Keep firing until I order a stand down—clear?"

"Clear, sir."

"No avoidable friendly casualties—are we all clear on that?"

All four lieutenants whispered, "Clear."

"Let's make this happen gentlemen."

CAPTAIN "PYRO" PERCY STIRLING, DR. LAYTON Winthrop, the *King Duck's* Fire Control Team and their semi-reluctant guide in his nightshirt and bedroom slippers started down the rocky shoreline. Before they moved out the Greek pointed toward a building in the distance—a whitewashed two-story structure.

The structure was easily visible from the pier.

Dr. Winthrop said, "That building is your objective, Captain. Our guide says it was the Italian barracks during the years they occupied the island. Now the 999th have taken it over."

Capt. Stirling said, "Strolling along out in the open in the moonlight on an enemy occupied island conducting our leaders' reconnaissance seems like a rather odd idea."

Dr. Winthrop said, "I would tend to agree."

Capt. Stirling was a legendary figure in Raiding Forces due primarily to his demolition adventures. He was also one of the unit's most skilled patrol leaders. His exploits in making things go *bang* tended to overshadow the fact he had been a troop leader from the day it was formed having seen as much action as anyone assigned.

And more than most.

He led his party inland for a short distance until they could parallel other buildings up close to cover their approach.

The Greek said something to Dr. Winthrop.

"Our guide claims there is no real need to steal up on the Germans. All the lights in their quarters are out. The Nazis are asleep."

Capt. Stirling said, "What makes him so sure of that?

Dr. Winthrop said, "Patmos is not under blackout restriction."

Capt. Stirling said, "We have a saying in Raiding Forces—'why take a chance?'"

Dr. Winthrop said, "A wise and prudent policy, Captain. One I heartily endorse."

Upon examination at close range not much was to be learned from observing the target. The barracks were in a simple rectangle two-story structure whitewashed like every other building on Patmos. Prior to the war the place had been a hostel catering to pilgrims who came to tour the Cave of the Apocalypse.

Capt. Stirling studied the objective and liked what he saw. There was no obstruction between the barracks and the bay. Most likely a location chosen to provide the pre-war paying guests with a view.

Naval gun support was not going to be a problem.

The barracks were located approximately twenty-five yards from any other building which allowed plenty of space to establish blocking positions with clear fields of fire. The terrain was flat, gently sloping toward the waterfront, with no dead ground.

An abandoned warehouse nearby would make the perfect Objective Rally Point/Release Point for his patrol when they came up. Without wasting time Capt. Stirling got on the radio and spoke to Acting Provisional Lieutenant Warthog Finley. Upon conclusion of their conversation the *King Duck* made way and steamed close inshore directly opposite the 999th barracks. The LCT dropped anchor and cleared for action.

Next Capt. Stirling contacted Brandy Seaborn. They spoke for a moment. She and Captain Penelope "Legs" Honeycutt-Parker crash-started their MAS boats and cruised over to take up station side-by-side off the port bow of the *King Duck.*

Now they had their Thunderbolts aimed at the target.

Capt. Stirling made note of the locations best suited for him to place blocking positions. He wanted to ensure none of the 999th escaped once the attack started. The most important consideration for the placement being to keep his men out of the line of fire from the navy.

Then he led the recon party back to the dock.

Dr. Winthrop took note of how skillfully Capt. Stirling conducted the reconnaissance and planned his displacements — and he was a tough grader. While the Professor knew no one understood all the mysteries of the Book of Revelation, one thing was clear. For the men of the 999th who had chosen to stay in their barracks and not go drinking tonight the Apocalypse was here and right now.

"Pyro" Percy was getting ready to blow them into kingdom come.

Hey, Presto!

COLONEL JOHN RANDAL SAID, "CAPTAIN HOOLIHAN, I want you to hold your six Royal Marines here at the dock to constitute our reserve. Stand by ready Butch, you're all we've got."

"Yes, sir."

"General McKoy where do you want to be?"

"I'll tag along with Captain Stirling anything's possible when Pyro swings into action."

Col. Randal said, "General Taylor?"

"I shall accompany General McKoy. I want the opportunity to observe the *King Duck's* pair of 88s in action. Their firepower in concert with the MAS boat's eight 20mm and twelve 50 caliber machine guns promise quite a show."

The extra 20mm guns, two per boat, were a recent upgrade after Brandy Seaborn had learned Thunderbolt mounts for U.S. Navy PT boats in the Pacific now came equipped with four Oerlikon cannon.

Col. Randal said, "In that case, I'll travel with Captain Jaxx."

Captain "Pyro" Percy Stirling and Captain Billy Jack Jaxx had their troops taking a knee in a semicircle around them as they issued their individual Op Orders. Up until now Col. Randal had been winging it by necessity. Once he assigned specific objectives the mission had snapped into tight focus.

His two subordinate commanders were doing it strictly by the book the way he expected—make that demanded.

There was one last detail to attend to. Col. Randal got on the radio and informed Acting Provisional Lieutenant Warthog Finley the signal to commence fire would be three green flares. An advantage of operations on tiny islands like Patmos was elevated visual signals could be seen by all parties at the same time no matter how widely scattered they might be.

While they waited for the orders to be completed, Captain Butch "Headhunter" Hoolihan said, "Sir, you will never guess who is on Commander Londos' caique."

"Who might that be?"

"Jackson Taylor, sir."

"You recovered his body?"

"Negative sir, Jackson alive and well. Make that almost well. He was found by nuns searching for one of their missing girls. My guess is that would be Cat."

Col. Randal said, "Lieutenant Taylor exhibited no vital signs—he was dead."

Capt. Hoolihan said, "Jackson said the nuns believed he had drowned too. They sent for a priest instead of a doctor. When he came back to life the sisters were convinced they were witness to a miraculous event."

"Really?"

"Jackson claims the monastery is making plans to erect a shrine on the beach to memorialize the miracle."

Col. Randal said, "I'll never live this down."

Lieutenant General "Geronimo" Joe McKoy said, "Look on the bright side, John. Now you get to tell the man he was awarded the Navy Cross—posthumously."

Capt. Jaxx walked over. "Sir, my people are ready to move out."

"Stand by. I want to see Captain Stirling off first."

"Yes, sir."

Capt. Stirling arrived. "The MAS boats and the *King Duck* are on station for a fire mission. My people are ready to depart, sir."

Col. Randal said, "Move out now. Wait for the signal to engage—three greens. Light 'em up, Captain."

The instant he said it Col. Randal realized that was a dangerous order to give to "Pyro" Percy.

"Yes, sir."

Col. Randal said, "OK Jack, let's do this!"

With no fanfare both units stepped off in the direction of their objectives. Now Raiding Forces was conducting a movement to contact. An entirely different proposition from patrolling or a leader's recon.

Anticipation was thick in the air.

The men were professionals. Everyone knew his job. Tonight all the extensive training and years of special operations combat experience were being brought to bear with each man executing his individual assignment during the movement to perfection.

King was on point with Lieutenant Jake Novak behind him in the slack position. Capt. Jaxx was third in the file in the patrol leader's slot. Col. Randal was next with the Fire Control Party so he could have access to their radio. The formation for the approach to the ORP was patrol in file with teams in file. This allowed the troops to move stealthily along the wall of the buildings in single file staying in the shadows. Lieutenant Clint Hays' team came next, followed by Lieutenant Ricky Mascuch's.

It seemed like the patrol had only been moving a few minutes when it was halted. Word was whispered down the column, "ORP."

Now the waiting game began. Capt. Stirling had to reach his Objective Rally Point before they could continue. Col. Randal handed his flare pistol to Master Sergeant Mack Beckwith with three green flares.

"On my command put these up."

"Yes, sir."

The leader of the Fire Control Party said, "Captain Stirling reports he has reached his ORP, sir."

"Radio him to deploy his teams and give me a sit rep when they're in position."

"Yes, sir."

Col. Randal ordered, "OK, Jack you're cleared to go. Move up and release your teams."

This sounded like a simple command but that was deceptive. Lt. Hays needed to cross the street in order to travel around behind the bar. Streets are classified as "Danger Areas." Crossing one exposes the people doing the crossing to visual observation and/or enemy fire if an alert sentry spots the movement.

There are two techniques for crossing a Danger Area. The most popular—because it is how Hollywood directors depict it in war movies—is to move up to the Danger Area, set out security left and right, then send security across left and right on the far side—while the remainder of the patrol waits for the security elements to get into position. Then the men cross over one person at a time.

Makes for a great action scene on the silver screen.

The downside to this technique is the patrol leader has to place security out on the near side of the Danger Area and on the far side—on both flanks on both sides simultaneously. Security has to be put in place and then brought in—a lot of movement and all that takes time. If the enemy should become aware of the crossing at any point while it's in progress, the patrol leader is faced with the prospect of having part of his troops on one side of the Danger Area and part on the other side with a firefight in progress.

In military terms that is officially "not good." At best it's a SNAFU. With every chance of turning into a full on FUBAR.

The second—less glamorous—way to cross a Danger Area is to bring everyone up on line. Then on signal have the men all take one or two steps out in the open and be across. With tactics beauty is what works. The second online technique is almost foolproof just not very flashy.

Capt. Jaxx was a lot of things but he was not a showboat. He issued Lt. Hays, one of his SOG officers, detailed instructions on how to conduct his Danger Area crossing. The best patrol leaders never take anything for granted or leave anything to chance. No matter how experienced his subordinate team leader may be.

Lt. Hays moved his people two blocks down the street to attain some degree of separation from the bar. Then he brought the men up on line. After checking to make sure there were no Germans outside the tavern he slapped the stock of his .30 M1 Carbine with the palm of his hand three times.

On the third slap everyone stood up took two large strides across the street and were back up against the wall of the building on the far side—fast. If a German had seen them it happened so rapidly he might mistake what he saw as nothing more than a cloud passing across the moon or his imagination.

Considering there was not a sober 999th trooper in the village it was possible.

While Lt. Hays was traveling, Lt. Mascuch moved his people into position single file directly across the street from the bar. Private First Class Norvel "Horn Dog" Hansen led staying flat up against the wall in the shadow. When everyone was in place the men assumed a prone firing position and waited.

Across from the Rangers the bright lights would destroy the night vision of the people inside the bar looking out the windows or of anyone who walked outside. The Germans had virtually no chance of spotting them lying in wait only a few feet away across from the bar.

Once Lt. Mascuch's team was in place PFC Hansen continued on alone making his way up the street for a block. Then he crossed over and worked his way back and around the side of the tavern. There was a window sure enough. He could see Germans inside.

His orders dictated he would need to remain in place and cover it.

Inside PFC Hansen observed a woman dancing on the bar. She was naked. He took up his one-man blocking position as ordered and settled in to enjoy the show.

Those 999th guys knew how to party.

Lt. Hays' team followed King and Lt. Novak as they led the way around back behind the bar, dropping off one of the Rangers to cover a window at the end of the building. In the back were two fairly large windows but it was not possible to see through them into the main room because of interior walls.

There was also a back door.

King unwound his rope with a grappling hook and tossed it up on the roof. It failed to catch and slid down the tiles. Unperturbed he tried again but the hook still did not attain purchase.

The third time was the trick. King pulled on the rope with his full body weight lifting himself off the ground to set the hooks. Then he hand-over-handed up onto the roof.

Lt. Novak waited until the Merc was on top then he went up the rope.

Capt. Jaxx had given a great deal of thought to each individual assignment. Selecting Jake the Snake to back up King on the roof was classic "Right Man, Right Job" attention to detail. In the short time the former 509th officer had been with Raiding Forces he had established a reputation for being an aggressive officer who could be counted on in a tight situation.

Lt. Hays was the perfect choice to command the rear blocking position because of his high level of experience in SOG. He enjoyed Capt. Jaxx's full confidence and was used to operating semi-independently making his own tactical decisions within the framework of a larger operation.

No small talent.

Lt. Mascuch was the right officer to set up the base of fire out front of the bar. Capt. Jaxx as well as Col. Randal and MSgt Beckwith would be on hand to keep an eye on him during his first combat action. They would be evaluating the GOYA's performance. Tonight was an opportunity for him to demonstrate what he was capable of.

PFC Hansen—how much trouble could he get into all by himself securing the far end of the building? Capt. Jaxx was beginning to have second thoughts on that one. Horn Dog all alone…

Waiting for his element leaders to have time to move into position Col. Randal was tuned in, clicked on, very aware—almost relaxed. He was allowing Capt. Jaxx to do his job with no interference which required a great deal of self-discipline.

Col. Randal knew it was a fact you go to war with the army you have—not the army you want. These Raiding Forces operators tonight consisted of the first people to make it back from Benevento. They had been hastily thrown together to form a composite unit serving under officers they may or may not have worked directly with before.

One, Lt. Mascuch, was a completely unknown quantity.

While not optimum for unit cohesion it did not seem to matter much to these veterans. The Rangers were performing like a precision drill team. Col. Randal was well pleased with the way the operation was unfolding.

The Fire Control Team leader said, "Captain Stirling reports his team is in position standing by to execute, sir."

Three red blinks came from the rooftop as King signaled with his hook-nosed flashlight.

Col. Randal said, "Sergeant Major."

MSgt. Beckwith pointed the Very flare pistol back in the general direction of the 999th barracks where he thought the *King Duck* might be located offshore. Then he fired the three green flares as fast as he could reload the stubby little sawed-off shotgun looking single-barreled signaling device. The flares *whooshed* into the sky. When they reached the apex of their trajectory tiny white canopies cracked open one by one.

The green flares ignited as they floated to earth burning brightly swinging back and forth under their parachutes.

Capt. Jaxx was standing with Col. Randal, Lt. Mascuch and Lieutenant Theodore Hamilton in the middle of what was essentially a firing line aimed directly at the front of the bar. Like Lt. Novak they could see people inside moving around through two large picture windows. The Nazis were not aware Raiding Forces was out there.

The experience had a strange quality about it.

The instant the first flare left the barrel of MSgt. Beckwith's signal gun, Capt. Jaxx ordered, "Do it now, stud."

Lt. Hamilton aimed Col. Randal's 45mm Brixia shoulder-fired mortar dead center at one of the plate glass windows and pulled the trigger.

CAPTAIN "PYRO" PERCY STIRLING LED HIS PATROL up the coastline to the abandoned building he had designated to be his Objective Rally Point/Release Point. He had Lieutenant General "Geronimo" Joe McKoy, Major General James "Baldie" Taylor, and Doctor Layton Winthrop strap-hanging as observers. Not that it mattered having them along. The way he was planning to take down the 999th troop barracks the more the merrier.

No one was going to get in the way.

Besides both generals were professional trigger pullers. Dr. Winthrop was armed with the .30 M1 Carbine Captain Billy Jack Jaxx had given him. He seemed to know how to handle it.

The movement to the ORP only took a few minutes. Capt. Stirling pointed out to Lieutenant Dan Bonham where he wanted him to set up his blocking positions. One to cover the rear and the other the far side of the building. The most important aspect of their locations was to be where they could prevent anyone from escaping while at the same time not being on the gun target line of either the *King Duck* or the MAS boats.

This was important.

To get into position Lt. Bonham would have to send a four-man party completely around behind the barracks to the far end of the building. While that was taking place he would set up an eight-man block under his command at an angle to cover the rear but *not* directly behind the target. The idea was to have the entire back side covered by fire at all times with no gaps.

Neither blocking position would be within twenty-five yards of the barracks. When the balloon went up the incoming fire was going to be "Danger Close." The tank gunners would be firing HE which should explode inside the barracks. However all the weapons on the Thunderbolt mounts were capable of shooting entirely through the building and that was a concern.

No troops should be allowed on the gun target line until the *King Duck* reported "End of Mission."

It was imperative for the troops to remain prone in their exact positions until given orders to move because they were within the blasting radius of the 88 HE rounds. The idea was for any shrapnel not contained inside the building to fly over their heads.

In military circles it is said that "hope is not a plan of action" but sometimes that is all a commander has to work with.

Capt. Stirling and the men in his command party, plus the straphangers, would be covering the near side of the building from the ORP. He would be responsible for ordering Acting Provisional Lieutenant Warthog Finley to cease-fire by putting up a red over green flare.

The traditional Commando signal indicating success.

ACTING PROVISIONAL LIEUTENANT WARTHOG Finley was on the bridge of the *King Duck* pacing back and forth like a caged tiger while his sailors tried their best to stay out of his way. Skipper Finley was a man of action.

Waiting around was not his style.

All advanced preparation had been taken to make this a successful shoot. Now there was nothing else to do but stand by. The wait seemed to be taking forever.

The main guns of the two Tiger tanks were leveled on the 999th barracks. Each tank had twenty rounds stacked up on the deck next to it. There was no way possible they were all going to be needed for this fire mission.

A Tiger tank normally carried 92 rounds split equally between High Explosive (HE) and Anti-Tank (AT). The HE round was also referred to at times as High Explosive Anti-Tank (HEAT) but that was for tank versus tank warfare. Since there was almost no likelihood of the LCT engaging enemy panzers in the Aegean any reference to anti-tank was dropped from the high explosive acronym though it did creep back into conversation from time to time.

Skipper Finley had discussed the German TO&E ammunition ratio with Vice Admiral Sir Randolph "Razor" Ransom. The Razor pointed out the vast majority of fire missions the *King Duck* would be tasked to perform would be ship-to-shore bombardments against point-type targets. The possibility of a ship-to-ship engagement was not out of the question though probably rare.

The Razor recommended a 90% HE to 10% AT ratio. If a small Kriegsmarine craft like an E-boat took a direct hit from an 88 mm HE round that would be a fight-ending event. Should Skipper Finley run into an enemy destroyer or larger warship, then that was going to be an entirely different story—no matter what ammunition he had onboard.

More important than the distribution of ammunition was the stability question. To shoot a cannon from a ship with accuracy the vessel has to be a stable platform. There was nothing to tell Skipper Finley how to solve that problem.

Once again he had sought out VAdm. Ransom's advice.

In earlier years as a young sub-lieutenant the Razor had served on the Nile in what the Royal Navy described as the "River War." The naval gunnery officers of the day operating from improvised barges and locally acquired riverboats solved the ship-to-shore gun stability problem by simply stowing extra anchors onboard. When a fire mission was called for along the banks of the Nile the mud hooks were put over the side to hold the gun barge in place.

Occam's razor again.

Skipper Finley conducted tests to determine how many additional anchors he needed—six per side—problem solved.

Brandy Seaborn and Captain Penelope "Legs" Honeycutt-Parker were on station. Their crews were closed up at Battle Stations. Like the *King Duck* the two MAS boats had antiaircraft .303Vickers K and .50 Browning M-2 aka "Ma Deuce" machine guns mounted in every conceivable location. Tonight only the Tiger tank's 88s and the Thunderbolt mounted 20mms and .50 calibers would be engaging because they could be locked down on target. With friendly troops in the immediate vicinity and a

Danger Close fire mission, this was no time for free guns to be spraying the area.

Every possible effort was being made to minimize friendly casualties.

There was one last detail. Lieutenant Randy "Hornblower" Seaborn's PT boat was stationed at the mouth of the narrow entrance of the bay. His mission was to provide rear security while the other three fighting craft were occupied reducing the target ashore. Lt. Seaborn would have much preferred to be closed up with the MAS boats to take part in the engagement. However, because his boat was the only one armed with torpedoes deploying it to guard the entry to the bay was the right tactical decision.

In fact Hornblower suggested it.

THE 45MM GRENADE LIEUTENANT THEODORE Hamilton fired from Colonel John Randal's field expedient shoulder-fired Brixia mortar made a not very warlike *Blooooop*! The distance was so close there was an almost instantaneous crash of broken glass followed by a muffled *Whuuuuump* as the fat little shell detonated inside the building. Screams erupted from the revelers but they were immediately drowned out by the instantaneous response by the Rangers to Lieutenant Ricky Mascuch's verbal command "FIRE!"

Gunfire erupted in an explosion of individual weapons all engaging at once. The sound was an extraordinarily loud roar of full auto and semi-auto weapons consisting of .30 M1 Garand Rifles, .30 M1 Carbines, .30 Baby Browning Automatic Rifles, highly modified .30 1919 Browning Light Machine Guns aka

Stingers, the odd .45 Thompson submachine gun and a number of 9mm submachine guns of various makes and models.

At point blank range in the confined space of a cobblestone street lined with commercial buildings the sound was magnified. No matter how many times Col. Randal heard an ambush initiated he was always impressed by the power of the combined weapons engaging and the volume of fire his men could put out. And while this was, by definition, technically not an ambush—it was an attack, the Nazis inside the bar on the receiving end would have been hard pressed to differentiate between the two.

Lt. Hamilton had pumped three additional .45 mm rounds into the tavern before the first of the hand grenades Lieutenant Jake Novak and King were dropping down the chimney started cooking off. Glass shattered. The building visibly vibrated at every explosion.

Col. Randal said, "Jack."

Captain Billy Jack Jaxx ordered, "Grazing fire, Lieutenant."

Lt. Mascuch shouted, "AIM LOW PEOPLE!"

The troops responded by firing at the sidewalk running along the front of the building. Since military ball ammunition is full metal jacket the rounds hit the concrete and ricocheted inside. Tracers started a number of small blazes. There was such a massive concentration of rounds slamming into the bar a visible heat wave was rising above the stream of bullets converging on the place.

The sound of the combined weapons was a constant unrelenting roar like a giant waterfall only angrier.

Up on the roof Lt. Novak and King had run out of grenades. Jake the Snake poked the barrel of his .45 Thompson submachine gun down the chimney and held back the trigger letting off the weapon's entire thirty-round box magazine. When he ran out of ammunition the Merc stepped in with his 9mm Beretta MAB-38, stuck it in the chimney, and let the SMG run full auto.

Around the far side of the tavern, Private First Class Norvel "Horn Dog" Hansen took dead aim at the naked dancer with his .30 Baby BAR. His orders were to engage the instant he heard breaking glass from the street. He may have jumped the gun slightly commencing fire on hearing the initial *Blooooop* of the 45mm Brixia *before* its round impacted the window.

Horn Dog liked strippers as much as anyone, probably more than most, but providing aid and comfort to the enemy was an overreach of his tolerance for bad behavior. How much actual aid the hookers were supplying was questionable. But they were knowingly and willingly providing a lot of comfort.

PFC Hansen knew the Geneva Accords said you could not do that . . . or he was pretty sure it did.

He blew the dancer completely off the bar.

On the other end of the building Ranger Private Willie Johannsen was firing into a window with his .30 M1 Garand. Some of his rounds traveled the length of the bar and exited through the wall in PFC Hansen's direction. This was more than Horn Dog had signed on for but he maintained his position and continued to engage.

Around back, Captain Clint Hays and his team stood to their guns and waited. When the firing commenced nothing happened for a brief two-second count. Then a mob of people came barreling out the back door.

"LET 'EM HAVE IT!"

A wall of fire greeted the fleeing partyers. The ones in front were mowed down but the panicked crowd behind kept surging forward. Some tried running into other rooms and jumping out the windows, crashing through the glass.

A few of the Rangers shifted their aim briefly then went back to the primary target.

With Capt. Hays in back, Lt. Mascuch in front, PFC Hansen and Pvt. Johannsen on the ends, King and Lt. Novak on the roof, the building was boxed in. The 999th and their camp followers were trapped. No one was going to make it out of the bar alive.

Men were shouting. Women were screaming.

But those sounds were overpowered by the point-blank automatic weapons fire.

Around front the constant roar of the Raiding Forces' weapons never slacked off. Col. Randal was well satisfied with his men's textbook fire discipline. He had heard Capt. Hays engage. The Rangers were performing like they were on a training exercise which is how they were supposed to do it.

He considered ordering check fire.

Then decided to let the shooting run a little longer.

THE *KING DUCK*'S TWO TIGER TANKS COMMENCED fire simultaneously the instant the first green flare cracked open. The twin *BOOOOMs* of the 88mm main guns rolled across the bay. The MAS boat's Thunderbolt gunners engaged immediately. Guns on Brandy's boat getting off first. The muzzle flashes from the mix of 20mm fast-firing cannon and the massed .50 caliber machine guns lit up the night.

The fire was so intense it was blinding to look directly at the bow of the two MAS boats.

Captain "Pyro" Percy Stirling fired an illumination flare into the sky over the barracks. The burning white phosphorus sparkler cracked open and slowly floated down casting eerie shadows on the ground. He put up another and another, creating a pale, artificial daylight.

The idea was to turn night into day so no one could possibly escape.

The German 88 was a versatile weapon. The cannon was designed to be the main gun on panzers, an artillery field piece, an antitank weapon, an antiaircraft gun and it had been mounted on railway trains.

But probably the 88 had never been intended to be a ship-to-shore naval gun.

The two rounds from the pair of Tigers on the *King Duck* were fired at virtually point-blank range. They smashed through the walls of the barracks at ground level. The HE rounds detonated inside with a flash that could be seen through all the downstairs windows. The twin thunderclap explosions broke every piece of glass on the ground floor and some upstairs.

Lieutenant General "Geronimo" Joe McKoy had one of Waldo's cigars clenched in his teeth as he watched the show. He was rightfully impressed.

"That's what I call firepower."

Major General James "Baldie" Taylor said, "Glad I was not in there asleep."

Doctor Layton Winthrop said, "Whose idea was it to mount tanks on an LCT?"

Lt. Gen. McKoy said, "Whoever it was they deserve a medal."

The first burst of gunfire from the MAS boat's Thunderbolts slammed into the barracks with the odd crunching sound of softball-sized hail impacting a tile roof. Unlike a hailstorm the volume of rounds striking the structure did not build up to a crescendo. The Thunderbolts started out going wide open full bore and maintained an even pace—a constant, unrelenting sound not unlike a pair of monster-sized circular saws at a sawmill only lower pitched.

And louder.

The front of the barracks was completely covered in pockmarks. One second it sported a clean, white-washed two-story wall. The next the building was dimpled by hundreds of bullet holes.

Just like that.

Hey, Presto!

Dr. Layton said, "In the '30s the Greek Government on Patmos decreed all buildings be painted with a white limestone-based paint because the public administrators believed, erroneously as it turned out, that it had antibacterial qualities."

It was not uncommon for people to make observations totally unrelated to the events taking place in the middle of a firefight.

Lt. Gen. McKoy said, "Look at those bad boys go."

Maj. Gen. Taylor said, "Amazing volume of fire Thunderbolts deliver. The recent upgrade of the additional pairs 20mm's is certainly noticeable."

The two generals—with all their combined experience—were awed. The stream of rounds poured in relentlessly. Massive overkill—or maybe not depending on your personal view. When it came to fire support Lt. Gen. McKoy had long been a proponent of the principle, "Too much ain't enough."

A concept wholeheartedly endorsed by Raiding Forces.

From the angle Capt. Stirling had established his blocking position the blizzard of rounds from the two Thunderbolts flashed past directly to their front. Seemingly millions of bullets as big around as a cigar—those being the light caliber rounds, were slamming into the barracks tearing the place apart.

Each bullet broke the sound barrier as it cracked by. The noise, up this close and personal, was nothing at all like the sound any of the Rangers had ever experienced. A million firecrackers going off an inch from their ears.

The Tiger tank's 88s HE rounds kept slamming in and exploding doing massive structural damage.

Firing broke out from the blocking positions behind the barracks and to the far side. A few of the Nazis had somehow survived the initial burst of fire and were making a frenzied attempt to get away. There was no escape. Capt. Stirling had planned well. Illuminated by artificial light created by the flares overhead, the Nazis were shot down the instant they made a move.

As with Captain Billy Jack Jaxx's takedown of the 999th's bar this was a textbook example of a Raiding Forces style attack on a point-type target.

Gather intelligence on the objective, make a plan of action, issue a clear concise order, conduct a stealthy movement to contact. Then utilizing the element of surprise, bring force on force, concentrate the maximum amount of firepower on the target, light it up—let no one escape.

Lt. Gen. McKoy often voiced one of his hard learned principals of war, "Never give the opposition the opportunity to fight again another day".

Col. Randal adhered to the policy, "Never send a man where you can send a bullet."

Raiding Forces operators had their own thought: "Recon by fire."

Capt. Stirling put up a green flare and then a red that arched over it—end of mission.

There was pretty much nothing left of the barracks except a pile of rubble. The roof was down and the second story floor caved in. There were likely no survivors inside, but that remained to be seen.

Lt. Gen. McKoy said, "Those boys shoulda' stayed in prison."

COLONEL JOHN RANDAL SAID, “JACK.”

Captain Billy Jack Jaxx gave the order, “Lieutenant Mascuch—check fire.”

“CEASE FIRE!

While the initial burst of firing had commenced as one highly disciplined burst, the cease-fire was ragged. It took longer to convince everyone to stop shooting. The hostility between Raiding Forces and the German units they were facing in the Aegean had reached the boiling point. It had all added up—the executions, rapes, the abuse of the Greeks, the killings of the Vulnerable Points Wing men, Lieutenant Bentley St. Ledger and ten-year-old Lucas, and Major the Lady Jane Seaborn having to swim to Turkey with her dog.

Raiding Forces took the attack on Lady Jane personally…they were outraged.

"The First Rule is There Ain’t No Rules" had never been intended to advocate ignoring the rules of engagement for ground warfare. It was meant to encourage creativity where tactics were concerned and prevent Raiding Forces from getting bogged down in by-the-book constraints.

Until, that is, the Nazis had abandoned the Geneva Convention in the Aegean. Now Rule No. 1 was being interpreted to mean exactly what it said.

The troops wanted to get in a last burst or two. As long as another element was not preparing to maneuver that was fair enough with Col. Randal. He felt the same way.

Lieutenant Ricky Mascuch shouted, “CEASE FIRE” again.

Then Capt. Jaxx and Master Sergeant Mack Beckwith advanced across the street at a slow walk. They moved up carefully to the shot-out plate glass windows on either side of the door. Both men pulled the pin on a grenade and then tossed them inside.

WHUUUUUMP WHUUUUUMP

Two more followed.

WHUUUUUMP WHUUUUUMP

In the back of the building Captain Clint Hays kept his people in position for any late-breaking developments. King and Lieutenant Jake Novak hopped off the roof onto the street. Lt. Mascuch strolled across to inspect the results.

Around the side Private First Class Norvel "Horn Dog" Hansen moved up and stuck the barrel of his .30 Baby BAR through the shattered glass resting it on the window sill. Taking out a cigarette he surveyed the damage inside. Casualties littered the floor of the bar—men and women. Maybe forty-plus people all up by his rough count.

Col. Randal and King made entry and shot every Nazi in the head.

14
THROWING IN THE TOWEL

BRANDY SEABORN'S MAS BOAT WAS POUNDING toward Leros. They were nearly three hours behind schedule. Colonel John Randal was standing next to her on the bridge. Captain Penelope "Legs" Honeycutt-Parker was closed up behind in her MAS boat. The two craft were the only vessels making the trip. Lieutenant Randy "Hornblower" Seaborn's PT boat was still at Patmos guarding the entrance to the bay.

There was good reason to use the MAS boats tonight. The Kriegsmarine had seized quite a number of the torpedo boats from the Marina Regia when the Italians capitulated. Some MAS boat squadrons were continuing to serve with the Germans preferring the Nazis to the Allies. In addition, there were reports of incidents where MAS boat crews mutinied, killed their officers and went over to the Kriegsmarine.

So there was a very real possibility the German seaborne forces invading Leros might not see anything unusual about two Italian torpedo boats in the waters off the island. The plan was to land Col. Randal and his party then for Brandy's boat to go under camouflage while Capt. Honeycutt-Parker proceeded to another location to do the same thing.

This was not the original idea. But plans change. All things considered it was a risky move.

Current thinking was for Brandy to bring off as many members of the SBS and the LRDG as possible during daylight hours and transport them to Patmos—another calculated risk. From a different location Capt. Honeycutt-Parker would extract select personnel from A Company, 1st Battalion, King's Own Royal Regiment who had served in Strike Force at RAF Habbaniya.

Strike Force had been a local formation raised by Col. Randal recruited from men out of the1st KORR battalion flown in to help defend the RAF base during the Golden Square Rebellion. They had served well. And now he intended to bring as many of them out of harm's way as possible even though he had no authorization to do so.

The following night Veronica Paige's MI-9 caiques accompanied by Lieutenant Commander Adrian Seligman and Commander Andreas Londos aboard their caiques would follow the MAS boats from Patmos back to Leros. SBS and LRDG guides recruited from the men brought off during the initial extraction would be on board the caiques to direct them to predetermined pick-up points. The hope was to bring off 300 highly skilled operators from the two Special Operations units.

Originally the thought had been for Col. Randal, Major General James "Baldie" Taylor, and King to make the first trip, move inland, locate Lieutenant Colonel John "Jake" Easonsmith, LRDG, and Major the Earl Lord George Jellicoe, SBS and effect the immediate withdrawal of as many of their troops as possible on the first lift out. It was a plan held in secret between the two units and Raiding Forces. Col. Randal had decided on it and briefed the two Special Operations officers when he toured the island.

It is a military maxim that no plan survives the first shot. Col. Randal had not found that to always be true. However Raiding Forces, which frequently operated with limited advanced intelligence, quite often had plans bite the dust *before* the first shot was fired. That was where improvising and adapting came into play.

It paid to be flexible.

Upon learning there were no other German troops anywhere else on Patmos to neutralize, Captain Billy Jack Jaxx insisted he be allowed to accompany Col. Randal to Leros. As did Master Sergeant Mack Beckwith. The Sergeant Major viewed it his right to travel with the commanding officer at all times, period.

No ifs, ands or buts—non-negotiable.

Unfortunately the long-standing army tradition of the sergeant major always traveling with his commanding officer was not always observed 100% of the time in Raiding Forces. From time to time due to exigent circumstances the Sergeant Major was needed to fill a leadership position in a combat role or because Col. Randal was whisked away to someplace like Camp Mackall or OSS Headquarters in Washington.

Being thin on the ground following the Benevento drop, every Raiding Forces officer or NCO had to do his duty whether or not it strictly conformed to military occupational specialty, job description or ancient custom. And that included Raiding Forces' Sergeant Major though every effort was made to accord him the privilege whenever possible.

The former Raiding Forces senior NCO, Sergeant Major Mike "March or Die" Mikkalis, now one of the MI-9 caique skippers commanding the good ship *Santa Claus*, also decided to come along to Leros with Col. Randal. He did not know the first thing about being the master of a sailing vessel but he had always wanted to be a pirate. So when Raiding Forces moved to

Castelrozzo, Sgt. Maj. Mikkalis midnight requisitioned a Greek caique (which may not have been strictly legal) and press-ganged its owner to be his helmsman.

Veronica Paige gave him a job in MI-9 Escape.

No one ever claimed Sgt. Maj. Mikkalis was not a good problem solver.

Lieutenant Theodore Hamilton wanted to be included in the party as well but he made the mistake of saying so. That was where Col. Randal drew the line. Major the Lady Jane Seaborn was going to be less than thrilled when she found out he had let The Great Teddy expand his role on Patmos to the degree he had.

Maj. Gen. Taylor and King were aboard Capt. Honeycutt-Parker's boat. As they approached Leros it would break off to the last known location of the 1st Battalion, King's Own Royal Regiment on the northern portion of the central section of the island. King had been at RAF Habbaniya. He knew the Strike Force people Col. Randal wanted brought off. Maj. Gen. Taylor was along to pull rank when the inevitable objection of troops being withdrawn from the KORR in the middle of a battle was raised.

Capt. Honeycutt-Parker's new orders were to load her passengers immediately and return to Patmos independently at her own chosen speed—also high risk.

If anyone thought it odd Col. Randal and his party were traveling to Leros during a major German invasion complete with Kriegsmarine naval shore bombardments and continuous around-the-clock Luftwaffe airstrikes, they did not mention it.

He was going in to get his men and there was no stopping him.

The thing was, as Mandy Paige had pointed out, not all the troops knew they were his men and some, like the LRDG, had no real desire to be assigned to Raiding Forces.

One other strap-hanger was onboard—Private First Class Norvel "Horn Dog" Hansen.

MSgt. Beckwith arrived on the bridge with the private in tow.

"Sir, we have a stowaway."

Col. Randal said, "Let's hear it, Hansen."

"I was present when you were issuing your orders prior to sailing, Colonel. You assigned King a mission on the north part of the island. When Captain Jaxx requested to make the trip I knew you two would end up together somewhere sooner or later.

"I came along to pull your personal security, sir."

"All right then Horn Dog. In that case, I've got a job for you."

It had nothing to do with being a bodyguard.

IN THE DISTANCE, LEROS SWAM INTO SIGHT. AT FIRST it looked like the typical thunderstorm at sea with sudden flashes of lightning and the faint sound of thunder. That was an illusion. The flashes were Kriegsmarine naval gunfire and the thunder was the sound of bombs exploding.

As the MAS boats got closer streams of red tracers could be seen arching into the sky. The British used red while the Germans favored white and green. The glowing tracer rounds would stream into the sky seeming to be chasing each other then blink out like lightning bugs.

The sound of the battle became louder and louder. Kriegsmarine naval guns were being answered by Leros's primarily Italian-manned artillery. Strings of bombs went *WHUUUUMP, WHUUUUMP, WHUUUMP* accompanied by brilliant flashes very, very fast, like a string of flashbulbs.

Colonel John Randal knew from his previous inspection tour of Leros there was a fractured command structure on the island. Originally, the two senior officers were the Italian Regia Marina's Captain Luigi Mascherpa, and British Major General Frank Brittorous. The Italian requested through his chain of command that he be promoted in order that the British general would not outrank him.

And that was done.

Then Maj. Gen. Brittorous issued an order—an ultimatum, decreeing that he alone commanded all troops on Fortress Leros—British and Italian. His counterpart, the newly promoted Admiral Luigi Mascherpa, was offended. He refused direct contact with his counterpart. No longer on speaking terms with the Italians—having to deal with them through an intermediary, Maj. Gen. Brittorous also managed in short order to lose the confidence of the British officers and men under his command.

When the bombing started he would disappear for long periods of time. Into a cave? Like on Malta?

Finally, a senior officer was dispatched to GHQ Middle East ostensibly to give a report on the state of the island's preparations to resist invasion. In fact his assignment was to ask for Maj. Gen. Brittorous to be recalled.

And that was done.

As a result two things occurred, neither of which was a positive development. Brigadier Robert Tilney, an officer with limited infantry experience, assumed command. Admiral Mascherpa, who believed he was senior, refused to accept the indignity of reporting to an officer of a lower date of rank.

Communications between the British and Italian senior command, never good, broke down completely.

There was another serious problem unrelated to military politics. It only became apparent when the German amphibious landing force was approaching shore. The Italian coastal batteries proved incapable of hitting anything. If they had, the poorly executed German seaborne invasion would have been wiped out before it made it to the beach.

All parties British, Italian and German agreed on that assessment.

On the bridge of her MAS boat Brandy Seaborn said, “Sparks has been monitoring radio transmissions from Leros for the last twelve hours.”

Col. Randal said, “Give me a report.”

“Order, counter order and disorder.”

“What does that mean?”

“Brigadier Tilney has no idea what he is doing.”

“What makes you say that, Brandy?”

“The Brigadier is creating more problems than he is solving. Our units are ordered to attack an objective. They attack and capture it. Then they are ordered to withdraw only to be ordered to retake it again later.

“A significant amount of the traffic on the net is coming from commanding officers complaining no one at Leros Fortress Headquarters seems to know what the situation is or if they do—not passing on the information.”

Col. Randal valued her input. Brandy was not an alarmist. What she voiced was not an opinion.

It was a professional assessment not to be taken lightly.

Brandy said, “I realize I shall not be able to talk you out of anything John, but what you are planning is a bad idea. Leros has catastrophe written all over it. Father says it is a house of cards.”

Col. Randal said, “That’s what he told me.”

Brandy said, “I do not want you on the island when the cards fall down, handsome.”

Col. Randal said, “That makes two of us.”

The sounds coming from the island no longer resembled a thunderstorm. Astern Captain Penelope "Legs" Honeycutt-Parker broke away turning north on her independent mission.

The lookout reported an enemy ship off the starboard bow. Col. Randal immediately raised his Zeiss binoculars to study it. He saw a Kriegsmarine barge crammed with soldiers entering the same bay they were. Brandy ordered a reduction in speed not wanting to overtake the Germans, then swung in behind and followed the landing craft in.

Keeping station on an enemy boat intent on making an amphibious assault in the same vicinity the Raiding Forces party was planning to put ashore seemed a little over the top. Even for as convoluted a situation as they were sailing into. Col. Randal thought it was a gutsy move on Brandy's part.

The sights and sounds of the battle intensified.

Brandy's MAS boat was slated to make landfall below Rachi Ridge almost exactly halfway between the beaches of the two-pronged German seaborne invasion. The rugged strip between Gourna and Alimia bays was the narrowest point on the island.

Major the Earl Lord George Jellicoe's headquarters was in the area somewhere.

The Kriegsmarine landing craft curled away to a beach farther south. Brandy stood boldly on for a rocky promontory. The site was reasonably safe. No German amphibious troops would be landing anywhere nearby because of the terrain ashore—no beach, a near cliff to be negotiated.

After studying the surroundings Brandy was tempted to forgo camouflage netting and hide in plain sight. In the event the need arose the MAS boat could make a faster getaway without it.

She ran the idea past Col. Randal.

"Your call, Skipper."

"If we're spotted under camouflage after BMNT the game is up anyway."

"Good point."

"In that case we shall rely on 'confusion to the enemy' and 'the fog of war'—Father's favorite toasts."

Col. Randal said, "Works for me."

He trusted her judgment.

Captain Billy Jack Jaxx, Captain Butch "Headhunter" Hoolihan, Sergeant Major Mike "March or Die" Mikkalis, Master Sergeant Mack Beckwith and Private First Class Norvel "Horn Dog" Hansen gathered around Col. Randal to conduct last-minute coordination before going ashore.

"Sergeant Major, you'll remain here to establish the preboarding assembly point. Keep the men under tight control. Load when Brandy gives the word—you're in charge of the ground element."

"Roger, sir."

"Captain Jaxx, Captain Hoolihan, Sergeant Major Mikkalis and Private Hansen—you will accompany me to Major Jellicoe's HQ. The first contingent of SBS should be standing by ready to move to the boat. That's your job Hansen—to escort the troops back here to Sergeant Major Beckwith.

"Then return to pick up another group."

"Yes, sir."

"Brandy, as soon as you declare a max load for your MAS boat shove off for Patmos. Sergeant Major, you and Hansen will remain behind. We'll keep shuffling people down to you here at the AP for the next boatload.

"Is that clear?"

"Clear sir!"

"Sergeant Major, you'll need to select a hide as more troops come in. Since Brandy has elected not to put up her camouflage nets maybe you can use 'em. You don't want to attract any undue attention to this location."

"Roger, sir."

"Brandy, screen the evacuees as they board. We're only taking SBS and LRDG from this location—clear?"

"Understood."

"Questions?"

PFC Hansen said, "When do we extract, Colonel?"

"Last boat out tomorrow night or maybe the next."

Uh-oh, this mission was turning out to be a little hairier than Horn Dog bargained for.

ORIGINALLY THE IDEA WAS TO GO ASHORE AND hold in place until dawn before moving out to Major the Earl Lord George Jellicoe's SBS Command Post. Being behind schedule and landing with BMNT only thirty minutes away Colonel John Randal decided not to wait. There was a crooked finger running up the rugged incline that was almost directly on the azimuth they needed to travel. After setting the course on the bezel ring of his U.S. Army-issue lensatic compass they moved out.

Order of march was Captain Billy Jack Jaxx, Col. Randal, Captain Butch "Headhunter" Hoolihan, Sergeant Major Mike "March or Die" Mikkalis, and Private First Class Norvel "Horn Dog" Hansen. They moved in single file as dictated by the narrowness of the steep terrain feature. The finger had vertical drop-offs on either side. The patrol had only traveled a few yards working their way up the incline when they came upon the canopy of a Webrmacht-issue RZ-20 parachute laying on the ground. It was wet and had not deployed—a full-on Roman Candle, which are rare.

German paratroops do not utilize reserves.

A Fallschirmjäger lay dead in his harness.

The patrol halted while Capt. Jaxx searched the German for documents. Then they began moving again. As he came by PFC Hansen scooped up the man's 9mm Walther P-38.

The Nazi was otherwise unarmed.

Fallschirmjägers dropped their primary weapons in door bundles or wing-mounted canisters.

This late in the war, Col. Randal thought the Nazis would have learned better. German generals were widely advertised to be the world's most brilliant military strategists. Some claimed them to be the best tacticians. But they were not infallible. Dropping paratroopers into battle equipped only with sidearms and making them search for their primary weapons dropped separately in canisters—what British Airborne Forces called a "container light equipment" or CLEs—was worse than command malfeasance.

It was murder.

The patrol moved on for a short distance when a pistol shot rang out off the right side downhill approximately ten yards down the slope. Everyone dropped to the ground except Col. Randal.

He spotted the muzzle flash.

Instinctively, the 9mm Beretta MAB-38 snapped to his shoulder like one of the bespoke shotguns Beretta was famous for. Also like a Beretta's over and under sporting gun the SMG had two triggers. The front trigger was semi-auto. The second full auto.

The second full auto trigger was serrated. The shooter could know by touch which one he was about to engage. The serrations were a custom feature lost on most users in the stress of a firefight.

But not Col. Randal.

He had carried a Beretta MAB-38 from his first days in Abyssinia.

As the SMG came up Col. Randal's finger instinctively went to the serrated trigger strictly by reflex. He unleashed a short crisp burst of three rounds. No more pistol shots were heard.

Capt. Jaxx moved out again.

Traveling up the narrow finger they passed six more abandoned RZ-20 parachutes—arguably the worst military parachute ever adopted by any army worldwide. For reasons unknown prior to the war the Germans copied the RZ-20 from the Italians. Two more dead Nazi paratroopers were encountered both with wet canopies that failed to deploy.

There had to be a story behind the wet parachutes but Col. Randal had no idea what it could be.

Had the Fallschirmjägers packed their chutes outside on an airstrip and been caught in a rainstorm? Jumping a wet canopy was clearly a bad idea—lesson noted and learned.

Once on top the ground gradually started to level out. The sky was beginning to lighten. Now the crackle of small arms fire could be heard in the distance.

Col. Randal instructed Capt. Jaxx to veer left to bring him back on azimuth. Land navigation, while moving in the direction of an ongoing firefight, when you do not know the exact location of the friendly or enemy forces in your direction of march is not something to be undertaken lightly.

At this point Col. Randal knew the invasion of Leros was not a big battle. He was hearing small meeting-type engagements that flared up briefly then died away. Only to have another similar contact take place a few minutes later somewhere else.

It was not what he had expected.

The Germans were engaging or being engaged as they moved inland when and where they were encountered by individuals or small groups of defenders. Missing was a major ground attack by the Germans who seemed to have mismanaged the initial phases of their invasion. Also missing was a coordinated counterattack by the British who were clearly mismanaging the defense.

The defenders were failing to capitalize on their superior numbers.

Like Brandy said, that could mean a lack of central command and control.

The ability to interpret battle sounds is a fundamental skill that only comes from combat experience. Not everyone can do it and the subject cannot be taught. Military schools do not even try. But after more than six years of war Col. Randal could "read" a battlefield from a distance almost as well as if he were physically present.

The lack of a rapid counterattack was a serious tactical error.

In Col. Randal's opinion the best place to stop an amphibious landing is at the water's edge when the invaders are at their weakest. The way to accomplish that was for the defending commander to marshal his forces and launch an immediate counterattack with everything he had. An all-out battle should be in progress on the landing beaches.

That was not happening.

Similarly, paratroops, especially Germans, are most vulnerable the moment they touch down because Fallschirmjägers jump armed only with sidearms. They should never be allowed to recover their primary weapons. Or given the opportunity to assemble.

There was no sign of any organized response to the enemy drop.

What Col. Randal was hearing did not make military sense. There had been months to prepare for the invasion everyone knew was coming. Why no counteroffensive?

A pistol shot rang out then Capt. Jaxx fired a burst from his .30 Baby BAR. Col. Randal shifted slightly to see around him and observed a dead Nazi paratrooper on the ground gripping a 9mm Walther P-38. A bone was sticking out of the Fallschirmjäger's left leg through his pants above the knee pad.

The result of a PLF gone wrong.

The awkward face-first belly-buster descent German paratroops had to make, due to the poor design of their RZ-20 parachute harnesses, forced them to wear heavy-duty elbow and knee pads. Not only did German paratroopers come down face first but then they had to execute a forward roll PLF—which could not be easy.

Col. Randal did not know that for sure having never made one—with no intention of ever intentionally trying.

Capt. Jaxx said, "Takes a tough hombre to be a Fallschirmjäger, sir."

"Roger that."

The dead German was wearing a 1st Battalion Fallschirmjäger Regiment, 22 Air Landing Division shoulder insignia. The division was primarily a glider outfit stationed on Crete with a reputation for brutality against civilians. Its commander, General Friedrich-Wilhelm Müller, was known as the "Butcher of Crete." He was the man who had ordered the execution of the Italian officers on Kos.

The division contained one regiment of paratroopers totaling approximately 1,500 men. Except for a company-sized Brandenburger unit flown in from Italy for the invasion of Kos they constituted the only German parachute troops in the Aegean.

From his map study of the island and knowledge of enemy forces in theatre Col. Randal knew the airborne operation underway could not be large in scale. Due to the rugged nature of the terrain on Leros there were no suitable sites for major glider landings. So slightly more than 1,500 Fallschirmjägers were all that were ever going to be dropping on the island.

Col. Randal had read Brigadier Tilney's Enemy Threat Assessment. He knew the general was not anticipating any German airborne assault. That was a mistake. A drop had taken place on Kos only thirty miles away.

Unknown to Col. Randal, because he was not cleared to know the source of the intelligence, an Ultra Secret Enigma radio intercept outlining the details of a jump to include the 22nd Air Landing Divisions timetable had been provided to Brig. Tilney.

He chose to ignore it.

While 1,500 Fallschirmjägers were not enough to influence the outcome of the battle in any major way they could be disruptive. Worse, the visual effect German paratroopers had on the British and Italian defender's morale could not be overstated.

It was a shock.

As the sky lightened, a grim sight at the top of the ridge came into view. Dead Fallschirmjägers from yesterday's drop littered the ground. Some were dangling from trees still in their parachutes. They had been shot by the SBS/LRDG Mobile Reserve Force (MRF) commanded by Captain Alan Redfern, recently arrived from the fighting on Kos.

Typical of the state of disorganization on Leros, the island's MRF consisted of a mere twenty-four men. The Germans dropped almost on top of them. From the look of things the tiny band of SBS operators had fought back with everything they had. The Fallschirmjägers paid a heavy price for their choice of drop zones.

So did the British. Captain Redfern was killed.

Col. Randal gave Capt. Jaxx another azimuth correction.

The patrol traveled approximately a quarter of a mile before they heard the command, "Halt!"

Not knowing the challenge and/or countersign, Capt. Jaxx instantly responded, "Raiding Forces—Colonel Randal."

Captain Anders Lassen, SBS, now in command of the MRF said, "Who are you trying to fool, Fritz? You are not bloody Colonel Randal."

Not good.

It was lucky the MRF had not opened fire.

Col. Randal said, "Well I am. We're here to pull you men off of Leros. Stand down."

"In that case advance and be recognized—carefully now."

Capt. Lassen recognized Col. Randal by sight. After Plans Division failure to find suitable maritime targets the SBS was attached to the SAS. Until the Special Air Service was broken up following Colonel David Stirling's capture.

SBS operators had participated in a number of gun jeep patrols in conjunction with Raiding Forces.

Col. Randal said, "What happened here, Captain?"

Capt. Lassen said, "Germans parachuted in late yesterday, sir. Landed right in front of us. We enjoyed what you Yanks call a turkey shoot."

"I can see that."

"The Boche moved off southeast in the direction of Brigadier Tilney's Command Post," Capt. Lassen said. "With any luck they will find it—one can only hope, sir."

He sounded like he meant it.

Having studied every document U.S. and British intelligence could provide on German Generaloberst Kurt Student, Chief of German Airborne Troops, Col. Randal knew one of his techniques for assembly after a combat parachute drop was what he called the "Ink Spot Method."

Fallschirmjägers were dropped with the expectation the jump would be scattered. Then little groups of paratroopers—"ink spots," would band together and keep on banding together until there would eventually be one big pool.

That was likely what the Germans were attempting to do.

The concept was similar to what Col. Randal had recommended to the Swing Board but not exactly the same . . . he was looking for a different result—preplanned chaos.

But there was no question . . . the Ink Spot Method worked.

Capt. Lassen said, "The bloody Cheshire's had a company here with us. The sight of the German parachutists must have reminded their CO of pressing business elsewhere. He ordered a retrograde movement of his troops without bothering to fire a shot.

Col. Randal said, "Where can I find Major Jellicoe?"

Capt. Lassen said, "The Major anticipated you would be coming, Colonel. He went to bring in some of our people positioned to the north of here by order of bloody Fortress Leros Command."

Col. Randal said, "Can you reach him by radio?"

"Negative, sir, our communications are in shambles."

Col. Randal said, "Did the Major brief you on the plan to extract the SBS?"

Capt. Lassen said, "That he did sir. When the invasion began Major Jellicoe sent out runners with the prearranged code for all detachment leaders and their troops to rally on SBS HQ. Like I said he went in search of some of our men who have been with the KORR."

In the distance the sound of Luftwaffe airstrikes and Kriegsmarine naval gunfire intensified as they were talking.

Sporadic return artillery fire could be heard. Compared to the furious German bombardment the British and Italian response sounded uninspiring.

Col. Randal said, "Captain Hoolihan, you go with Captain Lassen to SBS headquarters and start shuttling people to this location—this is the Initial Assembly/Release Point.

"Sergeant Major Mikkalis, you're in charge of the extraction from here. Organize the groups into small parties and send 'em down to Sergeant Major Beckwith with Hansen. Don't overload him all at once."

"Sir!"

Capt. Hoolihan said, "Where will you be, Colonel?"

"Captain Jaxx and I are going to locate Major Jellicoe."

"Sir, that is not . . ."

Col. Randal said, "The invasion is gaining momentum, Butch. With Tilney's lack of an urgent response to the landings things on Leros are about to get complicated fast. We don't have time to waste."

"Yes, sir."

"Captain Lassen, I'm putting you in charge of making sure all your people report in to SBS HQ for extraction. I don't want any SBS or LRDG personnel left behind. If there's any problem, Captain Hoolihan's senior.

"Is that clear?"

"It is, sir."

"Horn Dog repeat these orders I'm about to give you back to me."

"Yes, sir, Colonel."

"Guide these Mobile Reserve Force personnel down to Sergeant Major Beckwith's holding position. They are to board immediately. You inform Mrs. Seaborn I said to sail when as many people are loaded as her boat can carry at speed—clear?

"Clear, sir—I guide the SBS down to the boat. The Sergeant Major's to load 'em up. Mrs. Seaborn's to head for Patmos as soon as she determines she's full but not overloaded."

Col. Randal said, "Tell her to bring both MAS boats and all the caiques back to this location tonight. It's now the Primary Extraction Point. Is that clear?"

"Clear, sir—Mrs. Seaborn's to bring all boats back here tonight. This is the Primary Extraction Point."

This was a change of mission—having all the boats assemble at one location. Col. Randal had learned the hard way when sending a verbal message it was always a good idea to have the messenger repeat it back before letting him go dashing off.

Sometimes in the heat of the moment the response came back garbled beyond recognition."

PFC Hansen said to the first group of four SBS operators, "Follow me, men."

COLONEL JOHN RANDAL AND CAPTAIN BILLY JACK Jaxx moved out for Mount Appetici where elements of the 1st Battalion King's Own Royal Regiment were reported to be located. The idea was not to go all the way to the mountain but to use it as a navigational reference point. At a certain place to be determined they would break off and travel down to the battalion command post located on the coast where it was thought Major the Earl Lord George Jellicoe might be found.

At the present time there had not been either a German seaborne landing or a parachute drop in the northern quadrant of the center section of the island. A Company, the KORR unit the Habbaniya Strike Force had been drawn from, was believed to be in a position overlooking the bay where Captain "Legs"

Honeycutt-Parker's MAS boat should have docked by now. There were too many uncertainties for Col. Randal to feel completely confident about being able to locate Major Lord Jellicoe in the time he had to work with.

If only one operator was brought off Leros it needed to be the SBS commander.

Col. Randal and Capt. Jaxx traveled approximately three miles cross-country. Luckily they found an abandoned track heading in the right direction. The two were making good time across the rough terrain.

Ju-87 Stuka dive bombers could be seen working over targets in the distance but not much was going on in the direction they were moving. The air offensive was focused primarily around Portolano and the two Nazi landing beaches. In those places the sound of bombing interspersed with naval gunfire was continuous.

Col. Randal and Capt. Jaxx were making their way toward Rachi Ridge when a flight of four enemy Ju-87 Stuka dive bombers swept over low coming in from the southwest. They were spraying machine gun fire indiscriminately as they came. Right behind were six lumbering Ju-52 transports with paratroops spilling out.

It happened so quickly there was no time to react.

Unknown to Col. Randal and Capt. Jaxx they were under observation by Maj. Lord Jellicoe from a position on the military crest of the ridge 100 yards away. His SBS operators and a platoon of the 1st Battalion King's Own Royal Rifles attached to him began engaging the Fallschirmjägers.

Their gunfire was the first indication British troops were in the area.

The immediate problem for Col. Randal and Capt. Jaxx was a German stick of paratroopers exiting their aircraft directly over their heads. Something made out of camouflage material appeared under the fuselage of the Junkers troop transport. It billowed out into a giant mushroom beneath which the figure of a Nazi dangling down looked small and helpless. On came the rest of the Fallschirmjägers charging the door—fifteen in total.

The Germans dived out head first, hands outstretched, which was the technique Fallschirmjägers employed because of the configuration of the RZ-20 parachute's risers being connected to the parachute's harness in the small of the back.

The worst of all possible designs.

The jump took place so fast Col. Randal and Capt. Jaxx did not have time to take cover. Caught in the open there was no option for them but to stand their ground and fire on the enemy parachutists descending directly above them.

The Fallschirmjägers were ridiculously easy targets.

Because of the mountainous terrain the Junkers pilots were not able to fly as low as they would have liked. The winds coming in off the Aegean were gusting in excess of the 13-knot maximum generally recommended for parachute operations. And for reasons of their own the Ju-52s were not flying a tight formation.

As a result most of the drop was widely dispersed.

The stick that had exited directly over their heads was not. It was in a tight compact formation.

Col. Randal fired short crisp bursts from his Beretta MAB-38, aiming carefully using the smooth semiautomatic trigger—taking his time in hurry—the way Lieutenant General "Geronimo" McKoy preached. Every third round in the magazine was a tracer making getting on target simple. The Fallschirmjägers were well within the range of his 9mm Beretta M-38 from the moment they exited the aircraft.

Capt. Jaxx had his .30 Baby BAR to his shoulder—also firing with the weapons selector switch on semiautomatic, coolly transitioning from target to target. It was a lot like shooting doves coming in to a stock tank. You had to pick a single target—not fire at the flock. Only doves flew faster and were a lot smaller target.

The trick to hitting the Fallschirmjägers was to lead them low but not by much.

The math was simple: a parachutist falls approximately twenty feet per second. Due to the terrain the Germans were jumping at about 1,000 feet maybe less. Which meant Col. Randal and Capt. Jaxx did not have much time to kill all fifteen Fallschirmjägers.

Not that either of them was thinking about arithmetic.

In progress all around in every direction was what appeared to be a company-sized drop. The Luftwaffe transport pilots made a bad job of it. The jump was not helped by the breeze that gusted in from the Aegean from time to time.

One stick landed in the sea.

Firing was constant all along the ridge line. Streams of red tracers crisscrossed the sky. As the initial paralyzing psychological impact of the sight of German paratroopers wore off, Maj. Lord Jellicoe's men began fighting for all they were worth.

The Fallschirmjägers had jumped into a death trap.

Instead of an assembly area the DZ became a kill zone. Some jumpers were hit in the air. A few were ensnared in trees and shot as they hung in their harness. Others were drug by parachutes that did not collapse due to the gusting wind.

One Nazi became entangled in a power line dangling down like a puppet.

This was such an inviting target . . . almost all the defenders on the ridge shifted their fire to concentrate on him.

Lowering his binoculars, Maj. Lord Jellicoe shouted, "He's dead you bloody fools! Shift your fires!"

The SBS commander's troops were badly outnumbered. At least initially. So it was imperative to kill as many of the Nazis as possible before they were able to reach their equipment containers, recover their primary weapons and get organized. No one wanted the Germans to be able to fight back.

In the middle of the DZ, while continuing to fire, Capt. Jaxx edged over until he and Col. Randal were more or less standing back-to-back. Raiding Forces were used to being surrounded. But nothing like this.

Col. Randal's 40-round magazine clicked on empty as a Fallschirmjäger was burning in almost directly on top of him. Since he had been counting his rounds fired it was no surprise. In addition he always loaded tracers for the last three to visually alert him he was out. With no time to reload he dropped the submachine gun, to draw one of his Colt. 38 Supers.

A German coming down right on top of him. Because of the awkward prone position the German was forced to assume after his parachute deployed Col. Randal was staring him straight in the face as he was coming down. The enraged Nazi looked like he wanted to tear him apart with his bare hands—the man had blue eyes.

Col. Randal pulled the trigger at the range of about two feet. He had to step aside to avoid being hit by the jumper's body when it slammed into the ground. It was so close he became entangled in the RZ-20 parachute's lines when the chute collapsed.

Now both Colt 38 Supers were out.

Parachutes kept descending.

Behind him Capt. Jaxx was firing steadily carefully calling his shots.

Col. Randal shot a Fallschirmjäger who landed right in front of him with one of his pistols at point blank range.

Then shot another attempting to do one of their acrobatic front roll PLFs off to the side with his other pistol. Col. Randal was experiencing the familiar out-of-body sensation. Events he knew were happening lightning fast seemed to be taking place in slow motion.

His vision was enhanced.

Sounds were not having much effect. He was not really paying attention to them.

With no time to deliberate, Col. Randal was in a rhythm acquiring targets and shooting. But even though he was in a hurry to engage one and move on to another it did not feel like he was rushing his shots.

Parachutes and jumpers were swirling around.

A Nazi landed face first and Capt. Jaxx shot him with the last round in his magazine which he had also loaded with a tracer to be a visual signal. Without looking down he changed magazines on his .30 Baby BAR never taking his eyes off the sky—exactly like a dove hunter.

Col. Randal turned and shot a Nazi who crashed in behind Capt. Jaxx, almost between them—the fight was close and fast.

The firing from the ridge intensified. The SBS/LRDG and King's Own were over the initial shock. Now they were fighting hard to kill as many German paratroopers as possible, as fast as they could. Maj. Lord Jellicoe had his men under tight control. His troops were putting out highly effective small arms fire.

Aimed—not "spray and pray."

One of the Ju-52 transports, caught in a vector of red tracers streamed a contrail of white smoke, winged over, crashed and exploded.

With no more Fallschirmjägers landing in their immediate vicinity, Col. Randal and Capt. Jaxx went to ground. The only cover immediately available was in a shallow ditch barely deep enough to put them in defilade. But beggars could not be choosers. With Maj. Lord Jellicoe's people blazing away this was no time to be standing around above ground risking being taken for Germans.

Capt. Jaxx said, "Nobody's ever going to believe our story—wing shooting Nazis. How many did you get, sir?"

Col. Randal said, "I have no idea."

Capt. Jaxx said, "Don't ever let anyone talk us into making a daylight combat jump, sir."

Col. Randal said, "Roger—hold that thought, Captain.

Dead and wounded Fallschirmjägers littered the DZ, some hung from trees in the distance shot in their harnesses, the riddled jumper entangled in the power lines was still dangling, others were being dragged by their parachutes across rough ground and over rocks. The few Germans who landed unscathed were making frenzied attempts to extricate themselves from their parachutes before being chopped down by streams of red tracers.

The constant volume of fire from the ridge continued undiminished.

Three Fallschirmjägers, desperate to recover their weapons from the containers, ran by chasing a CLE being dragged by its parachute. Before Col. Randal could engage a burst from one of the King's Own tripod-mounted .303 Vickers Medium Machine guns cut them down.

Capt. Jaxx said, "How many bad guys do you estimate dropped, sir?"

Col. Randal said, “Seemed like a million —couldn’t have been more than a company.”

Capt. Jaxx said, “It’s a good thing we didn’t do anything stupid, Colonel.”

Col. Randal said, “You mean like invading a place that’s being invaded.”

Capt. Jaxx said, “So much for slipping ashore covertly, retrieving our people and sneaking back out with no one the wiser. Want to make God smile? Have a plan, sir.”

Jack Cool.

PRIVATE FIRST CLASS NORVEL “HORN DOG” HANSEN was leading the third group of Special Boat Section men down the bluff to Brandy Seaborn’s MAS boat. There were four men in the party. The idea was to keep the numbers small in hopes of not drawing attention to the extraction in progress. There was no Kriegsmarine naval activity in the immediate area but the Luftwaffe ruled the sky.

PFC Hansen led the men down the razor-sharp switchback finger. It was tougher going down than coming up. One misstep and you could find yourself pitching off the side in for a long fall. The unstable footing did not make things any easier. The SBS were eager to get off the island. They were used to taking the fight to the enemy on their own terms not being in a line infantry defensive battle.

The idea of becoming a POW did not sit well with them.

The way the process worked PFC Hansen led the troops down to where Master Sergeant Mack Beckwith had organized an assembly point. Once they arrived the Sergeant Major took charge of the group. He was responsible for holding them in place until such time as Brandy gave the word for the men to load aboard the MAS boat.

The assignment was not the bodyguard work Horn Dog had in mind when he stowed away. The trips up and down the hill were hard work. The goal was to extract approximately 300 SBS and LRDG personnel. Three hundred divided by four men per trip equaled seventy-five trips. And that was only counting one way.

Multiplied by two he was looking at a big number. PFC. Hansen was not good with math word problems. He made a couple of incorrect fundamental assumptions that skewed the numbers. However, Horn Dog was correct in calculating that he was going to have to make a lot of trips up and down that narrow switchback.

Coming from behind heading out to sea two Ju-87s flew directly overhead at low level strafing as they passed. The Stuka was a dive bomber but it did carry two 7.92mm machine guns in the wings and another pair for the rear-facing gunner in the back. While this was anemic firepower when compared to a P-38 Lightning or a Supermarine Spitfire, getting shot at by eight machine guns from an altitude of twenty-five feet did not offer anything to recommend the experience.

One second the column was moving along; the next it was down in a hail of machine gun fire with the four SBS men wounded. PFC Hansen searched himself frantically but he could not find any signs of an entrance or exit wound. He was pretty sure that was impossible.

Each of those machine guns had a cyclic rate of 1,200 rounds per minute. Each one fired so fast that the sound of the gunfire was like cloth being ripped. There was no way he was not hit.

He checked again—not a scratch.

None of the SBS men were dead. One was ambulatory. The other two had wounds of varying degrees of seriousness. No one appeared to be bleeding out but that could be deceiving.

Horn Dog knew this was a mass casualty event. The kind doctors describe as a triage situation. That meant he was going to have to make a hard decision with no time for second guessing.

If there were any good options he could not think of what they might be.

PFC Hansen told the wounded SBS operator who was able to walk, "I'm going to carry the gut shot guy down the hill. We need to get him medical attention fast. While I'm gone you start patching up these other two.

"I'll be back."

The problem was the most seriously wounded SBS operator was bigger than PFC Hansen. There was nothing to be done about that. He stood up, hoisted the man across his shoulders in a fireman's carry, nearly buckled under the weight, then started staggering downhill trying hard not to fall.

The Sergeant Major's assembly point was a long way down.

After only a few steps Horn Dog was reasonably sure he did not have 150 trips like this one in him—he might not have this one.

What seemed a lifetime later, PFC Hansen stumbled into the AP and collapsed. In an attempt to revive him, MSgt. Beckwith poured water in his face from a canteen.

"Why didn't you shout for help, Horn Dog?"

"Don't know, Sergeant Major. I was in a blackout."

Alerted a casualty had arrived at the assembly point Brandy dispatched her medical rating ashore then came to check on the wounded SAS operator for herself.

When the Sergeant Major was able to sort out the details of what had happened he took off up the bluff at a dead run. Horn Dog struggled off the ground and lurched after him. He had to crawl part way up the steepest parts.

The SBS men in the party were his responsibility—Col. Randal was counting on him.

CAPTAIN BUTCH “HEADHUNTER” HOOLIHAN AND Captain Anders Lassen split up and went in search of Special Boat Section and Long Range Desert Group operators to bring to the SBS Headquarters to assemble for extraction. The initial phase of locating them went relatively smoothly. Both Lieutenant Colonel John “Jake” Easonsmith and Major the Earl Lord George Jellicoe had briefed their troops on what to do once the invasion started—move to the AP at SBS HQ.

Groups of men were encountered making their way there.

Capt. Hoolihan came upon a party of LRDG who were the bearers of bad news. Lt. Col. Easonsmith had been killed. Now command of the unit fell on Major Lloyd Owen. The problem was he was not on the island.

Capt. Hoolihan said, “Where is Major Owen?”

Corporal Maynard Plimken said, “Somewhere off the coast of Turkey in a caique attempting to keep in touch by radio, sir.”

“Who is in command here?”

“I am not sure Dunkirk was more organized than this show, sir.”

The farther south Capt. Hoolihan traveled the more intense the sounds of fighting became. Swarms of Ju-87 dive bombers were everywhere, strafing and bombing everything that moved.

From what he was seeing it was clear the Germans had established a lodgment ashore and were attempting to build it up.

Capt. Hoolihan and his guide came to the top of a hill and straight ahead spotted what he estimated to be a company of German infantry heading inland. In the distance, other Nazi troops were on the move. The invasion was gaining momentum.

No officer in Raiding Forces was more experienced than the Headhunter. His orders were to rescue certain special operations personnel. Not get captured.

He made a command decision.

There was nothing more to be done here.

COLONEL JOHN RANDAL, MAJOR THE EARL LORD George Jellicoe and Captain Billy Jack Jaxx arrived at 1st Battalion, King's Own Royal Regiment Headquarters. Major General James "Baldie" Taylor and King were there. The battalion commander was absent having gone to inspect one of his companies following the German parachute landing.

That made their mission easier. He was not present to object. Thirty-three men who had served in the Habbaniya Strike Force were assembled. Col. Randal was pleased to see the unit's former commanding officer Major Valentine Fabian—he had been promoted.

Col. Randal said, "Get your Strike Force people onboard Captain Honeycutt-Parker's boat, Major."

"Sir, I . . ."

"Do it now. That's an order. I want you on board as well."

Captain Penelope "Legs" Honeycutt-Parker had been at Habbaniya during the siege. She greeted Maj. Fabian and his men like long-lost friends. With the eighteen SBS and LRDG operators Maj. Lord Jellicoe had with him it was going to be a tight fit.

Col. Randal and Maj. Gen. Taylor held a brief discussion.

Maj. Gen. Taylor said, "You need to come out now, Colonel. With German paratroopers scattered between here and SBS HQ and the possibility of an additional seaborne landing, it is entirely too dangerous for you to be moving cross country at this point."

King said, "He's right, Chief."

Col. Randal said, "I know."

He was not happy.

Capt. Honeycutt-Parker wasted no time putting to sea. Tarps were broken out to conceal the troops on deck in the event of a flyover by the Luftwaffe. Exhausted from five days of constant airstrikes and fighting, the men lay down and went to sleep.

Making the run to Patmos in broad daylight was a risk but then so was waiting for dark. The MAS boat was screaming across the sea at maximum speed with Capt. Honeycutt-Parker at the helm. Col. Randal was standing next to her in the cockpit, not pleased about leaving his Raiding Forces people behind.

Sparks came up from below. "Mrs. Seaborn reports she has departed Leros with forty-three PAX—four of them wounded who require medical attention, Skipper."

Capt. Honeycutt-Parker said, "Keep me informed of any other incoming messages."

Before Sparks could acknowledge the order, the lookout on the stern called out, "Enemy aircraft Red one-three-five degrees!"

In the Royal Navy "Red" meant left—or port side.

Col. Randal wheeled around and spotted a pair of Ju-87 Stukas up high dropping into an attack run. Parker glanced over her shoulder. Apparently these two Nazi pilots did not consider they might be attacking a friendly Regia Marina craft loyal to Germany. Or maybe they did not like Italians.

Capt. Honeycutt-Parker had antiaircraft machine guns bristling all over the MAS boat, but its main armament was the Elco Mk 15 Thunderbolt mount with its six M2 Browning .50 caliber machine guns and four .20mm Oerlikon fast-firing cannon. The problem was the Thunderbolt could not be elevated to be used in an air defense.

The Stukas dive sirens were screaming. The planes were coming straight down at a 90-degree angle, 500 to 600 miles per hour.

Col. Randal shouted, "Out from under the tarps, men. Stand by to commence fire on my command!"

The troops wasted no time complying with the order.

The Stukas' dive sirens were earsplitting terror weapons designed to strike fear into the hearts of those about to be bombed. It would be fair to say there was a certain amount of trepidation onboard the MAS boat.

Capt. Honeycutt-Parker said, "Order the men not to stand up, John. We are in for a wild ride."

"Everybody down—sitting position only!"

Capt. Jaxx arrived in the cockpit with his .30 Baby BAR he had stashed in Capt. Honeycutt- Parker's cabin when he came onboard.

"No problem Colonel the Ju-87 is obsolete."

"Somebody needs to tell that to the Luftwaffe."

Capt. Honeycutt-Parker pushed a button activating a series of loud whoops.

Every sailor manning a machine gun commenced fire. There was no need for Col. Randal to give the order to the passengers. The men were already blazing away at the lead Stuka.

When the plane looked close enough for its prop to give them a haircut, Capt. Honeycutt-Parker chopped the motor. No one was expecting that. The MAS boat did not exactly come to a screeching halt but it did dramatically reduce speed.

Parker put the helm all the way over hard to starboard and went to full speed ahead. It was a good thing no one on deck was up on their feet. The MAS boat seemed to stand on its side powering into the turn.

The lead Stuka was at the point of releasing its bombs when she made the maneuver but now the pilot realized he was going to overshoot his target. He corrected. A Ju-87 can dive at 90 degrees, straight down, but that is as far as it can go.

It cannot do 91 degrees.

The plane crashed where the boat would have been. The Ju-87 made a sickening metallic-sounding *WHOOOOOMP!*

Then was swallowed by the sea leaving a circle of foam.

The sailors shifted their machine gun fire to the second Stuka. The troops on deck followed suit shouting and blazing away as fast as they could operate their weapons. Tracers were seen striking the dive bomber but to no effect.

Even so the pilot had to be disheartened by the turn of events. He pickled his bombs early, pulled out of the dive and turned for home. Twin explosions erupted twenty yards away off the starboard bow blowing up fifty-foot geysers of seawater.

All they killed were fish.

Capt. Jaxx said, "I think I got a piece of him."

Col. Randal said, "Nice job, Legs."

He had never called her that before—to her face.

WHEN THE MAS BOAT ENTERED THE PROTECTED harbor at Patmos, Brandy Seaborn was already there unloading her contingent of troops. Lieutenant Theodore Hamilton was on hand standing by to put up her boat's camouflage. She waved him off.

"I shall be making a quick turnaround, Lieutenant."

Colonel John Randal noticed the Black Cat under netting not far away. The Catalina was not supposed to be there. Neither was Major the Lady Jane Seaborn.

She was at the dock when Parker pulled in.

When Col. Randal stepped off the MAS boat the two acted like they barely knew each other—as usual in public. To say he was displeased Lady Jane was on Patmos would have been a major understatement—but trying not to show it.

Vice Admiral Sir Randolph "Razor" Ransom walked up.

He was not supposed to be there either.

VAdm. Ransom said, "After you took off for Leros Jane had one of the Special Duties pilots at RFHQ fly Dr. Milam and a surgical team to Castelrozzo. As soon as the Catalina arrived back from making your drop Beverly and Pam had the plane refueled. We loaded aboard and flew back here to Patmos.

"Jane insisted on coming."

"I see."

Lady Jane gifted him one of her best-grade heart-attack smiles—she knew how to deal with him.

Major General James "Baldie" Taylor walked over with Lieutenant General "Geronimo" Joe McKoy.

VAdm. Ransom said, "Give me a report."

Maj. Gen. Taylor said, "Fortress Leros Headquarters has lost control of the battle. Communications between the maneuver elements of the 234th Brigade have completely broken down. The Italians are not fighting with any enthusiasm. Subordinate commanders are openly complaining about not being kept informed of developments.

"Need I continue Admiral?"

Coming from a senior MI-6 intelligence officer whose specialty was evaluating the military capability of foreign armies—allied, neutral and enemy—this was a damning analysis.

Col. Randal said, "Except for the Italians our troops are fighting hard, Admiral . . ."

Maj. Gen. Taylor said, "We outnumber the Nazis at least three to one but Brigadier Tilney has proven incapable of taking advantage of the lopsided odds in our favor."

VAdm. Ransom said, "For your information, gentlemen, Tilney has asked the Germans for terms."

Col. Randal said, "Giving up?"

VAdm. Ransom said, "Incredible as it sounds our signals intelligence people intercepted a communique from General Müller to his on-scene commanders discussing plans to evacuate their troops—the Germans believe they are losing the battle."

Capt. Jaxx said, "Throwing in the towel—that's crazy, sir."

Maj. Gen. Taylor said, "A national disgrace—a mistake to have placed Tilney in command."

Lt. Gen. McKoy said, "You couldn't make this up."

Col. Randal said, "I've got to go back . . ."

VAdm. Ransom said, "Negative Colonel—Brandy and Parker shall be returning to bring our Raiding Forces people out. You stand down.

"That is an order."

"Sir . . ."

VAdm. Ransom said, "I am not risking Small Raids Inc.'s Deputy Commander on a lost cause.

Leros is an MI-9 Escape operation now—the ball is in Mrs. Paige's court."

"Sir, I'd like you to reconsider."

VAdm. Ransom said, "I do not believe you fully comprehend the consequences of Fortress Leros surrendering, Colonel. Now Castelrozzo is the only island remaining in our possession. Odds are ABC shall have to be evacuated as well.

"We lost the war in the Aegean today."

~ ~

THE MISSION CONTINUES IN

–ECONOMY OF FORCE –

BOOK XVI IN THE RAIDING FORCES SERIES

COMING SOON

~ ~

The Raiding Forces series continues all the way to VE Day.
To be on our notification list for the next book, contact
phil@philward.com

ABBREVIATIONS
Orders & Awards

Bt	Baronet
CB	Companion of the Bath
CMG	Companion of the Order of St. Michael & St. George
DCM	Distinguished Conduct Medal—Awarded to noncommissioned officers for distinguished conduct in action in the field
DFC	Distinguished Flying Cross (Royal Air Force)
DSC	Distinguished Service Cross (Royal Navy)
DSM	Distinguished Service Medal—Awarded to ranks up to and including Chief Petty
DSO	Distinguished Service Order
GC	George Cross
GCB	Grand Cross in the Order of the Bath
GM	George Medal
KBE	Knight Commander of the Most Excellent Order of the British Empire
KCVO	Knight Commander of the Royal Victorian Order
LG	Lady Companion of the Order of the Garter
MC	Military Cross
MM	Military Medal
MVO	Member of the Royal Victorian Order
OBE	Order of the British Empire
SS	Silver Star Medal (U.S. Armed Forces)
VC	Victoria Cross

THE WAR THAT NEVER WAS
ACRONYMS

1 KORR	First Battalion Kings Own Royal Regiment
2 RIF	Second Royal Irish Fusiliers
2 RWKR	Second Royal West Kent Regiment
4 REKR	Fourth Royal East Kent Regiment of the Buffs
ABC	Advanced Base Castelrozzo (RFHQ)
AO	Area of Operation
AP	Armor Piercing
AP	Assembly Point
AT	Anti-Tank
AWOL	Absent Without Leave
BAR	Browning Automatic Rifle
BOQ	Bachelor Officers Quarters
BMNT	Beginning Morning Nautical Twilight
BOAC	British Overseas Airways Corporation
CBI	China Burma India
CG	Commander General
CLE	Container Light Equipment
CO	Commanding Officer
CP	Command Post
CSA	Confederate States Army
DRT	Dead Right There
DTTP	Doctrine, Tactics, Techniques, and Procedure
DZ	Drop Zone
E&E	Escape & Evasion
EM	Enlisted Man/Men
FANY	First Aid Nursing Yeomanry
FMFM	Fleet Marine Force Manual
FUBAR	Fouled Up Beyond All Recognition
GHQ	General Headquarters

GIR	Glider Infantry Regiment
GOYA	Get Off Your Ass / Great Outstanding Young Americans
GSS	Greek Sacred Squadron
HE	High Explosive
HEAT	High Explosive Anti-Tank
HQ	Headquarters
IO	Intelligence officer
IP	Initial Point
KIA	Killed in Action
LCT	Landing Craft Tank
LD	Line of Departure
LMG	Light Machine Gun
LRDG	Long Range Desert Group
LSF	Levant Schooner Flotilla
MAGTFS	Marine Air-Ground Task Forces
MAS boat	*Motoscafo armato silurante,* torpedo armed motorboat (Italian)
MEHQ	Middle East Command Headquarters
METT-TC	Mission, enemy, terrain, troops, time and civilian concerns
MGB	Motor Gun boat
MIA	Missing in Action
MP	Military Police
MRF	Mobile Reserve Force
OPCON	Operational Control
ORP	Objective Rally Point
OSS	Office of Strategic Services (The Outfit)
PAX	Passengers
PBY	Patrol Bomber, the "Y" denotes the manufacturer, Consolidated Aircraft Co.
PIB	Parachute Infantry Battalion

PIR	Parachute Infantry Regiment
PLF	Parachute Landing Fall
POW	Prisoner of War
PT	Patrol Torpedo (boat)
PWE	Political Warfare Executive
RAC	Royal Armoured Corps
RAF	Royal Air Force
RM	Royal Marine
RNSDD	Royal Navy Submarine Deception Devices Mark 1
RNVR	Royal Navy Volunteer Reserve
RON	Remain Overnight Position
RTO	Radio Operator
SAS	Special Air Service
SBS	Special Boat Section
SMG	Small Machine Gun
SNAFU	Situation Normal All Fouled Up
SOE	Special Operations Executive
SOG	Small Operations Group
SOP	Standard Operating Procedure
TDY	Temporary Duty
TOC	Tactical Operations Center
TO&E	Table of Organization and Equipment
TOT	Time On Target
TTC	Troop Transport Command
TWX	Teletypewriter Exchange
USAAF	United States Army Air Force
USMC	United States Marine Corps
VPW	Vulnerable Points Wing
WIA	Wounded in Action

THE WAR THAT NEVER WAS
LIST OF CHARACTERS

ACM Sir Arthur Tedder, DSO, OBE, DFC
Admiral Inigo Campioni
Admiral Luigi Mascherpa
Acting Provisional Lt. "Skipper" Warthog Finley, OBE, DSO, DSC, RNPS
Alex "Cat" Gataki
Alexandra (Mandy) Paige, OBE, RM
Beverly Blackwell, SS
Brandy Seaborn, GC
Brig. Dudley Clarke
Brig. Raymond J. "R. J." Maunsell
Brig. Robert Tilney
Brig. Gen. William "Wild Bill" Donovan
Capt. Alan Redfern
Capt. Anders Lassen
Capt. Billy Jack Jaxx, MC, SSM
Capt. Butch "Headhunter" Hoolihan, DSO, MC, MM, RM
Capt. Cord Granger
Capt. Cuthbert Bowlby, RN, aka "Curly"
Capt. M. H. S. McDonald, aka Snow White
Capt. Ian "Jock" Lapraik
Capt. Karen Montgomery
Capt. Lionel Chatterhorn
Capt. Oliver Fernsby
Capt. Pamala Plum-Martin, DSO, OBE, DFC, RM
Capt. Penelope "Legs" Honeycutt-Parker, OBE, GM, RM
Capt. Preston Butterfield III
Capt. "Pyro" Percy Stirling, DSO, MC
Capt. Roy Kidd, MC
Capt. Stephanie Fawcett-Tatum, RM

Cdr. Andreas Londos
Christos
Col. Longmore
Col. Douglas Turnbull
Col. John Randal, DSO, OBE, DSC, MC
Col. P. Ernest Gabel
Corp. Leslie Cooper
Corp. Maynard Plimken
Corp. Sid Billingslea
Corp. Tom Murphy aka "Murph the Surf"
Flanigan
Guns
Happy
King
Lana Turner
Lt. Bentley St. Ledger, RM
Lt. Clint Hays
Lt. Dan Bonham
Lt. George Paspati
Lt. Jake Novak aka Jake the Snake
Lt. Randy "Hornblower" Seaborn, DSO, OBE, DSC, RN
Lt. Ricky Mascuch
Lt. Theodore "The Great Teddy" Hamilton, OBE
Lt. Windell Mead
Lt. Col. John "Jake" Easonsmith, DSO, MC
Lt. Col. Sir Terry "Zorro" Stone, KBE, DSO, MC
Lt. Gen. "Geronimo" Joe McKoy, OBE
Lt. Gen. Lesley McNair
Lt. Cdr. Adrian Seligman
LtJG Jackson Taylor, USNR
Lucas
Maj. Baltimore "Mongo" Farquhar, MC
Maj. Clive Adair
Maj. Jack Dance
Maj. Lloyd Owen

Maj. Valentine Fabian
Maj. Zargo
Maj. Gen Matthew B. Ridgway
Maj. Gen. Elbridge Chapman
Maj. Gen. George Griner
Maj. Gen. James "Baldie" Taylor, OBE
Maj. Gen. Joseph Swing
Maj. Gen. Sam Houston "Bronc" Blackwell
Maj. Gen. William Miley
Maj. Gen. William "Bill" Lee
Maj. the Earl Lord George Jellicoe, DSO, MC
Maj. the Lady Jane Seaborn, LG, OBE, RM
MSgt. Mack Beckwith
Nikolas
Officer Diakos
PFC Norvel Hansen aka "Horn Dog"
Professor Layton Winthrop
Pvt. Donny Masterson
Pvt. Tommy Berkowitz
Ranger Pvt. Willie Johannsen
Red the Flying Clipper Girl
Rikke (Rocky) Runborg
Rita Hayworth
Scout Lionel Fenwick
Scout Munro Ferguson
Sgt. Fred Waltmier
Sgt. Maj. Mike "March or Die" Mikkalis, DSM, MM
SS-Hauptsturmführer Gretchen von Coffenhauser
TSgt. Luke Volkmann
VAdm. Sir Randolph "Razor" Ransom, VC, KCB, DSO, OBE, DSC, RN
Veronica Paige, OBE
Waldo Treywick

ABOUT THE AUTHOR

Phil Ward is a decorated combat veteran commissioned at age nineteen. A former instructor at the Army Ranger School, he has had a lifelong interest in small unit tactics and special operations. He lives in Texas on a mountain overlooking Lake Austin.

~ ~

Other books in the Raiding Forces Series:

Those Who Dare

Dead Eagles

Blood Wings

Roman Candle

Guerrilla Command

Necessary Force

Desert Patrol

Private Army

Africa 1941

The Sharp End

Raiding Rommel

Strategic Services

The Tip of the Sword

Always So Few

The War That Never Was

Economy of Force

www.ingramcontent.com/pod-product-compliance
Lightning Source LLC
Chambersburg PA
CBHW020304030826
48979CB00027B/2102/J

* 9 7 8 0 9 8 9 5 9 2 2 3 9 *